THE COMMODORE

Patrick O'Brian is the author of the acclaimed Aubrey-Maturin tales and the biographer of Joseph Banks and Picasso. His first novel, *Testimonies*, and his *Collected Short Stories* have recently been reprinted by HarperCollins. He translated many works from French into English, among them the novels and memoirs of Simone de Beauvoir and the first volume of Jean Lacouture's biography of Charles de Gaulle. In 1995 he was the first recipient of the Heywood Hill Prize for a lifetime's contribution to literature. In the same year he was awarded the CBE. In 1997 he was awarded an honorary doctorate of letters by Trinity College, Dublin. He died in January 2000 at the age of 85.

The Works of Patrick O'Brian

*The Aubrey–Maturin Novels
in order of publication*

MASTER AND COMMANDER
POST CAPTAIN
HMS SURPRISE
THE MAURITIUS COMMAND
DESOLATION ISLAND
THE FORTUNE OF WAR
THE SURGEON'S MATE
THE IONIAN MISSION
TREASON'S HARBOUR
THE FAR SIDE OF THE WORLD
THE REVERSE OF THE MEDAL
THE LETTER OF MARQUE
THE THIRTEEN-GUN SALUTE
THE NUTMEG OF CONSOLATION
CLARISSA OAKES
THE WINE-DARK SEA
THE COMMODORE
THE YELLOW ADMIRAL
THE HUNDRED DAYS
BLUE AT THE MIZZEN

Novels

TESTIMONIES
THE CATALANS
THE GOLDEN OCEAN
THE UNKNOWN SHORE
RICHARD TEMPLE
CAESAR
HUSSEIN

Tales

THE LAST POOL
THE WALKER
LYING IN THE SUN
THE CHIAN WINE
COLLECTED SHORT STORIES

Biography

PICASSO
JOSEPH BANKS

Anthology

A BOOK OF VOYAGES

PATRICK O'BRIAN

The Commodore

HarperCollins*Publishers*

HarperCollins*Publishers*
77–85 Fulham Palace Road,
Hammersmith, London w6 8jb

www.**fire**and**water**.com

This paperback edition 2003
3 5 7 9 8 6 4

Previously published in B-format paperback
by HarperCollins 1997
Reprinted seven times

Previously published in paperback by HarperCollins 1995

First published in Great Britain by
HarperCollins*Publishers* 1994

Copyright © Patrick O'Brian 1994

Patrick O'Brian asserts the moral right to
be identified as the author of this work

ISBN 0 00 649932 5

Set in Imprint by
Rowland Phototypesetting Ltd,
Bury St Edmunds, Suffolk

Printed and bound in Great Britain by
Clays Ltd, St Ives plc

CONTENTS

FOR MARY, WITH LOVE

The sails of a square-rigged ship, hung out to dry in a calm.

1 Flying jib	12 Mainsail, or course
2 Jib	13 Maintopsail
3 Fore topmast staysail	14 Main topgallant
4 Fore staysail	15 Mizzen staysail
5 Foresail, or course	16 Mizzen topmast staysail
6 Fore topsail	17 Mizzen topgallant staysail
7 Fore topgallant	18 Mizzen sail
8 Mainstaysail	19 Spanker
9 Main topmast staysail	20 Mizzen topsail
10 Middle staysail	21 Mizzen topgallant
11 Main topgallant staysail	

Chapter One

Thick weather in the chops of the Channel and a dirty night, with the strong north-east wind bringing rain from the low sky and racing cloud: Ushant somewhere away on the starboard bow, the Scillies to larboard, but never a light, never a star to be seen; and no observation for the last four days.

The two homeward-bound ships, Jack Aubrey's *Surprise*, an elderly twenty-eight-gun frigate sold out of the service some years ago but now, as His Majesty's hired vessel *Surprise*, completing a long confidential mission for Government, and HMS *Berenice*, Captain Heneage Dundas, an even older but somewhat less worn sixty-four-gun two-decker, together with her tender the *Ringle*, an American schooner of the kind known as a Baltimore clipper, had been sailing in company ever since they met north and east of Cape Horn, about a hundred degrees of latitude or six thousand sea-miles away in a straight line, if straight lines had any meaning at all in a voyage governed entirely by the wind, the first coming from Peru and the coast of Chile, the second from New South Wales.

The *Berenice* had found the *Surprise* much battered by an encounter with a heavy American frigate: even more so by a lightning-stroke that had shattered her mainmast and, far worse, deprived her of her rudder. The two captains had been boys together, midshipmen and lieutenants: very old shipmates and very intimate friends indeed. The *Berenice* had supplied the *Surprise* with spars, cordage, storage and a remarkably efficient Pakenham substitute rudder made of spare topmasts; and the two ship's companies, in spite of an initial stiffness arising from the *Surprise*'s somewhat irregular status, agreed very well together after two ardent cricket-matches on the island of Ascension, where a proper rudder was shipped, and there was a great deal of ship-visiting as all three lay with loose flapping sails in the dol-drums, a sweltering fortnight with melted tar dripping from the yards. Though unconscionably long, it was a most com-panionable voyage, particularly as the *Surprise* was able to do away with much of the invidious difference between deliverer and delivered by providing the sickly and under-manned *Berenice* with a surgeon, her own having been lost, together with his only mate, when their boat overturned not ten yards from the ship – neither could swim, and each seized the other with fatal energy – so that her people, sadly reduced by Sydney pox and Cape Horn scurvy, were left to the care of an illiterate but fearless loblolly-boy; and to provide her not merely with an ordinary naval surgeon, equipped with little more than a certificate from the Sick and Hurt Board, but with a full-blown physician in the person of Stephen Maturin, the author of a standard work on the diseases of seamen, a Fellow of the Royal Society with doctorates from Dublin and Paris, a gentleman fluent in Latin and Greek (such a comfort to his patients), a particular friend of Captain Aubrey's and, though this was known to very few, one of the Admiralty's – indeed of the Ministry's – most valued advisers on Spanish and Spanish-American affairs: in short an intelligence-agent, though on a wholly independent and voluntary basis.

Yet a surgeon, even if he may also be a physician with a physical bob and a gold-headed cane who has been called in to treat Prince William, the Duke of Clarence, is not a mainmast, still less a rudder: he may uphold the people's spirits and relieve their pain, but he can neither propel nor steer the ship; the Surprises had therefore every reason to feel loving gratitude towards the Berenices, and since they knew the difference between right and wrong at sea they made full acknowledgment of their obligations as they passed through the frigid, temperate and torrid zones and so to the

2

merely wet and disagreeable climate of home waters; but at no time could they be brought to love the *Berenice* herself.

Their feelings were shared by the crew of the *Ringle*, very much so indeed; for both the frigate and the schooner were quite exceptionally weatherly vessels, fast, capable of sailing very close to the wind – the schooner wonderfully close – and almost innocent of leeway, while the much larger and more powerful two-decker was but a slug on a bowline. She got along well enough when the breeze was abaft the beam – she liked it plumb on the quarter best – but as it came forward so her people exchanged anxious looks; and when at last studdingsails could no longer stand and when the ship was hauled close to the wind, the bowlines twanging taut, all their exertions could not bring her to within six points, nor prevent her sagging most disgracefully to leeward, like a drunken crab.

Most unhappily she had been compelled to behave in this manner for several days now, ever since an accurate observation had told them that they could set about painting ship, renewing the blacking on the yards and polishing everything that could be induced to take a shine, so that they might strike soundings fully prepared to sail home in glory. But for all of these days the breeze had been contrary, and although the *Surprise* – even more so the schooner – could have beaten up to good effect, working a great way to windward, they had been kept back by their unweatherly companion. And now they were far into this dirty night, this filthy goddam night, with their beautifully painted topsides being spoilt by spray, when they might have been bowsing up their jibs ashore; or at least the Surprises might, they being from Shelmerston, a little place much closer than the *Berenice*'s Portsmouth.

Feeling ran high, especially on the *Surprise*'s quarterdeck, where an unusually vicious blast, cutting against the tide on its turn, had soaked all hands; but below, in the great cabin, the two captains sat unmoved as the *Berenice* floundered along under topsails and courses, shipping a great deal of water and drifting to leeward at her usual horrid rate, while the *Surprise* kept exactly in her due station astern with no more than double-reefed topsails and a jib half in, and the *Ringle* even less. Both men knew that all seamanship could do was being done, and a long professional career had taught them not only to accept the inevitable but not to fret about it. Even before they struck soundings Heneage Dundas had suggested that the *Surprise* should ignore naval convention and part company, going ahead as fast as she chose.

'She ain't carrying dispatches,' replied Jack with a frown – a ship carrying them was excused from all ordinary decencies or politeness; forbidden indeed to delay for even a minute – so there the matter rested; and now, Dundas having dined and supped aboard the frigate, they sat there with a broad-bottomed decanter of port between them, half-hearing the stroke of the sea on the larboard bow and then on the starboard when the ship had gone about on yet another of her long legs, and the hanging lamp swung over the locker, intermittently lighting a backgammon board, a sea-going board with the men still held by their pegs in Jack Aubrey's improbable winning position.

'Well, you shall have her,' said Dundas, emptying his glass. 'And you shall have her with all her gear and her ground-tackle too.'

'Come, that is handsome in you, Hen,' said Jack. 'Thank you kindly.'

'But I will say this, Jack: you have the most infernal luck. You had no right even to save your gammon.'

'It was a damned near-run thing, I must admit,' said Jack, modestly; then after a pause he laughed and said, 'I remember your using those very words in the old *Bellerophon*, before we had our battle.'

'So I did,' cried Dundas. 'So I did. Lord, that was a great while ago.'

'I still bear the scar,' said Jack. He pushed up his sleeve, and there on his brown forearm was a long white line.

'How it comes back,' said Dundas; and between them,

drinking port, they retold the tale, with minute details coming fresh to their minds. As youngsters, under the charge of the gunner of the *Bellerophon*, 74, in the West Indies, they had played the same game. Jack, with his infernal luck, had won on that occasion too: Dundas claimed his revenge, and lost again, again on a throw of double six. Harsh words, such as cheat, liar, sodomite, booby and God-damned lubber flew about; and since fighting over a chest, the usual way of settling such disagreements in many ships, was strictly forbidden in the *Bellerophon*, it was agreed that as gentlemen could not possibly tolerate such language they should fight a duel. During the afternoon watch the first lieutenant, who dearly loved a white-scoured deck, found that the ship was almost out of the best kind of sand, and he sent Mr Aubrey away in the blue cutter to fetch some from an island at the convergence of two currents where the finest and most even grain was found. Mr Dundas accompanied him, carrying two newly-sharpened cutlasses in a sailcloth parcel, and when the hands had been set to work with shovels the two little boys retired behind a dune, unwrapped the parcel, saluted gravely, and set about each other. Half a dozen passes, the blades clashing, and when Jack cried out 'Oh Hen, what have you done?' Dundas gazed for a moment at the spurting blood, burst into tears, whipped off his shirt and bound up the wound as best he could. When they crept aboard a most unfortunately idle, becalmed and staring *Bellerophon*, their explanations, widely different and in both cases so weak that they could not be attempted to be believed, were brushed aside, and their captain flogged them severely on the bare breech. 'How we howled,' said Dundas. 'You were shriller than I was,' said Jack. 'Very like a hyena.'

Killick, his steward, had long since turned in, so Jack fetched more port himself; and after they had been drinking it for some time he noticed that Dundas was growing curiously silent.

Orders and bosun's pipes on deck, and the *Surprise* came smoothly about with no more than the watch, settling easily on the starboard tack.

'Jack,' said Dundas at last, in a tone that Jack had heard before, 'this is perhaps an improper moment, while I am swilling your capital wine . . . but you did speak of some charming prizes in the Pacific.'

'Certainly I did. We were required to act as a privateer, you know, and since I could not disobey my instructions we took not only some whalers, which we sold on the coast, but also a vile great pirate fairly stuffed with what she had taken out of a score of other ships: maybe two score.'

'Well, I tell you what it is, Jack. The glass is rising, as I dare say you have noticed.' Jack nodded, looking at his friend's embarrassed face with real compunction. 'That is to say, it is likely the weather will clear, with the wind backing west and even south of west: tomorrow or the next day we should run up the Channel and then we shall part company at last, with you putting into Shelmerston and me carrying right on to Pompey.' This, though eminently true, called for some further observation if it were to make much sense; but Dundas seemed incapable of going on. He hung his head, a pitiful attitude for so distinguished a commander.

'Perhaps you have a girl aboard that you would like landed somewhere else?' suggested Jack.

'Not this time,' said Dundas. 'No. Jack, the fact of the matter is that as soon as the *Berenice* makes her number and it is known in the town that she is at hand the tipstaffs will come swarming out of their holes and the moment I set foot on shore I shall be arrested – arrested for debt and carried off to a sponging-house. I suppose you could not lend me a thousand guineas? It is a terrible lot of money, I know. I am ashamed to ask for it.'

'In course I could. As I told you, I am amazingly flush – Crocus is my second name. But would a thousand be enough? What was the debt? It would be a pity to spoil the ship for a . . .'

'Oh, it would be amply enough, I am sure; and I am prodigiously obliged to you, Jack. I dare not come down on Melville at this point: it would be different if he loved me as much as he loves you, but the last time he showed me out of the door he called me an infernal trundle-thrift whore-monger and condemned me to this vile New Holland voyage in the *Berenice*.' Heneage's elder brother, Lord Melville, was at the head of the Admiralty, and he could do such things. 'No. The judgment was for five hundred odd – the same young person, I am sorry to say, or rather her infamous attorney – but even with legal charges and interest I am sure a thousand would cover it handsomely.'

They talked about arrest for debt, sheriff's officers, sponging-houses and the like for some time, with profound and dear-bought knowledge of the subject, and after a while Jack agreed that a thousand would see his friend clear until he could draw his long-overdue pay and see the factor who looked after his Scottish estate: with a vessel as slow and unwieldy and unlucky as the *Berenice* there could be no question of prize-money, above all on such an unpromising voyage.

'How happy you make me feel, Jack,' said Dundas. 'A draft on Hoare's – for you bank with Hoare's, as I well remember – will be like Ajax's shield when I go ashore.'

'There is nothing like gold for satisfying an attorney out of hand.'

'Truer word you never spoke, dear Jack. But even if you had gold – you will never tell me you have gold, English gold, Jack? – it would take hours to tell out a thousand guineas.'

'God love you, Hen. All this morning and much of this afternoon Tom, Adams and I were counting and weighing like a gang of usurers, making up bags for the final sharing-out when we drop anchor in Shelmerston. The Doctor helped too, nipping about among our heaps and taking out all the ancient coins – there were some of Julius Caesar and Nebu-chadnezzar, I think, and he clasped an Irish piece called an Inchiquin pistole to his bosom, laughing with pleasure – but he threw us out of our count and I was obliged to beg him to go away, far, far away. When he had gone we sorted and

7

counted, sorted and counted and weighed, only finishing just before dinner. Those large bags on the left of the stern-window locker hold a thousand guineas apiece – they are part of the ship's share – while the smaller bags hold mohurs, ducats, louis d'ors, joes and all kinds of foreign gold by weight of five hundred each, and the chests all along the side and down in the bread-room hold sacks of a hundred in silver, also by weight: there are so many that the ship is a good strake by the stern, and I shall be glad when they are better stowed. Take one of those thousands on the left, then. I can make up the sum in a moment from the rest, but silver would be much too heavy for you to carry.'

'God bless you, Jack,' said Dundas, hefting the comfortable bag in his hand. 'Even this weighs well over a stone, ha, ha, ha!' and as he spoke four bells struck, four bells in the grave-yard watch. This was almost immediately followed by an exchange of orders and distant cries on deck: they were not the routine noises that preceded going about, however, and both captains listened intently, Heneage still holding the bag poised in his hand, like a Christmas pudding. Some moments later a wet, one-armed midshipman burst in and cried, 'Beg pardon, sir, but Mr Wilkins desires his compliments and duty and there is a ship about two miles to windward, he thinks a seventy-four, in any case a two-decker, and he don't quite like her answer to the private signal.'

'Thank you, Mr Reade,' said Jack. 'I shall be on deck directly.'

'And pray be so good as to rouse out my bargemen,' called Dundas, stuffing the bag into his shirt and buttoning his waistcoat over it. And when Reade had vanished at a run, 'Jack, infinite thanks: I must get back to my ship. Clear and come within hail' – he was the senior captain – 'and short-handed though *Berenice* is, I believe the two of us can take on any seventy-four afloat.'

Out on the cold wet quarterdeck Jack's eyes grew used to the comparative darkness as Dundas groped awkwardly down into the tossing barge, clasping his anxious belly as he went. Comparative darkness, for now an old hunchbacked moon was sending enough light through the low cloud for him to make out a blur of white to windward, a blur that resolved itself into topsails and courses as he focused his glass, and a double row of lit gunports. But it was the hoist that fixed almost the whole of his attention, the reply to the private signal that distinguished friend from foe. It was a string of three lanterns, the topmost winking steadily: there should have been four.

'I replied *do not understand your signal*, sir,' said Wilkins, 'but she still keeps this one hoisted.'

Jack nodded. 'Clear for action and make sail to close the *Berenice*,' he said.

'All hands and beat to quarters,' roared Wilkins to the bosun's enchanted mate. 'Forward there, forward: forestaysail and full jib.'

The *Surprise* was in very good order: she had seen a great deal of action and she was kept in high training for a great deal more; she could change from a darkling ship, three parts asleep, to a brilliantly-lit man-of-war with guns run out, hammocks in the netting, magazines opened and protected with fearnought screens, and every man in his accustomed, appointed station together with all his mates, ready to give battle at the word of command. But she could not do so in silence, and it was the roar of the drum, the muffled thunder of four hundred feet and the screech of trucks that started Stephen Maturin from his profound and rosy peace.

He had left Jack and Dundas quite early, for he was something of a check on their flow of reminiscences; and in any case very highly detailed accounts of war at sea reduced him almost to tears after the first hour. They had drunk the usual Saturday toast of sweethearts and wives, and the civil Dundas had added particular compliments to Sophie and Diana, pledging both in bumpers, bottoms up. This meant that Stephen, an abstemious, meagre creature, weighing nine stone and odd ounces, far exceeded his usual two or three glasses, and although he had meant to retire to the rarely-used cabin below to which he was entitled as the ship's surgeon rather than the more spacious, airier place he usually shared with Jack, and there, after his evening rounds, to lie reading, the wine, without making him drunk, had to some extent affected his concentration, and as the book he was reading – Clousaz' *Examen de Pyrrhonisme* – called for a great deal he put it down at the end of a chapter, aware that he had made nothing of the last paragraph, lay back in his swinging cot and instantly returned to thinking about his wife and daughter, the first a spirited young woman called Diana with black hair and blue eyes, a splendid rider, and the second Brigid, a child he had longed for this many a year but whom he had not yet seen. This reverie was very usual with him, and it required no sort of concentration at all, but rather the reverse, being a series of images, sometimes imprecise, sometimes intensely vivid, of conversations, real or imaginary, and of an indefinite sense of present happiness. Yet tonight for the first time in all this very long parting – no less than a complete circumnavigation of the world by sea, with a great deal happening on land as well – there was a subtle difference, a change of key. At any moment now, he had learnt, they might *strike soundings*, an expression that in itself had a chilling quality, quite apart from its meaning; and the fact itself brought what had been a vague futurity into the almost immediate present. Now it was not so much a question of wandering in past felicity as of reflecting upon the reality he would meet in a few days' time or even less if the wind came fair.

He looked forward to seeing Diana and Brigid with the utmost eagerness, of course, as he had for thousands and thousands of miles; but now this eagerness was mixed with an apprehension that he could not or would not readily name. For almost the whole of this enormous voyage they had been out of touch: he knew that his daughter had been born and that Diana had bought Barham Down, a large, remote house with excellent stabling, good pasture and plenty of gallops – great stretches of down – for the Arabs she intended to breed; but apart from that virtually nothing.

Years had passed, and years had a bad name: a verse of Horace floated into his mind:

> *Singula de nobis anni praedantur euntes;*
> *eripuere jocos, Venerem, convivia, ludum . . .*

and for a moment he tried to make a tolerable English version; but his

> *The years in passing rob us of our delight,*
> *of merriment and carnal love, of each in turn,*
> *all sport and dining out . . .*

did not please him and he abandoned the attempt.

In any case things were not yet quite so desperate: although Venus might be a somewhat remote and flickering planet he still loved a cheerful dinner among friends and a severe, close-fought game of whist or fives. Yet changed he had to some degree, of that there was no doubt: more and more, for example, it seemed to him that the proper study of mankind was man rather than beetle or even bird.

He had changed: of course he had changed, and probably more than he knew. It was inevitable. What kind of Diana would he find, and how would they agree? She had married him mostly out of friendship – she *liked* him very well – perhaps to some degree out of pity, he having loved her so long: he was not at all agreeable to look at and from the physical point of view he had never been much of a lover – a state of affairs much influenced by years of addiction to opium, which he neither smoked nor ate but drank in the form of the alcoholic tincture of laudanum, sometimes, in his despair over Diana, reaching heroic doses. Diana, on the other hand, had never taken so much as a drachm, not a scruple of opium, nor anything else to diminish her naturally ardent temperament.

As the night wore on he worried himself foolishly, as one will in the dark with vitality low and courage, reasoning power and common sense all at their lowest ebb: at times he comforted himself with the reflexion that Brigid was there, a great bond between them; at others he said that the image of Diana as a mother was perfectly absurd; and he longed for the old tincture to ease the torment of his mind. He did possess a substitute in the leaves of the coca plant, much esteemed in Peru for the tranquil euphoria they produced when chewed; but they had the disadvantage of utterly banishing sleep, and sleep was what he wanted more than anything else in the world.

Somehow, at some point, he must have attained it, since the drum's echoing beat to quarters jerked him up from the depths. In most respects he remained a wholly unimproved landsman in spite of many years at sea, but there were a few naval characteristics to be found in him. Almost all had to do with his function as a naval surgeon, and even before his mind was fully aware of the situation his legs were hurrying him towards his action-station below and right aft on the orlop deck. It being cold as well as damp in the stuffy, fetid triangular hole that he occupied he had turned in all standing, so that he had only to put on an apron to be ready for duty. On reaching the sick-berth he found his loblolly-boy, a large and powerful, almost monoglot Munsterman called Padeen, hauling two chests together under the great lantern to make an operating-table. 'God and Mary be with you, Padeen,' he said in Irish. 'God and Mary and Patrick be with your honour,' said Padeen. 'Is there to be a battle at all?'

'The Dear knows. How are Williams and Ellis?'

These were the two invalids in the starboard sick-berth, whom Padeen had been sitting with. They had been sparring, in a spirit of fun, with loggerheads, those massy iron balls with long handles to be carried red-hot from the fire and plunged into buckets of tar or pitch so that the substance might be melted with no risk of flame. 'They are sober now, sir; and penitent, the creatures.'

'I shall look at them, when we have everything ready,'

said Stephen, beginning to range saws, scalpels, ligatures and tourniquets. Fabien, his assistant, joined him, followed by two little girls, Emily and Sarah: they were only just awake, and they would have been a sleepy pink had they not been extremely black. They had been found long ago on a Melanesian island whose other inhabitants had all been wiped out by the smallpox brought by a visiting whaler; and since they were then too ill and wretched to look after themselves in that charnel-house of a village, Stephen had brought them away. They did not attend at the very horrible surgery that he was sometimes obliged to carry out, but their small, delicate hands were wonderfully skilful at bandaging. They looked after those who had been operated upon, and the convalescents; they were also very useful to Dr Maturin in his frequent dissections of natural specimens, having no trace of squeamishness. They had entirely forgotten the language of Sweeting Island, apart from counting in it as they skipped, but they spoke perfect English, quarterdeck with never an oath or the much more earthy and emphatic lower-deck version, as occasion required.

Between them they laid out all the material that might be needed during an action and after it: lint, bandages, splints; the purely surgical instruments such as catlings, bistouries and retractors; and their grim companions, the gags and the leather-covered chains. When all these were arranged in their due order, the essentials within reach of the surgeon's hand and himself tied into his apron, they relaxed and listened with the utmost attention, trying to piece through the general confused run of the water alongside the ship, the voice of the eddy on the windward side of the rudder, and the reverberation of the taut rigging transmitted to the hull, to hear some sound that might tell them what was afoot. None came, and presently their sense of urgency diminished. The little girls sat on the deck outside the lantern's strong ring of light, silently playing the game in which an outstretched hand represented a sheet of paper, a stone, or a pair of scissors. Stephen walked into the other berth, looked at his patients and asked them how they did. 'Prime, sir,' they answered, and thanked him kindly.

'Well, I am glad of that,' he said. 'Yet although they were good clean breaks, immobilized at once, it will be long before you can go aloft, or dance upon the green, if ever we get home, which God send.'

'Amen, amen, sir,' they answered together.

'But how did you ever come to be so indiscreet and thoughtless as to beat one another with those vile great loggerheads?'

'It was only in fun, sir, like we sometimes do, meaning no harm. One has a swipe and the other dodges, turn and turn about.'

'In all my experience of the sea I have never heard of such a dreadful practice.'

The patients looked meek, avoiding one another's eyes; and presently Ellis said, 'It all depends on the ship, sir. We often used to play in the *Agamemnon*; and my father, which he was carpenter's crew in the old *George*, had a real set-to, real serious, with a forecastleman that called him a . . .'

'Called him what?'

'I hardly like to say it.'

'Murmur it in my ear,' said Stephen, bending low.

'A nymph,' whispered Ellis.

'Did he indeed, the wicked dog? How did it end, so?'

'Well, sir, they were at right loggerheads, like I said – the whole forecastle agreed it was right – and my dad fetched him such a crack they had to take his leg off that very evening, much mangled. But it was a blessing to the poor bugger in the end. Having but one leg left, Captain the Honourable Byron, who was always very good to his men, got him a cook's warrant, and he lived till he was drowned on the Coromandel coast.'

'Sir,' cried Reade in the doorway, with a covered can of coffee in his hand, 'the Captain sends this with his compliments to raise your spirits and soften the blow. There is to be no action after all. The vessel to windward proved to be

14

that famous, seamanlike ship of the line *Thunderer*, seventy-four. She hauled her wind, not liking the look of us, and in doing so some of the more brilliant officers aboard, those who could count above three, I mean, made out that she had a false signal flying: one lantern short.'

'Must they not be flogged round the fleet?'

'I am afraid not, sir. They say they are senior to us, which is quite true; that any possible inconvenience is regretted; and that Captain Dundas, Captain Aubrey and Dr Maturin are desired to breakfast aboard. Lord, sir, I should not be in that signal-lieutenant's shoes for instant promotion to flag-rank.'

Most of the exchanges that Reade reported were more or less imaginary, and in any case they had been slowly, laboriously transmitted through dense rain by hoists of lights variously arranged; but the breakfast invitation, which was true enough, was repeated at first light by flags and again by a sodden midshipman in a boat; and the two captains, together with Dr Maturin, came alongside just before eight bells in the morning watch, ravenous, cold, wet, indignant. Their host, an elderly man called Fellowes, was in much greater danger of promotion to flag-rank than Reade, being so high on the post-captain's list that the next batch of admirals to be gazetted must necessarily include him as a rear-admiral of the blue squadron unless by some unspeakable misfortune he should be yellowed – attached to no particular squadron and given no command. But this unspeakable misfortune might be now at hand. The *Thunderer*'s wretched signal-lieutenant, now confined to his cabin, had aroused a perfectly justified rage in two quite eminent bosoms: the son of a former First Lord and the brother of the present holder of that awful office, in the first place; and in the second that of the Tory member of parliament for Milport. Captain Aubrey might represent no more than a handful of bur-gesses, all tenants on his cousin's estate (it was a family seat) but his vote in the House counted as much as that of the member for the county. The ill-will of either of these gentle-men might have a horribly yellowing effect. And then there was this Dr Maturin, after whom the Admiralty official the *Thunderer* was carrying to Gibraltar had asked with such curious insistence . . . had he not been called in to treat Prince William?

Captain Fellowes greeted his guests with the utmost cor-diality, with apologies, explanations, and a breakfast-table covered with all the luxuries that a ship only a few days outward-bound could offer: beef-steaks; mutton-chops; bacon; eggs in all their charming variety; soft-tack, crusty or toasted; mushrooms; pork sausages; a veal and ham pie; fresh butter; fresh milk; fresh cream, even; tea and cocoa: every-thing except the coffee that Jack's and Stephen's souls longed for.

Mr Philips, the black-clad Admiralty official, Stephen's neighbour, said, 'I do not suppose you have seen the most recent *Proceedings of the Royal Society*. I have the volume hot from the press in my cabin, and should be charmed to show it to you.' Stephen said that he should be very happy, and Philips went on, 'May I help you to one of these kip-pered herrings, sir? They are uncommon fat and unctuous.'

'You are very good, sir,' said Stephen, 'but I believe I must refrain. They would increase my thirst.' And in a low confidential tone (in fact they knew one another quite well enough for such a remark), 'Would there never be a drop of coffee, at all?'

'I hope so,' said Philips, and he asked the passing steward.

'Oh no, sir. Oh no. This is a cocoa-ship, sir; though tea is countenanced.'

'Coffee relaxes the fibres,' called out the *Thunderer*'s sur-geon in an authoritative voice. 'I always recommend cocoa.'

'Coffee?' cried Captain Fellowes. 'Would the gentleman like coffee? Featherstonehaugh, run along and see whether the wardroom or the gun-room has any.'

'Coffee relaxes the fibres,' said the surgeon again, rather louder. 'That is a scientific fact.'

'Perhaps the Doctor might like to have his fibres relaxed,' said Captain Dundas. 'I am sure I should, having stood to all night.'

'Mr McAber,' called Captain Fellowes down the table to his first lieutenant, 'pray be so good as to encourage Featherstonehaugh in his search.'

But no amount of zeal could find what did not exist. Stephen protested that it did not signify – it was of no consequence – there was always (God willing) another day – and that if he might be indulged in a cup of small beer it would go admirably with this pickled salmon. And when at last the uncomfortable meal was over he walked off to Philips' cabin to see the new volume of the *Proceedings*.

'How is Sir Joseph?' he asked when they were alone, referring to his close friend and hierarchical superior the head of naval intelligence.

'He is physically well,' said Philips, 'and perhaps a little stouter than when you last saw him: but he is worried. I shall not venture to say what about: you know how cloisonné these matters are with us, if I may use the expression.'

'We say *bulkheaded* in the Navy,' observed Stephen.

'Bulkheaded? Thank you, sir, thank you: a far better term. But this letter' – drawing it from an inner pocket – 'will no doubt tell you.'

'I am obliged to you,' said Stephen, glancing at the black Admiralty seal with its fouled anchor. 'Now please be so good as to give me a detailed account of events since last February, when I had an intelligence report from the Spanish.'

Philips looked down, reflected for a while, and said, 'I wish I could tell you a happier tale. There is progress in Spain, to be sure, but everywhere else there are diplomatic reverses; and everywhere he keeps finding resources in allies, men, money, ships and naval stores, which we cannot do, or only with great and ruinous difficulty. We are stretched to the uttermost, and may break: he seems indestructible. Things are going so badly that if he delivers one more knock-down blow we may have to ask for conditions. Let me take Europe country by country . . .'

He was dealing with the success of Buonaparte's agents in Wallachia when a lieutenant came in with the news that as soon as the Doctor was in the *Berenice*'s barge the captains would be piped over the side: they were making their farewells this very minute. 'And the wind is backing, too,' he added. 'You will have a drier pull.'

Drier it might have been, but not for those who habitually stood on the lowest of the steps on the ship's side, holding on to the entering ropes and pondering until she rolled and the sea rose, soaking him, this time farther than the waist. Stephen came aboard the *Surprise* dripping, as usual; and as usual Killick, worn thin and old and preternaturally shrewish by the task of looking after both the Captain and the Doctor, a feckless pair with their clothes and their limbs, seized him and fairly propelled him into the sleeping cabin, crying, 'Your best breeches, too – your only decent breeches – take off your drawers too, sir, if you please – we don't want no bleeding colds in the head – and now put on this here gown and dry your feet – sopping, fairly sopping – with this here towel and I will find you something reasonably warm. God love us, where's your wig?'

'In my bosom, Killick,' answered Stephen in a conciliating tone. 'It is protecting my watch, itself wrapped in a handkerchief.'

'Wig in his bosom – wig in his bosom,' muttered Killick as he gathered up the clothes. 'Bedlam ain't in it.'

Jack had shot up the side far quicker than his surgeon, and now he called from the great cabin, 'Why, Stephen, have you . . .' Then, recollecting that his friend disliked being asked if he had got wet, he coughed and went on in a very cheerful, incongruously cheerful, voice '. . . ever had such a miserable God-damned breakfast? Small beer; and greasy mutton-chops on a cold plate. A cold plate, forsooth. I have eaten better in a Dutch herring-buss off the Texel. And not a single God-damned letter – not a note – not so much as a tailor's bill. But never mind. The wind is backing. It is already come north-north-east, and if it carries on another couple of points or so we shall be in Shelmerston by Wednesday, in spite of the *Berenice*.'

'Had you any reason to expect letters, brother?'

'Of course I had. When we were putting in to Fayal for water we exchanged numbers with *Weasel* as she cleared the point, homeward-bound. She was sure to report us, and I had hoped for something at least. But no, not a word, though Dundas had a great package. Such a package, ha, ha, ha! Oh Lord, Stephen,' he said, coming in, for the half-naked Maturin was as free from shame as his ancestor, the sinless Adam. 'But I beg pardon. I am interrupting you' – glancing at the letter in Stephen's hand.

'Never in life, my dear. Tell me what makes you so happy in spite of your disappointment.'

Jack sat close by him and, in a voice intended to be so low that it would escape Killick's attentive ear – a vain hope – he said, 'Heneage's letter had such a charming piece about me. Melville said he was so happy to hear that *Surprise* was almost in home water – had always thought it magnanimous in me – that was his very word, Stephen: magnanimous – to accept such an irregular command in spite of having been so shabbily used, and that now he had the opportunity of expressing his sense of my merits – of my *merits*, Stephen: do you hear me, there? – by offering me a neat little squadron that was putting together to cruise off the West African coast with some fast-sailing sloops to intercept slavers – you would approve of that, Stephen – and perhaps three frigates and a couple of seventy-fours in case of what he called certain eventualities. And I should be a *first-class* commodore, Stephen, with a broad swallow-tailed burgee, a captain under me and a pennant-lieutenant, not like that hard-labour Mauritius campaign, when I almost had to win the anchor myself as a mere second-class dogsbody. Oh ha, ha, ha, Stephen! I can't tell you how happy it makes me: I can take care of Tom – he'll never be made post else: this is his only chance. And there is no mad hurry. We shall have a month and more at home, long enough for Sophie and Diana to get sick of us. Ha, ha – Shelmerston – pull ashore, leap into a post-chaise from the Crown and astonish them all at Ashgrove! What do you say to a pot of coffee at last?'

'With all my heart: and Jack, let me give you joy in the highest degree of your splendid command' – shaking his hand – 'but as for Shelmerston, why, listen, Jack,' said Stephen, who had deciphered Sir Joseph's double-coded message from memory alone, 'I must be in town as quickly as ever I can fly. I shall have to forgo Shelmerston for now and stay with the *Berenice*. Not only is she on her way, whereas you will have to turn to the left for a considerable distance, but only an inhuman brute could go ashore after such an absence, kiss a cheek or two and then leap into a chaise. This, however, I can perfectly well do in Plymouth, where never a cheek awaits me.'

Jack looked at him keenly, saw that he was not to be shifted, and called out, 'Killick. Killick, there.'

'What now?' replied Killick, surprisingly close at hand.

'Light along a pot of coffee. D'you hear me, there?'

'Aye aye, sir: pot of coffee it is.'

The order had been long expected, the kettle was hot, the berries ground; and the elegant pot came gleaming in a few minutes later, scenting the whole cabin. Of all the many virtues, Preserved Killick possessed only two, polishing silver and making coffee; but these he possessed to such a high degree that for those who liked their plate brilliant and their coffee prompt, freely roasted, freshly ground and piping hot it was worth putting up with his countless vices.

They carried their cups into the great cabin and sat on the cushioned bench – in fact a series of lockers – that ran the whole width of the noble sweep of stern-windows, and Jack said, 'I am heartily sorry for it. Our homecoming will not be the same, no, not by a very long chalk. Though you must know best, in course. But when you say as quick as ever you can fly, do you mean it literally?'

'I do too.'

'Then why not go in the *Ringle*? Even if the wind don't back another point she will sail straight to Pompey as it lays, without going about, and get there at least twice as fast as that poor old knacker's yard of a *Berenice*.' Then seeing Stephen's look of surprise he poured him another cup and went on, 'I never told you – there was no time last night or this morning, with that ass, that *thundering* great ass, playing off his humours – but I won her from Heneage after supper: a throw of sixes when I was on the very point of being gammoned. He had already borne six men, but he could not re-enter for a great while; and so I won. Tom and Reade and Bonden will run you up-Channel – they handle her beautifully – and I will add a few hands that don't belong to Shelmerston.'

Stephen made a few customary protests, but very few, since he was thoroughly used to both the Navy's generosity and rapid decision. Jack swallowed another cup and hurried off, bawling for his gig.

Alone in the great cabin Stephen reflected upon Sir Joseph's message. It required him to proceed to London without the loss of a minute, and it did so even more briefly than was usual. Joseph Blaine hated prolixity almost as much as he hated Napoleon Buonaparte, yet this extreme curtness perplexed Stephen until, recalling times past, he turned the half-sheet over and there on the lower left-hand corner found the faintly-pencilled letter pi, signifying many. In this case it meant the Committee, a body made up of the leading men in the intelligence service and the Foreign Office that had sent him to Peru to forestall or rather to outstrip the French in their attempt at winning over the chiefs of the movement for independence from Spain. Clearly they wanted to know what he had accomplished, and in all probability this extreme haste meant that they were having some difficulty in representing the matter in a favourable or even a tolerable light to their Spanish allies. He ran through the long series of complicated events that would make up his account, and as he did so he gazed at the frigate's wake, a wake, all things considered, that had now attained a perfectly enormous length.

He was still reflecting when Tom Pullings, the ship's nominal captain – nominal, because of an inept scheme for disguising the *Surprise* as a privateer under the command of an unemployed half-pay officer in order to deceive the Spaniards – came in and cried, 'There you are, Doctor. Such news! *Berenice* hove to and struck soundings clear not half a glass ago, and the *Ringle* will be alongside directly. Killick, Killick, there. The Doctor's sea-chest as quick as you like.'

He had scarcely left to see to his own before Jack came swarming aboard again by the stern ladder. 'There you are, Stephen,' he cried. 'Heneage hove his ship to and struck soundings clear – white sand and small shells – and all is laid along aboard the schooner. Killick, ho. Killick, there. The Doctor's sea-chest . . .'

'Which I done it, ain't I?' Killick's voice quivered with indignation. 'All corded up: nightshirt on top; slippers; common check shirt and trousers for the run up to the South Foreland; white shirt and neckcloth for London and decent black breeches; best wig tucked down in the right-hand forward corner.' He stumped off, and could be heard shoving the chest about, telling his mate 'to look alive, there, Bill.'

'As for my collections,' said Stephen, referring to the many barrels and crates in the hold, containing the specimens of an ardent natural philosopher whose interests ranged from cryptogams to the larger mammals, by way of insects, reptiles and birds, above all birds, and who had travelled thousands upon thousands of miles, 'I confide them entirely to you. And there are the little girls. Jemmy Ducks has a wife in the village, I believe?'

'He had the equivalent, or at least he had when we sailed; and I do not suppose Sarah and Emily would know the odds. Anyhow, I shall see them stowed until you come back. You will be coming back, I collect?'

'Certainly: I shall post down as soon as ever I can. I should be very sorry to see my Titicaca grebe decay.'

'Schooner alongside, if you please, sir,' said Bonden, Jack's coxswain and a very old friend: Stephen had taught him to read.

'And Jack, you will salute Diana most affectionately for me, I beg; and assure her that if I had my will . . .'

'Come, sir, if you please,' said Tom Pullings. 'Schooner's alongside and we are fending off something cruel, in this ugly cross-sea.'

They got him over safely, dry and uncrushed, though somewhat winded from having leapt, against all advice, as the schooner was on her lively rise. He had not been aboard her when she was the *Berenice*'s tender, for although he did contemplate her from time to time with a certain mitigated interest, his own little green-painted skiff was infinitely more suitable for moving about, exploring the immediate surface of the ocean and the modest depths within reach of his net on those occasions when the ships were becalmed. Now he found her motion much brisker than that of the *Surprise*, six or seven times heavier, and he walked carefully aft to the larboard main shrouds, where he seemed to be in no man's way and where he was firmly supported by the aftermost pair. In the meantime the hands forward had flattened in the jib so that the *Ringle*'s head paid off: a moment later the foresail and then the mainsail rose; the sheet came right aft and she leant over to leeward, moving faster and faster. Stephen clung on, strangely exhilarated; he meant to pluck out his handkerchief and wave to his friends, but before he could get at it with any safety they were racing past the *Berenice*, which really seemed to be standing still, though she had a respectable bow-wave and a fine spread of canvas.

Heneage Dundas took off his hat and called out something, kind and cheerful no doubt but the wind bore it away: Stephen raised a hand in salute – a rash move, for the next moment he was dashed from his hold, coming up against the powerful Barret Bonden, who was at the tiller – the schooner had no wheel. Without allowing the *Ringle* to deviate from her course for an instant Bonden seized the Doctor with his left hand and passed him to Joe Plaice, who made him fast, though with a reasonable latitude of movement, to an eye-bolt on the transom.

Here he collected himself and settled in moderate comfort quite soon, looking directly aft; and to his astonishment he saw that the *Berenice* and *Surprise* were already a great way off. The people on their forecastles were small, diminishing as he watched, individually unrecognizable apart from Awkward Davies with his red waistcoat. By now the *Ringle* had set her foretopsail (she was after all a topsail schooner) and with the breeze more than two points free – two points for her, since she could lie closer than five from the wind, whereas even that weatherly ship the *Surprise*, being square-rigged, could not do better than six, while the poor fat *Berenice* could barely manage seven, and that at the cost of immense leeway – she fairly tore along, a delight to all hands aboard.

Presently the two ships were hull-down except on the top of the rise, white against the dark grey of the clouds. Stephen saw them go about, standing towards Ushant and growing smaller still, for unless the wind backed farther still, they, unlike the *Ringle*, were condemned to beat up, tack upon tack. He watched them with a strange medley of feelings: the *Berenice* was a kindly ship and one in which he had spent many a pleasant evening with Jack, Dundas and Kearney, the first lieutenant, playing keen but perfectly civil whist, or merely in discursive uncontentious rambling talk about ports, local manners, and naval supplies, from China to Peru, all from personal experience; but the *Surprise* had been his home for longer than he could easily recall. There had been intervals ashore and intervals in other ships; but he had probably lived in her longer than in any other dwelling he had known, his having been a wandering, unfixed life.

* * *

It was three days before the breeze finally relented, backing into the west and even south of west, a leading wind for those bound up-Channel; and in the afternoon watch of that day, being arrived at the height of Shelmerston, the *Surprise* and the *Berenice* parted company at last, each cheering the other with the heartiest good will.

The *Surprise* steered west under topgallantsails, a lovely sight, trim, new-painted, with all her people, even the watch on deck, in shore-going rig as brilliant as so long an absence allowed – bright blue jackets with brass buttons, white duck trousers, embroidered shirts, little pumps with bows, Barcelona neckerchiefs. The long, meticulously exact final sharing-out of the gains from the privateering side of the voyage had taken all morning, as grave as a high court, under the supervision of all commissioned officers, all warrant officers, and representatives of the four parts of the ship. The single-share man's dividend amounted to £364 6s. 8d, and even the little girls, who by general agreement were allowed a half share to be divided between them, had more pieces of eight than they could easily count, the pieces going at 4/6d. It was a grave, long-drawn out ceremony, but now grog and dinner had intervened, diminishing the solemnity, and many of the hands walked about, clashing their loaded pockets and laughing for mere pleasure as the ship sailed easily in on the making tide towards that infinitely familiar shore.

They had to check her way well before the entrance to the harbour, lying there to a stream-anchor with brailed-up topsails until there should be enough water on the bar to let the deep-laden frigate over without a scrape, and the people lined her side, gazing landwards. More than half of them were from Shelmerston, and they pointed out all changes and everything that remained as it had always been.

Some of the few Anglicans aboard cried out that the weather-vane on their parish church, a basking-shark, had had its tail renewed: the old squeak might have gone, never to be heard again. But others took great comfort in the low, square tower, whose Norman severity had been softened by several hundred years of rain and south-west gales: no alteration that even the keenest eyes could make out. Most of the villagers however belonged to one or another of the Nonconformist sects that flourished there; and of these the Sethians were the richest and most influential. They drew the utmost satisfaction from their high-perched chapel, whose white marble, decorated with huge gleaming brass inlays, now caught the sun, gleaming through a gap in the veiled and watery sky. It had benefited much from a former voyage in which Captain Aubrey captured, among other prizes, a ship with her hold crammed with great leather bottles of quicksilver, and it was destined to benefit to a still greater extent from this even more prosperous venture.

Just what form the splendour should take was not yet decided, but as they surveyed the land there was some talk of spires. A Knipperdolling, an Anabaptist, standing within a yard or so, one of the few hands whose imperfect digestion made him fractious after meals, gave it as his opinion that spires smacked of Popery. In spite of the general cheerfulness aboard this might have led to discord if William Burrowes, an elderly forecastleman of great authority, had not called out, in a voice that reminded all hands of the proper tone on great occasions, 'There is old Sandby's sail-loft, as bloody awkward as ever, with that cruel great overhang and no crane.'

This led to a general enumeration of houses, shops and inns unchanged; yet gradually the mood of exultation fell; a certain uneasiness became apparent – there was nobody going in and out of the Crown, which was against nature; all the inshore fishing-boats were drawn up; there was no one standing staring on the beach, though anybody with a glass, and there were glasses by the score in Shelmerston, could not only recognize the ship but also see the great silver-gilt candlestick taken from a pirate in the Great South Sea and now hoisted to her main topgallant masthead: what was amiss? The uneasiness spread slowly and many would have nothing whatsoever to do with it: but when a thick-witted oaf called Harris said that it reminded him of Sweeting Island in the Pacific, where all the people had died suddenly, leaving only Sarah and Emily, everyone turned upon him with surprising ferocity – he might stash that; he might stow his gob; or in the sea-going phrase, he 'might bugger off', taking his ugly black-poxed carcass with him, and his face like an ill-scrubbed hammock.

'Man the capstan,' called Jack, as the first drops fell.

They won the stream-anchor with no pain at all, the hands crowding to the bars and thrusting with enormous force; and as soon as it was catted the tide swung the ship's head inshore. They filled the foretopsails, gliding smoothly over the bar with a fathom to spare. And as they came in so an aged, aged man with his face in a bandage pushed off, a small boy sculling over the stern.

'What ship is that?' he hailed in a high shrill creaking old voice, one hand to his ear.

'*Surprise*,' replied Jack in the silence.

'Where do you hail from?'

'Shelmerston: last from Fayal.'

'*Surprise*. That's right: *Surprise*,' said the very old man, nodding. 'Do you have a young fellow named John Somers aboard?'

The silence continued for a moment. John Somers had been drowned off the Horn.

'Speak up, young Somers,' said Jack in a low voice.

'Grandad,' called John's brother. 'I am William. John was . . . John was called to Heaven. I am his younger brother, Grandad.'

'William? William? Yes. I know ee,' said the old man with little or no emotion.

'How is Mum?' asked William.

'Dead and buried this year and more.'

'Let go the anchor,' called Jack Aubrey.

While the ship was being made safe and the boats were getting over the side someone asked the boy who he was. 'Art Compton,' he said.

'Then you are my nephew,' exclaimed Peter Wills. 'I have a poll parrot for Alice. How are they all at home, and where is everybody?'

'They are well enough, I reckon, Uncle Peter. They are all gone off to see Jack Singleton and his mates hanged, over to Worsley. I was left behind to look after Cousin Somers here. Which we drew straws.'

'Red cutter away,' cried Jack, and so on through the frigate's boats. They pulled ashore through the increasing drizzle, and Jack went straight to the Crown, leading the little girls by the hand and knocking until a decrepit caretaking ostler came to open the door.

The rain cleared well before sunset, and with the return of the ordinary people and the Shelmerston whores from the hanging – seven men and a child on one gibbet, a sight that had drawn the whole county – the little town grew more cheerful by far, in spite of the news of more deaths, of some quite unlooked-for births and some frank desertions, more cheerful, with fiddles in most of the inns and ale-houses and visiting from cottage to cottage with presents in a truly wonderful abundance.

But by the time the Crown and all the other houses along the strand were full of noise and light and tumbling anecdote, Jack, having left Sarah and Emily with Mrs Jemmy, a fat, gasping lady, was travelling as fast as a chaise and four could carry him over good roads towards Ashgrove Cottage.

His massive sea-chest was lashed on behind, of course, but his most recent present for Sophie, a suit of the finest Madeira lace, could not bear crushing, and it travelled on his knee. This caused him to sit rather stiffly, yet even so he went to sleep now and then, the last time after the senior post-boy, having left the main road, asked him for an exact direction. Jack gave it to him, made him repeat it, and dropped off again, as sailors will, in five minutes, wondering whether anyone would still be awake at home.

Half an hour later the sound of hooves changed and died away, the motion ceased and Jack started into full wakefulness, astonished by the blaze of light in his house, or not so much in his house itself as on the other side of the stable-yard into which the chaise had wandered. At one time Jack, in a temporary period of wealth, had launched into the breeding and training of race-horses, of which he considered himself as good a judge as any in the Navy, and this splendid brick-paved yard and the handsome buildings all round dated from that time. The light gleamed from the handsomest of them all, a double coach-house: it poured out into the murky night, with song, laughter and the sound of loud, animated conversation, too loud for the arrival of the chaise to be noticed within.

Jack picked up the suit of lace, which he had been treading on for the last few miles, settled with the post-boys, desired them to carry his chest out of the rain and walked in. A voice cried, 'It's the Captain', the cheerful din died quite away apart from a single woman's voice deaf to anything but its own story, 'So I says to him "You silly bugger, ain't you ever seen a girl do a . . ."' and a song far in the background 'Wherever I roam I long and I long and I long for my home.'

Hawker, the groom, came up with a nervous smile and said, 'Welcome home, sir, and please to forgive us this liberty. It was Abel Crawley's birthday, and all the ladies being away, we thought you would not mind –' He gestured towards Abel Crawley, now seventy-nine to the day, dead-drunk and speechless, apparently dead: he had been a fore-castleman in one of Lieutenant Aubrey's earlier ships, the *Arethusa*; and indeed nearly all the men present had been Jack's shipmates at one time or another, and most were incapacitated. Their companions were what would have been expected, the short thick girls or youngish women known as Portsmouth brutes: the mule-cart that had brought them stood at the far end of the yard.

In the keenness of his disappointment Jack felt inclined to top it the holy Joe for a moment, but he only said, 'Where is Mrs Aubrey?'

'Why, at Woolcombe, sir, with the children and all the servants apart from Ellen Pratt. And Mrs Williams and her friend Mrs Morris are at the Bath.'

'Well, tell Ellen to make me supper and get a bed ready.'

'Sir, not to tell a lie, Ellen is somewhat overtook: but I will grill you a steak directly, and a Welsh rabbit; and Jennings will make you up a bed. Only I am afraid you will have to drink beer, sir: which Mrs Williams locked up the wine-cellar.'

In the morning Jack made his own coffee and ate a number of eggs with toasted bread in the kitchen. He had no heart to look round the shut-up house – it was meaningless without Sophie in it – but he did make a quick tour of his garden – no longer his, alas, but now the child of some alien spade – before walking into the yard. 'Tell me, Hawker, what horses have we in the stable?' he asked.

'Only Abhorson, sir.'

'What is Abhorson?'

'A black gelding, sir: sixteen hands, past mark of mouth.'

'What is he doing here?'

'He belongs to Mr Briggs, sir, the Honourable Mrs Morris's manservant. There ain't no stabling at their place in Bath, so when they are there the nag stays here; when they are here Briggs rides to Bath every so often.'

'Is he up to my weight?'

'Oh yes, sir: a strong, big-boned animal. But today he is full of beans, and may be nappy.'

'Never mind. How are his shoes?'

'New all round last week, sir. Which Mrs Williams is very particular about Briggs's horse,' said the groom with a curious emphasis. 'So is the Honourable Mrs Morris too, for that matter.'

'Very well. Have him at the door in five minutes, will you? And see if you can find me a cloak. We shall have rain before ever I reach Dorset.'

Abhorson was indeed a powerful brute, but with his heavy common head and small eyes he looked neither intelligent nor handsome: he flung away from Jack's caress and made an irregular crab-like movement so that the groom at his head was towed sideways and Jack, trying to mount, went hop, hop, hop half across the yard before swinging into the saddle.

He had not been on a horse since he was in Java, half a world away; but once there, with the leather creaking agreeably under him and his feet well in the stirrups, he felt pleasantly at home; and although Abhorson was undoubtedly nappy, inclined to indulge in such capers as tossing his head, snorting very violently and going along in a silly mincing diagonal gait, Jack's powerful hands and knees had their effect, and by the time the rain or rather the drizzle began they were travelling quite well together through the new plantations. Jack was possessed with admiration at the lovely growth of his trees, far beyond what he had expected and in very beautiful fresh leaf; but this was only the forefront of his mind: all the deeper part that was not taken up with the idea of Woolcombe, the family house he had recently inherited, and with Sophie and the children in it, kept revolving the delightful prospect of his squadron, the Royal Navy's unattached ships and officers perpetually forming fresh combinations of possibility. 'But I shall certainly keep the *Ringle* as my tender,' he observed aloud.

The drizzle increased to downright rain. He returned from these very happy speculations – he was a man unusually gifted for happiness when happiness was at all possible: and now it was flooding in from every side – and told Abhorson to cheer up, for it could not last long, coming down so hard. The horse was moving with a dogged, sullen pace, but he moved his ears as though there were at least some communication, and Jack twisted round to get at the cloak rolled up behind the saddle.

As he did so a blackbird shot across the road right under the horse's nose, cackling loud. Abhorson gave a violent sideways leap, a turning leap that threw Jack with perfect ease – a heavy, heavy fall, Jack's head hitting the stone that marked his boundary.

31

Chapter Two

'Good morning to you,' said Stephen. 'My name is Maturin, and I have an appointment with Sir Joseph Blaine.'

'Good morning, sir,' replied the porter. 'Pray be so good as to take a seat. James, show the gentleman into the second waiting-room.'

This was not that famous place, looking out over the court and so through the screen into Whitehall, in which generation after generation of naval officers had waited, usually in the hope of promotion or at any rate of an appointment to a ship, but a far smaller, far more discreet little room with only one chair in it; and Stephen had barely had time to sit down before the inner door opened. Sir Joseph, a portly man with a pale, glabrous and usually anxious, work-worn face, hurried in, smiling, looking thoroughly pleased. He took both Stephen's hands, crying, 'Why, Stephen, how very, *very* happy I am to see you! How are you, my dear sir? How do you do after all these countless miles and days?'

'Very well, I thank you, dear Joseph; but I wish I could see you less pale and harried and overworked. Do you sleep? Do you eat at all?'

'Sleep is difficult, I must confess; yet I still eat tolerably well. Will you join me this evening at Black's? Do join me, and you will see: I always sup on a boiled fowl with oyster sauce and a pint of our claret.'

'I shall happily watch you,' said Stephen, 'but for my own part I have already bespoke turbot and a bottle of Sillery.' He felt in his pocket and went on, 'Pray accept this offering.' He passed over a dirty handkerchief, and eagerly unwrapping it Sir Joseph cried, '*Eupator ingens*! How very kind of you to remember – a splendid specimen indeed – such generosity – I wonder you can bear to part with him.' He set the creature down, gazed at it and murmured, 'So now at last I am the possessor of the noblest beetle in creation.'

The door opened again and a severely official face said, 'The gentlemen are beginning to arrive, Sir Joseph.'

'Thank you, Mr Heller,' said Sir Joseph. 'I shall be with them before the striking of the clock.' The door closed. 'The Committee, of course,' he said to Stephen. He wrapped the beetle very carefully in his own handkerchief, gave back the first, and went on, 'Now I must speak to you as a public servant: the First Lord bids me tell you that a small squadron is intended for Captain Aubrey. He is to hoist a broad pennant and cruise off the west coast of Africa to protect our merchantmen and discourage the slave-trade. The slavers are of many nationalities, they carry a large variety of protections and they may be accompanied by men-of-war; so clearly he needs not only an eminent surgeon but also a linguist and a man steeped in political intelligence; and it is hoped that these characters may be united in the same amiable person. Yet there is the possibility of certain eventualities and since I know that – without its affecting our friendship in any way – there are subjects on which we are not wholly in agreement, I think it proper to ask, if I may, where your heart would lie if the French intended another descent on Ireland. Believe me, this is a question primarily designed to preserve you from the possibility of a painful state of indecision and reserve.'

'No indecision at all, my dear. I should do everything in my power to take, sink, burn or destroy them. The French, with their present horrible system, would be utterly intolerable in Ireland – look at Switzerland, look at the Italian states . . . No, no, no, as you are aware, I do very strongly feel that each nation should govern itself. It may be said that the Irish have not been very good at it – the annals make the saddest reading in the world, and an O'Brien, no less, Turlough O'Brien, King of Thomond, sacked Clonmacnois itself. But that is not really to the point: my own house may be unswept in places, but it is my own, and I will thank no stranger for putting it in order: least of all if he is an ugly, false, impious thief of a black Corsican.'

'Thank you, Stephen,' said Sir Joseph shaking his hand. 'I did so hope that that was what you would say. Now we must go and meet the Committee.'

'You know what I have to tell them, sure?'

'Yes, yes. I feel for you extremely.'

It was clear from the atmosphere of the Committee meeting that its other members were also aware of his mission's outcome – indeed, in its broadest outlines the outcome was perfectly obvious, since Peru was still part of the Spanish empire, but he nevertheless gave them a succinct account, to which most of them listened intelligently, asking a few pertinent questions in the course of his narrative and rather more when he had finished.

After he had dealt with the points they raised, Mr Preston of the Foreign Office, who had been taking notes throughout, said, 'Dr Maturin, may I beg you to listen to this very brief summary I have been making for the minister and to correct any mistakes I may have committed?' Stephen bowed, and Preston went on, 'Dr Maturin, appearing before the Committee, stated that after the ship in which he was travelling, a hired vessel, his own property, duly licensed as a letter of marque, had left Sydney Cove, her commander received instructions to proceed to Moahu, where two or perhaps three rival factions were at war. He was to ally himself with the most amenable, ensure his supremacy and annex the island before pursuing his course for South America. This was accomplished, and shortly afterwards an American privateer was captured . . .'

'Forgive me, sir, if I interrupt you at this point,' said Stephen. 'I am afraid I must have expressed myself badly. The ship in question, the ship in which I was then embarked, was the *Nutmeg of Consolation*, not my *Surprise*, which we met by appointment off the Salibabu Passage and in which we sailed on to Peru. The *Nutmeg* was provided by the Governor of Java, to replace the frigate *Diane*, in which the late Mr Fox and I had the happiness of concluding a treaty with the Sultan of Pulo Prabang . . .' There was a general murmur of approval at this, and Mr Preston looked at Stephen with an unofficial and even affectionate smile. '. . . and the conflict in Moahu was between the island's legitimate queen and a discontented chief aided by some white mercenaries and a Frenchman called Dutourd, a wealthy visionary who wished to set up a democratic paradise at the cost of slaughtering those who disagreed with him and who had bought, armed and manned a ship in America to effect this purpose. In this case morality and expediency happily coincided: the *Nutmeg* defeated the discontented chief and captured both Dutourd and his ship. But there was no question of annexation. The queen entered into an alliance with King George III, gratefully accepting his protection, no more. And as for the American privateer, the *Franklin* as Monsieur Dutourd called her, it appeared that she did not in fact enjoy that status, Dutourd having omitted to take out letters of marque, so that his capturing British whalers made a pirate of him: this at all events was the opinion of the *Surprise*'s commander, who decided to carry him back to England so that the question might be settled by the proper judges.'

'Thank you, sir. I shall make all this clear,' said Mr Preston, writing fast. Then he went on with his abstract, dealing with Stephen's encounter with the resident agent in Lima, his very successful conversation with high ecclesiastics and military men, particularly General Hurtado, all of them committed to independence and many to the abolition of slavery; the escape of the captured Dutourd, his contacts with the French mission engaged on a similar but much less successful, much less well-funded errand; his denunciation of Stephen as a British agent; and the cry of 'foreign gold' raised by the opponents of independence, a cry, which, taken up by the hired mobs, made Stephen's exactly-timed scheme, based on the temporary absence of the viceroy, quite impossible, since General Hurtado refused to act, and Hurtado alone could move the necessary troops.

'It must have been the cruellest blow,' observed Colonel Warren, the head of army intelligence.

'It was, indeed,' said Stephen.

'Had Dutourd any reason to suppose that you were in fact a British agent?' asked another member.

'He had not. But I was obliged to speak French when I was treating his wounded men after they had been captured; presently he almost certainly remembered meeting me in Paris; and intuition, coupled with very strong personal dislike and a desire to do harm no doubt did the rest – it was an accusation that would have passed unnoticed, disregarded in any other climate, but once the anti-independentists had seized upon it, public opinion changed entirely.'

After a silence the representative of the Treasury said, 'It is my duty to observe that very large sums of money in various forms were placed at Dr Maturin's disposal, and to ask him whether it was possible to preserve any part, such as the easily transportable drafts and bonds that had not yet been exchanged.'

'It is not without a certain complacency that I can tell the gentleman,' said Stephen, 'that the gold, which was to have been parcelled out among the various regiments on Wednesday had Hurtado not cried off on Tuesday, remains, apart from a few hundred pounds' worth of douceurs, in the hands of our agent in Lima; while the paper obligations, bonds and the like are now aboard the little vessel that brought me up to the Pool, in a case under the immediate eye of her captain.' Certain members of the Committee were unable to conceal a look of intense satisfaction, and Stephen perceived that some other costly scheme would now once more be possible. He added, 'As for the gold, our agent in Peru is of opinion – and I entirely agree with him, for what my

36

view is worth – that it would be far more usefully employed in the kingdom of Chile, where Don Bernado O'Higgins had such a following. Finally I may observe that our agent has shipping interests, and can undertake to remove the cumbrous metal.'

'Speaking of cumbrous metal,' said Blaine, as they walked down Whitehall together, 'you could do me such a kindness, if you mean to return to Shelmerston in the tender; and with this brisk wind settled in the north-east she would carry you there quicker and in much more comfort than a coach. No changing, either.'

'Please to name the service in question.'

'It is the carrying of a statue I have promised a friend in Weymouth; an impossible object for a waggon, but a mere trifle for a ship.'

Stephen, extremely unwilling not to post straight down to Barham and Diana, stopped a passing hackney-coach, and with his hand on the door-handle he asked, 'What would it weigh, at all? This is only a very little small thin sharp-bodied vessel.'

'In the nature of three ton, I suppose; a little small thin porphyry Jove.'

'Listen, my dear: may I say by all means – very happy – unless Captain Pullings says it must necessarily plunge through the schooner's bottom? I am on my way to see Mrs Broad in the Liberties of the Savoy – you remember Mrs Broad of the Grapes?'

'Certainly: my best compliments to her, if you please.'

'And from the Grapes it is no distance at all to the Pool.'

'Until this evening, then,' called Blaine, withdrawing hastily to the wall as a coach and four came cantering up, spraying filth wide on either hand.

Mrs Broad and Stephen were old friends. He kept a room up one pair of stairs the year round, even when he was in another hemisphere; he had a cupboard for his skeletons and presses for all manner of things that he might need –

instruments, specimens, books, the unfinished manuscript of a work in lithotomy, a large number of old letters and used envelopes with notes on the back – when he was in London, and she was thoroughly used to his ways as well as Padeen's, who acted as his servant on shore, wearing breeches with silver buckles, of which he was inordinately, sinfully proud. She had known the Doctor for so long and in such difficult circumstances that nothing surprised her very much: it had been bears in the coal-hole and laundry before now, and badgers rescued from a baiting in the farther outhouse, as well as some very odd dissections indeed; and the suggestion of two little girls did not worry her particularly, however black and Popish they might be. She wept to hear how and why they had been taken from their native island; but having wiped her eyes she comforted Stephen's apprehensions by saying, 'Lord bless you, Doctor, they will be happy enough here. We have every colour in the Liberties, black, grey, brown and yellow, everything except perhaps bright blue; and they can run about in the churchyard or watch the traffic in the Strand. But oh dear me, sir, what will you think of me? I have never asked after Mrs Maturin. How does your good lady do, sir? And Miss Brigid, bless her?'

'I have not seen them yet, Mrs Broad. I had to come straight up from the chops of the Channel in the tender, while Captain Aubrey went ashore. But I may go down in the tender tomorrow: the wind sits perfectly; or I may take a chaise.'

'Well, at least you will have supper here, and sleep in your room. Lucy and I have been airing it ever since Padeen came and made us understand you was not far off. "Clo' clo' clo'," he said, the way he had, poor fellow; and seeing me look stupid, Lucy cried, "He means the Doctor is near at hand," and we all laughed. Oh dear me, how we laughed. And we put warm, lavendered sheets on the bed.'

'Sup I cannot, Mrs Broad, for I am pledged to Sir Joseph Blaine, who sends you his compliments: but sleep I will, most happily. It would be best to give me the front-door key, for I may be late. But now I must run down to the Pool.'

He walked into Black's, and there was Blaine, standing in front of the hall fire with his coat-tails over his elbows and his bottom exposed to the blaze. 'Captain Pullings says she can very well manage three tons,' said Stephen, 'but since he must sail on the turn of the tide he wonders very much how you will get your image aboard in time.'

'Oh, what capital news! There will be no difficulty whatso-ever, since it is already at Somerset House, and we have an ordnance barge that will bring it alongside in a trice. In a trice. Stephen, ain't you clemmed? This north-easter makes me so hungry that I should be pettish if it were anyone but you.'

'I am of your way of thinking entirely. Let us go up at once.'

They ate eagerly, almost in silence for some time, like old table-companions.

'Come, that is better,' said Sir Joseph, putting some of his fowl's bones on a side-plate. 'Now I am more nearly human; though by no means satisfied yet. I shall certainly eat a Welsh rabbit, and probably a good many petits fours with my coffee. How did you find Mrs Broad?'

'Blooming, I thank you; and she sends her duty. She is a very good creature, you know.'

'I am sure of it.'

'We brought back two little girls, Sarah and Emily, from a Melanesian island where all the people but for them had been destroyed by the smallpox caught from a passing whaler. They could not be left there to die slowly – they were already very much reduced – so I took them on board. Perhaps it would have been kinder to knock them on the head directly.'

'It is said that one must beware of pity,' observed Sir Joseph.

'At the time it seemed to me that there was no choice; but since then it has puzzled me extremely to know what to do with them. I should like them to be brought up understanding how a house is run, but not as servants; to have reasonable dowries –'

'Dowries. For my infinite good luck your fortune is intact,' said Blaine with a laugh, since at the very beginning of this prodigious voyage an exasperated Stephen had sent him a letter with a power of attorney, begging him to transfer his wealth from the huge, slow, impersonal, negligent but solvent London house that looked after it to a small country bank that ceased payment a few months later, the depositors getting fourpence in the pound – a letter that in his agitation he had failed to sign with anything but his Christian name. This omission rendered the power of attorney invalid, but it accounted firstly for Blaine's and Maturin's most unusual custom of calling one another Stephen and Joseph, and secondly for Stephen's still being a man of uncommon substance. 'And as I remember it was nearly all in gold,' Blaine continued.

'So it was; and so it is, for the greater part, still in my godfather's iron-bound chests. I changed only a small proportion, for current expenses. Reasonable dowries, then, in case they choose to marry rather than lead apes in Hell. To marry, perhaps, some skilled and thinking artisan, a clockmaker for example, or one that makes scientific instruments: possibly an apothecary or a surgeon or a preparer of specimens for anatomy-classes: Catholic, of course. Certainly not a sailor. A sailor, who may be absent for years, throws impossible strains on his wife. If she is a woman of any degree of temperament at all there is of course the question of chastity; and in either case there is that of command or perhaps I should say of decision. A woman who has been running a household, perhaps an estate, acquires an authority and a power of decision that she is not always willing to renounce: nor indeed should she always do so, since men are not invariably born with innate financial wisdom; and those who have spent most of their time at sea may be far less well acquainted with business by land than a sensible woman. Then again there is the bringing-up of children . . .' Stephen prosed away until he noticed that Sir Joseph's attention was almost entirely taken up with his Welsh rabbit, and perhaps with some anxieties that he had brought away with him from the Admiralty.

He stopped, and in the silence Blaine said, 'Very true. There is little to be said for the marriage of a sailor; or for any other man, if it come to that. As for the perpetuation of the human race, there are times when it seems to me that the world would be far, far better if the race were to die out. We have made such a sorry piece of work of it – everything for happiness, and misery everywhere. Even in spite of my boiled fowl and my pint of claret and your company I find my spirits much oppressed.' He glanced round the room, still well filled with members, some of them at tables quite close, and said, 'But of course I speak as a bachelor, and it suddenly comes to me that you are now a married man: it was inhuman of me to delay you with my porphyry Jove. Of course, you did not land at Shelmerston and post away into Hampshire with Jack Aubrey, so of course you have not seen Diana or had any news of her, or of Mrs Oakes?'

'I have not,' replied Stephen, wondering a little at Blaine's emphasis.

'Shall we take our coffee in the library?'

'By all means. It is the finest room in the club.'

Fine and even splendid it was, but its three great lustres shone upon books, comfortable chairs and Turkey carpet alone: never a member there.

'Stephen,' said Joseph, when the waiter had left them with a pot of coffee, a tray of petits fours and a decanter of cognac, 'I did not think it right to tell you what is in my mind in a public office, however closed the room. These hypothetical ears may be no more than one of the hallucinations of a mind too long and too closely engaged on what for lack of a better word I shall call intelligence, but they may exist, and that is why I am so happy that we are sitting together here in this warm and well padded desert.' He poured coffee and absent-mindedly ate half a dozen little meringues. 'Your private letters asked me to take care of Clarissa Oakes and told me about her exceptional fund of information.' Clarissa, a young gentlewoman reduced to beggary, had worked in a fashionable brothel within a musket-shot of the clubs in St James's Street, where she was well placed for learning a great many curious facts. 'I did take care of her, getting poor young Oakes his promotion and a ship, and when he was killed I took her down to Diana. Her fund of information was indeed exceptional and with her help we quickly identified the limping gentleman with the Garter who was connected with those wicked buggers Wray and Ledward.' The wicked buggers – and Blaine used the gross word literally – had been concerned with passing secret intelligence, particularly naval intelligence, to the enemy; they had been betrayed by a French agent, and after many changes of fortune Stephen had cut them both to pieces in an East Indian dissecting-room.

'Unhappily he turned out to be a hemi-demi royal, the Duke of Habachtsthal. He was brought up mainly in England, but he has a little principality close to Hanover and a much larger estate on the Rhine, both now occupied by the French, of course, and ideally suited for French blackmail. The old King was very fond of him and if he had been a marrying man, which he is not, he might perhaps have had one of our princesses: but even without, he is very nearly untouchable.'

'If I do not mistake he has high army rank – perhaps only honorary – and considerable influence.'

'Yes. He acts as adviser to several bodies, and through his aide-de-camp Colonel Blagden he may be said to sit on some important committees.' A pause, in which they both drank brandy, and then Blaine went on, 'Of course, there was no possibility of direct proceedings against him without absolutely cast-iron evidence like that we had against Ledward and Wray: and this we do not possess. However, we did make a good deal of distant thunder. You would never believe, Stephen, what Byzantine ways Whitehall possesses of conveying a threat, of causing it to echo from wall to wall until it reaches the intended ear.'

'What effect did it have?'

'Excellent, to begin with. Information had been going across, as in Ledward's time, and it stopped abruptly. But presently our gentleman came to a better understanding of his own impunity, and last month we lost the greater part of a West Indies convoy. More than that, he is a very old court and ministry hand and I believe he has traced the threat back to its source or is near to doing so. I am afraid of his resentment, both for myself and you: he was very much attached to Ledward, and even, in their strange fashion, to Wray. He is a bitterly revengeful man . . . I am by no means sure of all this, Stephen; but there are one or two things that increase my feeling of uneasiness, however weak, illogical and even superstitious it may be. One is that both Montague and his cousin St Leger seem to be fighting shy of me, as I dare say you noticed at the Committee, when I . . .'

A member in a bright blue coat with shining buttons walked in: he peered myopically at them, came a little nearer, and called out, 'Sir Joseph, you have not seen Edward Cadogan, by any chance?'

'No, sir, I have not,' said Blaine.

'Then I shall have to look in the billiard-room.'

The door closed behind him and Blaine poured more brandy. 'Then again, you will remember you asked me to arrange pardons for both Mrs Oakes and your Padeen for the crime of returning from Botany Bay without leave. It seemed to me a matter of no difficulty: Clarissa is the widow of a sea-officer killed in a very creditable action, and in the right quarters I could mention unusual services rendered to Intelligence; while your interest with the Admiralty and some of your more illustrious patients would surely cover poor Padeen. But my unofficial approaches have not been satisfactory – strange delays – a hint of unavowed reluctance. I do not like to press a direct request, still less present it in writing, until I am sure of a favourable response. I had thought of abandoning the usual channels and applying to the Duke of Sussex, seeing that you and he are both fellows of the Royal Society and founder-members of the Council Against Slavery, but he is gone to Lisbon; and the first stages in a matter of this kind must be by word of mouth.'

'Certainly,' said Stephen.

'In any event,' said Blaine after a pause for consideration, 'this second instance is no more than academic. If the two in question do not advertise their presence the likelihood of their being disturbed is utterly remote; and I cite their case only as an example of the tainting effect of an important man's dislike. *If* he has made his aversion evident – *if* he has cried, "That old fool Blaine at the Admiralty," let us say – the news would spread; I should become at least slightly leprous, and no man in his senses would hurry to do me a favour. That is all. I do not intend to imply any direct malignity extending beyond me and perhaps you, if indeed that malignity exists at all, and is not the figment of a fagged-out mind and an overwrought imagination.'

Stephen took out a soft pouch made of llama-skin. 'These are the leaves of *Erythroxylon coca*, the cuca or coca shrub,' he said. 'I have used them for a great while, and so have most of the inhabitants of Peru. If you roll them into a moderate ball in your mouth, then add a little of this lime and so thrust it into your cheek, chewing gently from time to time, you will experience first an agreeable warm tingling of your tongue, the inner lining of your cheeks and the border of your larynx, followed by an increasingly remark-able and evident clarity of mind, a serenity, and a perception that almost all worries are of little real consequence, most of them being the result of confused, anxious and generally fallacious notions that crowd and increase in direct pro-portion to the decline of pure single-minded reason. I should not advise the taking of it now, if you value your night's sleep, since it tends to keep one awake; but do try it in the morning. It is the most virtuous of leaves.'

'If it diminishes anxiety by even a half per cent, pray let me have it at once,' said Blaine. 'The Dutch Duke is not the least of my cares, but he is much outweighed in real importance by the situation in the Adriatic, and in Malta once again, to say nothing of the present crisis in the Levant.'

The *Ringle* stood in to Shelmerston on the very last breath of the expiring north-east breeze, crossed the bar and dropped anchor inside the *Surprise*, whose thin crew of ship-keepers greeted her with the expected cries: 'Where had they been? What had they been a-doing of? Bowsing up their jibs, no doubt. The slow coach could have come down quicker. The waggon would have beat them by half a day.'

Stephen, Tom Pullings, Sarah, Emily and Padeen hurried ashore, piled into two chaises and set off directly for Ash-grove. But in spite of all their haste, express letters, signals and orders travelling by semaphore from the Admiralty roof to Portsmouth had preceded them, and it was with the third of these in her hand that Mrs Williams, a short, thick, red-faced woman, now redder than usual with excitement, said to her daughter Sophie Aubrey, "The *Ringle* passed Port-land Bill at half-past four, so Dr Maturin is sure to be here this afternoon. I think it my duty – and Mrs Morris agrees with me – to tell Captain Aubrey the whole of Diana's disgraceful misconduct, so that he may break it gently to his friend.'

'Mama,' said Sophie firmly, 'I beg you will do no such thing. You know he is to lie quiet, and Dr Gowers said . . .'

'Dr Gowers, ma'am, if you please,' said the butler.

'Good morning, ladies,' said Gowers. 'I will just have a look at the Captain, if you please, and then we can attend to the children.'

'He is as well as can be expected,' he said, coming down the stairs, 'but he must be kept perfectly quiet, with the

45

room still darkened; and perhaps he could be read to in a low voice. Blair's sermons, or Young's *Night Thoughts* would answer very well. There has been far too much mental agitation recently. And he is to take three of these drops in a little water every hour. Soup this evening, not too thick; and perhaps a little cheese. No beef or mutton, of course.' He and Sophie hurried away to Charlotte, Fanny and George, who, immediately upon their hasty arrival from Dorset, had seen fit to come down with a high fever, a noisy cough, headache, restlessness, thirst, and a tendency to complain.

When they had gone, Mrs Williams walked softly into her son-in-law's room, sat by his bed, and asked him how he did. Having heard that he was pretty well and that he looked forward to seeing Stephen Maturin, she coughed, drew her chair nearer and said, 'Captain, in order that you should be able to break the dreadful news gradually and gently to your poor unfortunate friend, I think it my duty to tell you that since the birth of this idiot child Diana has been drinking heavily. She has been driving about the countryside, dining with people as far as twenty miles away, sometimes fast, raffish people like the Willises, frequently going to balls and ridottos in Portsmouth, and perpetually fox-hunting sometimes without even a groom to accompany her. She is no sort of a mother to the poor little girl, and if it were not for her friend, this Mrs Oakes, the child would be left entirely to the care of the servants. And worse still,' she said, lowering her voice, 'worse still, Mr Aubrey – I say this of my own niece with the greatest reluctance, as you may imagine – worse still, there are doubts about her conduct. I say *doubts*, but . . . Among others Colonel Hoskins has been frequently mentioned, and Mrs Hoskins no longer returns Diana's calls. Mrs Morris says – but here she is. Come in, Selina, dear.'

'Oh Captain Aubrey, I am afraid I have sad news for you,' cried Selina Morris, 'but I think you ought to know. I think it only right to tell you: it is only too easy to nourish a viper in one's bosom. Just now, on information received from our man Frederick Briggs, I caught Preserved Killick making off by the back lane to the servants' quarters with a hamper of wine. "Where did you get that hamper of wine, Killick?" I asked him, and in his rough, bold way, without so much as a ma'am he replied, "Which the Captain gave it me," and walked doggedly on. I called out that I should report him this minute and hurried to be here before the hamper could be concealed or huddled back into the cellar. I am quite out of breath, I declare.'

'That was kind of you, Mrs Morris,' said Jack, 'but in fact I did give him the hamper.'

'Oh indeed? Well, my intention was good, I am sure: and I ran all the way. My father had no notion of giving . . .' But feeling that the notions of her father were of no great consequence in this case, although he was a peer, she withdrew, making discontented motions with her shoulders, arms, buttocks.

'But as I was saying before dear Selina came on her mistaken but very well-meant errand, the greatest cause for general comment and disapproval was Diana's almost open – what shall I call it? – liaison with Mr Wilson, who managed her stud – a most improper occupation for a woman, even a married woman, by the way – a fine upstanding man with red whiskers – though not to compare with Selina's Briggs – who lived if not in the same house then at least very close and in an isolated part of the country. When last I saw her, which is now some time ago, since I never fail to speak my mind to my niece, which instead of attending to admonition she resents – she always was a most undutiful girl . . .'

'But you told me yourself that she provided the capital for your present concern.'

'Perhaps she did. But the money meant nothing to her – quite apart from her enormous winnings, Dr M left her far, far too much at her own uncontrolled, unsupervised disposal – and in any case Selina and I will pay it back presently. However, last time we saw her, Mrs Morris was certain that she was with child; and now we hear that the horses are all sent up to London, that the grooms are turned away, and that she has gone off herself, no doubt with her handsome manager. You must break it gently to your poor friend, or he will run mad.'

'I shall certainly do nothing of the kind.'

Jack's silence had quite persuaded Mrs Williams that he was in full agreement. 'Upon my word,' she cried in her indignation, 'then I shall do it myself.'

'If you presume to speak to him on this subject,' said Jack in a low tone that nevertheless carried full conviction, 'you and Mrs Morris and your servant Briggs will leave this house within the hour.'

Mrs Williams had changed much during his absence, but not so much that she could bring herself to renounce free board and lodging in a comfortable house whenever she chose to claim it. She closed her lips tight, and pale with anger left the room with much the same gestures as her friend.

Jack lay back. He was far too happy to be angry for long: he had already heard a good deal of what she said about Diana; during the voyage Sophie's letters, far spaced-out though they were, had kept him aware of the general situation; and although he knew that Diana's views on sexual morality were rather like his own, he did not believe a tenth part of this gossip – particularly he did not believe that she had run off with the man who managed her stud. And although he did very much regret Stephen's inevitable heavy, heavy disappointment over the daughter he had so looked forward to, he felt that the marriage itself would hold together. It had always done so hitherto, in spite of being subjected to extraordinary strains.

Happiness and grief were both active in his mind, and partly to escape the confusion, as well as the guilt of joy at such a time, he deliberately reflected on the change in Mrs Williams. Diana, like many of her friends, had always been willing to back her judgment of a horse with a bet, and having staked a large sum at thirty-five to one on the animal that won the St Leger two years ago she found herself with several thousand to spare. Part of her stake had been made up of small amounts, like the cook's half-guinea, rising to twenty-five for old Lady West whose husband, like Diana's father, had been a cavalry officer, but most had been the five-guinea bets laid by tolerably well-to-do widow ladies in Bath who delighted in gambling – sums that the big, reliable London offices would not trouble with, while the small local men – sad riff-raff – could not be trusted. When she had paid all these happy creatures, she suggested that her aunt, at that time penniless and oh so meek, should take over the whole undertaking, but for a profit, being her own betting office – here was the connexion, ready at hand, and Diana would show her how to keep a book. Just where the Hon. Mrs Morris came in he could not recollect, but she added much to the respectability of the concern; while her servant, a tall man in a black coat who looked like a dissenting minister and who expected other servants to call him Mr Briggs, had been employed by a race-horse owner and was very well acquainted with the subject. The two ladies' conversation could never have recommended them anywhere, but they were accepted members of that world, and their respectability, combined with reliability, discretion and convenience, caused their undertaking to prosper. How Mrs Williams reconciled her occupation with her former rigid principles Jack could not tell: but the principles had never prevented her, in the days of her wealth, from making an eager search for investments that would give her a very high yield – an attorney who offered her a certain thirty-one per cent return had been her undoing – and perhaps it was all part of the same thing. At all events she now grew steadily richer, and steadily more unpleasant. Jack was revolving this in his mind, an aphorism just out of reach, when he heard the sound of wheels on the drive, the opening and closing of carriage doors, steps on the gravel, more voices raised quite high, steps in the corridor, and Stephen opened the door of the room in which Jack's bed had been set up.

'Why, my poor Jack,' he exclaimed, but in little more than a whisper, 'how sorry I am to see you brought so low, my dear. Do your ears and eyes hurt you, now? Can you bear talking at all?'

'To be sure I can, Stephen,' said Jack, quite loud. 'It is much better today; and I am so glad to see you. But as for my being brought low, it is only my head; my heart is bounding about like a lamb. I had such a signal on Wednesday morning, brought up post-haste from the port-admiral, that valuable man. Such a signal . . . but tell me, how did your journey go? Was all well in town?'

'Very well, I thank you. Sir Joseph asked me to bring a statue down for a friend at Weymouth, so I came back with Tom in the *Ringle*, picking Sarah and Emily up at Shelmerston and coming on by chaise. Tom came along with us, for orders. You can hear him roaring on the terrace. I mean to take the girls on to Barham to see Diana for a while, and then to carry them up to the Grapes, to live with Mrs Broad. But Jack, your house is in a strange turmoil, I find. Will I go and bid Tom bring up all standing?'

'Never in life. I am sorry for the din – that screeching is Sophie from upstairs, I think, talking to him – but the fact of the matter is, the children have reported sick, the three of 'em, and with me laid up, the place is all ahoo. Would you like to hear about my signal, Stephen?'

'If you please.'

'Well, I am to have *Bellona*, seventy-four, with a broad pennant and Tom as captain under me; *Terrible*, another seventy-four; and three frigates, one of which is sure to be the *Pyramus*; and perhaps half a dozen sloops, for the cruise off Africa that Heneage Dundas told me of. Ain't you amazed? I was, I promise you. I thought it was just one of those things people throw out, far too good to be true.'

'I give you all the joy in the world of your command, my dear: long, long may it prosper.'

'You will come with me, Stephen, will you not? It is mostly for putting down the slave-trade, you remember; and by the twenty-fifth of next month all should be assembled, manned and equipped.'

'I should be very happy. But now, my dear Commodore, I must go and look at your children. I promised poor distracted Sophie so to do while your medical man was there, so that we might lay our physical heads together. I also promised not to tire you. Then I must hurry on to Barham: if I am not there by dark Diana will think we have been overturned in some remote, ill-favoured ditch.'

Jack's spirits fell at once. He hesitated, and said, 'It is quite a while since Sophie has seen her – some disagreement with Diana's aunt, I believe. But Stephen, do not be disappointed if she is away. Nobody knew we were coming back, you know.'

Stephen smiled and said, 'Diana and I will come and see you on your feet in a few days' time, I hope; but in the meanwhile I shall desire Dr Gowers to prescribe a little hellebore to calm the turbulence of your spirits and procure a healing equanimity. God bless, now.'

In the hall he found Tom Pullings, entirely alone, leaping and making antic gestures: on hearing Stephen he span round, showing a face of such laughing delight that the Devil himself could not have failed to smile. 'Can I see the Captain now, do you think?' he asked.

'You may; but do not speak loud, do not agitate his mind.'

Pullings took his elbow in an iron grip and whispered, 'He is to hoist a broad pennant in *Bellona*, and he has named me to be captain under him – he has made me post! I am a post-captain! I never thought it could happen.'

Stephen shook his hand and said, 'I am so happy. At this rate, Tom, I shall live to congratulate you on your flag.'

'Thank you, thank you, sir,' called Tom after him as he hurried up the stairs. 'I have never heard a sentiment so well expressed; nor with such elegance and wit, neither.'

'Sophie, my love,' said Stephen, kissing her on both cheeks, 'you are in the most charming bloom, joy: but there is some degree of nervous tension, even a hint of febrility.

I believe, Dr Gowers, that we might profitably exhibit a modest dose of hellebore for Mrs Aubrey as well as for the Commodore.'

'The Commodore,' murmured Sophie, squeezing his arm.

They looked at the children, all struck dumb for the moment, and presently Stephen said, 'I quite agree with my colleague. This is an advanced state of the commencement of measles: look at the swollen, bloated appearance of poor Charlotte's face.'

'I am not Charlotte. I am Fanny; and my face is neither swollen nor bloated.'

'Oh Fanny, for shame,' cried her mother, in great distress, tears starting from her eyes.

'So bloated and so swollen that the eruption cannot be long delayed: but I am sorry that it should be the measles, since I cannot bring my little girls up to see the invalids. Like many other black people they have no protection against the disease, and frequently succumb. And now, dear Sophie, I must go and collect them: do not move, I beg.' And privately in her ear, 'I am so very happy about Jack.'

On the stairs he murmured to himself, 'Presently I shall see a little face that is neither swollen nor bloated; one that is incapable of such a gross reply.'

In the drawing-room he found no one but Mrs Williams, still simmering with ill-temper.

'Where are Sarah and Emily?' he asked.

'The little niggers? I sent them to the kitchen, where they belong,' said Mrs Williams. 'When I came in they neither curtseyed nor called me ma'am. And when I said, "Don't you know you must not just say good day and no more as if you was addressing the cat and don't you know you must curtsey to a gentlewoman?" they only looked at one another and shook their heads.'

'You are to consider, ma'am,' said Stephen, 'that they have spent much of their life aboard a man-of-war, where there are no gentlewomen to be addressed, and where curtseys, if they exist, are reserved for officers.'

Mrs Williams sniffed, and then said, 'They are your property, I collect; and if so, I must inform you that no slaves can be countenanced in England, so that you are likely to lose your price. In the colonies, yes: but we must always remember that England is a free country and that as soon as slaves set foot on English soil they too are free: as a foreigner you cannot of course understand our love of liberty. But we must never forget to look closely at all sides of a bargain, or we may find ourselves buying a mare's nest.' Ill nature and ill temper urged her to add something about charity beginning at home, since a moment's reflection on their clothes and uncowed manners suggested that they might be protégées rather than bond-servants, but angry though she was she did not dare go farther, and after contemplating her for a moment with his pale eyes Stephen took up his hat, bowed, said 'Servant, ma'am,' and hurried off to the kitchen, where he found the little girls telling two superannuated ship's cooks about the glories of the green ice they had seen off the Horn.

For the rest of the journey they were very quiet, gazing at the wonderfully unfamiliar English countryside in the gentle evening light. So was Stephen. His mind, like Jack's, was confused by a variety of strong emotions – intense anticipation and a dread he did not choose to name – and like Jack he took refuge in reflecting upon Mrs Williams. There was not only the change from the broken-spirited poor relation, perpetually aware of her dependence, back to her former degree of assurance – though not indeed of dominance: Sophie had grown much stronger – and of indignant self-righteousness; there was also a change in that earlier being, with a barely definable raffishness superadded, an ease in throwing herself into a comfortable chair, an occasional absurdly inappropriate gross or at least ungenteel and totally incongruous expression, as though by handling bets she had absorbed some of the coarse side of the turf. 'It would not surprise me if she has taken to putting gin in her tea,' he said, 'and to the use of snuff.'

Shortly after this the rain began to fall; the landscape vanished, and Emily went to sleep on Padeen's knee. The postilion drew up to light his lamps inside the carriage, begged pardon, asked the direction again, and drove on slowly, clop, clop, clop. After a mile or so and a shouted exchange with a farm-cart the postilion stopped again, came to the door, begged pardon and feared they had taken the wrong lane. He would have to turn when he found a gate into a field. This happened once or twice, but not long after sunset they found themselves in the familiar high bare country rising to Barham Down.

The carriage drew up before the great middle door; no lights to be seen within. The little girls woke, anxious, dismayed; Padeen began unstrapping the baggage; Stephen rang the bell and knocked, his heart beating high.

No answer, but somewhere in the back of the house, perhaps the kitchen, a dog began to bark. He knocked again, the queer feeling in his bosom: pulled the bell-wire; and the bell itself could be heard ringing far inside.

A light through the cracks of the door; it opened on the chain and Clarissa's voice asked, 'Who is there?'

'Stephen Maturin, my dear. I am sorry we are so late.'

The chain came off with a rattle and the door swung wide, showing Clarissa with a lantern on a table by her side and a horse-pistol in her hand. 'Oh how very glad I am to see you,' she cried, yet with a certain embarrassment in her joy. She carefully uncocked the pistol – evidently loaded and for use – laid it on the table and held out her hand. 'Nonsense,' he cried, 'we embrace,' and kissed her.

'You have not changed,' she said, smiling, and stood back, motioning him in.

'You are alone, I doubt?' said he, not moving but with his eyes searching the long dark hall and his ears on the strain.

'Yes . . . yes,' she answered hesitantly. 'Well, but for Brigid.'

He went out, settled with the post-boy and came back with

the little girls, Padeen following with the baggage. 'Here are some old shipmates, Clarissa,' he said, leading them forward. 'Sarah and Emily, you must make your bobs to Mrs Oakes, and ask her how she does.'

'How do you do, ma'am?' they said in unison.

'Very well indeed, my dears,' she replied, kissing them. She shook Padeen's hand, and although they had not agreed very well when they sailed together in the *Nutmeg* the travellers now felt much drawn to a well-known face and a familiar voice in these utterly strange and foreign surroundings. Not only was the country strange – nothing of shipboard about it, nothing of the pleasures of a port, filled with unknown people who might fly out at you – but this particular house was quite outside their experience. It was in fact an unusual building, tall, gaunt and cold, one of the few large old houses that had not been altered in the last two centuries, so that the great hall ran right up the whole height to the roof, sombre indeed on such an evening and by the light of a single lantern.

Clarissa led them slowly, almost as it were reluctantly, quite through its length and then turned right-handed into a carpeted room with candles and a fire. A small girl was building card-houses on a table near the grate.

Clarissa murmured, 'Do not mind if she does not speak,' and Stephen could feel the controlled anguish in her voice.

The girl at the table was lit by the fire and two candles: she was three-quarters turned towards Stephen and he saw a slim fair-haired child, quite extraordinarily beautiful: but with a disquieting, elfin, changeling beauty. Her movements as she handled the cards were perfectly coordinated; she glanced at Stephen and the others for a moment without the least interest, almost without ceasing to place her cards, and then carried on with the fifth storey.

'Come, my dear, and pay your duty to your father,' said Clarissa, taking her gently by the hand and leading her, unresisting, to Stephen. There she made her bob, standing as straight as a wand, and with only a slight shrinking away she allowed her face to be kissed. Then she was led to the others; their names were clearly stated; they too made their bobs and Brigid walked easily back to her card-house, unconscious of their smiling black faces, though she did look straight up into Padeen's for a moment.

'Padeen,' said Clarissa, 'will you go down that long corridor, now? The first door on your right hand' – she held up her right hand – 'is the kitchen, and there you will find Mrs Warren and Nellie. Please give them this note.'

Stephen sat in an elbow-chair away from the light, watching his daughter. Clarissa asked Sarah and Emily about their journey, about Ashgrove and about their clothes. They all sat on a sofa, talking away readily enough as their shyness wore off; but their eyes were fixed on the slight, wholly self-possessed, self-absorbed figure by the hearth.

Mrs Warren and Nellie took some time to appear, since they had to fetch clean aprons and caps to be presented to the Doctor – the master of the house, after all. An ancient white-muzzled kitchen dog shuffled in after them and the first relief to Stephen's quite extraordinary pain – extraordinary in that he had never known any of the same nature or the same intensity – came when the old dog sniffed at the back of Brigid's leg and without stopping her left hand's delicate motion she reached down with the other to scratch his forehead, while something of pleasure showed through her gravity. Otherwise nothing disturbed her indifference. She saw her tall card-house fall, the tottering victim of a draught, with perfect composure; she ate her bread and milk together with Emily and Sarah, unmoved by their presence; and after a good-night ceremony in which Stephen blessed her she went off to bed with neither reluctance nor complaint. He observed with still another kind of pang that if ever their eyes met hers moved directly on, as they might have moved on from those of a marble bust, or of a creature devoid of interest, since it belonged to a different order.

* * *

'Can she speak at all?' he asked when he and Clarissa were sitting at the dining-table – cold chicken and ham, cheese, and an apple-pie: the servants sent off to bed long since. 'I am not sure,' said Clarissa. 'On occasion I have heard her doing something very like it; but she always stops when I come in.'

'How much does she understand?'

'Almost everything, I believe. And unless she is in one of her bad days she is very good and biddable.'

'Affectionate, would you say?'

'I like to think so. Indeed, it is probable; but the signs are hard to make out.'

Stephen ate wolfishly for a while, and cutting himself another piece of cheese he said, 'Will you tell me about Diana? I mean, what you feel you can properly say.' Clarissa looked at him doubtfully. 'I do not mean lovers or anything you cannot tell of a friend. For you were friends, I believe?'

'Yes. She was very kind when Oakes was at sea, and kinder still when he was killed; although by that time it was already perfectly clear that Brigid was not like ordinary people, which distressed her extremely, so that she drank too much and might then speak wildly and be indiscreet. But she was very kind. She taught me to ride: such joy. Very kind, and I am not an ungrateful creature, you know,' said Clarissa, laying her hand on Stephen's arm. 'But there were reserves. I believe she was deeply convinced that I was or had been your mistress. When I protested my complete indifference where such matters were concerned she only smiled politely, repeating that catch-phrase *Les hommes, c'est difficile de s'endormir sans*; and I could not prove my point with the confidences that you so kindly listened to on that remote island when we were aboard the *Nutmeg*, dear ship. Confidences, I may say, that I have never made to anyone but you, and never shall: and as you and Sir Joseph advised, for the world in general I am a governess who disliked her employment in New South Wales and ran away with a sailor.'

'When do you suppose her unhappiness began?'

'Oh, very early; well before I knew her. I believe she missed you cruelly. And from what I have heard the birth was worse than usual – an interminable labour and a fool of a man-midwife. The baby was put out to nurse, of course. When it came back it looked enchanting and she thought she would certainly love it. But already there was this total indifference. The child wished neither to love nor to be loved. Diana had never come across anything of the kind and she was completely bewildered as well as being wounded to the heart. When I came I think it was some relief, but it was not nearly enough and she grew more and more unhappy and often difficult. Her aunt Williams was very unkind indeed, I believe. And as time went on there was no improvement in Brigid: rather the reverse. The indifference grew to positive aversion, and even to a cold dislike.'

'Did any of my letters reach her?'

'None while I was here: none except that which Oakes and I brought back, of course. They would have been of the greatest help. She began to give up hope: so many ships are lost. And yet she dreaded your return. Obviously. Presently she took against this house: you would not have wished her to buy it; and indeed it is cold, lonely and inconvenient. The horses she loved almost until the end, but then suddenly she told me that she was giving up the stud, though it was quite successful, and the next week they were all sent up to Tattersalls with Mr Wilson, the manager, all except a stallion and two mares who went into the North Country – I forget the name of the house. Near Doncaster. All the grooms except for old Smith, who was to look after my little Arab and the pony and trap, were dismissed, though I know she wrote about among her friends to find new places for them; and she begged me to stay on here with Brigid until she could make arrangements. She left me a quantity of money and said she would write. I did hear from her once, in Harrogate; but not since.'

'She never was a letter-writer.'

'No. Yet she did write one that I was to give to you,

should the frigate bring you home. Would you like to see it now?'

'If you would be so good.'

While she was away he rolled himself a large ball of coca-leaves; before she opened the door again he tossed them into the fire.

'I am sorry to have been so long,' she said. 'Please open it at once, if you wish. I will bring some port, if I can find it.'

Stephen, he read, *I know you loathe women who have no fortitude, but I have not the courage to bear it any longer. If you come back, if ever you come back, do not, do not despise me.*

Clarissa returned with a decanter. They neither of them spoke for a while: the rain could be heard pouring from the eaves. Eventually Stephen poured the wine, and coming back to the commonplace world he said, 'Clarissa, I am infinitely obliged to you for staying and looking after my daughter. I must go to town with Sarah and Emily tomorrow but if I may I shall leave Padeen here with you. Now that the house is empty it is not fit you should be here with no more than one elderly groom. I have promised to be back at Ashgrove a week before the squadron sails, and by then I hope we can make better arrangements.' There was always Bath, he said, speaking somewhat at random, and the coast of Sussex; while Gosport offered a pleasant naval society, for really so isolated a place as Barham Down would weigh upon an angel's spirits, in time. Clarissa agreed that the house itself was cold, dark and sad, but it did have glorious rides about it: she had grown much attached to riding.

'Sure, a cheerful horse is a delightful, understanding companion,' said Stephen with something of a smile. 'But now, my dear, when we have drunk our port – and a very decent bottle it is – I should like to retire, if I may. Where am I to sleep?' He heard himself utter the question: almost immediately he saw that it was, that it might be, equivocal and his mind turned quickly in foolish circles.

Clarissa remained silent, looking grave. 'I have been thinking,' she said. 'Nellie and I turned out Diana's room on Friday. A mouse had made her nest between one of the bedposts and the curtain, a soft round ball with five pink creatures inside. She ran off, of course, but we left the nest in a box, and when she came back I closed the lid and carried them away to the hay-loft. For the moment I could not remember whether we made up the bed again, but now I am quite certain of it. New sheets and clean curtains.'

Chapter Three

'Papa,' shouted Fanny as she ran, still two hundred yards from the coach-house, 'Papa, your uniform is come.'

'Fan,' cried Charlotte, the fatter twin, several lengths behind, 'you are not to bawl out like that. And Miss O'Hara will hear you. You are to wait for me. Wait, oh do wait.' Her sister flitted on however, and Charlotte, coming to a halt, clapped her right hand behind her ear, in the manner of her old friend Amos Dray hailing the foretop in a gale of wind, and roared, 'Papa. Papa there, your admiral's uniform is come.' Then, hoarse with the effort, she added in little more than an ordinary shout, 'Oh George, shame on you,' for at this moment her little brother came racing into the stable-yard from the far end. With a better sense of timing and distance he had cut across the kitchen-garden, burst through the gooseberries regardless of their thorns, and had dropped from the wall into the back lane: now ran at full speed into the coach-house, where he gasped out, 'Papa. Oh sir. Your uniform is come. In Jennings' own dog-cart.'

'Thankee, George,' said his father. 'Jennings is always punctual. I do love a man that is true to his hour. Hold this strap, will you?' He had been home long enough for the children to have grown quite used to him again; and now his daughters rushed in without the least ceremony, repeating the news as though vehemence and a wealth of detail – who saw the dog-cart first and from what distance: the colour of the horse and of the packages: their number and shape – would restore something to its freshness.

'Yes, my dears,' said Jack, smiling at them – they were pleasant hoydens, between childhood and adolescence, almost pretty, and sometimes as graceful as foals – 'George told me. Clap on to the buckle, there.'

He was wholly unmoved, and with some indignation Charlotte cried, 'Well, ain't you going to come and try it on? Mama said you would certainly come and try it on.'

'There is no need. Everything was in order at the last fitting, bar a few buttons to be shifted and the epaulettes. Yet I may come up when George and I have finished this surcingle.'

'Then please may we open the epaulette-case? We have never seen an admiral's epaulette close to; but Miss O'Hara says we must not touch it on any pretext whatsoever without permission; and Mama has gone to fetch Granny and Mrs Morris.'

'Oh Papa, won't you come up and put on just the undress coat?'

'Please, sir,' cried George, 'please may I see the presentation sword again? You will certainly wear your presentation sword in full dress: that's poz.'

Jack ran up the ladder into the loft for an awl and a hank of saddler's twine.

'Well, bloody George,' murmured Fanny, looking at his gooseberry wounds, 'you will cop it if Miss O'Hara sees you. Stand over and I'll wipe you with my handkerchief.'

Charlotte directed her voice into the loft and called, 'Mama will be amazingly disappointed if you do not come up, sir.'

By the time Sophie returned with her mother and Mrs Morris, Jack was in the blue chamber, which had a dressing-room that opened off it; and in this dressing-room Killick, with a fanatical glee and without waiting for any man's permission, had laid out the contents of all the tailor's parcels: although in himself he was as dirty, slovenly and sea-bucolic as it was possible to be in the Navy, he delighted in ceremony (for a grand dinner he would sit polishing the silver until three in the morning) and even more in fine uniform. Jack had gratified him much in the first, possessing a fair amount of plate and then having been presented with a truly magnificent dinner-service by the West Indies merchants; but hitherto he had almost always been a disappointment in the second, patching up old coats and breeches, and having them turned when they were too threadbare. (It was true that during most of Killick's servitude Mr Aubrey had been extremely poor and often deep in debt.)

But now the case was altered: superfine broadcloth in every direction; a dazzling abundance of gold lace; white lapels; the new button with a crown over the fouled anchor all agleam; undeniable cocked hats; a variety of magnificent swords and a plain heavy sabre for boarding; two bands of distinction-lace; a star on the gorgeous epaulette, heavy with bullion; white kerseymere waistcoats and breeches; white silk stockings; black shoes with silver buckles.

Having passed through the plain 'undress' stage – pretty splendid, nevertheless – Jack came out of the dressing-room in all the glory of a flag-officer, his hair powdered, the Nile medal gleaming on his lace jabot, and his laced hat adorned with the diamond spray given him by the Grand Turk, a spray that was made to quiver and sparkle by a little clockwork heart. 'Behold the Queen of the May,' he said.

'Oh very fine!' cried the ladies; and even Mrs Williams and her friend, who had been sitting there with pursed lips, disapproving of such expense, were quite melted, adding,

'Glorious, superb: superb: superb.'

'Huzzay, huzzay,' cried George. 'Oh, to be an admiral!'

'How I wish Helen Needham could see him,' said Charlotte. 'That would clap a stopper over her prating about the General and his plume.'

'Fan,' said Sophie, rearranging her husband's neckcloth and smoothing the golden fringe of an epaulette, 'run and ask Miss O'Hara whether she would like to come.'

A clock in the corridor struck the hour, followed by several others at different levels, the last of all being the slow deep chime from the stable-yard. 'God's my life,' cried Jack whipping off his coat and hurrying into the dressing-room. 'Captain Hervey will be here.'

'Oh don't throw it on the floor,' called Sophie. 'And do please, *please* take care of those stockings as you pull them off. Killick, make him take the stockings off by the band.'

When the men had gone, thundering down the stairs, Jack dressed as a plain country gentleman rather than a sea-going peacock and Killick looking as usual like a lean, cantankerous and out of work ratcatcher, the ladies walked into Sophie's boudoir. Mrs Williams and her friend sat together on an elegant satinwood love-seat with entwined hearts for a back, and Sophie in a low, comfortable elbow-chair with a basket of stockings to be darned beside it.

She rang for tea, but before it came her mother and Mrs Morris had resumed their habitual looks of disapproval. 'What is all this we hear about those *extremely* expensive garments forming part or indeed parcel of an *admiral*'s uniform? Surely Mr Aubrey cannot be so thoughtless and indiscreet as to assume a rank superior to his own, a *flag-rank* no less?' The mention of high authority always brought a pious, respectful look to Mrs Williams' face: before it had quite faded she interrupted Sophie's answer with the words, 'I remember a great while ago, that he called himself captain when he was really only a commander.'

'Mama,' said Sophie in a stronger voice than was usual with her, 'I believe you mistake: in the service we always call a commander captain out of courtesy; while a commodore of the first class, that is to say a commodore with a captain, a post-captain, under him, in this case Mr Pullings . . .'

'Yes, yes, honest Tom Pullings,' said Mrs Williams with a condescending smile –

'. . . is absolutely required, not just by courtesy but by Admiralty rules, to wear the uniform of a rear-admiral. So there,' she added, sotto voce but not altogether unheard, as the tea-tray came in.

Even at Ashgrove, a tolerably well-run house with a strong tradition of promptness and order, tea entailed a fair amount of turmoil; but in time the older women were quiet at last, absorbed in stirring their sugar, and Sophie was about to make some remark when Mrs Williams, with that prescience sometimes found in mothers, cut her short with the words, 'And what is all this about inquiries being made in the village concerning Barham Down?'

'I know nothing about them, Mama.'

'Briggs heard that there had been a man in the ale-house asking about Barham Down and those that lived there, a man like a lawyer's clerk. And since he had to go there on some business to do with rat-poison he asked the landlord what was afoot; and it appeared that most of these questions were about Mrs Oakes. Not about Diana. It was not a matter of gathering evidence for a criminal conversation case or a divorce with Diana as the guilty party as I thought straight away, but something to do with Mrs Oakes: debts, I have little doubt. But it is also possible that Mr Wilson the manager had a wife somewhere . . .'

Sophie had been brought up so straight-laced that she possessed no very exact notion of how babies were made in the first place or born in the second until she learnt from personal and startling experience; and one of the changes in her mother that surprised her most was this strong, almost obsessive and sometimes singularly specific interest – disapproving interest of course – in who went, or wanted to go, to bed with whom: an interest fully shared by Mrs Morris, so that the two of them would go over the details of any fresh trial for crim. con. for an hour or more. She was reflecting on this when she heard her mother say '. . . so of course I borrowed the gig and called, Briggs driving all the way up that steep, stony road to Barham. She was denied, but I insisted – said I wanted to see the child, my own grand-niece after all, my own flesh and blood. So I was admitted. I thought she was far too expensively dressed for a mere lieutenant's widow, and her cap was outré: I believe she has some pretensions to looks. Well. I questioned her pretty closely, I can tell you – what was her maiden name? Who were her employers in New South Wales? Did she teach the harp? – Nothing so graceful as the harp – When did this curious – I did not say *alleged* – marriage take place? She was evasive – short, unsatisfactory answers – and when I told her of it, saying I expected more openness, she positively turned me out of the house. But I was not going to be put down like that by a chit worth no more than fifty pounds a year if that and I said I should come back. In Diana's absence I have a right to supervise the bringing-up and welfare of the child. If there is an undesirable connexion in that house, she must be removed. I shall speak to my man of business, and I shall say . . .'

'You are forgetting, Mama,' said Sophie when the torrent paused, 'you are forgetting that Dr Maturin is his daughter's natural guardian.'

'Dr Maturin – Dr Maturin – pooh, pooh – here today and gone tomorrow: he has been away six weeks at least. *He* cannot oversee the welfare of his child,' said Mrs Williams. 'I shall have myself appointed supervisor.'

'We expect him tomorrow afternoon,' said Sophie. 'His bedroom is ready: he is staying here, not at Barham, to be nearer the squadron during these last important days.'

Stephen rode towards Ashgrove Cottage, sombre from his long and unsuccessful journey to the North Country, sombre from his stop at Barham, where he had heard of Mrs Williams' barbarity; but with a sombreness shot through and through with a brilliant gleam. In a small square room upstairs at Barham, overlooking the now almost empty stables, Diana had put a good many of his papers and specimens: a dry little room, in which they might be preserved. On the other side of the passage another room, sometimes called the nursery, held a number of unused dolls, a rocking-horse, hoops, large coloured balls and the like; and as he sat arranging these papers and sheet after sheet of a hortus siccus collected in the East Indies and sent home from Sydney, he heard Padeen's voice from across the way.

When Padeen was speaking Irish he stammered very much less – hardly at all if he were not nervous – and now he was discoursing as fluently as could be: 'That's the better – bless the good peg – a little higher – oh, the black thief, he missed the stroke – four it is – now for the five – glorious St Kevin, I have the five itself . . .'

This was usual enough. Padeen alone often talked aloud when he was throwing dice or knuckle-bones or mending a net. Stephen did not so much listen as be aware of the homely, agreeable sound: but abruptly he stiffened. The paper dropped from his hand. It was exactly as though he had heard a faint childish voice cry 'Twelve!' or something very like it. Twelve in Irish, of course. With the utmost caution he stood up and set his door on the jar, with a book either side to prevent it moving.

'For shame, Breed, honey,' said Padeen, 'it is a dó dhéag you must say. Listen, sweetheart, listen again will you now? A haon, a dó, a trí, a ceathir, a cúig, a sé, a seacht, a hocht, a naoi, a deich, a haon déag, *a dó dhéag*, with a noise like yia, yia. Now, a haon, a dó . . .'

The little high voice piped, 'A haon, a dó . . .' and so right through to 'a dó dhéag,' which she said with just Padeen's Munster intonation.

'There's a golden lamb, God and Mary and Patrick bless you,' said Padeen kissing her. 'Now let you throw the hoop on the four, which will make twelve altogether so it will too: since eight and four is twelve for evermore.'

The dinner-bell clashed on Stephen's intensely listening ear with a most shocking effect – a galvanic effect. It scattered his wits strangely, and he had not fully recovered them before the passage outside creaked under Padeen's step: he was a big man, as tall though perhaps not as broad-shouldered as Jack Aubrey: and it was clear that he was carrying the child – they talked in a murmur, each into the other's ear.

Dinner was a silent meal, and after a while Clarissa said, 'I should not have told you about Mrs Williams: it has taken your appetite away. But she forced her way into Brigid's room, crying that a good shake would cure this sort of trouble; and her clamour shocked the child.'

'Sure, it angered me to hear of her conduct, the strong self-willed unruly shrew; but you were wholly and entirely right to let me know. If you had not done so she might have repeated the intrusion, with all the damage that would ensue: now I can deal with it.' He stirred his wine with a fork for some little while; recollected himself, looked attentively at the fork, wiped it on his napkin, laid it square on the table and said, 'No. It was not anger that took my appetite away but delight. I heard Brigid speak clear and plain, talking to Padeen.'

'Oh I am so glad. But . . .' she hesitated '. . . did it make sense?'

'It did indeed.'

'I have heard them too. So has Nellie. But only when they were quite away by themselves – they were always together, you know – in the hay-loft, or with the hens and the black sow. We thought it was only gibberish, the sort of language that children make up.'

'It is the pure Irish they speak.'

'I am *so* glad,' said Clarissa again.

'Listen,' said Stephen, 'I think the balance is exceedingly delicate at this point and I dare not make any move at all – dare not rush blundering in. I must reflect, and consult with colleagues who know much more than I do: there is Dr Willis in Portsmouth. There is the great Dr Llers of Barcelona. For the now, I beg you will take no notice, no notice at all. Let the flower open.'

Some time later he said, 'How happy I am you told me of that woman. At the present juncture her ignorant violence might wreck, spoil, desecrate . . . I shall cope with her.'

'How shall you do that?' asked Clarissa after a pause.

'I am contemplating on the means,' said Stephen; but the pale, reserved ferocity of his expression faded entirely with the entry of Nellie with the pudding and Padeen with Brigid.

She sat there on her high-cushioned chair and as Stephen helped her to gooseberry fool she turned her face to him. He thought he saw a distinct look of acceptance, but he dared not speak directly. It was only when the meal was nearly over that he said, in Irish, 'Padeen, let you bring the little mare in twelve minutes,' and the words brought a quick turn of the small fair head, ordinarily immobile, absorbed in an inner world.

The little mare carried him with a long easy stride down the miles of bare upland road, along the turnpike for a while and so to the lane leading up through Jack Aubrey's plantations to the knoll on which he had built his observatory: for Captain Aubrey was not only an officer professionally concerned with celestial navigation but also a disinterested astronomer and, although one would never have suspected it from his honest, open face, a mathematician: a late-developing mathematician it is true, but one of sufficient eminence to have his papers on nutations and the Jovian satellites published in the *Philosophical Transactions* and translated in several learned journals on the Continent.

Jack had just closed the door of this building and he was standing on its step contemplating the English Channel when Stephen came in sight, round the last upward curve. 'Ho, Stephen,' he hailed, though the distance was not great. 'Have you come back? What a splendid fellow you are, upon my sacred honour! True to your day and almost to your hour. I dare say you could not wait to see the squadron – a glorious sight! Although it is nothing like what I promised you in the first place – no squadron ever is. I have been gloating over them this last half hour, ever since *Pyramus* came in.' And indeed the slide of the revolving copper dome was pointing directly down at Portsmouth, Spithead and St Helens. 'Should you like to have a look? It would not be the least trouble . . .' He glanced at Stephen's mount, paused, and in quite another tone he went on, 'But Lord, how I rattle on about my own affairs. Forgive me,

Stephen. How do you do? I hope your journey was . . . ?'

'I am well, I thank you, Jack: and I am happy to see that your head is mended, though you look sadly worn. But my journey did not answer as I could have wished. I had hoped to find Diana; and I did not. I came upon some of her horses, however: this is one.'

'I recognized her,' said Jack, caressing the mare. 'And I too had hoped . . .'

'No. She had sold two mares and a stallion to a man that breeds running horses near Doncaster. He very kindly let me have Lalla here, but he had little notion of Diana's move-ments apart from Ripon and Thirsk, where she had friends: she had spoken of Ulster, too, where Frances lives.'

He swung out of the saddle and they walked slowly on towards the stables. 'But that is of no great account. Do you remember Pratt, the thief-taker?'

'By God, I should think I do,' cried Jack: and well he might. Earlier in his career he had been accused of rigging the Stock Exchange, and Pratt, who as the son of a gaoler had spent much of his childhood among thieves and who had improved his knowledge of the underworld by serving with the Bow Street runners before setting up on his own account, had acted for Jack and his lawyers, finding an essen-tial witness in a masterly fashion – masterly but inefficacious since the witness's face, upon which identification depended, had been as one might say erased.

'Well, I have retained Pratt and his colleagues to find her out and I have little doubt of their eventual success. I do not mean to persecute her, you understand, brother: it is because she is labouring under two separate misunderstand-ings, both of which I wish to remove, an act that can be done only by word of mouth.'

'Of course. Certainly,' said Jack, to fill the silence; and the mare, turning her head, gazed at them with her lustrous Arabian eyes, blowing gently on them as she did so.

'You know about Brigid, of course. She is called an idiot, which is wholly incorrect: hers is a particular form of development, slower than most; but Diana does not know this. She believes there is idiocy, which she cannot bear . . .' Jack too had a horror of anything like insanity, and a word almost escaped him. '. . . and feeling no doubt that her reluctant presence was not only useless but positively harmful, she went away. She believes that I should blame her for doing so: that is the first misunderstanding. The second is, as I said, that she believes in this idiocy, and I wish to tell her that she is mistaken. Children of this kind are rarer than true idiots – who, I may say, can be told at a glance – but they are not very uncommon. There are two of them in Padeen's village in the County Kerry – they are called leanaí sídhe in Ireland – and both were I will not say cured but brought into this world rather than another. They were taken at the critical moment. Padeen is the sort of person who can do this. He is strangely gifted.'

'I remember him taking a trapped cat in his hand and undoing the jaws with never a scratch: and there was the savage stone-horse we took out for the Sultan.'

'Just so: and many another example. But in this particular development, in Brigid's particular development, the balance is extremely delicate: it may go either way. The circumstances – the physical environment itself – are so exceptional. I must consult with Dr Willis: I must write to Dr Llers in Barcelona, the great expert in these matters. Yet in any case Mrs Williams must be kept away. She called and savaged Clarissa with impertinent questions and then insisted on seeing the child, her grand-niece: she frightened her, offering to give her a great shaking if she would not speak. I am happy to say that Clarissa put her out of the house directly.'

'I have a great esteem for Clarissa Oakes.'

'So have I. But that woman shall not go to Barham again. I must have a word with her.'

They were almost in the stable-yard, and Jack said, 'In point of fact she and Mrs Morris are waiting for you: I said you would be here today, and they are waiting for you. They are in a great taking.'

'What's amiss?'

'Their man Briggs played the informer once too often: the hands caught him in Trump's Lane, coming back from the ale-house, and beat him. Black night, no words; only a din like a great puppy being whipped.'

'Oh Dr Maturin,' cried the three children more or less in unison, as they came running in from a side-walk. 'There you are. You have arrived! Grand-mama posted us by the gazebo to look out for you. She and Mrs Morris beg you to come at once. Briggs was set upon and terribly beaten by the Hampton Blacks . . .'

'Mr Owen the apothecary has plastered him and says he may live; but we doubt it.'

'Please may we take you there at once? We were promised fourpence if we took you at once. Papa will look after the horse, will you not, dear Papa?'

'She is a mare, stupid. An Arab, sir, I believe?'

Stephen walked in, and when he had endured their clamour, indignation and circumstantial account for some considerable time, he desired the ladies to leave him with the patient. He made his examination: here indeed was a truly swollen, bloated face, and back and buttocks strongly marked with rope's-end and cobbing-board; but no broken bones, no incised or lacerated wounds. Stephen was surprised that a man long accustomed to the race-course should be so upset by these moderate degrees of violence; yet Briggs was quite prostrated – fright almost amounting to terror, dignity shattered, a sense of total outrage, and perhaps something close to abject cowardice. Stephen approved Mr Owen's dressings, prescribed a few harmless comfortable medicines and crossed the passage to where the anxious ladies sat.

'He needs quietness, a dim light, and undemanding company,' he said. 'If Mrs Morris would be so good as to sit with him, I will explain the treatment to my aunt Williams, since our relationship allows me to use medical terms and expressions that I should be embarrassed to employ in the presence of any other lady.'

'They have not cut him, have they?' cried Mrs Williams when they were alone. 'I trust that was not what you meant when you said embarrassed.'

'No, ma'am,' said Stephen. 'You will not have an eunuch on your hands.'

'I am so glad,' said Mrs Williams. 'I have heard that robbers often do it to people who resist them. They do it out of spite, knowing that gentlemen do so hold to their . . . you understand me.'

'Is it known who the robbers were?'

'We are pretty sure, and I am going to lay an information with Sir John Wriothesley, the justice of the peace. At first we half-suspected the seamen he had very properly caused to be admonished, yet Mr Aubrey, *Commodore* Aubrey, flatly denied it; and he is practically a flag-officer. But then it came out that they had black faces, so it is obviously the gang called the Hampton Blacks, who always blacken their faces when they go out at night to poach the deer. They may very well have known that he often carries considerable sums to and from Bath for us.'

'Did they take anything?'

'No. He clung so bravely to his watch and money that they got nothing at all.'

'Very well. Let him be kept quiet and dosed regularly, and I think I may assert that you will find him as good as ever in seven days' time.'

'He is in no danger, then?' cried Mrs Williams. 'So I may send and countermand the priest? He will not charge if he is told in time, I am sure. Mr Briggs is a Papist, you know.' Stephen bowed. Mrs Williams said, 'What a relief,' and rang the bell for some madeira for the Doctor.

As he drank it – Jack always had capital madeira – she said in a musing voice, 'Not that I have anything against Papists. Did you ever hear of Mrs Thrale?' Stephen bowed again. 'Well, *she* married one, after her husband died, a man

73

of somewhat lower rank, and even a foreigner; but now she is received everywhere, I understand.'

'No doubt. Here is a brief list of the necessary measures and doses, which I desire you will adhere to with the utmost regularity. And now, ma'am, I wish to speak to you of my daughter Brigid. As you are aware, her mental health is delicate; but you probably do not know that its progress has now reached a critical stage at which any shock or setback may prove disastrous. I must therefore beg that for the present your kindly-intended visits to Barham may cease.'

'Am I not to see my own flesh and blood? My own grand-niece? Believe me, Dr Maturin,' cried Mrs Williams, her voice reaching its metallic, dominant ring, 'these childish, self-willed, stubborn, obstinate fancies are best dealt with firmly: a good shaking, the black hole, bread and water and perhaps the whip answer very well and at no cost: though to be sure you are a physician and everything in that line is free.'

'I should be sorry to forbid you my house,' said Stephen.

But Mrs Williams, well launched, carried straight on: 'And let me tell you, sir, that I cannot at all approve of the young person in charge of her at present. Naturally it was my duty to ask her a few questions to satisfy myself of her suitability; but all I got was short answers, unsatisfactory replies. A very repulsive reserve, a confidence and self-sufficiency, a want of submissive respect that quite shocked me. And there are rumours of debts, inquiries in the village, questionable morality . . .'

'I am perfectly well acquainted with the lady's ante-cedents,' said Stephen in a more determined voice, 'and I am perfectly well satisfied with Mrs Oakes's qualifications as a person to look after my daughter; so let us have no more of this, if you please.'

'I ought to be appointed guardian, with a right of inspection when you are away on these interminable voyages. I certainly have a moral right to visit; and a legal one too, I am sure.'

'I do not agree. And if, as I do not suppose possible now that I have made my views clear, you were so unwise as to commit a trespass, you would not only be ejected by my powerful, dangerous Irish servant, but you would lay yourself open to a most determined prosecution – a prosecution not only for trespass but also for keeping, and having kept, an unlicensed betting office. Furthermore, the least hint of such an indiscretion would infallibly lead to your man Briggs being pressed into the Navy and sent aboard a ship full of common and often violent sailors, none of whom has any reason to love him, a ship bound for the deadly West Indies, or perhaps for Botany Bay.'

'Sir,' cried George, intercepting him in the garden, 'Papa says would you like to take a quick glance at the squadron while there is still some light on the sea.'

'I should like it of all things,' said Stephen. 'George, here is a three-shilling piece for thee.'

'Oh thank you, sir. Thank you very much. We never got our fourpence, but now Amos is just going down to Hampton and I shall go with him and fairly gorge . . .' His words were lost in the distance.

'Come in, Stephen,' called Jack from the depths, the very moderate depths, of the observatory. 'I have the glass just so. Mind the cantilever – Oh never touch that sprocket – take care of the eye-piece box, if you please – never mind: I shall pick them up and clean them later – now slide in here and sit square on the stool: *square on the stool*, there – leave that screw alone, for God's sake – hold on to the turret-casing, if you must hold on. It will be easier when your eyes have grown accustomed to the gloom: gloom for contrast, you understand. There: sit tight. I have shipped cross-wires, as you see – no, get your eye right into the eye-piece, Stephen: what a fellow you are – in point of fact they are stretched threads of spider's web, exactly placed. Ingenious, ain't it? Herschel's sister showed me how to do it. The focus is right for my good eye, but if you find it blurred, turn this screw' – guiding his fingers – 'until it is sharp. For the moment there is very little turbulence. The telescope is exactly pointed, so never touch anything else, whatever you do.'

Stephen squared himself still more, thrust his eye even deeper into the eye-piece, drew several deep breaths, and timidly turned the screw. Instantly the cross-lines showed clear, and at their intersection, broadside on, there was a ship of the line, sharp and distinct, in another world, another though familiar dimension: her topsails were hanging loose to dry and many of her people were over the side on stages, painting ship, but this did not take away from her beauty, nor from the sense of concentrated power. It made a living ship of her, a ship with no collective self-consciousness and anxiety, holding her breath for her portrait or an admiral's inspection.

'Now there is the great elegant ship of the world,' said Stephen. 'A seventy-four, I make no doubt?'

'Well done, Stephen,' cried Jack, and if he had been speaking to any other man he would have clapped him on the back. 'A noble seventy-four she is. And that red swallow-tail burgee is my broad pennant. The Admiral sent his flag-lieutenant particularly desiring me to hoist it, which I took very kindly. One has to have permission, you know.'

'So she is the *Bellona*, the chief argosy of your command! Huzzay, huzza! I congratulate you, Jack. Why, I declare, she has a poop, which adds much to her dignity.'

'And not only dignity but safety too. When you are on the quarterdeck in a hot action with a really malignant enemy firing great guns and small arms, it is a wonderful comfort to have a solid poop behind you.'

'For my part I prefer to be far, far below. Pray show me the rest of the squadron.'

'There is *Pyramus*,' said Jack, moving the glass very slightly until the cross-lines rested on a fine thirty-eight-gun frigate. 'She is like the French *Belle Poule*, you know. Frank Holden has her now, a fine dashing fellow; but I doubt we shall keep her. There are nasty rumours of her being sent off on a cruise of her own and being replaced by something smaller, older, slower. I am afraid the air is beginning to shimmer down over the harbour and Gosport,' he went on, turning the telescope and guiding it by the finder, 'but if you focus again for your eyesight I think you will make out a ship creeping along by Priddy's Hard. She is the *Stately*, sixty-four: she was given me when the *Terrible*, our other seventy-four, was suddenly and very unfairly snatched away; and I am afraid we shall certainly keep *her*. A sixty-four-gun ship is a very pitiful craft, Stephen; worse in a way than the horrible old *Leopard*, with a mere fifty. In *her* we could run from the Dutch seventy-four without a blush, crack on until all sneered again with a clear conscience; but a sixty-four would have to turn and fight or feel dishonoured. *Stately*'s captain, William Duff – you remember Billy Duff in Malta, Stephen? – does all he possibly can, but . . . Alas, the light is going. The sun has dipped. I can just make out the *Aurora*, twenty-eight, and the *Orestes* brig, but they are fading, and I shall have to tell you about them when we have had something to eat. You must be cruel sharp-set.'

'With the blessing I shall see them all tomorrow. I must be aboard early, to attend to my assistants and medical supplies. How many are we in all?'

'To tell you the truth, Stephen, I do not know. There is so much chopping and changing. We are still a frigate short; it is just possible that we may lose the *Pyramus*; the sloops and brigs come and go; and the date is perpetually postponed. I should never have insisted on your coming back so soon. After all, I have known the Navy all my life, and never, never, has any squadron put to sea on the date the port-admiral or commodore was told in the first place. Nor with the same ships. But now, upon my word, you must and shall be fed. Sophie complains that she saw nothing of you, because of the children's measles – keeps mentioning it. We will drag her from her accounts and sit down comfortably with a dish of muffins. You shall see the squadron by early morning light, before breakfast, if it don't rain; and then we can ride down to Pompey.'

Stephen had been put to sleep in his usual room, far from children and noise, away in that corner of the house which looked down to the orchard and the bowling-green, and in spite of his long absence it was so familiar to him that when he woke about three he made his way to the window almost as quickly as if dawn had already broken, opened it and walked out on to the balcony. The moon had set: there was barely a star to be seen. The still air was delightfully fresh with falling dew, and a late nightingale, in indifferent voice, was uttering a routine jug-jug far down in Jack's plantations; closer at hand, and more agreeable by far, nightjars churred in the orchard, two of them, or perhaps three, the sound rising and falling, intertwining so that the source could not be made out for sure. There were few birds he preferred to nightjars, but it was not they that had brought him out of bed: he stood leaning on the balcony rail and presently Jack Aubrey, in a summerhouse by the bowling-green, began again, playing very gently in the darkness, improvising wholly for himself, dreaming away on his violin with a mastery that Stephen had never heard equalled, though they had played together for years and years.

Like many other sailors Jack Aubrey had long dreamed of lying in his warm bed all night long; yet although he could now do so with a clear conscience he often rose at unChristian hours, particularly if he were moved by strong emotion, and crept from his bedroom in a watch-coat, to walk about the house or into the stables or to pace the bowling-green. Sometimes he took his fiddle with him. He was in fact a better player than Stephen, and now that he was using his precious Guarnieri rather than a robust sea-going fiddle the difference was still more evident: but the Guarnieri did not account for the whole of it, nor anything like. Jack certainly concealed his excellence when they were playing together, keeping to Stephen's mediocre level: this had become perfectly clear when Stephen's hands were at last recovered from the thumb-screws and other implements applied by French counter-intelligence officers in Minorca; but on reflexion Stephen thought it had been the case much earlier, since quite apart from his delicacy at that period, Jack hated showing away.

Now, in the warm night, there was no one to be comforted, kept in countenance, no one who could scorn him for virtuosity, and he could let himself go entirely; and as the grave and subtle music wound on and on, Stephen once more contemplated on the apparent contradiction between the big, cheerful, florid sea-officer whom most people liked on sight but who would never have been described as subtle or capable of subtlety by any one of them (except perhaps his surviving opponents in battle) and the intricate, reflective music he was now creating. So utterly unlike his limited vocabulary in words, at times verging upon the inarticulate.

'My hands have now regained the moderate ability they possessed before I was captured,' observed Maturin, 'but his have gone on to a point I never thought he could reach: his hands and his mind. I am amazed. In his own way he is the secret man of the world; but I wish his music were happier.'

In the early morning light however he was plain Jack Aubrey, and as they walked over the dew towards his observatory he said, 'If I had not officially appointed Adams my secretary I should ask him to stay here and help Sophie with her papers. The Woolcombe estate is nothing much – poor spewy land, most of it – but it is amazingly troublesome, with some uncommon wicked tenants, poachers to a man, and she tries to look after it all herself, to say nothing of this place, and the infernal income-tax, the poor-rate, the tithes – what is that bird?'

'It is a shrike, a great grey shrike. Some say wariangle.'

'Yes. Cousin Edward's keeper calls them that: he showed me a nest when I was a boy. But speaking of tithes, we have a new parson, Mr Hinksey. Do you remember him?'

'I do not. Unless he was the gentleman I met once or twice in my booksellers, and who was good enough to carry some naval essays down to Sophie.'

'He was the man that made addresses to her when we were taking poor Mr Stanhope to the East Indies, to Kampong. Mrs Williams thought the world of him: such a gentleman-like parson, with a good living and five or even six hundred a year of his own. He was something at Oxford: a wrangler, perhaps. Do they have wranglers at Oxford, Stephen?'

'I rather believe it is the other place: at Oxford I think they only have fornicatores, but I may well be mistaken.'

'Well, it was something creditable, in any event. And she declares the reason he has never married is that Sophie broke his heart, running off to marry me. But now here he is, installed in our rectory these eighteen months at least: ain't it amazing?'

'I have rarely been more astonished.'

'I was perfectly prepared to hate him, of course, but he is such an open, friendly, agreeable fellow, a very fair horseman and an uncommon good bat, that I could not succeed. A big, well-built man, six foot odd; and he used to box at college: he has a broken nose.'

'That is a recommendation, sure.'

'Well, it does mean he cannot decently prate away in the evangelical line, like some parsons and some of our blue-light officers with their pious tracts. And he has come over from time to time, when Sophie's mama or Sophie herself was quite at a loss with their sums, which I take very civil. But Lord, how I wander. I was talking about Adams: now as you know very well there is a world of difference between a flag-officer's secretary and a captain's clerk, and having appointed him I cannot in decency ask him to stay ashore and help Sophie; but I shall certainly desire him to look about among his friends in Plymouth and Gosport. Here we are. Stephen, mind the ditch: tread in the middle of the plank. I brought you this roundabout way to show you a creeper I am trying to persuade to turn the pollard into a bower, but it seems to have been swallowed by the nettles. Now let me go in first and re-focus – there is a prodigious difference between a morning and an evening speculum, of course – and then you shall see all the squadron there is to be seen. Some of the brigs and a schooner or two are only to join us off Lisbon. You will not see them in their full detail, with the light coming from the east; but I hope you will get at least some notion.'

No man would ordinarily have associated Jack Aubrey with the idea of fuss; yet this was a special case. He had made the telescope, grinding seven mirrors before achieving the present masterpiece; he had invented the improved mounting as well as the singularly exact finder; and in this single instance he did fuss, trying to make it perform miracles, urging the sun to shed a diffused and even illumination, uttering otiose explanations.

Stephen disregarded his friend's anxious prattle, most of it deeply technical, dealing with diffraction, aberration and virtual images, and gazed upon the successive remote and silent visions as they appeared in the eyepiece.

First the splendid *Bellona*, in profile: some of her people were still washing the forecastle and all that was to be seen of the upper deck, while the afterguard and waisters flogged the poop and quarterdeck dry. 'Seventy-four guns, of course,' said Jack, 'a broadside weight of metal of nine hundred and twenty-six pounds: twenty-eight thirty-six pounders on the gundeck, twenty-eight eighteen pounders on the upper deck, two long twelves as chasers and six short, with ten thirty-two-pound carronades and four little ones for the poop.'

'That makes seventy-eight guns.'

'For shame, Stephen. Surely you must recall that we only make a notional reckoning for the carronades, when we count them in at all.'

'I beg pardon.'

'She is a Chatham ship: one thousand six hundred and

fifteen tons, gundeck a hundred and sixty-eight foot, beam forty-six foot nine; and she has a depth of nineteen foot nine in the hold, which I call really comfortable. With six months' stores she draws twenty-two foot nine, abaft. Less afore, of course.'

'When was she built?'

'In 1760,' said Jack in a somewhat unwilling, defensive voice. 'But you would not call her an *old* ship. *Victory* was laid down a year before, and she is pretty spry, I believe. She answered tolerably well at Trafalgar, they say. Besides, the *Bellona* was doubled and braced in the year five, and she is if anything better than new. Far better, with everything well shaken into position.'

'I beg pardon.'

'She was always an uncommonly weatherly ship – I remember her well in the West Indies when I was a boy – rolls easy, makes nine and even ten knots close-hauled on a brisk topgallant breeze, steers easy, wears quick, lies to perfectly well under maincourse and mizzen staysail, fore-reaching prodigiously all the while – amazing great wash.'

'I rejoice to hear it. Pray state the number of her crew.'

'The establishment is five hundred and ninety: I should think we are within a score or two of it, and I have great hopes of a draft from the Nore on Monday. But that is Tom's concern, you know; I only have to worry with the paper-work, the Admiralty, the Navy Board, the Port Admiral and the other captains belonging to the squadron. Now let me show you our other line-of-battle ship.' A little wheel turned: masts, yards, loose sails, rigging and stretches of pale gleaming water shot sideways through Stephen's field of vision: a sudden trembling halt, and there, as sharp, firm and distinct as Jack or any other telescope-maker could have wished, swam another two-decker, not sideways this time but seen from four points on her starboard bow, a three-quarter view that showed her exactly-squared yards to great advantage. Her sides were painted black and her gunports a fine clear blue, while above them ran a line of the same colour, a combination that gave Stephen's heart a strange wrench, it being so much favoured by Diana.

'That is *Stately*, the sixty-four,' said Jack. 'She was inflicted upon us when they took the *Terrible* away, as shabby a piece of favouritism and jobbery as the service has ever known.'

'Her captain is clearly a man of taste, however,' said Stephen.

'Well, I am no judge of taste: I am not a dilettanto. But if the Nelson checker was good enough for the great man himself, it is good enough for me.' Jack paused. 'And I tell you what, Stephen: I do not like saying anything behind anyone's back, but you are a medico, and that makes it different – you will understand. As you know, I hate the way sodomites are hanged or flogged round the fleet, and I like Duff: but you must not do it with the young foremast jacks, or discipline goes by the board. Duff is a pretty good seaman, and he does his best, but the *Stately* had taken all night to tow to her berth. And in any case, there really *is* an old ship for you: she may not have been launched until eighty-two, but she was on the Brest blockade for years and years, which wore her out before her time – those frightful south-westers lasting for weeks on end, with tremendous seas – and she has neither been doubled nor braced. She is now about as seaworthy as the Ark after Noah left her high and dry on the top of Ararat: perhaps the slowest of her miserable class, sagging to leeward so as to make even a midland ploughboy stare. Yet since we have to live with her, I will tell you she gauges one thousand three hundred and seventy tons: a hundred and fifty-nine foot six inches on the gundeck with a beam of forty-four foot four: she carries twenty-six twenty-four pounders, twenty-six eighteen-pounders, six nine-pounders and sixteen mixed carronades, a broadside of only seven hundred and ninety-two pounds against the *Terrible*'s thousand odd; and if she can manage to fire two in five minutes it is looked upon as a wonder. Let us look at something more cheerful.' Again the rushing blur. 'Oh,' cried Jack in a much happier voice, 'I had not expected her so soon. You recognize her, of course?' Stephen made no reply. 'The *Nimble* cutter, in which that good young fellow Michael Fitton brought us home from the Groyne. But I must not linger on her. Now here, look, is our prime jewel *Pyramus*, a really modern thirty-six-gun eighteen-pounder frigate, nine hundred and twenty tons, a hundred and forty-one foot on the gundeck, thirty-eight foot five beam, broadside weight of metal four hundred and sixty-seven pounds, crew of two hundred and fifty-nine in capital order, long together, thoroughly used to their captain, that fine, taut spirited fellow Frank Holden, and to their officers, some of whom have sailed with us.' He gazed at the ship with great approval, and then moved on. 'This is *Aurora*, our second frigate,' he said. 'Another antique, I am afraid: she was laid down in 1771 and she only carries twenty-four nine-pounders, as they did in those days, but I have an affection for her because of the *Surprise*, not that she is anything like so fast or weatherly or comfortable. Five hundred and ninety-six tons, a hundred and twenty foot six on the gundeck, and she probably has a hundred and fifty of her hundred and ninety-six complement by now: Francis Howard has her, the Grecian – but you know him perfectly well: we met off Lesbos. Now beyond her, towards St Helens, lie the *Camilla*, twenty, just a rated ship, *Orestes*, a brig-rigged sloop, and some other craft. I will tell you about them as we ride down, and indeed show you when we are there. But for now I should think you have had enough.'

'Not at all,' said Stephen, rising from his intolerably cramped position. 'It is a far more imposing command than I had imagined, and far more glorious.'

'It is, ain't it?' said Jack, guiding him out of the observatory. 'Even without the *Terrible* and in spite of our old crocks it is a very fine squadron. I am as proud as Pontius Pilate. But, you know, it is a shocking responsibility. In Mauritius I had the Admiral behind me, even though he was rather far behind: here I shall be entirely alone.'

*   *   *

Sophie met them on their way up to the house. She was in strikingly good looks, but at the same time her expression was uneasy: she called out one of the reasons for this while they were still at some distance: Mama and Mrs Morris had gone back to Bath, taking Briggs with them; she had let them have the coach, but Bentley would bring it back as soon as the horses were rested. This was a far more decided action than Stephen had ever known her take; yet she did not seem to think it of much consequence. It was not the disposal of a coach and a pair of horses that was disturbing her mind, still less the absence of her mother.

'Oh,' cried Jack, with no more than a nod at the news, 'oh the smell of bacon and coffee: and even' – opening the door – 'of toasted soft-tack. There is no finer beginning to a day. And kippered herrings too!'

They sat down, just the three of them, in the breakfast-parlour, the pleasantest room in the house, and part of the original Ashgrove Cottage as it was before Jack Aubrey, during those spates of gold that sometimes reached the more fortunate commanders in that prize-taking war, had thrown out wings, stable-blocks, the double coach-house, bow-windows here and there, the corner balcony, and a row of cottages for old shipmates: just the three of them, for although the children were much loved and cherished they ate with Miss O'Hara, sitting quite straight, never touching the backs of their chairs, and speaking only when they were spoken to.

The fine plump kippers were soon dispatched, the first coffee-pot had been emptied, and Jack was silently engaged with his eggs and bacon, listening with half an ear to Stephen's minute and circumstantial account of the Madras fashion of making kedgeree, when Killick made his courtly entrance, jerked his chin in the direction of the Commodore and said, 'Which the Port Admiral's flag-lieutenant is come, and begs the favour. I told Awkward Davies to take his horse to the stable and put him in the welwet saloon.' Velvet had strong connotations of wealth and for Killick so had the word saloon; and since the front morning-room contained one vel-vet-covered chair and a few cushions nothing could induce him to call it anything else: only commissioned officers were ushered in.

'Oh,' said Jack, swallowing his coffee, 'forgive me, my dear. I shall be back in a moment. It is the weekly return, for sure.'

But minutes went by, and the toast grew cold: clearly something more complex than weekly returns was in question.

Sophie felt the second coffee-pot for warmth, nodded, and poured Stephen yet another cup. 'How pleasant to see you sitting there again,' she said. 'I have hardly had you to myself for five minutes, even after all this dreadfully long absence, thousands and thousands and thousands of miles. Nor Jack either. Always messages from the Admiral, or people coming to ask for appointments or to have their boy taken aboard one of the ships. And then although he is so delighted with this splendid command – it must lead to a flag, Stephen, must it not? – he is sadly worried too, above all with this perpetual chopping and changing. There are worries about Parliament as well, and the Woolcombe estate . . . Oh, Stephen, we were so much happier when we were poor. Now there is so much to do and so much to worry about and the loathsome bank that will not answer letters that there is no time even to talk as we used. Only next Thursday there is a dinner for all the captains, although it is our anniversary: and someone is sure to get drunk. Tell me, how do you find him, after all these weeks?'

'More worn than I could wish,' said Stephen, looking at her.

'Yes,' said Sophie, and she paused before going on, 'and there is something on his mind. He is not the same. It is not only the ships and all the business: besides, the invalu-able Mr Adams takes a great deal of that off his hands. No. There is a sort of reserve . . . it is not that he is in the least unkind . . . but you might almost say a coldness. No. That would be an absurd exaggeration. But he often sleeps in his study because of the paper-work or because he is out late. And even when he does not he gets up at night and walks about until the morning.'

In this most unpromising conversation Stephen could find nothing better to say than, 'Perhaps he will be happier once he gets to sea,' which earned him a reproachful look. Both were poised to say something almost certainly unfortunate when Jack came in from seeing the flag-lieutenant off, the remains of a farewell smile still on his face. It died entirely as he said, 'I am afraid I was right about *Pyramus*. She is to be taken away from the squadron, and we are to have the *Thames* instead. The *Thames*, a thirty-two gun twelve-pounder ship.'

'Only four guns less than *Pyramus*,' observed Sophie, in one of those ill-fated attempts at comfort.

'Certainly. But her two and thirty guns are only twelve-pounders, as against *Pyramus*'s eighteens: and her broadside weight of metal is a mere three hundred pounds as against four hundred and sixty-seven. But whining will do no good. Come, Stephen, we must be away. Is there another cup of coffee?'

'Oh dear,' cried Sophie, 'I am afraid there is not. But it will not take five minutes to make another pot.' She rang the bell: but she rang in vain. Jack was already on the wing, urging Stephen through the door before him. 'You will not forget that the Fanshaws and Miss Liza and Mr Hinksey are coming to dinner?' she called.

'I shall try to be back in time,' replied Jack. 'But if the Admiral keeps me you will make my excuses, if you please. Fanshaw will certainly understand.'

They rode down through what was now quite a respectable wood, Stephen on his neat little mare, Jack on a new and powerful bay gelding. He broke a longish silence to say, 'I was telling you about that parson, Hinksey, yesterday.'

'You said you could not hate him, as I recall.'

'Just so. But although I could not manage a full-blown hatred, now that I am so God-damned vexed at losing *Pyramus* I will tell you that I cannot like him neither. He comes far too often for my taste; and he walks about the house as though ... once I found him sitting in my own particular chair, and although he jumped up directly with a very proper excuse it put me out amazingly. And he and Sophie talk about things that happened when I was at sea. There is your wariangle again, carrying a mouse, upon my word.'

Stephen spoke of shrikes he had known, particularly the woodchat shrike of his boyhood, at some length; and he offered to show Jack the difference between the chiffchaff and the willow-wren, several of which were flitting about in the leaves just overhead. But finding that the Commodore was sunk in a grim reverie, perhaps on the subject of frigates, inferior ships of the line, and the criminal levity of those who sent some thousands of men to sea with no consistent plan, no intelligent preparation, no adequate forewarning, he refrained.

They rode in silence as far as the bridge to Portsea Island, where Jack cried, 'Good Lord, we are at the bridge already. Stephen, you have lost your tongue, I find: you have been in a deep study: we are already at the bridge.' The discovery pleased him disproportionately; so did the proof of the gelding's remarkably easy pace. He had digested his ill-humour, and they rode through the familiar, squalid outskirts of the town, through the still more squalid streets quite cheerfully and so to the Keppel's Head, the favourite inn of Jack's days as a midshipman. Here they put up their horses and walked on to the Hard as the clocks were striking ten: Bonden was waiting for them, with many a well-known smiling face among Jack's bargemen, and they pulled with the exactly-dipped oars and the stately pace of a flag-officer's boat, scorning the smallcraft that threaded the great harbour in all directions.

A long pull, since the *Bellona* was lying right over by Haslar, and Stephen's mind, lulled by the steady rhythm, swam far, far back to woodchat shrikes again, to the sun-baked Catalan side of his childhood; and he was thinking in the language when Jack, to his coxswain's disappointment, said, 'Larboard.'

This was no time to be worrying a busy ship, still taking in stores, still somewhat shorthanded, with a ceremonial arrival on the starboard side; but it grieved Bonden, who, like Killick, dearly loved pomp and ceremony where his officer was concerned, dearly relished the stamp and clash of the Marines presenting arms when Jack was piped aboard to a quarterdeck full of attentive officers and midshipmen, and who had hoped that Stephen might be shown the Commodore's present glory. Yet since he had no choice he brought the barge round, in order that Jack might join his ship discreetly.

Discreetly, but not unnoticed. Of course the boat had been seen putting off, and of course Captain Pullings was there to receive him, and of course there were side-boys, scrubbed pink, offering man-ropes as he came nimbly up, which was just as well, since he was immediately followed by Dr Maturin, as impervious to sea-lore as Mr Aubrey was to elegant literature – more so, indeed, since Jack had read *Macbeth* aloud, enchanting his daughters, not long since, while Stephen had not thought of ships or the sea since he set foot on shore, and had contrived to forget almost all of what little he had ever acquired: furthermore, he had only been aroused from his dreamlike state a moment before, when the barge came alongside and the even motion stopped. Bonden and most of the bargemen were well acquainted with his occasional absences and perfectly aware of the weakness of his nautical acquirements; and although the sea was duck-pond calm they anxiously propped him from behind adjuring him 'to clap on to them man-ropes sir, them padded things' and placing his feet successively on the steps; and they got him aboard dryfoot – something of a triumph.

Yet once there he stared about in a very simple, moon-struck fashion. For a great while now, and the whole breadth of the world, his ship had been a small frigate; and although, years before, he had been in a ship of the line for a short while the recollection had entirely faded: his scale was that of the *Surprise*, and the hugeness of the *Bellona*, the presence of a poop and of all these people quite bewildered him. He was at a disadvantage, and his face took on a cold, withdrawn expression; but his old friend Tom Pullings, now advancing to shake his hand and welcome him aboard, was even better acquainted with the Doctor's vagaries than the bargemen, and speaking very loud and clear, told him that two of his assistant surgeons had reported aboard last night and were now waiting for him in the sick-berth: perhaps he would like to see them before Tom named the officers to him. 'Mr Wetherby,' he said to a fresh-faced youngster in brand-new uniform, 'pray show the Doctor to the sick-berth.'

Down to the upper deck with its long ranges of eighteen-pounders on either side; down again by the after-ladderway to the gundeck, dim at present with the gunports closed for painting – 'That is where I live, sir,' said the youngster, pointing to the gun-room. Stephen was in civilian clothes; he presented no marks whatsoever of following the sea in any capacity, and the child explained things to him. 'I am not yet rated midshipman, you know, sir, so I mess with the gunner with half a dozen other coves, and the gunner's wife is very good to us. She shows us how to mend our clothes. Now, sir' – guiding Stephen forward – 'Here – pray mind your step – beyond that piece of screen is where the people sleep, all of them jam-packed, chock-a-block, when hammocks are piped down. And the screened bit is what we call the sick-berth.'

In the darkness stood two figures, dim themselves, but clearly nervous. 'Good morning, gentlemen,' said Stephen. 'I am the ship's surgeon, Maturin.'

'Good morning, sir,' they replied, and the first assistant said, 'My name is Smith, sir, William Smith, formerly of the *Serapis* and of the hospital at Bridgetown.'

The second, blushing, said that he was Alexander Macaulay, that after his apprenticeship he had studied at Guy's, where he was dresser to Mr Findlay for nearly five months: this was his first appointment.

'And are we indeed in the *Bellona*'s sick-berth?' asked Stephen, shocked. 'Mr Wetherby, be so good as to jump up to the quarterdeck and ask the officer of the watch if I may have a gunport open.'

He had barely spoken before there was a creak, a heave, and the nearest port rose up, letting in a square flood of light and showing two beaming faces, Joe Plaice and Michael Kelly, both Jack Aubrey's followers since the time of his first command, the brig *Sophie*, and both very old friends of Stephen's.

'Joe Plaice and Michael Kelly,' said Stephen, shaking their hands through the gunport, 'I rejoice to see you. Joe, how is the headpiece?'

The seamen looked sharply up at some order from on high. 'Aye aye, sir,' they cried to the distant officer, winked privately at Stephen, and vanished.

Stephen returned to the immediate abomination. 'Can such things be?' he cried, looking at the partially folded canvas screen, the few bare cots, a little more hanging sailcloth, ragged at the bottom, and then the vast cavern of the lower deck, empty now but for the rows of thirty-two-pounders and the mess tables hanging between them, but crammed at night with all the hundreds of seamen and Marines apart from the watch on deck, snoring and breathing, above all breathing the very small quantities of air and exhaling it in a vitiated condition pernicious to themselves and even more so to invalids. 'Can such things be? It is archaic: it belongs to the Dark Ages. This is the unhealthiest part of the ship – unbreathable air – impossible for a sick man to go to the head – hands trampling to and fro, shouting and bawling, at every meal, every change of the watch – and the present stench, although the deck has been cleaned: for it is still wet, another evil point.' He sniffed, sniffed again, and recognized both the scent and the distant hurdles: the ship's pigs, right forward, in their sty. He had heard of it in ships of the past and he had seen it once, at the very beginning of his career. 'This cannot be. Where are the men in the sick-list?'

'I believe they were all removed to Haslar, sir, when the late surgeon died. An alcoholic coma, I am told.'

'Infamous,' said Stephen, not so much at the alcoholic coma as at the monstrous surroundings. 'Let us look at the dispensary, and then I can make my report. Mr Wetherby, pray show the way.'

The child led them forward to a ladderway, from which the sty was even clearer, the smell much stronger – the pigs looked up at them, their little intelligent eyes full of curiosity – down into the darkness of the orlop, beneath the water line, where by the faint gleam of reflected light that filtered down through grating after grating and by an occasional lantern they groped aft to the cockpit, the midshipmen's berth, a noisy, noisome place. There were only four young gentlemen, one ape and a bulldog in it at present, but they could be heard a great way off, and the youngster said, 'I should not dare go in, sir, if you was not with me. Mind your step, I beg.'

'What would happen, were you to go in?' asked Stephen.

'The oldsters and the master's mates would scrag me, sir, and feed me to the bulldog.' He opened the door and stood aside.

'Gentlemen, good day,' said Stephen into the abrupt silence.

They were disparate creatures: one a dark, fierce-looking man sitting on the deck trying to read by a purser's dip; two gangling youths with their wrists and ankles starting from their clothes; and a devilish little fourteen-year-old trying to show the ape how to stand on its head. But they instantly saw that it would not do to play off their humours on this visitor and they returned his greetings, standing up with what grace they could summon, while the devilish boy quite unnecessarily strangled the bulldog, advancing to pay its respects. Stephen looked round the cockpit, which was his action-station and which would be his operating-theatre in the event of a battle: a fine spacious theatre, since it ordinarily housed a score of young men – and walked on aft.

'Oh sir,' cried Mr Wetherby again, 'pray mind your step.' And well might he cry: the hatch to the after powder-room was open, and the gunner's face framed in it, a foot above the deck. The face, ordinarily grave, spread in a smile and his right hand reached up. 'Why, Doctor,' he cried, 'we heard you was coming, and right glad we were. Rowley, gunner's mate in the old *Worcester*.'

'Of course,' said Stephen, shaking his hand. 'A nasty splinter-wound in the gluteus maximus. How does it come along?'

'You would never know it, sir. I showed it to my old woman when I came home. I showed her the scar, what there was of it, and I said, "Kate, if you could sew as good as the Doctor, I should put you out to work, and live at my ease," ha, ha, ha!' With this he vanished like an inverted Jack-in-a-box, and the hatch clapped down over him.

Smith opened the dispensary door, and a strong light came out, coming from the operating lantern that hung within. 'I hope you will not think me over-busy, sir,' said he. 'But last night the purser told me that some stores had come down from the Sick and Hurt Board, and rather than leave them lying in his steward's care I have been putting them in the medicine-chest. I was still at it when your boat came alongside, so I left things as they were. I am afraid they will not all go in.' The hatch opened abruptly: the gunner's beaming face reappeared. 'I said, "Kate, if you could sew as well as the Doctor, I should put you out to work and live at my ease,"' and clapped to again over his laughter.

'You did perfectly well, Mr Smith,' said Stephen, looking into the miniature apothecary's shop with its drawers, bottle-racks and recesses. 'But I am afraid you are in the right of it. These' – nodding at the powders, dried roots, drugs, ointments, bandages, dressings, tourniquets and the like that covered the floor – 'will never go in. We shall be obliged to put – to *stow* – them in the starboard dispensary.'

'By your leave, sir,' said Smith after a hesitation, 'there is no starboard dispensary.'

'Jesus, Mary and Joseph,' cried Stephen. 'Five hundred and ninety souls to be dosed out of one miserable cupboard, four foot by three at the most! All, all of a piece throughout. Very well, gentlemen: be so good as to put them into my cabin here' – opening the door of a room measuring six foot by four – 'while I go and make my report to the Captain. Oh such a report, by God.'

'Why, Doctor, what's amiss?' cried Tom Pullings as he burst in upon them.

'Stephen, have you had a fall?' asked Jack, starting up and taking him by the arm, for he was unnaturally pale, and his eyes glared extremely.

He looked coldly at each in turn, and then in a carefully controlled voice he said, 'I have just discovered that this – this vessel, for I will not call it a vile hulk, has a sick-berth that would disgrace a Turk, a sick-berth that a parcel of Hottentots would blush for, so they would. It is a sick-berth so horrible that I cannot consent to be associated with it, and' – his voice now rising with passion – 'if it cannot be converted into something less like Golgotha, more designed to kill rather than to save, I wash my hands of it entirely.' He washed his hands, glaring at their shocked faces. 'I wash my hands, I say: the shame of the world.'

'Pray, Stephen, sit down,' said Jack gently, leading him to a chair. 'Pray sit down and drink a glass of wine. Do not be cross with us, I beg.'

Pullings was too upset to say anything, but he poured the madeira; and they both looked at Stephen with infinite concern. He was still pale, still furious. 'Have either of you ever been in this odious travesty of a sick-berth?' he asked, his glare piercing first the one and then the other. Oh, the

94

moral force of that wholly unfeigned wholly disinterested and righteous anger!

Jack slowly shook his head, his conscience clear on at least that point. Tom Pullings said, 'I suppose I must have walked through, on my way to see the pig-sties; but since all the invalids were discharged to the hospital before ever I came aboard there was nobody there: so I did not notice it was so very wrong.'

Stephen told them that a sick-berth with no peace, no light, no air, could not possibly be right in any particular whatsoever: he told them in vehement detail; and, his energy subsided a little, he told them that the only ship-of-the-line sick-berth he would consent to be associated with must of necessity banish the swine in favour of the Christian sick, must lie right forward under the forecastle, and must have light, air and access to the head according to the plan of the eminently ingenious and truly benevolent Admiral Markham.

'Doctor,' cried Tom, 'say but the word and I shall send for Chips and all his crew this moment. If you will direct them, you shall have your Markham sick-berth before the evening gun.'

The tension fell; Stephen took a little wine; his colour, though still disagreeably sallow, returned to a natural pallor rather than one blanched by fury; he smiled at them; and Captain Pullings sent for the carpenter.

'Stephen,' said Jack diffidently, 'I had thought of carrying you round the other ships, so that you might meet their captains and officers; but I dare say making a proper sick-berth would take up most of your time.'

'So it would too,' said Stephen, 'and all my energy. Tom, you have joiners of your own, have you not? I could wish to install a full dispensary there where the swine gambolled and wantoned at their ease, rather than send down to the after cockpit every time I need a black draught. Jack, I beg you will excuse me if I put off the meeting until your dinner for all these gentlemen.'

Chapter Four

When Captain Aubrey, his steward and coxswain were at sea, Ashgrove Cottage retained much of its naval quality because of their former shipmates who lived in and around the place, carrying out their usual duties of swabbing, scrubbing and painting everything in sight in as seamanlike a manner as their age and missing limbs would allow, to the admiration of all housewives within calling or gossiping distance; but the family house, Woolcombe, which Jack had recently inherited, always relapsed into a mere landsman's dwelling. Mrs Aubrey spent most of her time at Ashgrove, Woolcombe being left in the care of Manson, the hereditary butler, and a few servants on board wages.

Yet when Jack was at home, and when there was a good deal of entertaining – particularly polished civilian entertaining – to be done, Manson was brought up to Hampshire, where he had a wretched time of it. He did understand the chief duties of a butler admirably well, caring for the wine in the wood, ulling it, racking it, bottling it, cherishing the bottles and eventually decanting their contents, bringing the wine to table in excellent condition; and he performed the ornamental part of his functions with proper dignity. But the seamen did not value him a bean for any of his skills; they despised him for his neglect of Woolcombe, which was turned out only once a year, in spring, instead of every day at dawn; and they resented the least hint of any infringement upon their rights, privileges or sea-going customs.

The sound of one of these disagreements brought Sophie running nimbly to the dining-room on the day of the captains' dinner. As she opened the door the sound increased quite shockingly: Killick, his disagreeably yellow face now almost white with fury, had Manson in a corner, threatening him with a fish-slice and telling him in a high shrewish screech that he was not all that a good man should be – telling him with such a wealth of detail and such vehement obscenity that Sophie clapped the door behind her in case the children should hear. 'For shame, Killick, for shame!' she cried.

'Which he touched my silver,' replied Killick, his quivering fish-slice now pointing to the noble, gleaming spread on the dining-table. 'He shifted three spoons with his great greasy thumbs and I seen him hurr on this here slice.'

'I was only giving it the butler's rub.'

'Butler's . . .' began Killick with renewed fury.

'Hush, Killick,' said Sophie. 'The Commodore says you are to stand behind his chair in your best blue jacket and Manson behind him in his plum-coloured coat; and Bonden is to see to the proper gloves. Now hurry along, do. There is not a moment to lose.'

There was not, indeed. The invitations had been marked half-past three for four and she knew from long experience of naval punctuality that between thirty and thirty-five minutes after the hour there would be a sudden flood of guests. She glanced along the table, all ablaze, all exactly squared; rearranged one bowl of roses; and hurried off to put on a glorious dress made of the scarlet silk, Jack's present, that had survived its almost intolerably arduous voyage from Batavia unharmed.

She was sitting in the drawing-room looking beautiful and with what she hoped was a convincing appearance of calm, pleasurable anticipation when Jack led in the first of his captains, William Duff of the *Stately*, a tall, athletic, exceptionally good-looking man of perhaps thirty-five. He was followed by Tom Pullings and Howard of the *Aurora*; Thomas of the unwelcome *Thames*; Fitton of the *Nimble*; and presently the tale was complete – almost complete.

'Where is the Doctor?' she whispered to Killick as he

97

came by with a tray of glasses. He looked quickly about: his face changed from its unnatural expression of amiability, with a fixed smirk, to its more usual pinched severity, and with a secret nod he hurried out.

It was a long-established rule in the Navy that the higher a sailor rose in rank the later he was fed. As a midshipman Jack Aubrey, like the ratings, had eaten at noon. When he was made a lieutenant, he and his fellow-members of the wardroom mess dined at one; when he commanded his own ship he ate half an hour or even a full hour later; and now that he was, for the time being, a commodore with a squadron, it was thought proper that he should move on towards the admirals' still later hours. But his stomach, like those of his guests, was still a captain's. It had been sharp-set before three; it was ravenous at half-past; yawning and gaping with hunger. Conversation, though stimulated by Sophie's increasingly anxious efforts, by olives and little biscuits handed on trays by white-gloved bluejackets, by Plymouth gin, madeira and sherry, was tending to flag or grow somewhat forced when the door opened and Stephen made a curiously abrupt entrance, as though propelled from behind. He was in a decent black suit of clothes, his wig was powdered and set square on his head, his white neck-cloth was tied with perfect accuracy, so tight that he could scarcely breathe. He still looked somewhat amazed, but recovering in a moment he bowed to the company, and hurried over to make his apologies to Sophie: he had been 'contemplating on wariangles, and had overlooked the time.'

'Poor Stephen,' said she, smiling in the kindest way, 'you must be dreadfully hungry then. Gentlemen,' she called, rising, to the relief of one and all, 'shall we go in, leaving introductions for later?' And privately, 'Stephen, gorge yourself with soup and bread: the venison pasty may not be quite the thing.'

After the proper hesitations and yielding of precedence at the dining-room door, the table filled quickly, Sophie at one end and Jack at the other.

Stephen, as he had been desired, earnestly attacked the soup, a most uncommonly good dish made principally of pounded lobsters, with their carefully shelled claws aswim in the rosy mass, and when the first pangs were assuaged he gazed about the table. Since this was essentially a social gathering, convoked by Sophie, the seating was unorthodox from the service point of view, though she had respected seniority to the extent of placing William Duff on her husband's right, while on his left he had young Michael Fitton, the son of a former shipmate and close friend. For her own neighbours she had two exceptionally shy officers, Tom Pullings, who had an ugly wound and a countryman's voice, both of which made him uneasy in company, and Carlow of the *Orestes*, who had no reason for diffidence at all, being well connected and well educated, but who nevertheless hated dining out and who, she felt, needed taking care of.

Stephen gazed about. He was not a particularly social animal – a watcher rather than a partaker – but he did like to see his fellows and quite often he liked to listen to them. On his left there was Captain Duff, talking eagerly to Jack about Bentinck shrouds: Stephen could detect no sign whatsoever of the tastes attributed to him. Indeed he could have sworn that Duff would have been most attractive to women. Yet the same, he reflected, might have been said of Achilles. His mind wandered over the varieties of this aspect of sexuality – the comparatively straightforward Mediterranean approach; the very curious molly-shops around the Inns of Court; the sense of furtive guilt and obsession that seemed to increase with every five or ten degrees of northern latitude. On the other side of the table, not directly opposite Stephen but one place up, sat Francis Howard of the *Aurora*, perhaps the best Greek scholar in the Navy: he had spent three happy years in the eastern Mediterranean, collecting inscriptions, and Stephen had hoped to sit next to him. On Howard's right he saw Smith of the *Camilla* and Michael Fitton, both brown-faced, round-headed, cheerful, intelligent-looking young men of a kind quite usual in the service. They could never have been taken for soldiers. Why did the Navy attract men with round heads? What had the phrenologist Gall to say? Stephen's right-hand neighbour, Captain Thomas, was round-headed too, and deeply tanned: but he was neither young nor cheerful. After a very long career as a commander, chiefly in the West Indies, he had been made post into the *Eusebio*, 32, which was destroyed in the hurricane of 1809; and now he commanded the *Thames*. He was the oldest man present, and his authoritarian face was set in an expression of disapproval – perpetually cross. He was known in the service as the Purple Emperor.

'Sir,' murmured a familiar voice in Stephen's ear, 'you've got your sleeve in your dinner.' It was Plaice, forecastleman, wearing white gloves and a mess-servant's jacket.

'Thank you, Joe,' said Stephen, taking it out and mopping it busily, with an anxious look at Killick.

'Capital soup, sir,' said Duff, smiling at him.

'The true ambrosia, sir, in the right place,' said Stephen, 'but perhaps a little unctuous on black broadcloth. May I trouble you for a piece of bread? It may do better than my napkin.'

They talked away, agreeing very well; and when, after the first remove, a roast loin of veal was put down in front of Stephen, he said, 'Sir, allow me to cut you a piece.'

'You are very good, sir. There are few things I dread more than having to carve.'

'For you, sir?' asked Stephen, turning to Thomas.

'If you please,' said the Purple Emperor. 'Why, you slice as trim as a surgeon.'

'But then I *am* a surgeon, sir: so it is no virtue. The surgeon of the Commodore's flagship, if that is the right expression. My name is Maturin.'

Joe Plaice uttered a loud, coarse laugh, attempted to be smothered with a white kid glove. Stephen and Duff glanced back at him with a smile. Thomas looked furious. 'Oh, indeed,' he said, 'I had imagined that this was a dinner for commissioned officers, for officers in command,' and spoke no more.

'Sophie, my dear,' said Stephen next morning, 'that was a sumptuous feast you gave us. When next I see Father George I shall have to admit to the sin of greed, of deliberate, premeditated greed. I returned to the venison pasty not once but three times. So did Captain Duff. We encouraged one another.'

'I am so glad you enjoyed it,' said she, looking upon him fondly. 'But how I regret your having to sit next to that cross old stick. Jack says he is always finding fault, always against everything; and like many of those West Indies spit-and-polish captains he thinks that if he can drive his people so hard that they are able to shift topgallant masts in thirteen minutes and make all the brass shine like gold day and night they must necessarily beat any of the heavy Americans, to say nothing of the Frenchmen. He is going to try to persuade the Admiral to make an exchange.'

'If you please, sir, Captain Tom has the dog-cart at the door,' said George.

'But he said nine,' cried Stephen, bringing out his watch, his beloved Breguet. Although it was of the perpetual kind and more reliable than the Bank of England, he shook it twice. The platinum mass that kept it always wound gave a muffled answer, but the hands still said ten minutes past the hour. 'God's my life,' he said. 'It is ten minutes past the hour. Sophie, forgive me, I must run.'

As a commander and a post-captain Jack Aubrey had never discussed the officers of his own ship with Stephen: as a commodore he had told him about Duff, but rather in the medical line than otherwise. He might also have spoken of the Purple Emperor's shortcomings, since the earlier rule did not apply – Stephen and the Emperor were not mess-mates, more or less tied by a wardroom loyalty – but it was unlikely that he should do so right away.

Tom Pullings had no such inhibitions. He had known

Stephen since he was a midshipman and he had always talked to him without the least restraint. 'That cove should never have risen above master's mate,' he said as they drove towards Portsmouth on a sweet morning, talking about last night's dinner and their fellow guests. 'He should never have been given authority: he don't know what to do with it so he is for ever giving orders to show that he does. He is always ill-used, always in a rage with someone. You get fathers of families like that. Always someone due for a flogging or kept to bread and water or sent to bed for tittering at the wrong moment. He makes life hell for everyone else in the ship, and to judge by his vinegar headpiece it is not much better for himself. Him and his dignity! Lord Nelson never topped it the dignified don't-talk-to-me kind of nob. If you fart on this man's quarterdeck even to leeward as is but right you have insulted the King's representative. Bah. And he has never been in action.'

'To be fair, nor have most sea-officers.'

'No. But he thinks that those that have, hands and all, hold it against him and laugh behind his back: so he takes it out on *them*, as well as everybody else. How I hope the Commodore will get rid of him. We need a fighting captain in this squadron, not the first lieutenant of a royal yacht, with his double-blacked yards – a skipper whose people can fire their guns and who will follow him like the Sophies followed us – God love us, that was a day!' Tom laughed, remembering the tall side of the Spanish thirty-two-gun frigate and the way he and his fifty-three shipmates from the fourteen-gun sloop *Sophie* had swarmed up it after Jack Aubrey, defeating the three hundred and nineteen Spaniards aboard and carrying their ship a prize into Port Mahon.

'So it was, too,' said Stephen.

'What is more,' said Tom, 'the *Thames*'s gunner told our gunner they had not used up even their practice allowance this last eight months: the guns were rattled in and out now and then, but only in dumb-show; and he doubted – he fairly wept when he said so – they could fire two broadsides in five minutes. Anything for pretty decks and perfect paint.'

'Have you anything against Captain Thomas personally, Commodore?' asked the Admiral. 'Do you feel he may possibly lack conduct?'

'Oh not at all, sir. I have no doubt he is as brave as a . . .'

'A lion?'

'Just so. Thank you, sir. As brave as a lion. But I do feel so strongly that in this squadron gunnery is of the first importance; and a ship's company capable of firing at least three well-directed broadsides in five minutes cannot be suddenly improvised.'

'What makes you think the *Thames* cannot do so?'

'Her captain's statement that they have never timed themselves, and her gunner's returns, which show that even the trifling official allowance of powder and shot has not been expended.'

'Then you will have all the more to work them up with. No, Aubrey: I cannot shift the *Thames* and you will have to make do with what you possess. Which upon my word is pretty handsome for a young fellow of your age. I have never seen a ship in better order than *Thames* herself; and the Duke of Clarence said the same when he went aboard her at the Nore. In any case it is not a question of suddenly improvising anything at all. You will probably have several weeks before you are on your station, with the wind so wickedly fixed in the south-east. On the other hand, by way of compensation for taking *Pyramus* away, I mean to give you the *Laurel*; and what is more, I mean to give you your sailing-date at last. Wind and weather permitting, you will proceed to the rendezvous off the Berlings specified in your orders on Wednesday the fourteenth.'

'Oh thank you, sir. Thank you very much. I am most uncommonly obliged to you; and if I may take my leave at once I shall hurry aboard and set everything in train for Wednesday the fourteenth.'

'There is not a moment to lose,' said the Admiral, shaking him by the hand.

'Pass the word for Dr Maturin,' said the Commodore, and the word passed down through the echoing decks.

'Him and the Commodore have been tie-mates this many a year,' observed a seaman as it made its way along the orlop.

'What's a tie-mate, guv?' asked a landsman, newly pressed.

'Don't you know what a tie-mate is, cully?' asked the seaman with tolerant scorn. The landsman shook his heavy head: there were already seventeen thousand things he did not know, and their number increased daily. 'Well, you know what a pigtail is?' asked the seaman, showing his own, a massive queue that reached his buttocks, and speaking loud, as to a fool or a foreigner. The landsman nodded, looking a little more intelligent. 'Which it has to be unplaited, washed on account of the lice, combed, and plaited again for muster. And can you do it yourself, behind your back? Not in time for muster, mate. Not in time for Kingdom Come, neither. So you get a friend, like me and Billy Pitt, to do yours, you sitting on a cheese of wads at your ease, or maybe a bucket turned arsy-versy; and then you do his: for fair's fair, I say. And that is what we call tie-mates.'

'I heard of that Billy Pitt of yours,' said the landsman, narrowing his eyes.

Presently Stephen pitched upon the right ladder – the ship had at least one more floor than he had remembered – and found the Commodore and the Captain of the *Bellona* in the great cabin. They were smiling, and Jack said, 'Such pleasant news, Stephen. We are to have the *Laurel*, twenty-two, one of the new sixth-rates, amazingly quick in stays, and she is commanded by Dick Richards. You remember him, Stephen?'

'The unhappy boy so woefully afflicted with acne that they called him Spotted Dick? Indeed I do. An obstinate case, though not bad at heart.'

'The very man. I taught him gunnery: he laid a pretty chaser, and his gun-crews were the best in the ship – the best ship afloat. I had been growing very anxious. I have seen so many squadrons formed, delayed in port, delayed still longer, the date put off, put off again, and then, when their officers had all their stores aboard for say a six months' voyage, dispersed, the whole scheme given up, the commodore sent back among the mere post-captains and reduced to begging in the street, having spent his last guineas on a rear-admiral's gold lace.'

'When do we sail?'

'Stephen, do not be indiscreet, I beg. French spies may see all the bustle and report it by the countless smugglers, but so long as no one ever mentions the actual date, the ministry feels quite safe. All I can say is that there is not a moment to be lost. You must attend to your medical stores directly, and may the Lord have mercy on your soul.'

'Gentlemen,' said Stephen to his assistants in their splendid new sick-berth, full of light and air, furnished with capacious dispensaries, port and starboard, 'I believe we may now cross off the antimonials, jalap and camphire, the eight yards of Welsh linen bandage, and the twelve yards of finer linen, which sets us up for the first month, barring the tourniquets, the mercury, and the small list of alexipharmics that Beale is sending over tomorrow. So much for our official supplies. But I have added a certain number of comforts – they are in the cases on the left, together with a chest of portable soup infinitely superior to the Victualling Board's second-hand carpenter's glue – and a parcel of my own particular asafetida. It is imported for me by a Turkey merchant; and as you perhaps have noticed in spite of the sturgeon's bladder in which it is enclosed it is by far the most pungent, the most truly fetid, variety known to man. For you must know, gentlemen, that when the mariner is dosed, he likes to know that he has been dosed: with fifteen grains or even less of this valuable substance scenting him and the very air about him there can be no doubt of the matter; and such is the nature of the human mind that he experiences a far greater real benefit than the drug itself would provide, were it deprived of its stench.'

'May I ask, sir, where we are to stow it?'

'Why, Mr Smith,' said Stephen, 'I had thought it would scarcely be noticed in the midshipmen's berth.'

'But we live there, too,' cried Macaulay. 'We live and sleep there, sir.'

'You will be astonished to find how quickly it becomes indifferent, how quickly you grow used to what weak minds call the offensive odour, just as you grow accustomed to the motion of the billows. Now this second parcel, colleagues, is a substance more valuable by far than the most nauseous asafetida, or even perhaps than bark, quicksilver or opium. It does not yet figure in the London or even in the Dublin pharmacopeia; but presently it will be written in both, and in that of Edinburgh, in letters of gold.'

He opened the small, close-woven rush basket, lifted the tissue-paper and then the two layers of pale-green silk. The assistants looked attentively at the dried brown leaves within.

'These dried brown leaves, gentlemen,' said Stephen, 'come from the Peruvian bush *Erythroxylon coca*. I do not present them as a panacea, but I do assert that they possess very great virtues in cases of melancholia, morbid depression of spirits whether rational or irrational, and the restless uneasiness of mind that so very often accompanies fever: it brings about a euphory, a sense of well-being far more lucid, far superior in every way to that produced by opium; and it does so without causing that unhappy addiction we are all so well acquainted with. Admittedly, it does not procure sleep as opium does – a most unhealthy sleep, I may add – but on the other hand, the patient does not *require* sleep: his mind rests of itself in a remarkable calm clarity.'

'Is it in no way dangerous?' asked Smith.

'I heard of no untoward effects in my inquiries among

medical men,' said Stephen, 'though it is known, esteemed, and very generally used throughout Peru. So long as man is man, there is always the possibility of abuse, sure, just as there is with tea, coffee, tobacco, wine and of course ardent spirits among us: but I never heard of an instance in some weeks' or indeed months' residence among the Peruvians.'

'Is it prescribed as a specific for some Peruvian disorder, as a tonic, or as an alterative?' asked Macaulay.

'It is certainly used as a febrifuge and as a remedy for most ills,' said Stephen, 'but it is primarily taken as an enhancer of daily life, particularly by the labouring classes of men; for as well as the euphory I have spoken of, the coca also provides or perhaps I should say liberates great stores of energy, at the same time doing away with hunger for days on end. I have known thin spare men, no larger than myself, walk across mountainy country in piercing weather at a great altitude from sunrise to sunset, carrying burdens without fatigue, and without food. Yet although the uses of the coca-leaf are most evident among the poor, the field-labourers, the miners and the porters, they are even more striking among those who work with their heads. I have written all night, covering forty-three octavo pages, without mental exhaustion or even weariness, after a very hard day's journey; and I have heard well-authenticated reports of surgeons operating for twenty-four hours on end after a very shocking battle – operating with their abilities undiminished. But from the purely medical point of view, it seems to me that the most evident and immediate application is in everyday mental disturbance. I had great hopes of proving its value in my most recent voyage, but unhappily – I should not say *unhappily*, of course – all our people, officers, petty officers and seamen, were resolutely cheerful. Some frostbites off the Horn, the first hints of scurvy north of the Island, but no real depression, no moping, no sadness, no peevish quarrelling, rarely a cross word. It is true that they were buoyed up with thoughts of home, and we had been very fortunate in the matter of prizes; but their merriment among the ice-floes of the south, their merriment in the heaving, sticky sea of the doldrums with the sails hanging loose day after day, would have vexed a saint. Have we any case even approaching melancholia at present?'

'Well, sir,' said Smith doubtfully, 'a good many of the pressed men are low in their spirits, of course; but as for downright, clinical melancholia . . . I am sorry to disappoint you, sir.'

The young men, who had been bent over the leaves, sprung upright, and Stephen, turning, saw Captain Aubrey walk into the berth. 'Here's glory, upon my word,' cried he. 'Light and air in God's plenty. It would be a pleasure to be sick in such a place. But come,' – sniffing right and left – 'has something died here?'

'It has not,' said Stephen. 'The odour is that of the Smyrna asafetida, the most fetid of them all. In former times it was carried hung from the loftiest mast. Perhaps I might be indulged in some oiled silk, and a box lapped with lead, in which the bulk may be *struck* into the orlop, while I keep just a little small jar on this floor for our daily use.'

'By all means, Doctor,' said Jack. 'If you will come with me we can speak to Chips directly. There is a gentleman from the Sick and Hurt Board to see you in the cabin.'

The gentleman was not in fact from the Sick and Hurt Board, though he carried some of their official papers, but from the Admiralty itself, one of the more rarely seen officials in the department of naval intelligence, a gentleman often entrusted by its chief, Sir Joseph Blaine, with the most delicate missions. Neither acknowledged any former acquaintance even when Jack had left them alone. Mr Judd spoke firmly and authoritatively on some obscure points of medical administration, handed over the relevant documents with only the very slightest emphasis, and took his civil but distant leave.

Stephen walked straight into the quarter-gallery, and there, poised upon the seat of ease, he opened the packet. The papers were straightforward, devoid of interest, their only function being to contain the note that asked him to be in the beetle wood that afternoon if he possibly could, or to catch the bearer, who would stay at the Cock for half an hour, and appoint a very early meeting.

At this stage in the *Bellona*'s preparations Stephen was virtually a free agent. He looked in at the Cock, spoke to his man, took a chaise back to Ashgrove, saddled his mare and rode some miles towards Liss before branching off into a series of lanes, one of which would have brought him to a farm belonging to Sir Joseph if, before reaching it, he had not turned along a path leading through the roughest of rough and sandy pasture to a neglected wood, one of the few in England where an entomologist had a reasonable chance of finding that brilliant creature *Calosoma sycophanta*, as well as no less than three of the tiger beetles.

'I am so glad you were able to come,' cried Blaine, reaching up and shaking his hand. He led horse and rider down to a shaded bank, where Stephen dismounted, tethered Lalla by a long symbolic cord and sat down, contemplating his friend's pale and anxious face.

'I am so full of matter and so disturbed that I hardly know how to begin,' said Sir Joseph. 'The last time we met I told you that Habachtsthal was continuing Ledward's work in sending information to the French; that a threat of retribution was conveyed to him, a threat that checked his activity until he realized how hollow it was. I also told you that he was an exceptionally revengeful man and that I had reasons for suspecting that he saw me as the ultimate source of the threat. These suspicions were justified, and it grieves me beyond measure, Stephen, to say that he has also identified you as the destroyer of his friends Ledward and Wray, and Clarissa as the source of your information about him and therefore of mine.'

'Do you know how he did so?'

'The first was clear enough, from Wray's known hatred of you and Jack Aubrey and your presence in Pulo Prabang when they were killed. The second was more obscure . . .

but here I must branch off and hark back to that ugly, that very ugly affair which led to Captain Aubrey's being charged with rigging the Stock Exchange. It was engineered by criminals, of course: the swell mob, as they say, the same criminals as those who at one or two removes brought about the murder and the disfigurement of the witness whose testimony would have dismissed the accusation. You might think it a far cry from the Solicitor-General and a long-established, eminently respectable firm of lawyers to a band of criminals; but the eminently respectable know the less respectable and so down to the very dregs; and where *raison d'état* or what can be disguised as *raison d'état* is concerned I believe that even you would be astonished at what can happen. And I must tell you that by the same long and dirty road Habachtsthal's attorneys had brought him into more or less direct contact with a set of the same kind of fellows, if not the very same. Pratt, who is very well acquainted with that world, asserts that at least three belonged to the former group; and that one of them, a man called Bellerophon, murdered the accomplice who killed and mutilated the unhappy Palmer, in case your wealth might induce him to peach.'

'Pratt?' said Stephen.

'Yes. His acumen, honesty, and very particular qualifications impressed me deeply when you and I employed him, and I have entrusted him with several other inquiries since then, always to the department's satisfaction. He has associates now, all like himself, children of the gaol and often former Bow Street runners.'

'So he told me. He is working for me at present: or more probably two or three of his partners. It is a family investigation: I will tell you about it when we have finished with this.'

Sir Joseph bowed and said, 'He did not mention this to me, of course; but we did talk about you and Captain Aubrey. He has a great respect and liking for you: I might indeed say an affection. However . . .' He paused, gathered his anxious thoughts and went on, 'These men, perhaps with the help of some part of officialdom, together with the lowest stratum of crooked attorneys, have presented their employer with the following facts: that you have illegally brought back two unpardoned convicts from New South Wales, Patrick Colman and Clarissa Harvill, now Mrs Oakes; that you have sought, with me acting as go-between, to have them pardoned; but that since no pardon has yet been obtained you are still open to prosecution on an undeniable charge that leads not perhaps to death but at least to imprisonments and loss of all property. Furthermore they allege that the pardon we sued out for you long ago . . .'

'I believe you must explain that, Joseph.'

'Forgive me, Stephen. When first the department asked your advice on Catalan affairs it was told that you and some of your friends and relations had been concerned in the Irish rising of 1798, which might bring you within the catch-all "failure to denounce" and "association with malefactors" legislation. To protect you we had your name included in one of the wider pardons: I confess that it was a very great liberty; but it served our common cause. Without it I could not have shown you any confidential document without committing a crime, while at any point a malignant private prosecution might have robbed us of your invaluable help – private prosecutions are usual in these cases.'

Stephen nodded, and presently Blaine went on, 'But most unhappily these people appear to have had access to the document, and it is said that it may not be watertight – that if new evidence is produced you may still be taken up for treason. It seems that such evidence can still be procured, even now, in Dublin, where creatures like the infamous Sirr crawl about to this day – procured at no great price.'

In his agitation Blaine plucked a handkerchief from his pocket, a handkerchief in which there was entangled a sadly folded, crumpled envelope. 'I was forgetting,' he cried, holding out the paper. 'This should have been sent to you. It is your statement of the amount due to you for the hire of the *Surprise* in this recent voyage. The accountant disputes your addition on the first page as being too great by eighteen pence, and observes that in your grand total you have omitted the agreed sum of seventeen thousand pounds odd for hire, maintenance and repairs.'

In an undertone Stephen said, 'How life is diminished when you can forget or indeed even dismiss seventeen thousand pounds.'

Blaine paid no attention and continued, 'On reflexion I find that I have mis-stated the case, giving the impression that all this information is in Habachtsthal's possession. That is not so: he has the general notion but not the particulars. And from two sources I have learnt that the – what shall I call them? – the *gang* not only mean to make him pay very heavily for them, but then to blackmail him for having procured and used them. I am wholly indifferent to his fate, which is likely to be extremely uncomfortable: I am not to yours, and I must tell you with infinite concern that their more immediate project is to blackmail *you*. You are known to be wealthy, I am very sorry to say: you are known to be extremely vulnerable, if only because of Clarissa and Padeen and the thought of their forced return to New South Wales. The information reached me from two sources. It will not surprise you to learn that Pratt was one, but I think the second will astonish you – Lawrence, Jack Aubrey's counsel in the Stock Exchange case. He was as guarded and discreet as could be, but I gather that Habachtsthal has begun to find that he is far, far deeper entangled in this association with malefactors than he had expected, that they are not going to be satisfied with the fees agreed upon in the first place, and that whereas the sovereign ruler of even a very small German state can deal expeditiously with awkward customers in his own country, it will not answer here. The foolish man quarrelled with his own lawyer and now he is consulting right and left for means of protection; and that, directly or indirectly, is how Lawrence has come to understand the matter. He is perfectly aware of the position with regard to Clarissa and Padeen: he perfectly understands that the long delays in granting their otherwise routine pardon is part of a long-drawn-out manoeuvre against me, and through me, against you. He begs you to take the utmost care.'

'I have long had a great respect and esteem and liking for Brendan Lawrence,' said Stephen, 'and I am obliged to him for his kindness. He would not have offered any words of advice, at all?'

'He did indeed, this very morning. They exactly coincide with Pratt's, who came to tell me that on Monday a low attorney will at last have the authenticated papers from Newgate to complete the files proving Clarissa's transportation. And with mine, for what it is worth.'

'Pray let me know what you all think, will you, now?'

In the silence a jay pitched in the tree above their heads, a white poplar: it peered down, and seeing what they were flew off again with a harsh chattering.

'I hesitate to tell you,' said Blaine, looking full at Stephen. 'It sounds so wild and I might almost say romantic, excessive. However, we all agree that you should escape at once, taking your protégés with you and all the money you can lay your hands on. For once the charge against you is laid, once the Newgate records have made their way to the lawyers Habachtsthal is now employing, and once he has signed the denunciation that sets the legal process in train, your account with your banking-house is attached: you cannot touch it. We think you should hide and remain hidden at least until the Duke of Sussex returns, when my position will be much stronger, and when his kindness for you should make the pardons an ordinary matter of course: he far outweighs Habachtsthal in our Byzantium. But in the meantime it all hinges on Habachtsthal.'

The jay returned, circled round the grazing mare, and perched in the tree once more, grumbling for a while before it flew off again.

'It all hinges on him,' said Blaine. 'If he were eliminated he could do no favours and all this reluctance about pardons would vanish; and the moment they are granted the black-mailers have no hold on you whatsoever.' He fell silent, but his look conveyed all he meant it to convey.

'Certainly,' said Stephen. 'He is as much the enemy as Ledward was, and Wray, and some other men I have killed or caused to be killed with a tranquil conscience. But here the case is altered; and with my commitments in this country I do not think I can consider such a course.'

'I suppose not. But I very much regret it: for with the Garter gone, everything collapses. He is the one and only primum mobile. If he were dead all his revenge and all his influence would die with him. The case is a private prosecution: so it would die too. We should not have to wait for Sussex. I should not have to overcome your reluctance to turn to your old patient Prince William. And the department would be rid of a dangerous opponent – rid for good and all. However . . . as to money, Lawrence thinks you still have a great deal of it in gold?'

'Just so. I consulted him when I was last in town, and after considering what he told me about stocks and shares, annuities and land, I decided to leave it in the little chests that brought it from Spain. One of the partners showed them to me, in a vaulted strong-room under their house in the City.'

'Would you be prepared to sign a letter of attorney directed to some nominee guaranteed by Lawrence and myself so that it may be stored in a safe place?'

'I would, too.'

'We both thought so, and Lawrence prepared the paper: here is a pocket inkhorn and a pen. The bank will need some little time to get everything ready; and, you know, there is not a moment to lose.'

Chapter Five

'Why am I so nervous?' asked Stephen as he rode back towards Portsmouth. 'My mind is in a silly flutter – pursues no clear line – flies off. Why, oh why did I leave my pouch of leaves behind?' This was the perfect opportunity for them to show their powers, so very much superior to those of the poppy, which provided little more than a stupid tranquillity. 'Though there is something to be said for a stupid tranquillity at times,' he reflected, remembering that Petersfield possessed an apothecary's shop where, before now, he had purchased laudanum. 'Vade retro, Satanas,' he cried, dismissing the thought.

Clouds were piling high in the south-west; the evening was well advanced and night would fall earlier than usual, almost certainly bringing rain. He had abandoned his lanes long since and he was now steering for the main London to Portsmouth road, which he would strike a little above Petersfield: the broad, even verges would make his journey much quicker; he could not easily miss his way; and as Sir Joseph had said, with his pale smile, there was not indeed a moment to lose.

Since mood is so freely conveyed not only from person to person but from person to dog, cat, horse and the other way about, some part of his present state of mind derived from Lalla, though her unusual and nervous volatility arose from a cause that could not possibly have been more remote. The season of the year, her temperament, and a variety of other factors had inspired her with a notion that it would be delightful to meet with a fine upstanding stallion. She skipped as she went, sometimes dancing sideways, sometimes tossing her head: her views were evident to other members of her race, and poor rueful geldings rolled their eyes, while the only stone-horse they passed raced madly round and round his paddock, neighing; while a pretentious jack-ass uttered a huge sobbing cry that followed them beyond the cultivated land to the edge of a barren common where a broad lane joined their present road, the two running on to join the highway by a gallows. Pleased with her success, Lalla whinnied, arched her neck and curvetted to such a degree that Stephen cried, 'Avast, avast there. Belay. Why, Lalla, for shame,' and reined in hard to bring her to a halt at the foot of the gallows, always a point of interest for an anatomist, even one as deeply harassed as Maturin.

This ill-omened place at the junction of the lanes, with scrub on either hand, perfect for an ambush, had been chosen for the exhibition of awful examples; but they did not seem to have much deterrent effect, since they had to be renewed with such regularity that the two pairs of ravens from Selborne Hanger came over at least twice a week for fresh supplies. By now the light was too poor for Stephen to make any worthwhile observations; but at the edge of his field of vision he did catch a movement in the furze. It might have been a goat – there were several at large – but at the same moment he regretted a long, accurate revolving pistol, the gift of a French intelligence-agent, that he usually carried when he travelled by night.

He pushed Lalla forward, but she was hardly beyond the point where the two roads joined when there was a thunder of hoofs behind them. When he was riding Lalla, Stephen wore no spurs, he carried no whip: now he urged her on with knees, heels and all the moral force he could exert, yet she took shockingly little notice, barely reaching a hand-gallop. The hoofs came closer, closer: they were abreast on either side: a band of foolish unmounted ogling geldings, colts and farm horses from the common, as Lalla had obviously known from the beginning.

'Yet even so,' said Stephen, when the gateway was closed

behind them and they were trotting along the Portsmouth road, 'there is a gunsmith in Petersfield, and I believe I shall buy a pair of little pocket pistols.'

They baited at the Royal Oak: here Stephen found that he had forgotten not only Duhamel's weapon but his own money too, and it was only on the chance discovery of a seven-shilling piece that he had put in a side pocket as a curiosity that he was spared an embarrassing and perhaps thoroughly disagreeable experience. 'Joseph's message carried its shadow before it,' he reflected. 'Of course it did: I have rarely let my wits go so far astray.'

Riding on through the steady rain, he let his mind return to Duhamel, an agent who, ill-used and perhaps about to be sacrificed by his government, had changed sides, providing Stephen with proof of the treachery of Wray and Ledward. From Duhamel, whom he had thoroughly liked, he moved on to other agents, dwelling on the man they called McAnon, a well-placed Norman from Vauville who used to slip across to Alderney to see an unofficial wife, and who, like others in the same fragile posture, had been turned, all the more easily because he *hated* Buonaparte with a strong personal hatred both as a vulgar Italian upstart and as one who had refused his scheme for an improved system of telegraphic signals. McAnon, high in the communications department, had provided them with some very fine long-range forecasts, and it was he who lay behind the secret orders that Jack Aubrey would open when he reached a stated latitude and longitude, orders telling him that a French squadron of roughly equivalent strength, but accompanied by transports, would assemble at Lorient at a given date, and that with the help of three separate diversions it would sail as nearly as possible to a stated full moon. The intention of the French commander was to steer across as though for the West Indies, by way of deluding any possible observers, and then to head for the south-west coast of Ireland, there to land his troops on the shore of the Kenmare river or Bantry Bay, as time and weather and the movements of the Royal Navy served.

McAnon: a valuable man, though as Blaine had said, their hold on him was weaker now that the unofficial wife had taken to wearing hair-curlers in the daytime and to talking in a little girl's voice. Yet even so, it was probable that his loathing of the imperial régime, his enjoyment of the perilous game and his friendship for the man who dealt with him would keep him active and reliable. But how difficult it was to tell. There were some very intelligent men on the other side, wonderfully adept at poisoning the springs of intelligence: he remembered Abel, a devoted and wholly disinterested ally in Paris whose chiefs had *by accident* allowed him to see Admiral Duclerc's plan of an attack on a Baltic convoy, and shortly before his death he had sent it over in all good faith. Knowing the agent so well, Blaine's deputy – Blaine was in Portugal at the time – had acted at once: but to their astonishment the additional ships sent to guard the merchantmen found themselves heavily outnumbered. The convoy was terribly mauled, a gun-brig was taken, a sloop destroyed, and HMS *Melampus* was only saved by the descent of a providential fog, though with very heavy casualties, including Jack's friend her captain, the loss of two topmasts and grievous damage to her hull.

Difficult situations: difficult situations. And if Jack was still aboard there would be another within the hour. Commodore Aubrey was of course much overworked, as any man ordered to sea in so short a time, with such indifferent preparation and so many sudden changes, must necessarily be: yet he was better equipped than most for a situation of this kind. Like many big men he was not easily put out of temper; he did not use up much of his energy in expostulation; upon the whole he despised those who complained; and the entire course of his professional career had fitted him for his present role. On the other hand he was quite remarkably defenceless when it came to dealing with jealousy. It was an emotion he had apparently never known, at least not in its present consuming state, and it was one whose nature and development he scarcely seemed to recognize at all, so that he was unable to call upon intelligence for what help it can bring in these cases.

Stephen was well acquainted with this blindness where health was concerned – 'It is only a lump: it will soon go away' – and affections – 'She has certainly not received my letter. The posts are so slow these days, and very far from sure' – yet even so it surprised him in Jack Aubrey, a much more intelligent man than he seemed to those who did not know him well. With great concern he had watched the progress of the disease, the changes in the atmosphere at Ashgrove Cottage, where Mr Hinksey continued to call with the most unlucky regularity, often appearing a few moments before Jack left, and the beginning of a change in the *Bellona*. Jack was still very kind to him, and in matters to do with the squadron he was perfectly agreeable to those around him; but every now and then a sudden rigour, a peremptory tone startled those who had served with him before and made his new subordinates look at him rather uneasily. Were they to sail with another St Vincent, otherwise known as Old Jarvey or even as Old Nick for his ferociously taut discipline?

Clearly, this particular and in Stephen's opinion totally unnecessary trial was telling on Jack Aubrey's temper most severely. Stephen regretted the whole foolish matter extremely, the suffering of the two chiefly concerned and of those around them, the utter impossibility of playing the kind intervening friend who puts everything right with a few quiet, understanding words, perhaps conveyed parabolically; and at this juncture his regret was singularly immediate – a personal, directly interested regret – since he was going to ask a favour that even an uncommonly well-disposed, unhurried, and benevolent naval commander would hesitate to grant, let alone a man in the throes of readying a squadron for the sea with a half-acknowledged monster at the same time devouring him within.

Lalla stopped and looked round at him: was she to go into Portsmouth or carry on by the back lane home? 'To the left, hussy,' he said, pushing his knee into her side. He had not yet quite forgiven her for making such a fool of him by the gallows; but by the time they reached the Keppel's Head he relented, and he ordered her bran-mash with treacle in it, her favourite indulgence, before going out on the Hard in search of a boat, since the ostler had told him that Jack's horse was still in the stable.

'*Bellona*'s a great way over, sir,' said the boatman, 'and you will have a long, wet pull. Would you like this here piece of sailcloth, since you have forgot your cloak?'

In spite of the sailcloth Stephen was wet to the skin well before they reached the ship. As they approached her busy, well-lit side the boatman observed that *Thames*'s barge was at her starboard chains. 'Look at 'em, like a parcel of popinjays,' he said, nodding at Captain Thomas's bargemen, all dressed in the same showy garments like a band of damp Merry Andrews. 'I dare say it's larboard for you, sir?'

'Certainly,' said Stephen. 'And were you to call out that I should like a small convenient ladder, if it is available, I should be obliged.'

'The boat ahoy,' called the *Bellona*.

'Ho,' replied the boat.

'Coming here?' asked the *Bellona*.

'No, no,' said the boatman, meaning thereby that he *was* coming there, but that he had grasped, without much difficulty, that his passenger was not a commissioned officer; and then, raising his voice, 'The gentleman would be obliged for a small convenient ladder, if available.'

This was received with a startled silence for an even longer moment than the boatman had hoped, and he was filling his lungs, suppressing his mirth, for a repetition, when a number of familiar voices called out that the Doctor was not to move – he would slip in the rain – he was to stay there – they would bring him aboard.

This they did, Surprises to a man: on deck they plucked at his clothing and told him he was wet, wet through – why had he not put on his cloak? With the wind in the south-west, he ought always to put on his cloak.

He was making his way aft when Captain Pullings intercepted him. 'Oh Doctor,' said he, 'the Commodore is engaged at the moment – will not you shift your coat, at least? You will catch your death, else. Mr Somers' – this to the officer of the watch – 'stand by: any minute now.'

'Mr Dove,' said Somers to the bosun, 'stand by. Any minute now.'

A bosun's mate leant over the rail, looking down into the barge; he caught the coxswain's eye and gave an unofficial nod, full of significance.

A door right aft opened: a deep voice, now no longer muffled, said in a tone of strong displeasure, 'That is all I have to say: this will not occur again. Good day to you, sir.'

Captain Thomas came out, pale with emotion, carrying the *Thames*'s punishment register under his arm: he gave the officers on the quarterdeck little more than a nod as he was piped over the side with full ceremony.

With a knowing look, Tom Pullings said to Stephen, 'The cabin is clear now, Doctor, if you choose to go along.'

'There you are, Stephen,' cried Jack, looking up from his desk, a more natural smile doing away with the severity of his expression. 'Have you come back? God's my life, you are soaked quite through. Should you not change your shoes and stockings? It is always said that the feet are the weakest part. Take Achilles' heel – but you know all about Achilles' heel.'

'Presently. But for the moment, Jack . . .'

'Well, in any case take a dram to keep the wet out. Seawater does no harm, but rain is deadly stuff once it gets right in.' He swung round, took a case-bottle from the locker and poured them each a tot of rum, a glorious rum he had drawn from the wood in Trafalgar year. 'Lord, I needed that,' he said, putting down his glass. 'How I do loathe a steady indiscriminate flogger.' He glanced down at his papers, and the stony look returned.

'Jack', said Stephen, 'I have not chosen my moment well. I have a request. I have a favour to ask, and I could have wished to find you with a mind reposed. But you have clearly had a trying day.'

'Ask away, Stephen. I shall be no better-tempered tomorrow: ill-humour seems to have settled in my bosom' – striking it – 'much as the wind used to settle in the south-east and stay there when we were trying to claw out of Port Mahon, week after week.'

A silence: and in a harsh voice Stephen said, 'I should like to borrow the *Ringle*, if you please, with a proper crew, for a private voyage to London, as early as can be.'

Jack fixed him with a piercing stare that Stephen had never seen before. 'You know we sail on Wednesday's ebb?' he asked, having looked at Stephen's face in an objective manner.

'I do. But may I say that if the wind does not serve, I should certainly join you at the Groyne or off Finisterre.' Jack nodded. Stephen went on, 'I must add that this is an entirely personal need – a private emergency.'

'So I had gathered,' said Jack. 'Very well: you shall have her. But with the weather that promises, I doubt you can come down in time. Do you mean to spend long in town?'

'Only long enough to load some chests near the Tower.'

'How many tides do you reckon?'

'Tides? To tell you the truth, Jack, I had not thought of tides . . . and then,' he said in a low, diffident voice, 'I had hoped to put in to Shelmerston for perhaps a night.'

'I see.' Jack rang a bell. 'Could Captain Pullings spare him a minute?'

'Tom,' he said, 'the Doctor has occasion for the tender, to run up the London river directly. Let him have Bonden and Reade and as discreet a set of old shipmates as you can think of, enough for watch and watch with two to spare. He may not be able to rejoin before the Groyne or Finisterre. Let her be victualled for the Berlings with the utmost dispatch.'

'The utmost dispatch it is, sir,' said Tom, smiling.

'I am very deeply obliged to you, Jack, my dear,' said Stephen.

'There is no such thing as obligation between you and me, brother,' said Jack. And in another tone, 'It will take some little time – she is over by Gilkicker – but you should clear at the height of flood. I am sorry I was a trifle chuff to begin with. I have had an uncommon wearing day. So have you, by your look, if I may be so God-damned personal. What do you say to a pot of coffee?' Without waiting for an answer he rang the bell and said, 'Killick, large pot: and the Doctor will need half a dozen shirts put up, as well as a dry coat and stockings this minute.'

They drank their coffee and Jack said, 'Let me tell you about my rough day, apart from my battle with the Victualling Yard and that ass Thomas – he will end up like Pigot or Corbett if he goes on like this: food for the less particular fishes. I had gone ashore to see how my second chronometer was coming along, the Arnold, that needed cleaning, when I ran into Robert Morley of the *Blanche*. She lies at St Helens, fresh from Jamaica. I literally ran into him – he did not see where he was going – and knocked him into the kennel. I picked him up and dusted him, and carried him into the Keppel's Nob, where I called for a glass of shrub, which I knew Bob Morley had always liked. But he still looked horrid pale and I asked him was he hurt? Should I send for a surgeon? No, he said, he was perfectly well; and he leant on the table with the tears running down his face. His ship had come in before daylight and he had pulled ashore, hurrying up to their house for breakfast. Well, he found his wife six months gone with child: he had been away for two years. She was terrified. His father-in-law was there, an elderly parson, and he told Bob he was not to abuse her or be unkind. He was not to throw a stone unless he was sinless himself; and not even then if he was a good man. Now as you know very well, Bob Morley, though excellent company and a tolerable good seaman, has never set up for chastity any more than I have, though he carried things much farther. In the West Indies he always cruised with a miss aboard, and he allowed his officers and even mids so much liberty when he had the *Semiramis* that she was a floating bawdy-house – that the Admiral himself took notice of.'

'Her surgeon died of the pox.'

'Well, I tried to put this to Bob – I tried to say he could not decently blame anyone for doing what he so notoriously did himself. Of course he came out with the parrot-cry "Oh it is different for women."'

'What did you say to that?'

'I did not say I thought it was a mere scrub's reply, which I do, because he was in a very sad way, so I just suggested that it was the general cant – great nonsense – the act was the same for both – the only difference that a woman could bring a cuckoo into the nest and cheat the rightful chicks: but that could be dealt with by leaving the cuckoo out of your will.'

'Is that your considered view, brother?'

'Yes, it is,' said Jack, with a look of anguish, 'my deepest considered view. I have thought it over again and again. Fair is fair, you know,' he said with an attempt at a smile. 'I have always felt that very strongly.'

'I honour you for it.'

'I am glad of that: some would say it was sad stuff. Yet I do not think you will be so pleased when I tell you I said that if he wished I should go and ask the man in question to give him satisfaction.'

'But surely, Jack, there is a contradiction here? Decency – I will not say Christian charity – but at least decency on the one hand, and barbarous heathen revenge on the other?'

'Stephen, you have nothing whatsoever to say about barbarous heathen revenge: we both have bloody hands. We have both been out. And if there is an apparent contradiction, I can account for it like this: I feel – I deeply *know* – I am right in the first case; and I am almost as certain of it in the second. Did your mathematical studies ever reach to the quadratic equation, Stephen?'

'They did not reach to the far end of the multiplication table.'

'The quadratic equation involves the second power of the unknown quantity, but nothing greater. The square.'

'Oh, indeed?'

'And my point is this: a quadratic equation has two solutions, and each is right, demonstrably and provably right. There is an apparent but no real contradiction between the answers.'

Stephen felt that he was on dangerous ground; even if he had not been afraid of giving pain, his mind was so weary that although it teemed with objections it could barely formulate them. 'Jack,' he said in an entirely different voice, having reflected for a while, 'you mentioned the Berlings. Will you tell me about them, now?'

'Why,' said Jack, who understood him perfectly well, 'they are that group of rocks, or you might say islands, that rise up sheer out of the sea like mountain-tops a little south of the Farilhoes, some two leagues west-north-west of Cape Carveiro, in Portugal. They are quite dangerous in thick weather and many a ship on the Lisbon run has come to grief through not keeping a good offing and a good look-out by night. But they make a capital rendezvous if you don't choose to go over the infernal Tagus bar, hanging about for high water; and in moderate weather you can lie easy in their lee, fishing over the side for codlings.' He reflected, seeing the Berlings rising high from a warm calm Maytime sea. 'When I was a mid in *Bellerophon*,' he said, 'the Captain sent Mr Stevens the master to survey them, and he took me with him, knowing how I loved that kind of job. He was always very kind to me, or to any young fellow that had a bent for surveying. There is a great satisfaction in triangulation and taking bearing, Stephen.'

'I am sure of it.'

'I remember some very pretty cross-checks we made, all

agreeing exactly. And I remember the enormous clouds of sea-birds.'

'What sort?'

'Oh, every conceivable sort. You would know their names. The master said that a great many were petrels, I recall; but being startled, they did not fly as petrels usually do. And some had much more white about them than the common kind. They were startled because we pulled into an enormous cave that went on and on, and in the half-darkness they came flying out almost like black snow. And the cave went on and on, most uncommon tall overhead, and at last we saw light gleaming round a corner at the other end, for the cave went right through. At the far end the light came more slanting and we could make out innumerable bats . . .'

'Bats, Jack? You amaze me. Bats, so far from land? You did not take notice of them, I suppose?'

'We were busy taking soundings all the time, but I did notice that some were as big as partridges – well, quails – and some were small. I am quite certain that one had long ears. I saw it outlined against the mouth of the cave before it flew off.'

'How I long to spend an hour or two among them. Will you tell me about the surface of the rocks, the vegetation, the places where the birds were sitting, for I presume they had made their nests?'

'Certainly they had, and right on top of one another almost like the people in Seven Dials; but the petrels, as far as I could see, came mostly from the cave. It was full of crevices and ledges and holes.'

'What joy. But the vegetation, now; and a very rough description of the fowls themselves?'

They talked on until well after the evening gun, supping together and going back over that voyage to Portugal in the *Surprise* during which Stephen would dimly have perceived the Berlings had he been on deck, and in which, after their going ashore at Lisbon, they heard of Sam's being ordained

– Sam Panda, Jack's black love-child, begotten at the Cape – and they were still discussing his chances of a prelacy when the tender came alongside. Jack Aubrey was as solid a Protestant as ever abjured the Pope and the Pretender, but he was deeply attached to Sam, as well he might be, and he was now as expert in the intricacies of the Catholic hierarchy as he was in the succession of admirals. He was speaking eagerly of the Prothonotaries Apostolic and their varying rows of little violet buttons when Reade came in, took off his hat, and said, 'Tender hooked on, sir, if you please, and all is laid along,' this last, with a significant look at Stephen, meant that Killick had carried over a small valise holding all that he thought proper for Dr Maturin to wear during this absence, and a supply of shirts.

'Thank you, Mr Reade,' said Stephen: he hurried into the sleeping-cabin that he shared with Jack, put a considerable sum of money into his pocket, and a llama-skin pouch holding his coca-leaves and their necessary phial of vegetable ash into his bosom, together with the revolving pistol. 'Farewell, Jack,' he said, coming out, fastening his coat. 'Pray watch your bowels. There is something a trifle more liverish in your visage than I could wish for: should nothing occur this evening, desire Mr Smith to give you rhubarb tomorrow. My dear love to Sophie, of course. I shall be as quick as ever I can, so I shall. God bless, now.'

The sense of hurried urgency that had been with him ever since he received Sir Joseph's message, at some point now removed by a vast extent of space rather than of time, had revived as he groped his way down the *Bellona*'s side in the darkness; and now its long-frustrated desire was fulfilled, even beyond his hopes.

The wind, a strong reefed-topsail breeze in the south-west, was kicking up an odd little cross-sea in the harbour, and as Reade, who had brought the *Ringle* round to face Southsea Castle, filled his forestaysail, leaving the *Bellona*'s towering side and getting under way, the long low schooner took on a curious fidgeting motion like a horse held in, dancing on his toes, eager to be off.

The gaff rose, the foresail shivering and fluttering like an enormous washing-day; the sheet came hard aft, and at once the deck leaned sharply, the whole motion changing to a long, slightly pitching glide. She ran straight out of the harbour – Reade and Bonden had spent every spare hour they could and they handled her beautifully, with love – set her full mainsail and jib, and with Bonden at the helm and Reade at the con she raced for the ships moored off St Helens.

When Stephen came on deck – he had been desired to go below during these manoeuvres and to stow his belongings as well as he could with so little headroom – she had brought the wind on her starboard quarter: both great fore-and-aft sails were drum-tight, she had set her square foretopsail as well as everything the forward stays could bear, and now Reade, Bonden and two elderly Shelmerstonians were wondering whether they might venture upon a weather stud-dingsail.

The Shelmerstonians, Mould and Vaggers, were fine examples of what might be called nautical relativity: they were both Sethians and respected members of their congregation, yet neither had ever found any difficulty in reconciling the importation of uncustomed goods with the strictest probity in all personal dealings; and now one was saying that if the studdingsail in question had been the King's he would have risked it without hesitation, but since the clipper was Captain Aubrey's private property, why . . . and he shook his head. This kind of discussion was neither usual nor encouraged in the Royal Navy, but the present occasion was quite exceptional. Mould and Vaggers, not to put too fine a point upon it, were smugglers, and both their living and their freedom depended on their outsailing the Revenue cutters or the faster men-of-war that tried to detain them. They were the most successful smugglers in Shelmerston, and although they usually sailed in a lugger called the *Flying*

Childers they had also had great success in a topsail-schooner, not indeed as sharp-built as the *Ringle* but the fastest in home waters; their opinion on the studdingsail was therefore the opinion of eminent practitioners, and its authority was increased by the fact that they were not sailing again with Captain Aubrey because they needed wages. Far from it, indeed: all those who had shipped with him in the *Surprise* so long ago, and who had survived, had done so well in prize-money that if they wished they could set up as their own masters. Some preferred wild spending followed by extreme penury; but this was not the case with the serious men of the town, elders, deacons, presbyters of the many sects and chapels; and the reason for the continued presence of Mould, Vaggers and several of their friends was a revelation, perhaps illusory, certainly ill-timed, to the effect that polygamy was now allowed and indeed recommended to the Sethians of Shelmerston, a revelation so very ill-received by Mrs Mould and Mrs Vaggers (to speak only of them) that the *Bellona*, though a man-of-war, seemed a haven of peace.

Stephen had been aboard the clipper from time to time during their homeward voyage, but in calm weather, and in daylight. Now, as he came up the companion-ladder on to the dark, steep-sloping deck, he could not recognize his surroundings. Little could he see, and that little was unfamiliar – the great boom of the mainsail, the haze of white low to leeward meant nothing to him, and although on consideration he would almost certainly have made out the fundamental difference between fore-and-aft and square rig, he had no leisure to do so. His groping foot came up against a cleat, a chance caper of the deck flung him off his balance, and he trundled along until he came firmly against one of the *Ringle*'s carronades, to which he clung.

They picked him up with the usual sea-going questions – 'Was he hurt? Did he not know he must always keep one hand for himself and the other for the ship? Why had he not asked one of them to help him?'

For once he answered rather shortly, which made them stare, the Doctor being the meekest of landlubbers, always attentive to good advice and admonition, always grateful for being set on his feet again and if necessary helped below; but they were forgiving creatures, and when they understood that their old shipmate wished to stand there, near to what little prow the *Ringle* could be said to possess, where those sails did not obscure his view, stand there in the dark and the cold, they kindly told him that it would never do, not in this sort of a barky, which was more what might be called a racing-craft than a Christian schooner, with no more of a bulwark than would keep a kitten aboard – it would never do, without he was made fast to this here stanchion.

And so, fast to that there stanchion, he stood, hour after hour: and while one part of his being lived in this great rushing stream of air, with the dead-white bow-wave flying out, flung wide on his right hand, and the black, pale-flecked sea racing close below him, the whole in a vast and all-embracing medley of sound, the rest of him peered into the immediate future with all the acuity and concentration that he could bring to bear. Very early his hand had of itself reached for the pouch of coca-leaves, but he had deliberately checked the movement. 'This I justify on the grounds that although the present crisis seems to call for all possible clarity of thought and foresight, the leaves should be reserved in case another, even more exigent crisis, should arise; but I fear it may be mere superstition, the passionate desire to succeed overwhelming reason entirely, leaving mere sophistry behind.'

From time to time Reade or a seaman would come and ask him how he did, or tell him that that was Selsey Bill, or that the breeze was freshening a little – those were the lights of Worthing, New Shoreham . . .

Well on in the middle watch the stream of tide came more southward, so that great quantities of spindrift, spray and even green water swept across the low deck. Reade came forward with a cloak over his shoulder and begged Stephen to put it on. 'And don't you think, sir,' he said, 'that you should turn in? On the leeward bow that is Beachy, and round Beachy it will cut up rough. It worries the people to think of you getting soaked.'

'To tell you the truth, William, I do not mind it at all. Nothing could be more agreeable to my spirit than this all-pervading sense of speed – speed of air, sea, and rushing water. It is so very much more present in a boat like this than in a stolid great ship.'

'Why, sir, we *have* been clipping along at a very fair pace: ten knots most of the time, with points of twelve; and if the breeze don't die or box the compass we should have quite a tolerable run. But sir, will you not step below and take a little something?'

The little something was a dish of lobscouse: salt beef, biscuit, onions, potatoes, all pounded or cut up small, stewed close with a good deal of pepper and kept warm between hot bricks covered with a blanket for the graveyard watch: it went down extraordinarily well with a quart of beer, which they shared in the sea-going manner, passing the pot to and fro without ceremony.

'I do not like to tempt fate, sir,' said Reade, 'but I sometimes think that if only we could catch the early flood, we might make a truly extraordinary run, with never a check between the North Foreland and Sheerness, meeting the first of flood at the Nore and so straight up to London River, ha, ha. Old Mould did it once, in the *Flying Childers*, from off St Catherine's Point.'

'That would be very fine, sure.'

'And it would absolutely delight the Captain. He thinks the world of this craft, and he means to give her a fine-weather suit of the best Riga poldavy, including a square running-course. Now if you will excuse me, sir, I believe I must go on deck. Your berth is behind that hanging. Pray try to close an eye.'

Stephen did so, swimming presently into that series of inconsequential thoughts and half-memories that so often preceded sleep; and he woke from it again in a grey dimness to the sound of a fairly discreet cough, the clink of china, and the smell of coffee. 'God be with you, William,' he said, 'would that be coffee, at all?'

'Which it is Vaggers, sir,' said the seaman with the tray. 'The Captain is on deck, looking at the convoys. You never seen so many windbound ships. We are in the Downs.'

'How is the breeze, Vaggers? And shall we catch our tide?'

'Breeze holds true, sir. But as for the tide . . . nip and tuck, sir, nip and tuck. Though it will not be Mr Reade's fault if we miss it. He has been driving the clipper most zealous all night.'

He was driving it still when Stephen found him calling for a bonnet to the forestays, but he came over at once with civil enquiries and the assurance that this was not a real lull in the wind, only a slight blanketing from the South Foreland – 'we are well in with Deal, as you see' – and it would pick up again directly. 'And all those poor souls,' he said, waving out to sea, to the crowded anchorage of the Downs, 'are praying it may drop entirely and come round into the north-east. Some have been windbound for a fortnight and more: it often happens here. That is the West Indies convoy just this side the Gull Stream; and there, stretching right up to the North Foreland, those are the Mediterranean ships, a hundred sail of merchantmen at the very least. And towards the south Goodwin you can make out a group of Indiamen, all praying, no doubt.'

'It is not the number that pray, William, but the intensity of the prayer that is offered up, and of course its quality,' said Stephen. 'Purely mercantile considerations cannot expect to receive much notice in Heaven.'

'I am sure you are right, sir,' said Reade, and he rehearsed the names of the guardian men-of-war, studding the glum-grey sea with its white horses and intermittent showers from the low racing sky. '*Amethyst, Orion, Hercules, Dreadnought . . .*' unconsciously using a tone of voice more usual at the altar.

The North Foreland, and the *Ringle* hauled her wind, heading westward. 'Do you think,' asked Stephen at dinner, 'that we could be said to be within the estuary of the Thames?'

'I believe we may, sir,' said Reade, happy though red-eyed from want of sleep. 'And I believe we may almost say – though I touch wood – that we are not very likely to miss our tide.'

The Nore, and presently it became apparent even to Dr Maturin that the schooner's motion had changed, that she had in fact caught her tide, and that the first hint of the making flood was carrying her on a living stream. The remote shore, visible now on either side, drew somewhat closer; and after a while Reade handed over to Mould, disappointed as a polygamous patriarch, but the best Thames pilot among them. Mould told Stephen a great deal about the official men, all to their discredit, and presently he pointed out Muck Flat, on the northern shore, where a Trinity House branch pilot had run him aground in the year ninety-two. 'Well might you have called it Muck Flat by the time we had served him out.'

Although the breeze, the river and even those that used the river, including the heavy slow awkward and inclined to be abusive Thames barges, that felt they had priority over all the other craft in the stream, behaved well through that long winding day, Mould was in a sombre mood. Towards evening, when between showers the sky cleared beautifully, showing Greenwich in all its splendour, shining white and green on the river-bank, he jerked his chin in that direction and said, 'Greenwich. You would not believe, sir, the amount of money they screw out of poor hardworking seafaring men for that old chest of theirs. And who ever seen a penny piece out of it? Not Old Mould, any gate.'

'Lo, Greenwich, where many a shrew is in,' said Stephen, unthinking.

'Greenwich is bad enough, bad enough; there are some very disagreeable females in Greenwich. But it is nothing at all,' said Mould, his voice rising passionately as he caused the stout tiller to tremble under his hand, 'nothing at all, set against Shelmerston, for shrews. Take Mrs Mould, for instance . . .' He took Mrs Mould and handled her most severely, not only for her ignorant, illiberal, worldly rejection of the plurality of wives – 'Think of Abraham, sir: think of Solomon: remember Gideon – threescore and ten sons, and many wives!' – but also for a variety of shortcomings that it would scarcely be decent to name, all denounced with such vehemence that it would have been necessary to check him if a lighter more or less guided by an idiot boy with a single enormous oar had not drifted across the *Ringle*'s bows, so that her topsail was obliged to be backed at once, to take the way off her, and all sheets let fly, while every soul that could seize a spar fended off in an uproar of reprobation.

It was as though the din stunned both tide and breeze, for when at length the wretched lighter slanted off towards the farther shore, the *Ringle* no longer answered her helm, but slowly turned upon herself, facing the way she had come: for this was now slack-water, and presently the ebb would begin. Happily the calm was only the respite caused by the setting of the sun, and the reviving breeze carried them well up into the Pool before the downward current had gathered any real strength. Here, to the relief of all hands, they dropped anchor: Reade looked at his watch, laughed aloud, and gave the formal order 'Pipe to supper.'

There was a fair amount of traffic on the river – ship-visiting among the scores of merchantmen, citizens going about their business, parties of pleasure dropping down to Greenwich – and when he and the jubilant Reade had eaten their meal, a capon and a bottle of claret brought from the King's Head to celebrate their wonderful passage, Stephen hailed a passing wherry, which carried him to the Temple stairs.

But at Mr Lawrence's chambers he was confronted by a startled clerk who said that Mr Lawrence was not in the way – nobody had looked to see the Doctor for at least two days and Mr Lawrence had gone out of town – would not be back until tomorrow – late tomorrow. He would be so sorry to have missed the Doctor.

'He will not miss me at all,' said Stephen. 'I shall sleep at an inn called the Grapes in the Liberties of the Savoy, and I shall spend the early part of tomorrow buying various things and seeing friends. I shall dine at my club, which Mr Lawrence knows. I shall leave a message at the Grapes and at Black's to say where I can be found, if by any chance he should come back sooner than he expects. Otherwise I shall come here at the same time in the evening.'

'Very well, sir. And may I add, sir,' said the clerk in an undertone, 'that the goods have been looked after.'

Stephen was too late to find Sarah and Emily still up, but Mrs Broad gave him a most satisfactory account of their happiness, and they breakfasted with him in the morning, grinding the coffee themselves, bringing toast, kippers, marmalade, describing the wonders of London, perpetually interrupting one another, perpetually breaking off to ask whether he remembered Lima and the splendid organ there, the street lined with silver, the mountains and the snow, the green ice off Cape Horn.

'Mrs Broad,' he said on leaving the Grapes, 'if anyone should call from Mr Lawrence's chambers, be so good as to say that I shall be at Clementi's pianoforte warehouse until about three, and after that at my club.'

No message did in fact appear, but the time passed agreeably with Mr Hinksey, whom he met at Clementi's and who, after they had dined together at Black's, walked back with Stephen as far as the Temple Bar.

Lawrence was touchingly pleased to see him, obviously feeling very much more concern than his mere duty as Stephen's legal adviser required. 'I am so very glad you have taken our advice,' he said. 'Come in, come in. This is as disagreeable and potentially dangerous a situation as ever I have known. In here, if you please – forgive these papers and the cake. How happy I am that you are here. I had scarcely looked for you until tomorrow. You posted up, I presume?'

'I came by boat,' said Stephen. 'By sea,' he added, observing that his words had no effect whatsoever.

'Ah, indeed?' said Lawrence, for whom this astonishing fact was clearly much the same as a trip from Richmond or Hampton Court. 'A packet, no doubt?'

'No, sir. A private tender, belonging to Mr Aubrey, a vessel of astonishing powers of sailing. No other could have brought us to the Pool of London itself in a number of hours that escapes me for the moment but that filled my shipmates with admiration and astonishment.'

'So you have it yet, this boat. And in the Pool? So much the better. Pray sit down. How very glad I am to see you: I have been growing anxious. Allow me to cut you a piece of cake.' They sat at the crumb-covered table, and Lawrence fetched another glass. 'This is the madeira you sent me a couple of years ago,' he said.

They settled, drinking their wine and eating their cake, collecting themselves and as it were breathing.

'Sir Joseph brought me the documents signed,' said Lawrence. 'I am most obliged to you for your confidence.'

'I am infinitely more obliged to you for your advice and your help,' said Stephen.

Lawrence bowed and went on, 'I gave the bank formal warning within the hour, and then I sent for Pratt. Physical transfers of treasure call for a certain discretion at all times: even more so now, and in this case. I have been growing more anxious, as I say, and Pratt shared my anxiety: we neither of us have heard anything definite, but we have both heard of fresh consultations on the part of Habachtsthal's main lawyers, and of violent, indeed murderous disagreements among those criminals he has so imprudently employed as his agents.' He poured more wine, and said, 'I have taken it upon myself to spend some hundreds of your guineas.'

'Of course, of course. You could not oblige me more.'

'Pratt, who understands these things better than any man I know, caused your chests to be repacked in large cases marked Double-Refined Platina and removed to a lead, brass and copper warehouse on the river, by Irongate Stairs, where they can lie until you make arrangements to carry them away elsewhere. Or perhaps to ship them – I do not know your plans, of course. Is the tender of which you speak a ship, or a little pleasure-boat?'

'It is scarcely what the mariners would describe as a ship, but it is a commodious little vessel capable of a circumnavigation; and the Dear knows, I have carried more in less.'

It was no new thing for Dr Maturin's shipmates to load singular cargoes aboard the vessels he sailed in: giant squids on occasion, or little iron-bound chests of extraordinary weight. He was and always had been a singular gent; but they were used to his little ways – it was known that he carried out learned scientific and political tasks for Government – and although they were a little puzzled by the grim bruisers and former Bow Street runners who supervised the operation they took no umbrage and stowed the double-refined platina so that it would bring the clipper a trifle by the stern; and they were preparing to cast off in the first light when it was found that Arthur Mould was missing.

'Ain't he back yet?' asked Bonden. The other Sethians shook their heads, looking down. 'Joe,' said Bonden to the youngest member of the crew, 'cut along to Bedmaid Lane, first on the left going downstream, knock on the door of number six – a great big six in red – and ask for Mr Gideon Mould. The barky awaits his *pleasure*.'

'His *pleasure*, ha, ha, ha. That's right, cock,' said several of his mates. 'What a cove he is, that old Mould. He can't leave it alone.'

Mould, glum now, penniless, and anxious about the possible outcome of his repeated joys, returned: the *Ringle* hoisted her jib, shoved off from the wharf and stood out into the midstream at half-ebb, with a stiff breeze on her starboard beam, followed by a cry from a black man in a crimson gig: 'What ho, the Baltimore clipper oh!'

When all was settled and the river somewhat broader, less crowded, Reade found Stephen in the cabin and said, 'Please would you look at the log-book, sir? I have wrote it fair.'

'Very fair it is too, upon my faith,' said Stephen, looking at the neat column of dates, winds, and remarks.

'And here, sir, you see the *exact minute* of our dropping anchor in the Pool. Please would you sign, small and neat in the margin, with all the degrees you can think of, and FRS as well? They will never believe me, else.'

Stephen signed, and Reade, having gloated over the entry for a while, said, 'And don't we wish we may do the same going back? Oh no, not at all. Still, she is by the stern now, near half a strake, which is some comfort.'

'In what way is it a comfort, William?'

'Why, sir, she will beat to windward just that trifle better.' Seeing the blank stupidity on the Doctor's face he added, 'Had you not noticed it is still in the west-south-west?'

'I thought it was on our flank, the wind, our broad side, our starboard beam,' said Stephen. 'I particularly noticed it when my hat blew off. But then no doubt it is *we* that have turned rather than the breeze or indeed I may even say tempest. Do you suppose that we may be windbound like those unhappy convoys in the Downs, the sorrow and woe?'

'Oh no, sir, I hope not. I dare say the breeze will have changed by then – I have no doubt of it, indeed, from the tingling in my wound.'

But for all Reade's tingling – he had been wounded in the arm during an action with Dyaks in the East Indies, and Stephen had had to take it off – it was still blowing strong from the west-south-west as they passed the Nore again in the falling dusk; and all the way along from the North Foreland the whole length and breadth of the Downs glittered with the riding-lights of ships lying there with two or three cables ahead, windbound still, with many new arrivals. The wind grew stronger with the progress of the night, and in the middle watch four ships drove upon the Goodwin Sands.

The following week was among the most disagreeable that Stephen had ever known. Evening after evening promised relief; and every time the sun went down the promise proved false. There were slightly less dangerous lulls in the day, usually about noon, and a few hardy Deal boats would come out, trade at famine prices along the more sheltered merchantmen, and then put in, downwind, at Ramsgate; but even these were sometimes wrecked. Some days after the squadron must have sailed – for even Dr Maturin could see that ships lying off St Helens had a west-south-west wind on the beam rather than in their teeth like the unfortunate souls in the Downs – he embarked in one of these Deal boats for Ramsgate, half-determined to post across country to Barham. But sitting there in a music-shop and reflecting, he found that the uncertainties were too great. This was an enterprise that had to be carried out in one smooth sequence – easily or not at all – no wavering, no hesitation. There must be no *Ringle* arrived independently at a time unknown, no indiscreet loquacious messengers blundering about, no indefinite waiting, no widely aroused public curiosity.

'Now, sir, if you please,' said the shopman, 'I fear I must put up my shutters. There is an auction at Deal that I must attend.'

'Very well,' said Stephen, 'then I shall take this' – holding up Haydn's *Symphonie funèbre* – 'if you will be so good as to wrap it thoroughly; for I too must ride back to Deal, to regain my ship.'

'In that case, sir, pray come with me in my taxi-cart. I will fold the score into a double piece of oilskin, for I am afraid you will have but a wet trip in the boat.'

From this point until Saturday he returned to his coca-leaves, feeling that the din alone, the incessant though varied howling, shrieking and moaning of the wind, the perpetual thunder of the seas, justified the measure, quite apart from mental distress. He found that they had one very curious and unexpected effect: for whereas ordinarily he was a poor and hesitant reader of an orchestral score, he could now hear almost the entire band playing away together at his first run through the pages, not far from perfectly at the second and third. And of course the leaves also did what he had relied upon them to do, clarifying his mind, diminishing anxiety, largely doing away with hunger and sleep; yet on the third day he was aware of the impression that they were doing these things not to Stephen Maturin but to a somewhat inferior, apathetic, uninterested man who, though cleverer in some ways, thought Haydn of no great consequence. 'Can it be that I am over-indulging?' he asked, as he counted the leaves to ascertain his usual dose. 'Or may the incessant and violent pitching be the cause of this dismal change, the loss of joy?'

'Doctor,' cried William Reade, breaking in on his thoughts, 'this time I believe we can really hope. The glass has risen!'

Other vessels had noticed this – many an anxious eye had been fixed upon the barometer – and now there was a certain amount of activity in the road; but the wind was still too strong and too dead foul for any of the ships, the square-rigged ships, to think of moving in these narrow waters, though it gave signs of veering into the west and even north of west. About noon, a hoy, intently watched by the few other fore-and-aft rigged vessels in the Downs, got under way. For the first moments a squall hid her from the *Ringle*'s deck, and when it had passed she was seen to have carried away her sprit: her foresail had blown out of its bolt-rope and she was driving helpless through the lines of shipping, fouling many a hawser, cursed by all within earshot.

In the afternoon watch Bonden, coming below on a more or less convincing pretext, said to Reade, 'As I dare say you know, sir, some of our people were free-traders at one time. In course, they are reformed characters now, and would scorn an uncustomed keg of brandy or chest of tea; but they remember what they learnt in them wicked days. Mould and Vaggers were once in this very spot with just such a blow in their topsail schooner, and they say with the breeze not half a point west of this there is a passage at high tide for a very weatherly craft. They took it, being in a hurry: they passed between the Hammer and Anvil, cleared the Downs and so beat down-Channel as light as a fairy and put into Shelmerston the next day for supper, having met their friends off Gris Nez. And their barky,' he added, gazing at the horizon, 'was not as weatherly as ours.'

Reade did not reply at once. Like many other midshipmen, he had carried prizes into ports; but he had never had such a voyage as this, still less such a vessel. For half an hour he watched the weather-gage, and when it showed half a point in their favour he called for Mould and Vaggers.

'Mould and Vaggers,' he said in a deep, formal voice, 'with this breeze and at this state of the tide, could you undertake to pilot the tender through the passage?'

'Yes, sir,' they said, but they would have to look sharp: the ebb would start in half an hour.

The Ringles looked sharp. They were sick and tired of being rattled about like dried peas in a can, and they were very willing to show those lubbers in the Downs how seamen of the better sort dealt with situations of this kind. They won their anchors, hoisted a scrap of the jib, set the close-reefed mainsail and edged away through the shipping.

Mould was at the helm with three turns round the tiller; Vaggers and two friends at the mainsheet. There was a great deal of white water over the face of the sea, and with the beginning of ebb breakers showed wider on the edge of the sands. They were steering for a particular shoal, and already the sequence that gave this shoal its name was beginning to show: a roller would break on the right hand, shooting up a column of water that at low tide and with a strong swell and following wind would be flung across a twenty-yard channel, falling with a loud dead thump on the flat sand the other side, the Anvil. So far the Hammer was no more than a little ten-foot fountain, but the men's faces were tense as they approached it, for immediately after it came a dog-leg in the channel that had to be judged to the yard.

They were between Hammer and Anvil: the little fountain rose, sprinkling Stephen and Reade. 'Ready about,' said Mould. 'Helm's a-lee.' The schooner stayed to perfection, a smooth turn with never a check: Mould held her so, very close to the wind for a moment during which she forged somewhat ahead, and then let her fall off. They were through, clear of the narrows, clear of the Downs; and now, for a craft as weatherly as the *Ringle*, with plenty of sea-room, it was only a matter of a dozen long reaches for home.

Stephen Maturin, the clock of his appetite much dis-ordered by the use of coca-leaves (a strictly moderate use now, however, with the dose being administered to a person wholly recognizable as himself), walked into the dining-room at Barham while the meal was in full progress: that is to say when Clarissa had cracked the shell of her second boiled egg.

She was not a woman much given to shrieks or excla-mations, but she was not wholly above commonplace reac-tion and now she uttered a great 'Oh!' and quickly asked him was it he? And had he come back? before recovering herself, sitting down again and suggesting that he should have something to eat – an omelette was a matter of minutes, no more.

'Thank you, my dear, I dined on the road,' said Stephen, giving her a peck on each cheek. 'What a pleasant table this is,' he went on, as he sat down at her side. He had inherited an absurd amount of silver from his godfather, most of it Peruvian, sober, almost severe; and a gleaming river ran down the whole length.

'It is to celebrate the day I left New South Wales,' said Clarissa. 'Will you not take a glass of wine, at least?'

'I might, too,' said Stephen. 'A glass of wine would go

down very well. But listen, my dear. We must be off to Spain within the hour; so when you have eaten your egg and may it prosper you, perhaps you would put up just what you and Brigid will need for the voyage.'

Clarissa looked at him gravely, with the spoon poised between her egg and her mouth, but before she could speak there was a thundering on the stairs and in the corridor and Padeen and Brigid burst in. Padeen began a long stammering word that might have been chaise but that never came to an end, Brigid cried out 'Horses!' in English; and then, seeing Stephen, both fell silent, amazed.

After a pause of no more than half of a breath Padeen took Brigid by the hand and led her up to him: she looked at Stephen with a shy but quite open interest, even a smile, and slightly prompted she said, in clear high Irish, 'God and Mary be with you, my father,' holding up her face.

He kissed it, and said, 'God and Mary and Patrick be with you, my daughter. We are all going to Spain, the joy and delight.'

Padeen explained that they had been in the high back room netting a hammock before Brigid should be brought down for her pudding when they saw the Royal William's chaise come into the stable-yard with two horses they knew, Norman and Hamilton, and two horses they did not, borrowed no doubt from the Nalder Arms.

Mrs Warren brought in the pudding, flustered and upset by all this activity. She tied the child's bib rather sharply, squaring her in her chair, clapped the pudding down (common quaking pudding) and said to Clarissa, 'The post-boys say they are to water their horses and walk them up and down for an hour, no more. Am I to give them something to eat?'

'Bread, cheese, and a pint of beer for each,' said Clarissa. 'My dear Brigid, you are not to play with your food. What will your father think?'

Brigid had indeed been beating her pudding to make it quake in earnest, but she stopped at once and hung her head.

After a while she whispered in Irish, 'Would you like a little piece?'

'A very little piece, if you please,' said Stephen.

He contemplated Clarissa as she finished her egg. 'How I value that young woman for not asking questions,' he reflected. 'It is true that she is used to naval ways, and to leaving home, family, kittens, doves, pot-plants at a moment's notice – no tide must ever be missed, God forbid – but I am convinced that she does not need to ask: she understood the essentials when first our eyes met.'

All this he had known or strongly surmised at some level: the child, on the other hand, left him astonished, completely taken aback, at an enchanted loss. He had hoped and prayed with more than a hundredweight of candles judiciously shared among fifty-three saints for some perceptible progress: but now, and virtually at once, the child was living an outward life.

She finished her pudding, and showing her bare-scraped plate she asked if she might get down: she did so want to go and look at the chaise close to and touch it. This was in English of a sort, but then in a quiet and as it were confidential Irish she said to Stephen, 'And should *you* like to be shown the chaise? The chaise and four?'

'Honey, am I not after coming in it? It is warm with my warmth, like a chair. And we shall all set off in an hour, no more, when I have drunk up my coffee.'

The child laughed aloud. 'And may the Padeen and I sit on the little small seat high up behind, on the dickey?' she asked. 'Oh such happiness!'

Clarissa had never accumulated much in the way of personal property. Once she put her head in at the door and asked, 'Is it cold?'

'Bitter cold in the winter,' said Stephen, 'but never trouble your mind. We shall buy a suitable garment in Corunna, Avila, or Madrid itself. Take something against the wet in the north, however, and half-boots.'

He had barely had time to deal with the aged groom and

the women servants, paying them down six months' board-wages, giving instructions for the care of the livestock and the renewal of the laundry boiler, a bill that Mrs Aubrey would pay, before Padeen reported, 'All stowed aboard and roped, sir; and may the Brideen and I sit on the little, the little, on the little small . . . ?'

'You may,' said Stephen, walking out of the house. He opened the carriage door for Clarissa, called 'Bless you all,' to the servants gathered on the steps, and 'Give way' to the post-boys: the carriage rolled off.

'Will I explain the position?' asked Stephen.

'Padeen and I have been betrayed?'

'Just so.'

'Yes. There have been enquiries in the village: odd-looking men along the lane and even in the stable-yard.'

'It all turns on a question of revenge against me. The pardons I had asked for, the quite usual pardons for you and Padeen in a case like this, were not refused, but they were held up, delayed and delayed by ill-will. They will be granted I believe, and quite soon; but until then we are all much better out of the country, out of my enemy's reach. In any case I should like to have Brigid under the care of Dr Llers, who has had more success with children of her kind than any man in Europe. Not, the dear God be thanked beyond measure, that she seems to need the care of any medical man at all. The change is of the nature one usually associated with miracles alone.'

'It is utterly beyond my comprehension,' said Clarissa. 'Nothing I have ever known has given me such happiness – day after day, like a flower opening. She prattled for quite a while with Padeen and the animals, and now she does so with me and the maids: a little shy of English at first. To begin with she spoke it only to the cats and the sow.'

Stephen laughed with pleasure, an odd grating sound; and after a while he said, 'She will learn Spanish too, Castellano. I am sorry it will not be Catalan, a much finer, older, purer, more mellifluous language, with far greater writers – think of En Ramón Llull – but as Captain Aubrey often says, "You cannot both have a stitch in time and eat it." I mean to take you – or rather to send you under escort, since I cannot leave the ship – to the Benedictine house in Avila, where an aunt of my father's is Abbess, and where Dr Llers will be at hand. It is the easiest and kindest of disciplines there; the nuns are gentlewomen and several of them and the pensionnaires are English of the old Catholic families, or Irish; they have an excellent choir; and the convent owns three of the finest vineyards in Spain. I intend Padeen to go with you as your servant and as a continual source of springing life for Brideen. You will not be lonely there; and though your life may be rather dull, it will be safe.'

'I ask no more,' said Clarissa.

The chaise was on the smooth road now, not far from the turning to Ashgrove Cottage, and Brigid's voice could be heard exclaiming at the huge enormous great haycocks, bigger than she had ever seen in her life.

'Shall we have time to call on Mrs Aubrey to take leave?' asked Clarissa. 'It would surely be most improper to vanish with never a word. It would also look like a low-minded resentment.'

'We shall not,' said Stephen. 'Even as things are, the tide will be half out. There is not a moment to be lost.' He reflected, and presently he repeated the word *resentment* in a questioning tone.

'Yes,' said Clarissa. 'It was all most unfortunate. She has very kindly come to see Brigid and me from time to time, and a little while ago she sent a note saying she had a letter from Captain Aubrey in London with some news about my pension as an officer's widow and might she call. Since a friend of Diana's had given us a present of venison and since it was full moon and she all alone I asked her to dinner, together with Dr Hamish and Mr Hinksey, our parson. We laid things out with some degree of splendour – even that dreadful Killick could hardly have done better than Padeen – and I put on my very best dress. It was that glorious crimson Java silk which Captain Aubrey gave me to be married in.'

Stephen nodded. He remembered the incident perfectly: the cutting of a bolt of cloth that Jack Aubrey had bought from a Chinese merchant in Batavia with the help of the Governor's wife.

'Yes. But Mrs Aubrey walked in wearing exactly the same stuff. Cut a little more full, and gathered here; but exactly the same magnificent red. We stared at one another like a couple of ninnies, and before either of us could say anything the men arrived, first Hinksey and then the Doctor. But I knew with absolute certainty, as though it had been printed on her forehead, that she thought Aubrey had given me the cloth for services rendered and that she had come off with the fag-end of his mistress's leavings. The food was pretty good, as I remember; the wine was of your choosing – we drank an ancient Chambertin with the venison – and from time to time she remembered her manners and added some-thing to the general talk. But it was no good. The dinner, one of the few I have ever given, was a complete failure. Brigid was brought in when Mrs Aubrey and I went to the drawing-room, so there was no possibility of explanation even if I had felt inclined to make any, which by then I most certainly did not. Fortunately the men did not sit long over their wine, so the evening soon came to its miserable end. That is what I mean by resentment.'

Stephen nodded. 'There is nothing to say: only that I very deeply regret the unhappiness, all of it unnecessary. We are descending towards the sea.'

'The sea, the sea!' cried Brigid, leaping about in an ecstasy as they went down the shore to the waiting boat. 'Oh what a wonderful sea!' This was her first sight of it, and she was luckier than most. The tide was half out and from the har-bour mouth a small swell sent in a series of waves that broke in white fan after fan on the pure hard sand: the water itself was a living blue-green, perfectly clear. Very high overhead rode a sky of no determinate colour crowded with towering cumulus; on either hand the bay curved out in tawny cliffs, while from behind Shelmerston the remote and setting sun sent a warm, diffused, calm, even and comfortable light. She broke away, seizing three strands of sea-tangle and a piece of green fresh-curling weed, thrust them into her bosom and ran back. 'How do you do, sir?' she said to Bonden, offering her hand, and the boat's crew welcomed her with infinite benevolence. 'Let the Doctor's little maid sit up in the bows,' said Mould, and they passed her from hand to hand until she was perched on his folded jersey, calling out with delight as the boat shoved off.

'Mrs Oakes, ma'am, you are very welcome aboard,' said Reade, helping her up the side. 'And you too, my dear. Doctor, sir, you have caught your tide as pretty as could be. I had scarcely started looking at my watch. Ma'am, how I hope you have an appetite. Our friends in the town have brought us the noblest soles that ever yet were seen.' He showed them below, begging them to mind their heads, and returned to the deck.

The usual sounds followed their usual sequence – the cable coming aboard, the anchor being catted and fished, the boat run up to the davits; then even a moderately prac-tised ear could make out the sound of halliards in their blocks and the deck leaned over under their feet: the ship was filled with a universal living sound, a vibration.

'It is moving we are!' cried Brigid. She escaped from the cabin and ran up on deck. 'I must not behave like an old foolish mother-hen,' thought Stephen, but he followed her nevertheless, and sitting abaft the tiller he watched her risk life and limb, very gently restrained in her wilder excesses by Padeen and the seamen, kind and endlessly patient: at one point he saw her ascend to the fore crosstrees, clinging to the rough and scaley neck of old Mould.

She was the ideal traveller, indefatigable, delighted with everything; and though the *Ringle* met a fine west-south-west swell when she was clear of the land, a swell that cut up somewhat on meeting the tide, she felt not the slightest qualm, nor, apparently, fear of any kind. She did not mind getting wet, either, which was just as well, since the *Ringle* was sailing due south-west with the breeze two points free and the choppy seas were coming aboard in packets over the starboard bow, soaking her at regular intervals as she clung to the foremost shrouds, each packet, green or white, being signalled by a delighted shriek.

Eventually, with darkness gathering, she was brought aft and below, dried, put down in front of a bowl of lobscouse (the *Ringle*'s only dish, apart from skillygalee or burgoo) and desired to 'tuck in, mate, tuck in like a good 'un.' After two spoons she fell fast asleep, her head on the table, one hand still clutching a gnawed ship's biscuit, so fast asleep that she was obliged to be carried off, perfectly limp, sponged more or less, and lashed into a small hammock.

'Well, sir,' said Reade at supper, 'we could not have asked for a more prosperous breeze. This craft fairly loves the wind afore the beam and we have been making ten knots ever since we passed the Start with no more than what you see – no dimity, no gaff topsails even. I did suggest cracking on, ma'am, to show you just what she could do, but they would have none of it. There was no actual downright mutiny, just disapproving looks and shaking heads, and I was told it was felt the barky should sail sweet, this being the little maid's first trip: though I must say I do not think she would turn a hair if we were scudding under bare poles, in danger of being pooped every other minute. Now ma'am, a trifle of this apple tart? The carpenter's wife sent it down, one for his mess and one for ours, which I take very kind.'

'The merest trifle, if you please. I love a good apple tart, and this one looks superb; but I am so sleepy that I am liable to disgrace myself and fall over sideways. It is no doubt the effect of the sea air.'

No doubt at all. The sea air did the same for all three

passengers, who did not stir until the sun was well up, when they appeared, heavy-eyed, pale, and stupid, no one any better than the rest.

'Good morning, sir,' cried Reade, offensively bright. 'What a brilliant day! We had a wonderful run in the night, and close in by Ushant we spoke the *Briseis*: old Beaumont – you remember old Beaumont in the *Worcester*, sir? – was the officer of the watch, and he said some of the offshore squadron had exchanged signals with the Commodore on Thursday, standing south-west under an easy sail. But sir, I dare say you would like your breakfast. What will the little girl take?'

'What indeed? Mrs Oakes,' he called, 'pray what are children fed on?'

'Milk,' said Clarissa.

The *Ringle*'s people looked tolerably blank; and discipline aboard a private tender under a midshipman not being as rigid as it might have been in a ship of the line, they freely exchanged their views. 'If only I had thought,' said Slade, 'I should have brought a pailful along; and a pot of cream.'

'Cheese is particularly good for young female bones,' said the yeoman of the sheets. 'My cousin Sturgis would have lent us his goat.'

In the end it was decided that if ship's biscuit and small beer were rejected – and Mrs Oakes rejected both out of hand – then skillygalee was their only resource. Brigid therefore faced a bowl of very thin oatmeal gruel, sweetened with sugar and tempered with butter. She thought it the finest dish she had ever eaten, a more-than-birthday indulgence: she ate it up with naked greed and begged for more, and when at last she was told that she might get down skipped about the deck singing 'Skilly-galee, skillygaloo, skillygalee ooh hoo hoo hoo' with a persistence that only very good-natured men could have borne, as the Ringles did, until dinner changed the course of her mind. This being Thursday, she and all hands were allowed a pound of salt pork and half a pint of dried peas: a gallon of beer would also have made part of her ration, but she was advised not to insist upon it.

The breeze freshened in the afternoon: they took a reef in the foresail and the main, and the *Ringle* was filled with that happy sense of making a good passage: ten knots, ten and two fathoms, eleven knots, sir, if you please, watch after watch; and Brigid spent all her time in the bows, watching the schooner rise on the now much longer swell, race down, and split the next crest at great speed, flinging the spray to leeward in the most exhilarating fashion, always the same, always new. Once a line of porpoises crossed their hawse, rising and plunging like a single long black serpent; and once Stephen showed her a petrel, a little fluttering black bird that pittered on the white traces of broken waves; but otherwise the day was made up of strong diffused light, racing clouds with blue between, a vast grey sea, the continuous rush of wind and water, and a freshness that pervaded everything.

'You was born with sea-legs, my dear,' said Slade, as she came careering aft for supper.

'I shall never go ashore,' she replied.

Padeen slipped easily back into his place as a seaman, an ordinary seaman, for he did not possess the countless particular skills required to be rated able – skills he had, and many of them, but they were all to do with the land, he being profoundly a peasant, a peasant by breeding and inclination. Yet he was seaman enough to be perfectly at home aboard, and in the morning watch on Thursday Stephen found him fishing for mackerel in the *Ringle*'s bows.

It was still long before dawn: moderately thick weather with occasional showers, thunder out to sea: a long even swell: the wind quite strong in the west-north-west. The schooner had been making long, long boards, beating steadily into it, and now she was on the starboard tack, close in with the land, with the ironbound northern coast of Spain hitherto unseen. Well ahead on the larboard bow the Vares light, high on a cape that ran far out to sea, showed fiery orange when it was not obscured by the squalls; and it was said that this light attracted the fish so often to be found within this bay. Whether this was so or not, the middle watch had caught a fine basketful, and that was why the clipper had lingered a little longer on this tack, drawing somewhat closer to the shore. She was under reefed fore and main sails, with the jib half in, easily stemming the tide, which ran fast round the cape, but making no great way with regard to the land.

'You have not gone to bed, I find,' he said.

'Nor have I, indeed,' said Padeen. 'At the end of the watch I began thinking about the man that betrayed us, the informer, the Judas; and what with the fury and the dread of being sent back to Botany Bay there was no sleep in me at all.'

'The back of my hand to the informer,' said Stephen. 'Hell is filled with them seventeen deep. They are . . .' He was cut short by a triple flash of lightning and an almost simultaneous thunderclap over the cliff to leeward. 'There,' he went on, 'there is the coast of Spain itself.' Still more lightning showed it clear. 'And once you have set foot in that country, no man can take you up and send you back to that infamous place. In any event I am confident that within the year I shall get you your pardon, and then you can go wherever you please. But, Padeen, for the present I wish you to go with Brigid and Mrs Oakes to Avila, in Spain, to look after them. They are to live there in a convent where many other ladies stay with the nuns. And listen, now, Padeen, if you look after them faithfully for a year and a day, you shall have a small farm I own in Munster, near Sidheán na Gháire in the County Clare, with seventeen acres – seventeen *Irish* acres – of moderate land: it has a house with a slate roof, and at present there are three cows and an ass, pigs of course, and two hives of bees; and it has the right to cut seventeen loads of turf on the bog. Are you content, Padeen?'

'I am content, your honour, your discretion,' said Padeen

in a trembling voice. 'I should look after the Brideen for a thousand years and a day for nothing at all; but oh how I should love some land itself. My grandfather once owned nearly three acres, and rented two more . . .'

They talked about the land, the pleasures of farming, the delight of seeing things grow, of reaping and threshing; or rather Padeen talked, such a clear torrent of words as Stephen had not heard from him before; and the day broke, broke quite suddenly, the clouds tearing away in the first gleam of dawn.

'All hands, all hands!' roared Bonden right aft, and he and others ran beating on the hatches. 'All hands, all hands on deck!' Padeen, easily amazed, tripped Stephen with his rod and his basket of fishes and before they had recovered Reade was on deck in his nightshirt, giving orders. Half a mile astern, in the bay closed by Cape Vares, lay a three-masted lugger, long, low and black. She was heavily armed and heavily manned; she was already increasing sail.

Padeen had instantly run to his station at the fore-sheet. Stephen took up a post on the starboard quarter where he was reasonably out of the way: he could hear the rapid exchanges between Reade and the men whose opinion he asked; and he caught the hands' words as they worked or stood by. All agreed that the lugger was a Frenchman out of Douarnenez called the *Marie-Paule* – very fast: the Revenue cutters had never caught her – sometimes a privateer – privateer now, for certain sure, so full of hands – they might spare a Brixham trawler, but no one else, Christian, Turk or Jew – and François the skipper was a right bastard – a brass nine-pounder in the bows they served most uncommon well. All hands spoke very seriously, and they looked grave. He could not see Reade's expression – he was at the tiller with Bonden and his back was turned – but Bonden's was firm-set, composed.

Looking fore and aft Stephen assessed the position, the light strengthening every minute and the clipper heeling more and more as the sheets were hauled and belayed right aft. As far as his sea-going experience went there was no way out. A short mile ahead Cape Vares ran north into the sea: they could not clear its tip on this starboard tack: they must go about to gain an offing, and as they did so the big lugger must necessarily board them. She was coming up fast, full-packed with men.

Many a sea-chase had he known, as either hunter or quarry, and they had all been long, sometimes very long, a matter of days, with the tension great yet sustained, as it were spread out and more nearly bearable. Now it was to be a matter of minutes rather than hours or days: the clipper, her lee-rail buried in foam and a cloud of sail abroad, was already making ten knots and she must either strike that cape in four minutes or go about and receive the lugger on her starboard beam.

As these minutes passed he realized, with an extraordinary intensity, just what his fortune, lying in its chests below, meant to him and his daughter and to a thousand aspects of his life. It had not occurred to him that money could have such value – that he could prize it so much. Gulls drifted between the *Ringle* and the cape, waves breaking along its shore. He turned a haggard face to the men at the helm and as though he felt the look Reade glanced back at him. The young man's expression had something of that happy wildness Stephen had often seen in Jack Aubrey at times of crisis, and smiling he called, 'Stand by, Doctor. Watch out,' adding some words to Slade about a biscuit. Then he and Bonden, their hands on the triple-turned rope and the tiller, their eyes fixed to the leach of the foresail, eased the helm alee, and still more alee.

Stephen saw the dreadful shore of the cape, now so close, racing away to the left. He saw its seaward end appear, just clear of their larboard bow, at ten yards perhaps. He heard young Reade cry, 'Toss it hard.' Slade flung the biscuit, hit the rock, and in a roar of laughter they were past, round into the open sea.

The lugger fired an ineffectual gun and tacked, incapable

154

of weathering the cape, losing ground, impetus, and her prize. The pursuit continued for some hours, but by noon the lugger was hull-down in the east, hopelessly outsailed.

The *Ringle* carried on in a state of extraordinary good humour, often laughing, often reminding one another that 'they had weathered that old Cape Vares within biscuit-toss, ha, ha, ha!' Some tried to explain their triumph to Mrs Oakes and Brigid, but although they conveyed their happiness and sense of good fortune they had not fully succeeded before the *Ringle* opened the port of Corunna, or as some said, the Groyne.

As Stephen stood in the bows, smiling at the busy harbour and the town, Mould sidled casually up to him and out of the corner of his mouth he said, 'Me and my mates know the Groyne as well as we know Shelmerston: this is where we used to come for our brandy. And if so be you should like to have the goods landed *discreet*, as I might say, we know a party, dead honest, or he would have been scragged long since, that might answer.'

'Thank you, Mould, thank you very much for your kind suggestion but this time – *this time*, eh? – I mean to land them in all legality. And that is what I am going to tell the captain of the port and his people. But I am very much obliged to you and your friends for your good will.'

Some hours later Stephen, sitting in the cabin with a perfectly mute Reade and the two senior port authorities, said, 'And apart from the martial stores belonging to this vessel, the tender to His Britannic Majesty's ship *Bellona*, that you saw so recently, none of which constitutes merchandise, there is nothing except some treasure belonging to me personally, which I mean to lodge with the Bank of the Holy Ghost and of Commerce in this city – I am acquainted with don José Ruiz, its director, who shipped it to me in the first place. As it is in minted gold, in English guineas, it is of course exempt from duty.'

'Does it amount to a great deal?'

'The number of guineas I cannot tell, but the weight, I

believe, is somewhere between five and six tons. That is why I must beg you to do me the very great kindness of giving this vessel a berth against the quay, and, if you possibly can, to lend me a score of trustworthy able-bodied men to carry the chests. Here' – waving to two fat little canvas bags – 'I have put up a sum that I hope you will distribute as you think fit. May I take it that we are in agreement, gentlemen? For if so, I must hurry ashore, speak to don José about the gold, and then go straight up and pay my compliments to the Governor.'

'Oh sir,' they cried, 'the Governor is half way to Valladolid by now. He will be distracted with grief.'

'But Colonel don Patricio FitzGerald y Saavedra is still with us, I trust?'

'Oh certainly, certainly, don Patricio is with us still, and all his men.'

'Cousin Stephen!' cried the Colonel, 'how happy I am to see you. What good wind brings you to Galicia?'

'First tell me do I see you well and happy? Kindly used by Fortune?'

'Faith, her privates me: but never let a soldier complain. Pray carry on.'

'Well, now, Patrick, I have brought my daughter Brigid and the lady who looks after her, because I should like them to spend some time with Aunt Petronilla in Avila: they have a servant, Padeen Colman, but with the country so disturbed and the journey so long, and myself bound to part, I do not like to let them go alone, without a word of Spanish between them. Ruiz, at the bank, has bespoken a carriage with a French-speaking courier and the usual guards, but if you could lend me even half a dozen of your troopers and an officer you would oblige me extremely, and I should be oh so much happier, sailing away.'

The Colonel obliged him extremely; but no one looking at Stephen's face as he stood in the *Ringle*'s bows, watching eight horses draw a lumbering great coach up the hill behind Corunna, with a cavalry escort before and behind, and two hands waving white handkerchiefs, waving and waving until they were lost in the distance would have thought that he looked oh so much happier.

'Now, sir,' said Reade, in an embarrassed compassionate voice as Stephen came into the cabin, 'we mean to cast off our moorings the moment this hulking great Portuguese gets out of the way; but I do not believe, sir, that you ever told me our next rendezvous if we did not find the Commodore at the Groyne.'

'Did I not?' asked Stephen. He pondered, and pondered again. 'Jesus, Mary and Joseph,' he murmured, 'I have forgotten its name. The word is on the top back edge of my mind – it eludes me – petrels nest there: perhaps puffins – bats, in a vast great windy cave – some way out in the sea – islands – I have it: the Berlings! The Berlings it is, on my soul.'

Chapter Six

In the afternoon of Saturday, with the Berlings in sight on the larboard bow, the topgallant-sail breeze that had been bowling the *Ringle* along so handsomely since Cape Finisterre almost entirely deserted her, stunned perhaps by the roar of battle away in the south-west, to starboard.

The schooner, cleared for action, packed on more and more canvas, slanting down into what air there was towards the dimness on the starboard bow. Dr Maturin, torn from the rail where he had been observing the clouds of disturbed, uneasy sea-birds as they drifted in wide circles about their distant rocks, was sent below to that dim, cramped triangular space in which he would have to treat the wounded, single-handed, if the *Ringle* could work south-west in time to join the fray, the prodigious fray, judging from the din of full broadsides from line-of-battle ships, no less.

Mould, the oldest but the lightest hand aboard, a wizened sinner five feet tall, was at the masthead with a glass: the heady scent of powder was already drifting faint across the deck when he called, 'On deck, there. I can see over the smoke-band and the murk. It's only the squadron at target-practice. I see *Bellona*'s broad pennant. I see *Stately* clear.'

The kindly breeze revived as he spoke, sweeping aside the low-lying swathes of gun-smoke, revealing the entire force, now increased by two brigs and a schooner from Lisbon, and wafting the *Ringle* down at a fine pace towards her rendezvous.

Reade hurried below to release the Doctor. 'It was more like a real battle, a fleet engagement, than anything I have ever heard,' he said. 'If you take my glass you will see that they have been firing both sides, at different sets of targets towed down the line. Both sides! Have you ever known such a thing, sir?'

'Never,' replied Stephen, with the utmost truth. His action-station was in the cockpit or its equivalent: and although on certain clearly defined occasions when the drum had not beat to quarters he had been allowed to watch the officers, midshipmen and hands going through the great-gun exercises, he had never seen them going through the motions of fighting both sides of the ship at once. It rarely happened even in battle except when the engagement turned into a general mêlée, as it did at Trafalgar, and virtually never in practice, one of the reasons being the cost of powder. Government allowed a certain meagre ration, enough for only a trifling amount of practice with the guns actually firing: anything beyond this had to be paid for by the captain, and few captains were both thoroughly persuaded of the importance of gunnery and rich enough to buy the amount of powder needed to make a ship's company so expert that they could fire three well-directed broadsides in five minutes. Some, though like Thomas of the *Thames* reasonably well-to-do, felt that briskness in manoeuvre, shining brass, gleaming paintwork, well-blacked yards and natural British valour would answer for all purposes, and their great-gun exercise amounted to nothing more than running the guns in and out in dumb-show, never using even the Government allowance: most of these officers had seen little action or none at all. Jack Aubrey, on the other hand, had seen more fighting at sea than most; and he, like many of his friends, was convinced that no amount of courage would beat an enemy of roughly equal force who had the weather-gage and who could fire faster and more accurately. Further-more, he had seen the disastrous effect of not training the crew to fight both sides. Once, for example, when he was a passenger in HMS *Java* she had met the USS *Constitution*: at one point in the battle the American presented her vulner-able stern to the British ship, but the hands, who had been firing the starboard guns, had neither the wit nor above all the training to rake her effectively with those to larboard. The *Constitution* moved off almost unharmed, and although somewhat later the *Java*, full of spirit, tried to board her, it was no good. By the end of that December day the dismal *Java* was captured and burnt, while her surviving people, including Jack, were carried away prisoners to Boston.

Now he had money enough for a great deal of powder; and now, determined to have a squadron that could deal with any enemy of equal force, he had been conducting a great-gun exercise of heroic proportions, all his ships ranged in line of battle and firing at targets passing on either side at a cable's length, well within point-blank range.

As the *Ringle* approached the pennant-ship, lying to in the middle of the line, Stephen observed with some concern that although the surface of the ocean was as smooth as could be desired, with barely a ripple, its main body, the enormous liquid mass, was heaving with a long southern swell, a motion clearly visible among the boats along the *Bellona*'s side, for the Commodore had summoned the captains of the *Stately*, *Thames* and *Aurora*, and their barges were rising and falling to a surprising degree. As he knew only too well, it would be difficult for any but a prime seaman to get aboard without disgrace; yet while he was still reflecting on the problem the *Ringle* glided under the *Bellona*'s stern, ran gently up her larboard side and hooked on to her forechains.

'Mr Barlow,' called Reade to a master's mate on the fore-castle, 'a whip for the Doctor's dunnage, there. A stout whip, if you please,' he added with a certain emphasis.

A stout whip it was; and Stephen's belongings having been made fast he was directed to sit on his sea-chest, holding the rope with both hands. 'Hold fast, sir, and never look down,' said Reade; and then, at the top of the swell, he called, 'Way oh. Handsomely now: handsomely.' Stephen and his possessions rose, swung inboard, and touched the deck with no more bump than would have cracked an egg. He thanked the hands, looked sharply at one of the familiar faces, said,

'Why, Caley . . .' and gently seized the man's left ear, an ear that he had sewn back after it had been partially torn off by a playful companion. 'Very good,' he said, 'you heal as healthy as a young dog,' and walked aft along the larboard gangway, meeting half a dozen nods and becks from former shipmates, for nearly all the Surprises who were not settled in Shelmerston had joined their captain in the *Bellona*.

As he approached the quarterdeck he saw Captain Thomas of the *Thames* come out of the Commodore's cabin, looking furious: his face was an odd colour, the extreme pallor of anger under the tan making it resemble a mask. He was piped over the side with all due ceremony, making no acknowledgment whatsoever, in marked contrast to Duff of the *Stately* and Howard of the *Aurora*, who had set off in their barges immediately before him.

Stephen noticed looks of intelligence and privy smiles among the officers assembled in formal array on the quarterdeck, but as soon as the *Thames*'s boat had shoved off Tom Pullings turned from the entry port with a broad, candid, cheerful smile of a very different sort and hurried over, crying, 'Welcome aboard, dear Doctor, welcome aboard. We had not looked to see you so soon – what a charming surprise. Come and see the Capt – the Commodore. He will be so happy and relieved. But first let me name my second lieutenant – the premier is in the sick-list: not at all the thing – Lieutenant Harding, Dr Maturin.'

They shook hands, each looking at the other attentively – shipmates could make or mar even a short commission – and to the civil 'How do you do, sir?' the other replied 'Your servant, sir.'

This was the first time Stephen had seen Pullings in the infinitely coveted uniform of a post-captain, and as they walked aft he took notice of it: 'How well that coat becomes you, Tom.'

'Why sir,' said Pullings with a happy laugh, 'I must admit I love it dearly.'

They reached the Marine sentry and Pullings said, 'I will

leave you here, sir, and bring my report of the rates of fire as soon as they are wrote out fair. There is not a moment to lose, because half the meaning of the scribbles on the slate is still in my head and the other half in Mr Adams's.'

Stephen walked through the coach into the great cabin, smiling: but Jack sat right aft, staring out over the stern, both arms on his paper-covered desk; he sat motionless, and with such a look of stern unhappiness that Stephen's smile faded at once. He coughed. Jack whipped round, strong displeasure masking the unhappiness for an instant before he sprang up, as lithe as a much younger man: he seized Stephen with even more than his usual force, crying, 'God's my life, Stephen, how glad I am to see you! How is everything at home?'

'All well, as far as I am aware: but I came post-haste, you know.'

'Aye. Aye. Tell me about your run. You must have had leading winds all the way. The packet said you were still windbound in the Downs as late as last Tuesday – last Tuesday week, I mean. Lord, I am so happy to see you. Should you like some madeira and a biscuit? Sherry? Or perhaps a pot of coffee? What if we both had a pot of coffee?'

'By all means. That villain in the *Ringle*, though no doubt a capital seaman, has no notion of coffee. None at all, at all, the animal.'

'Killick. Killick, there,' called Jack.

'What now?' asked Killick, opening the door of the sleeping-cabin. He added 'Sir,' after a distinct pause; and directing a wintry smile at Stephen he said, 'I hope I see your honour well?'

'Very well, I thank you, Killick: and how are you?'

'Bearing up, sir, bearing up. But we have great responsibilities, wearing a broad pennant.'

'Light along a pot of coffee,' said Jack. 'And you must ship a cot for the Doctor.'

'Which I just been doing it, ain't I?' replied Killick, but

in a more subdued tone of grievance than usual, and not without an apprehensive look.

'So tell me about your run,' Jack went on. 'I am afraid I cut you short, in my hurry of spirits.'

'I shall not trouble you with my doings by land, apart from observing that the tender and her people behaved in the most exemplary manner, and that we put ashore at Shelmerston and then again at Corunna: but let me tell you that in spite of the strong and favourable wind that sometimes propelled us two hundred miles between one noon and the next, we saw . . .' He eagerly recited a list of birds, fishes, sea-going mammals (a pod of right whales among them), vegetables, crustaceans and other forms of life plucked from the surface or caught in a little trawl until he noticed a slackening in Jack's attention. 'Off Finisterre,' he went on, 'the breeze abandoned us for a while, and I may have seen a monk seal; but the wind soon answered our whistling and ran us down merrily until the Berlings came in sight and we heard the roaring of your guns. That excellent young man Reade hung out sails in all directions, so unwilling he was to miss the battle, as we supposed it to be; nor would he take them in when the breeze revived – the masts bent most amazingly. But, however, it turned out to be no more than the great-gun exercise on an heroic scale. I trust you found it satisfactory, my dear?'

'Stephen, it was a bloody shambles. It was indeed. But perhaps we shall do better another time. Tell me, you did not bring any letters when you came away from Shelmerston? From Ashgrove, I mean, in particular.'

'I did not,' said Stephen. 'I am truly sorry to be disappointing, but I had promised young Reade to catch the morning tide, the holy morning tide. Besides, as well as an eagerness to keep my appointment with you – one might even say apart from a sense of duty – I was travelling with my daughter and Clarissa Oakes, taking them to Spain, where an eminent authority is to be consulted; and I did not call: Clarissa and Sophie are not friends.'

'No. I know they ain't.'

'I am sorry to be disappointing,' said Stephen again, into the silence.

'Oh, never fret about that, Stephen,' cried Jack. 'You could not be disappointing. In any case I had one but the other day by the Lisbon packet, and a damned unpleasant letter it was. I will not say it made me uneasy, but . . .'

Stephen said inwardly, 'Brother, I have never seen you so destroyed but once, and that was when you were struck off the Navy List.'

'Come in,' called Jack.

'All laid along, sir,' said Tom Pullings. 'And here is the report on the exercise. I am afraid you will not be pleased.'

Jack glanced at the paper. 'No,' he said. 'No. It is not pleasing. Let us try to show them something rather better. Stephen, it is long since you watched a great-gun exercise, and I do not remember ever having shown you a ship firing both sides at targets. Should you like to watch?'

'I should like it of all things.'

As they walked out on to the quarterdeck Pullings gave the order to beat to arms, and above the thunder of the drum Jack said, 'It is just the main batteries, you understand, the gundeck and the upper deck, the thirty-two pounders and the eighteens.'

Even Dr Maturin could not have supposed that this was a normal great-gun exercise, with the hands called away from their ordinary occupation to run their pieces in and out three or four times before being dismissed. Not at all: it was meant, and everyone in the squadron knew it was meant, as an example of how these things should be done in battle: and everyone in the *Bellona* was exceedingly anxious that the pennant-ship's example should indeed be exemplary, for not only was there already a very high degree of pride in the barky, but even among those who had served with him from his very first command, a lumpish brig in the Mediterranean, there was a strong inclination to please the Commodore, or more exactly to avoid his displeasure, which could be devastating, above all at present. From an early hour Mr Meares, the gunner, his mate, the quarter-gunners and of course the gun-crews, first captain, second captain, sponger, fireman, sail-trimmers, boarders, powder-boys and Marines, had been titivating their pieces, greasing trucks, begging slush from the cooks to ease the blocks, arranging tackles and shot-garlands just so, while the mid-shipmen and officers in charge of stated divisions also fussed over every detail of powder-horns, wads, cartridge-cases, locks, works and the like: and this each crew did on both the starboard and larboard batteries, for although the *Bellona* had rather better than five hundred people aboard, that was not enough to provide men for each side, and a single crew had to serve two guns.

The crews, often captained by old Surprises, used to Jack Aubrey's ways, or at all events by men who had seen a great deal of action, had been formed as soon as Jack took command and they had practised together ever since. They should have been confident, but they were not. They settled their handkerchiefs round their heads, hitched their trousers, spat on their hands and stared out forward into the brilliant light over the smooth-heaving sea, their black, brown, or whitish deep-tanned upper parts unconsciously swaying with the heave of the deck as they waited for the signal-gun from the quarterdeck and the appearance of the targets.

'Very well, Mr Meares,' said Captain Pullings, and the shrill gun went off: its smoke had barely swept astern before the starboard target appeared, three masses of casks and worn-out sailcloth flying on upright spars, each representing the forecastle, waist and quarterdeck of a ship of the line, the whole towed on a long cablet by the boats of the squad-ron. And at a two-minute interval came the larboard set, also travelling at an easy pace within three hundred yards.

'From forward aft, fire as they bear,' called Pullings from the quarterdeck, and on the gundeck the second lieutenant echoed his words. Jack set his stop-watch.

Two long heaves, with the ship rolling seven degrees, all her teeth showing; and on the next rise the gundeck bow thirty-two pounder uttered its enormous sullen roar, shooting out a stab of flame that lit the whole jet of smoke, and its ball struck barrel-staves from the target: cheers down the line from both decks, but the bow-gun's crew had no time for such things – they held the gun at its full recoil, sponged, loaded with cartridge and then ball, rammed the wad home with furious speed, heaved the fifty-five-hundredweight monster out again with a crash and raced across to the larboard side, where the second captain had all ready for them to point their massive piece at the next. By this time the firing had run half way down both gun and upper decks on the starboard side. The shattering din, the billowing smoke had already confused Stephen's spirits and perception, but now the uproar redoubled as the larboard guns came into play and still another set of targets moved within range. He had an impression of enormous, overwhelming noise, shot through and through with fierce jets of intense, concentrated labour where he could see the gun-crews in the waist, shining with sweat as they heaved and pointed and fired their gun before leaping across to the other, never getting in one another's way, never stumbling – almost no words – gestures, nods immediately understood.

Then, with a last deliberate thirty-two pounder right aft, it was all over, and silence fell on the deafened world. The smoke-bank drifted to leeward, clear of the squadron. Jack looked at the anxious Tom and said, 'I am afraid it was not quite the equivalent of three broadsides in five minutes, Captain Pullings.'

'I am afraid not, sir,' said Tom, shaking his head.

'Yet it was not very far off; and we shall soon work up to something a little brisker,' Jack went on. 'And in any case it did give a general idea of what may be expected, a moderately good general idea. What did you make of it, Doctor?'

'I had no idea that fighting both sides was so very strenuous,' said Stephen in that rather loud voice usual after heavy gunfire, 'nor so very skilled and dangerous, with the cannon recoiling on either hand, with such shocking force. The single broadside I have seen often enough, and it called for surprising agility, but this passes all imagination. I watched them at their frightful task in the waist' – nothing over the quarterdeck barricade down to the upper-deck eighteen-pounders, now being housed and all their implements made fast – 'but below, in the gundeck itself, with those vast pieces booming in one's ear on either side and all the smoke, it must have been very like Hell itself.'

'Use makes master,' observed Jack. 'It is wonderful what one can grow accustomed to. Not many people could stand your saws and buckets of blood, but you do not turn a hair.' He turned to walk back to the cabin and Stephen was about to follow him when the senior assistant surgeon approached. 'Forgive me, sir,' he said, 'but we are much concerned at Mr Gray's condition – the first lieutenant – Macaulay thinks it may be a very sudden and acute attack of the stone; and with submission I agree.'

'I will come at once, Mr Smith,' said Stephen; and as they passed down, deck after deck, so the patient's strangled cries became more evident. Stephen's coming was some relief, and Gray stopped for the length of a quick examination – quick, since there was no doubt about the matter – but as soon as he was eased back the groaning began again, though he bit on sheet and blanket with all his strength, his body arched and quivering with the pain. Stephen nodded, went to his dispensary, took out his untouched tincture of laudanum (once his own solace and delight, and very nearly his destruction, it being a liquid form of opium) and some leeches, poured a dose that made his assistants stare, gave them instructions about instruments and bandages, placed half a dozen leeches, told the young men in Latin that he entirely agreed and that as soon as the patient was in a fit state – should he survive that far – he would operate, probably early in the morning. The carpenter would have the necessary chair prepared: there was a measured drawing in Archbold.

He returned to the quarterdeck and there paced for a while in the sweet evening. The squadron was standing south-south-east under an easy sail and from the forecastle of the *Stately*, next astern, came the sound of music, the hands dancing in the last dog-watch. At one point he saw Killick in the half-darkness, who said to him, 'There will be a rare old duck for supper tonight, sir,' in a kindly, protective tone before padding along the gangway to the forecastle: thence by way of the shrouds, he reached the foretop, that broad, comfortable platform high above the deck, with folded stud-dingsails for cushions and a splendid view of the leading ships steering for Africa under courses and single-reefed topsails beneath a sky already filling with stars. But Killick was as indifferent to the stars as he was to the beauty of the *Laurel*, the lovely little twenty-two-gun ship just ahead. He had come aloft by appointment, to one of the very few places in the ship (500 people and more in a space 170 feet long by 46 feet 9 inches wide at the most and almost entirely filled with stores, provisions, water, guns, powder and shot) where men could talk privately, to see his old friend Barret Bonden, with whom he had scarcely exchanged two words since the *Ringle* joined; and he looked at the young seamen who were also sitting there, playing draughts, with great displeasure.

'Bugger off, mates,' said Bonden to them, quite kindly, and they went at once, the authority of the Commodore's coxswain leaving them not a moment's choice.

'What cheer?' asked Killick, shaking Bonden's hand.

'All a-tanto,' replied Bonden, 'All a-tanto, thankee. But what's come over the barky?'

'You want to know what's come over the barky?'

'That's right, mate. Everything is changed. Anyone would think Old Nick was aboard, or Old Jarvey – wry looks, never a smile, officers nervous, people jumping to it like the day of doom or an admiral's inspection. She had not been really worked up, nor the people had not really shaken down when we left Pompey, but there were a power of old shipmates aboard, right seamen, and on the whole she was a happy ship. What has come over her?'

'Why,' said Killick, and he searched for a striking, even an epigrammatic reply; but eventually, giving up the attempt, he said, 'It's not just the Purple Emperor and his right discontented ship – which she could not meet a Yankee brig-of-war and take her if the brig was anything like smart – nor it's not that old *Stately* with her parcel of pouffes aboard; though all that helps. No. It is domestic infelicity that done it. Domestic infelicity that has overflowed into the barky, an awkward barky in any case, whatever you may say, with so many dead ignorant green hands, a heap of miserable pressed men, and a first lieutenant too sick to do his duty. Domestic infelicity.'

'What do you mean, with your domestic infelicity?' asked Bonden in a stern voice.

'I mean that the Capt – the Commodore and Mrs A have parted brass rags. That's what.'

'God Almighty,' whispered Bonden, sinking back against the top-rim, for Killick's words carried complete conviction for the moment. But after a pause he said, 'How do *you* know?'

'Well,' said Killick, 'you notice things. You can't help hearing things, and you put them together. No one can call me nosey . . .' Bonden made no comment. '. . . and no one can say I ain't got the Captain's best interests at heart.'

'That's right,' said Bonden.

'Well, while we was in the East Indies, and Botany bloody Bay, and Peru and so on, Mrs A looked after what we have here, at Ashgrove, in Hampshire, I mean; and she looked after the Woolcombe estate the Captain inherited from the General: which Mr Croft, Lawyer Croft, was not quite exactly in his intellects, being so ancient. And down there there is a family called Pengelley.'

'Pengelley. Yes, I remember them.'

'Now these Pengelleys had two farms on the estate, both held for his life by old Frank Pengelley: and the last time the Captain was ever in Dorset just before we set sail, old Pengelley told him he was worried about the lease if he should die before the ship came home – worried for his family, it being a lease for two lives and he being the second. His father's son, if you understand.' Bonden nodded. Leases for one, two or three lives were usual in his part of England too. 'Well, it seems that as the Captain was getting on his horse – that big flea-bitten grey, you remember? he said *he would see the young Pengelleys right*, by which old Frank understood his sons. But when old Frank died, which he did when we had not been gone a year, Mrs gave Weston Hay to his eldest boy William and Alton Hill, with all its sheep-walks, to young Frank, the old man's nephew and godson, leaving the other brother, Caleb, with nothing.'

'That Caleb was an idle drunken shiftless creature, no sort of a farmer. Though he had a pretty daughter.'

'Yes. But when we come home, it appeared that the Captain *did* mean sons when he said young Pengelleys, and he and Mrs had words about it. Many times and most severe. And about several other changes she had made: there were a lot of deaths down there in Dorset while we were away.' Killick hesitated, unable to see Bonden's expression in the darkness, but presently he went on. 'Yes, Caleb did have a pretty daughter, which her name was Nan: and Nan is a maid at Ashgrove. You know Ned Hart, as works in our garden?'

'Of course I do. Of course I do. We was shipmates. He lost a foot in the old *Worcester*.'

'Well, Ned and Nan want to marry. And if Caleb can get that there lease he says he will set them up. That is how I come to know so much: Nan tells Ned how Caleb goes to work, and Ned tells me, as someone that knows the Captain's mind.'

'Fair enough. But they would never part brass rags over a thing like that?'

'No. But one thing added to another and every time there was a disagreement, with hard words and ill-feeling. You remember Parson Hinksey?'

'The gentleman as courted Miss Sophie long ago, the cricketer?'

'Yes: well it turned out that it was Parson Hinksey as advised it – advised the lease and everything else, all the things they disagreed upon. He was over to Ashgrove at least every week all the time we were away, says Ned, and now he sat in the Captain's chair.'

'Oh,' said Bonden.

'Taken much notice of by Mother Williams and her tie-mate; and by the children. Looked up to.'

Bonden nodded gloomily: an unpromising state of affairs.

'So there was words, and Parson Hinksey always being brought up. And Parson Hinksey calling very frequent. But that was nothing, nothing, against what happened when the Captain was in London and she went to dinner over to Barham, where Mrs Oakes looks after the poor Doctor's little natural.'

'She ain't a natural . . . She's as pretty a little maid as ever I see – talks away to Padeen in their language, and quite like a Christian to us. Laughs when the barky ships a sea, goes aloft on old Mould's shoulders, never seasick – loves the sea. We just run her and Mrs Oakes across to the Groyne in the tender. A dear little maid, and the Doctor is as happy as . . .' Before he could hit upon the very type of happiness Killick went on, 'Just what happened Nan could not tell, but it was to do with that there silk the Captain bought in Java and that we made Mrs Oakes's wedding dress out of.'

'I sewed its bodice,' said Bonden.

'Well, that only took part of the bolt and the rest was brought home as intended in the first place. So Mrs A wore it to this dinner where there was Parson Hinksey and some other gent: and when she came back she tore it off – said she would never wear such a rag again – and gave it to her maid, who showed Nan a piece – had never seen such lovely stuff, she said.'

'I do not know what to make of that,' said Bonden.

'Nor did I,' said Killick. 'Not until it all came down through Mrs A's particular maid Clapton and her friends down to Nan. But it seems that when the Captain came back a day or so after this dinner there was a letter waiting for him about the lease that vexed him, and he checked Mrs A with seeing too much of Parson Hinksey, of thinking more of his advice than her husband's, and perhaps he said something else, being carried away, like. Anyway, it was far, far more than she could bear and she went for him like a Tartar, right savage – calling out that if he could use her so, and accuse her so, while she was wearing his trull's leavings and being civil to her, she would be damned if she had anything more to do with him and she took off her ring and told him he might – no, she never said that: she tossed it out of the window. But she might have said it, and worse: nobody ever thought she had so much spirit or fury in her, nor such a power of dragging him up and down, though with never a tear nor a foul word nor breaking things. Well, that was just before we sailed. He slept in the summerhouse the last few days and she in a dressing-room with a locked door; and there were no fond farewells at parting, though the children saw him to his boat and waved, and . . .'

A ship's boy put his head over the rail and said, 'Mr Killick, sir, Grimble asks is he to take up the duck or wait for you? Which Commodore's cook says it will spoil, else.'

'Killick,' said the Commodore, passing him an empty gravy-boat, 'tell my cook to fill this with something that very closely resembles gravy or take the consequences. Heaven and earth alike revolt against a parched and withered duck,' he added, addressing Stephen.

'If a duck lack unction, it forfeits all right to the name,' said Stephen. 'Yet here are some aiguillettes – what is the English for aiguillettes? – from the creature's inner flank that will go down well enough with a draught of this Hermitage.'

'I wish I could carve like that,' said Jack, watching Stephen's knife slice the long thin strips. 'My birds generally take to the air again, spreading fat in the most disastrous fashion over the table and the laps of my guests.'

'The only vessel I ever sailed turned ignominiously upside down,' said Stephen. 'Each man to his own trade, said Plato: that's justice.'

The gravy came, somewhat pale and thin, but adequate: Jack ate and drank. 'Surely you will have a little more?' he said. 'The bird lies before you, or what is left of it. And another glass of wine?'

'I will not. I have done quite well; and as I said, I must be tolerably Spartan. I shall probably have a busy day tomorrow, starting early. But I will join you when the port comes on.'

Jack ate on without embarrassment – they were very old friends, differing widely in size, weight, capacity, requirements – but without much appetite either.

Stephen said, 'Will I tell you another of Plato's observations?'

'Pray do,' said Jack, his smile briefly returning.

'It should please you, since you have a very pretty hand. Hinksey quoted it when I dined with him in London and we were discussing the bill of fare: "Calligraphy," said Plato, "is the physical manifestation of an architecture of the soul." That being so, mine must be a turf-and-wattle kind of soul, since my handwriting would be disowned by a backward cat; whereas yours, particularly on your charts, has a most elegant flow and clarity, the outward form of a soul that might have conceived the Parthenon.'

Jack made a civil bow, and pudding came in: spotted dog. He silently offered a slice to Stephen, who shook his head, and ate mechanically for a while, before pushing his plate away.

Killick brought the port, with bowls of almonds, walnuts and petits fours. Jack told him that he might turn in and stood up to lock the doors of both coach and sleeping-cabin after him, taking no notice of his shocked 'What, no coffee?'

'I did not know you had dined with Hinksey,' he said, sitting down again.

'Of course you did not. It was when I ran up to London in the tender, and you were already at sea. I ran into him in the back of Clementi's shop, where he was turning over scores – pianoforte and harpsichord. I found him very knowing, conversible on the subject of your old Bach, and carried him back to Black's, where we had a moderately good dinner. It would have been better if a table of soldiers had not started roaring and bawling. Still, we ended the evening very agreeably, prating about the Bendas in the library: we might play some of their duets that I brought with me when we have finished our wine.'

'Oh, Stephen,' said Jack, 'I have no more heart for music than I have for food. I have not touched my fiddle since we put to sea. But to go back to Hinksey, what do you think of him?'

'I find him very good company: he is a scholar and a gentleman, and he was very kind to Sophie while we were away.'

'Oh, I am much obliged to him, I know,' said Jack, and in a growling undertone he added, 'I only wish I may not be too deeply obliged to him – I wish I may not have to thank him for a set of horns.'

Stephen took no notice of this deep muttering: his mind was elsewhere. 'I remember,' he said at last. 'They were playing at the cricket, and someone struck or caught the ball in such a way that there was a general cry of approbation. My neighbour cried, "Who was it? Who was it?" springing up and down. "It was the handsome gentleman," said her companion. "Mr Hinksey." He is generally thought good-looking.'

'Handsome is as handsome does,' said Jack. 'I cannot imagine what they see in him.'

'Oh, with his athletic form – which you cannot deny – and his amiable qualities – he seems to me admirably adapted to please a young woman. Or a woman of a certain age, for that matter.'

'I cannot imagine what they see in him,' repeated Jack.

'Perhaps your imagination runs on different wheels, my dear: but, however that may be, it appears that Miss Smith, Miss Lucy Smith, sees so much that she has accepted his offer of marriage. This he told me, not without a certain modest triumph, at the end of our dinner: and before we parted he told me that the lady's father, one of the great men of the East India Company, so thoroughly approves the match that he has used all his influence to have Mr Hinksey appointed Bishop – Anglican bishop, of course – of Bombay. Perhaps Bombay – perhaps Madras or Calcutta – or possibly suffragan bishop – my mind was a little confused by the toasts we drank – but at all events a noble Indian establishment for him and his bride. Jack, we are still in the region of beer, are we not?'

'Beer? Oh yes, I dare say so . . . Stephen, I cannot tell you how glad I am you told me all this . . . So he is to be married? . . . I had been so afraid . . . Stephen, the port stands by you . . . I had been on the point of unbosoming myself . . . foolish, discreditable thoughts.'

'I rejoice you did not, brother. The closest friendship cannot stand such a strain: the results are invariably disastrous.'

'I am so happy,' observed Jack, after a moment; and indeed he could be seen swelling with it. 'But what was that about beer?'

'I asked whether we were still in the beer region, or domain, that part of the ocean in which the beer we bring from home and which we serve out daily at the absurd and criminal rate of a gallon – a *gallon*: eight pints! – a head, is still available. Has the beer not yet given way to the even more pernicious grog?'

'I believe we are still on beer. We do not usually run out

before we raise the Peak of Tenerife. Should you like some?'

'If you please. I particularly need a light, gentle sleep tonight; and beer, a respectable ship's beer, is the most virtuous hypnotic known to man.'

In time Jack returned with a quart can, from which they took alternate draughts as they sat gazing astern at the long-running wake in the moonlight.

'But you know,' said Jack, 'I made no direct accusations.'

'Brother,' said Stephen, 'you can give a woman a great wounding kick on the bottom and then assert you never slapped her face.'

Half a pint later Jack went on, 'Still, she really should not have said "your trull" when as you know very well I was perfectly innocent in that case.'

'In *that* case . . . on how many others were you not as guilty as ever your feeble powers would allow? For shame to quibble so. It *was* unfortunate; but it gives you no moral height at all. None whatsoever. Your only course is to crawl flat on your belly, roaring out Peccavi and beating your bosom. And I will tell you something, Jack: both you and Sophie are afflicted, deeply afflicted, with that accursed blemish jealousy, that most pernicious flaw, which sours all life both within and without; and if you do not heave your wind you may be hopelessly undone.'

'I have always prided myself on a perfect freedom from jealousy,' said Jack.

'For a great while I prided myself on my transcendent beauty, on much the same grounds; or even better,' said Stephen.

They finished their beer; and presently Stephen, coming back into the cabin from the quarter-gallery, said, 'But I am glad you did not open your mind: later you would have held it against me, and in any case I could not have given you the sympathy that you would have felt your right. In the morning I must almost certainly cut a man for the stone, and marital discord, above all that which is based upon misapprehensions, seems trifling in comparison with undergoing a lithotomy at sea and a probable death in extreme apprehension, inhuman suffering and distress of mind – the ultimate distress of mind.'

Chapter Seven

Mr Gray underwent the operation with the utmost fortitude. Physically he had no choice, since he was immovably attached to the dreadful chair, his legs wide apart and his bare belly open to the knife: the fortitude was on another plane altogether and although Stephen had cut many and many a patient – patient in the sense of sufferer – he had never known anything to equal Gray's steady voice, nor his perfectly coherent thanks when they cast off the leather-covered chains and his shockingly-marked pale glistening face sank back at last.

The loss of any patient grieved Stephen professionally and often personally and for a long time. He did not think he should lose Gray, although indeed the case had been almost desperate; but a sullen deep infection slowly gained in spite of all that Dr Maturin could do and they buried him in two thousand fathoms some time before the squadron picked up the north-east trades.

The wind, though steady, blew gently at first and the Commodore had an excellent proof of his ships' sailing qualities: when they were making their best way consonant with keeping station, the *Bellona* could give the *Stately* royals and lower studdingsails; the *Aurora* could outsail both two-deckers; but the *Thames* could only just keep up. It did not seem to Jack the fault of her hull, nor a want of activity when the hands raced aloft to loose sail, but rather the absence of anyone in authority who understood the finer points of sailing – sheets hauled aft by main force, the tack hard down, and bowlines fiddle-string taut whenever the breeze came a little forward of the beam was their universal maxim, though they still outshone all the rest in the matter of gleaming brass and paint; and it had to be admitted that they now fired their guns a little quicker, if not much more accurately. The smaller ships, Smith's twenty-gun *Camilla* and Dick Richardson's twenty-two-gun *Laurel*, were his delight, however. They were both excellently well handled and they both had many of the virtues of the dear *Surprise*, being good sea-boats, very weatherly, and almost as devoid of leeway as a square-rigged ship could possibly be.

'I will tell you what it is, Stephen,' said Jack, and they standing in the stern-gallery surrounded by gilt figures of a former age, the age of long waistcoats, 'the glass has shot up in a very whimsical fashion, and in these waters I have never known that happen without there followed a clock-calm or something close to it. In the last dog-watch – oh, Stephen, whenever I say that I remember your exquisitely beautiful explanation: that the short watch was so called because it was curtailed – *cur*-tailed – so *dog* – oh ha, ha, ha, ha – and I often laugh aloud. Well, if my calculations and Tom's and the master's are right, we should then cut the thirty-first parallel, and I must open my sealed orders. Our noon observation was so close that I really could have done so then, but I have a superstitious reverence for such things. How I hope there will be good news in them – orders to seek out the enemy – something like real wartime sailoring – with a squadron this size it would not be unusual – rather than skirmishing about for a parcel of miserable slavers . . .'

'Perhaps the miserable slaves may be worthy of consideration too,' observed Stephen.

'Oh, certainly; and I should very much dislike being a slave myself. But Nelson did say that if you abolished the trade . . .' He broke off, saying, 'However,' for this was one of the few points on which they wholly disagreed. 'Do you think, Stephen,' he went on after a moment during which the *Ringle* shot across their wake – she, being the *Bellona*'s tender, was not required to keep to any particular station, so long as she was always within hail, and Reade made the most of her delightful powers – 'Do not think that I am murmuring or discontented or ungrateful for having this splendid command. But I have thought, and reflected, and pondered . . .'

'Brother,' said Stephen, 'you grow prolix.'

'. . . and I believe it is too splendid for the work it is given. Besides, there are several things I have disliked about it almost from the beginning: it was booted abroad like any football, and the newspapers had pieces like "We learn from a gentleman very close to the Ministry that extremely strong measures against the odious traffic in Negroes have been decided to be made, and the gallant Captain Aubrey, determined that Freedom shall reign by sea as well as by land, has sailed with a powerful squadron," and the wretch names them all with complement and number of guns. And that paper, with the *Post* and the *Courier*, also pointed out, very truly, that this was the first time line-of-battle ships had ever been sent on such a mission. "A very great effort to stamp out this vile commerce in human flesh was to be made, which redounded much to the something of the Ministry." I read that in Lisbon; and then there were dozens more of the same kind. There has been a great deal of fuss and unnecessary talk, often very personal and unpleasant – flashy. How can we be expected to take them by surprise if it is shouted from the housetops? But what I really meant to say was that whether there is good news or no, I am sure as you can be of anything at sea that there will be little wind or none at all, and I mean to ask the post-captains to dinner. You cannot have an even half-efficient squadron without there is reasonable good understanding.'

'If you wish to reach a good understanding with the Purple Emperor, you have but to tell him of Lord Nelson, slavery and the Royal Navy. His surgeon consulted me about the imperial health: I went across to look at the patient, and he gave me his views on our mission: it was the greatest nonsense to try to guard a great stretch of coast from north to south with a squadron of our size. And even if we were confined to the general area of Whydah for example, no ship of the line and very few frigates could catch a slaver, except in very heavy weather. They were nearly all long low schooners, very weatherly, built above all for speed and handled by capital seamen. But even if that was not the case, what would be the point? The poor creatures, coming from all sorts of tribes in the interior, with no common language between them and often deadly hatred, were, upon being rescued, put down in Sierra Leone or some other crowded well-meaning place and told to till a plot – people who had never tilled anything in their lives and who ate different kinds of food. No, no. It was far better, far kinder, to let them take the rapid and easy middle passage, be landed quickly in the West Indies and sold to men who would not only look after them – anyone with any sense of his own interest takes care of what has cost him dear – but who might also make Christians of them, which was the kindest thing of all, since the slaves would be saved, while all those left in Africa or taken back to Africa must necessarily be damned. He then repeated your piece about the abolition of the slave-trade being the destruction of the Navy, and ended by saying that slavery was approved in Holy Writ. He was, however, firmly determined to carry out his orders to the very best of his ability, that being the duty of an officer.'

'What did you say to that, Stephen?'

'Faith, I said nothing – there were few intervals into which I could have slipped a word – but from time to time I made a noncommittal movement of my head. Then I prescribed him a dose that may have a mollifying effect: it will certainly purge his more malignant humours.'

'Perhaps he will be better company. It must be a weary life, being in a permanent state of rage or at least at half-cock.' Jack's ear caught the little ping of the chiming and repeating watch in Stephen's pocket. 'The last dog,' he cried, and walking into the cabin he rang for a midshipman. 'Mr Wetherby,' he said, 'be so good as to carry my compliments to Captain Pullings and say that I should like to know the distance made good since the noon observation.'

'Aye aye, sir,' said the young gentleman, and he came back in under a minute with a slip of paper. Jack looked at it, smiled, stepped into the master's day-cabin for a last check, and hurried to the iron box in his locker – pierced iron, weighted with lead, for documents that must not be taken, that must sink on being thrown overboard, sunk at once, beyond recovery: signals, codes, official letters. His secret orders were the most voluminous he had ever received, and he saw with keen pleasure that they included the remarks and observations of those commanders who had preceded him since 1808 with the same missions, for his own acquaintance with the coast was almost entirely confined to sailing past it as far off and as quickly as possible, an extraordinarily unhealthy part of the world and, close in, with variable winds or calms, and distressing currents.

But when he had turned them over he ran his eye down the orders themselves, and half way along his face glowed bright with pleasure. With extreme rapidity his glance seized the fact that having harassed the slavers, he was at a certain date and in a given longitude and latitude, to assemble the ships named in the margin and steer an appropriate course to intercept and destroy a French squadron that would sail from Brest at a given date, at first heading for the Azores and then in or about twenty-five degrees of west longitude changing course for Bantry Bay. All this was accompanied by a mass of qualifications, but Jack was used to them; he had grasped the essence in a moment and his eyes ran down to the paragraph that had ended so many of his orders: that in this undertaking he was to consult and advise with Dr Stephen Maturin (through whom more precise dates and positions might later be conveyed through suitable channels) on all points that might have a political or diplomatic significance. Disregarding the assurance (their Lordships' graceful finishing touch) that he must not fail in this or any part of it as he would answer the contrary at his peril, he called Stephen in from the great stern-gallery, the most engaging piece of naval architecture known to man, in fact. But hardly had the Doctor turned before the radiance in Jack's face, smile, eyes dropped by two or three powers: the French clearly intended another invasion of Ireland, or liberation as they put it, and he felt a little shy of broaching the matter. Stephen had never made his views vehemently, injuriously clear, but Jack knew very well that he preferred the English to stay in England and to leave the government of Ireland to the Irish.

Stephen saw the change in his face – a large essentially red face in spite of the tan in which his blue eyes shone with an uncommon brilliance, a face made for good humour – and the papers in his hand.

'You know all about this, I am sure, Stephen?' Stephen nodded. 'Anyhow, there is a paper for you' – holding it out – 'Shall we take a turn on the poop?'

Privacy, even for a commodore of the first class with a post-captain under him and a rear-admiral's hat, was a rare bird in the man-of-war, that intensely curious and gossiping community, above all in a man-of-war with such more than usually inquisitive hands as Killick and his mate Grimble, whose duties took them into holy places and who were extraordinarily knowing about which grating on which deck and with which wind was likely to carry voices best.

The poop, a fine lordly sweep of about fifty feet by twenty-eight, was soon cleared of the signal yeoman and his friends and Jack and Stephen paced the deck athwartships for a while.

'You are puzzled to know how to begin, my dear,' said Stephen after half a dozen turns, 'so I will tell you how it is. The Irish question, as people are coming to call it in the newspapers, can as I see it be solved by two simple measures, Catholic emancipation and the dissolution of the Union; and it is possible, *possible*, that this may come about in time without violence. But were the French to be there and busily arming the discontented there would be the very Devil to pay – endless violence – and it might even tip the balance, giving that infernal Buonaparte the victory. And where would Ireland be then? In a very much worse state, under an *efficient* and totally unscrupulous tyranny, Catholic only in name, and remarkably avid for spoil. Think of Rome, Venice, Switzerland, Malta . . . No. Though it would grieve many of my friends, I should, with all my heart, prevent a French landing. I have served long enough in the Navy to prefer the lesser of two weevils.'

'So you have, brother,' said Jack, looking at him affectionately. 'I am of course required and directed to advise with you on difficult points and I shall show you the whole set of papers presently, when you are at leisure – though in passing let me say that the Admiralty, having observed that the loss of men from disease was sometimes very great on the West African coast, said that in the early period a severely sick or diseased ship might collect a judicious number of invalids from other vessels and stretch away to Ascension Island, where refreshments were to be had in the form of turtles in the proper season, clear fresh water, and certain green plants.'

'Ah, Ascension . . .' said Stephen in a voice of longing.

'And they say that the present governor of Sierra Leone is my old shipmate James Wood. You remember James Wood, Stephen? He was shot through the throat at Porto Vecchio and talks in a wheeze: we went aboard him in the Downs when he had the *Hebe*, and he came to stay at Ashgrove.'

'The cheerful gentleman who filled his ship with such unconscionable amounts of rope and paint and the like?'

'Just so – no stickler for form – he loved to go to sea in a well-found ship, even if it meant conciliating the dockyard people to a surprising degree. And an uncommon keen hand at whist.'

'I remember him perfectly.'

'Of course you do, ' said Jack, smiling at the recollection of Captain Wood's jovial way with a bribe, his acquisition of one of the flagship's spare anchors. 'And since you know everything about the second part,' he continued in little more than a whisper, 'I shan't go on about it at all – not a word – tace is the Latin for a candlestick. But I will tell you about the first, about knocking the slavers on the head: we are required to make a great roaring din straight away and amaze all observers, as well as liberating as many slaves as possible. Now I have no experience of this particular service at all, and although I have glanced at the earlier commanders' tolerably meagre remarks I should still like to know a great deal more, and I believe asking questions is the only way of finding out. You cannot ask questions of a book or a report, but a word to the cove that wrote it would make everything clear. So I mean to summon all captains and ask them what they know; and then I shall invite them to dinner tomorrow.' He strode forward and called down to the quarterdeck 'Captain Pullings.'

'Sir?'

'Let us heave out the signal for all captains.'

'Aye aye, sir. Mr Miller' – to the officer of the watch – 'All captains.'

'Aye aye, sir. Mr Soames . . .' And so it went from signal lieutenant to the signal midshipman and thus to the yeoman of the signals himself, who had had plenty of time to prepare the hoist *All captains repair aboard pennant* that broke out at the *Bellona*'s masthead a moment later, to be echoed along the line by the repeating brigs and to spread consternation in many a cabin, where captains flung off their duck trousers and nankeen jackets – it was a hot day, with the breeze aft – and struggled sweating into white stockings, white breeches and white waistcoat, the whole topped with a blue broadcloth gold-laced coat.

They arrived in no particular order but in excellent time, only the *Thames*'s barge being somewhat late – her captain could be heard cursing his midshipman, his coxswain and 'that son of a bitch at bow-oar' for the best part of five minutes. When they were all assembled on the poop, which seemed to Jack an airier, more informal place than the quarterdeck, he said to them, 'Gentlemen, I must tell you that my orders require the squadron to make a very strong demonstration of force at our first arrival on the coast. I have the remarks and observations of earlier commodores on the station, but I should also like to question officers who have been on this service. Have any of you been engaged, or any of your officers?'

A general murmur, a looking at one another, and Jack, turning to Captain Thomas, who had long served in the West Indies and who owned property there, asked him whether he had anything particular to say.

'Why me?' cried Thomas. 'Why should I have anything particular to say about slavery?' Then, seeing the astonishment on the faces all round him, he checked himself, coughed, and went on, 'I ask pardon, sir, if I have spoken a little abruptly – I was put out by my bargemen's stupidity. No, I have nothing particular to say.' Here he checked again, and Stephen and Mr Adams's eyes met in a fleeting glance; the expression of neither altered in the least degree, but each was certain that the swallowed words were a eulogy of the trade and indeed of slavery itself.

'Well, I am sorry to have drawn a blank covert,' said Jack, looking round his captains' uniform stupidity. 'But my predecessors' reports make it perfectly clear that much of this service is inshore, smallcraft work, and I must desire all officers present to ensure that their boats are in very good order, with their crews thoroughly accustomed to stepping masts and proceeding under sail for considerable distances. Mr Howard, I believe I saw you lower down your launch in a most surprising brisk manner the day before yesterday.'

'Yes, sir,' said Howard, laughingly. 'It was the usual idiot ship's boy. He harpooned a bonito with such zeal that he flung himself out of the bridle-port on to the fish, the harpoon fast to his wrist. Fortunately the launch was in the act of being shifted, so we got her over the side straight away and saved our only decent weapon.'

'Well done,' said Jack, 'well done indeed. And the word

weapon reminds me: getting boats over the side quick and handling them well is very important, but it must not, *must not*, affect our great-gun exercises, which, as you will all admit, still leave something to be desired. Yet tomorrow is a somewhat exceptional day; and tomorrow I hope and trust the exercise will leave you all time enough to dine with me.'

Two bells, and Killick, his mate and three mess attendants walked carefully up the poop ladder, the first two carrying trays with decanters of all things proper to be drunk at such an hour, the others with glasses to drink them from.

As the captains were being piped over the side Stephen's friend Howard came, and standing by him said discreetly, 'Of course, Maturin, you know the Commodore infinitely better than I do: is he very exact and naval in his use of the word officer?'

'Fairly so, I believe: certainly punctilious in the use of rank and title. He could no more bear the Swedish knight than could Nelson. But he is the most reasonable of men.'

'To be sure. I was astonished at the cogency, sequence and clarity of his account of nutation at the Royal Society – Scholey took me – and for several days I believe I understood not only nutation but even the precession of the equinoxes.'

'Sure, he is the great astronomer of the world.'

'Yes. But my point is this: in the *Aurora* I have an elderly master's mate called Whewell. And a master's mate, as you know very well, is not an officer in our ordinary use of the word – a commission officer. He served his time, passed his public or quasi-public examination for lieutenant, but failed to pass for gentleman – in short, the examining officers, conferring in private, did not think him one, and so no commission was ever made out. Yet he is a good seaman and he knows a great deal about slave-ships and their ways.'

'Then I am perfectly certain that the Commodore would like to see him.'

'He could hardly ask better. Whewell was born in Jamaica, the son of a ship-owner: he first went to sea in one of his father's merchantmen, carrying goods and some slaves, and then Dick Harrison took him into the *Euterpe*, on the quarterdeck. During the peace he served in one of the Thomas's regular slavers as a mate, but he sickened of it and was glad to get back into the service, into John West's *Euryalus*, and then with me.'

'I did not know that Captain Thomas owned slavers.'

'It is a family concern; but he is extremely sensitive about it since the law abolished the trade – don't choose to have it known.'

Whewell was aboard within ten minutes in spite of having had to shave and change into his best uniform. He was a short, straight, round-headed man of about thirty-five, far from handsome: the smallpox had marked his face terribly, and where it was not pitted by the disease an exploding twelve-pounder cartridge-case had covered it with a dense sprinkling of black dots; furthermore his teeth were very bad, gapped and discoloured. Yet this positive ugliness did not account for his present position in the Navy – perhaps the most uncomfortable of them all – since as Jack knew very well midshipmen worse-looking by far had been given a commission on passing for lieutenant at Somerset House. No: the trouble was the yellow tinge in what complexion Whewell could be said to possess – the evident legacy of an African great-grandmother.

'Sit down, Mr Whewell,' said Jack, rising as he came into the great cabin. 'You are no doubt aware that our squadron is intended to put down the slave-trade, or at least to discourage it as much as possible. I am told that you have a considerable knowledge of the subject: pray give me a brief account of your experience. And Dr Maturin here would also like to know something of the matter: not the nautical side or the particular winds in the Bight of Benin, you understand, but the more general aspects.'

'Well, sir,' said Whewell, looking Jack straight in the face while he ordered his thoughts, 'I was born in Kingston, where my father owned some merchantmen, and when I was a boy I used often to go along in one or another of them, trading in the islands, up to the States or across to Africa, to Cape Palmas and right along into the Gulf, for palm-oil, gold if we could get it, Guinea pepper and elephants' teeth; and some negroes if they were offering, but not many, since we were not regular slavers, fitted up to deal with them by wholesale. So I came to know those waters, particularly in the Gulf, tolerably well. Then after some while my father told his old acquaintance Captain Harrison that I was wild to go aboard a man-of-war, and he very kindly took me on to his quarterdeck in *Euterpe*, lying in Kingston at the time. I served in her for three years and then followed my captain into the *Topaz*, where he rated me master's mate. That was just before the peace, when the ship was paid off at Chatham. I made my way back to Jamaica and took what I could find – my father had left off business by then – mostly small merchantmen to Guinea and south right down to Cabinda or over to Brazil. A few negroes, as before; but although I was thoroughly used to slavers and their ways, particularly the big Liverpool ships, I never sailed in one until I went aboard the *Elkins* in Montego Bay; and then, although the owners had made out she carried mixed cargoes, I saw she was a high flyer in that line the moment I set foot on deck.'

'How could you tell that, sir?' asked Stephen.

'Why, sir, her galley overflowed in every direction: ordinarily a ship has coppers enough to cook for the crew – in this case say thirty hands – but here they were calculated for keeping four or five hundred slaves alive for the four or five thousand miles of the middle passage: say a couple of months. And her water was in proportion. Then again she had a slave-deck, which was perfect proof.'

'I do not think I know the term.'

'Well, it is not a deck at all, in the sense of planking, but rather a set of gratings covering the whole space set aside for the slaves and letting air into it; and about two or two and a half feet under these gratings they sit, or squat, usually in rows running athwartships, the men forward, chained in pairs, and the women aft.'

'Even in two and a half feet they could barely sit upright, let alone stand.'

'No, sir. And it is often less.'

'How many might there be, at all?'

'Broadly speaking, as many as they can cram in. The usual reckoning is three for every ton the ship gauges, so the *Elkins*, that I was in, could stow five hundred, she being a hundred and seventy ton; and that may answer for a quick passage. But there are some that force them in so tight that if one man moves all must move; and then unless there are leading winds most of the way, the result is terrible.'

'When are they let out?'

'Never at all when they are within swimming distance of the land; at sea, by groups in the daytime.'

'What of cleanliness by night?'

'There is none, sir; none whatsoever. Some ships turn a hose on the filth and man the pumps in the forenoon watch, and some make the negroes clean up and then wash on deck – they are all stark naked – with vinegar in the water; but even so a slaver stinks a mile and more to leeward.'

'Surely,' said Stephen, 'with such filth, such crowding in such foul air and this heat, surely disease must ensue?'

'Yes, sir, it does. Even if the blacks have not suffered very much when they are captured and then marched down to the coast and kept in the barracoon, and even if they don't have to sit waiting cooped up on the slave-deck for a week or so until the cargo is completed, the flux very often starts the third or fourth day, about the time the sea-sickness stops, and then they generally start dying: sometimes, it seems, of mere misery. Even in a reasonably careful ship where they whipped the slaves that would not eat and made them run about the deck for the air and exercise, I have known twenty a day go over the side, a week out from Whydah. It is not reckoned extraordinary if a third of the cargo is lost.'

'Do no intelligent masters calculate that a more humane

policy might be more profitable? After all, a stout negro fetches from forty to sixty pounds at the auction block.'

'There are a few, sir: men that pride themselves on presenting prime stock, as they put it. Some even have fattening farms, with medical care. But most find it don't answer. The profits, even with a third loss, are so great now the trade is illegal, that they think it best to cram full every time, whatever the risk; and there is always the chance of a fair wind out of the Bight and a quick and healthy run.'

'What kind of vessels are they at present?' asked Jack.

'Well, sir, after the passing of the act abolishing the trade and the coming of the preventive squadron, most of the *ships* gave up. There are a few fast-sailing brigs on the Bahia or Rio voyage from the Bight – I say nothing about the old-fashioned Portuguese south of the line, because they are protected – but most of the slavers now are schooners, faster on a wind and more weatherly, from quite small craft up to the new three-hundred-ton Baltimore clippers, sailing under Spanish colours, often false, with a more or less American crew and a master that says he is a Spaniard, the Spaniards not being subject to our law. But now, since the preventive squadron was withdrawn, some of the old hands have come back, patching up their old ships, more or less, and making the Havana run. They usually know the coast very well, and the chiefs, and sometimes they run in where a stranger would not dare to go. Yet the larger craft have to load through the surf by canoes in many places. It is all inshore work on a very low coast all the way down to the Bight of Biafra, mangrove swamps and mud for hundreds of miles and mosquitoes so thick you can hardly breathe, particularly in the rainy season: though every now and then there are inlets, little gaps in the forest if you know where to look, and that is where the smaller schooners go, sometimes taking a full cargo aboard in a day.'

'Do you know the whole of the Coast, Mr Whewell?' asked Jack.

'I should not say I was a pilot for the country between

Cape Lopez and Benguela, sir, but I am pretty well acquainted with the rest.'

'Then let us look at this general chart, and work down from the north. I should like you to give me a rough idea of local conditions, currents, breezes of course, active markets and so on. Then another day, with Captain Pullings, the master, and my secretary to take notes, we will go over it all more thoroughly. Now here is Sierra Leone and Freetown . . . Doctor,' he called, 'you are very welcome to stay, if you choose; but I must warn you that from now on our discussion is likely to be purely nautical, dull work for a landsman.'

'What makes you think that I resemble a landsman, Commodore, I beg? I am salted to the bone; a pickled herring. But, however' – looking at his watch – 'my sick-berth calls me. Good day to you, Mr Whewell. One day I hope you will have time to tell me a little of the West African mammals: I believe there are no less than three species of pangolin.'

The next day was that of the Commodore's dinner to his captains, a day rendered wearisome beyond expression for those who lived aft by the incessant, ill-tempered and querulous activity of the Commodore's steward, Preserved Killick, his mate Grimble, the Commodore's and Captain's cooks, and as many hands as they could press into their service to turn out, scrub, swab, polish, replace and arrange with a truly forbidding rigour, the whole accompanied by a high-pitched nagging stream of abuse and complaint that drove Jack on to the quarterdeck, where once again he showed the youngsters the right way of handling a sextant and examined the midshipmen's berth on their knowledge of the chief navigational stars, and Stephen to the orlop, where he read through his assistants' notes until he was interrupted by a ship's boy who told him that the *Stately*'s surgeon had called to see him.

Mr Giffard and Stephen were fairly well acquainted –

well enough, in any case, for Giffard's initial embarrassment to persuade Stephen that this was not an ordinary visit nor a request for the loan of a carboy of Venice treacle or a hundredweight of portable soup and some lint. And indeed, after a tedious discussion of the trade wind, Giffard asked whether they might talk privately. Stephen led him back to the orlop, to his little cabin, and there Giffard said, 'This may be considered a proper subject for two medical men, I trust: I think I betray no confidences or offend against professional discretion when I say that our captain is a paederast, that he calls young foremast hands into his cabin by night, and that the officers are much concerned, since these youths are much favoured, which in time will destroy discipline altogether. It is already much loosened, but they hesitate to take any official action, which must necessarily result in ignominious hanging and throw great discredit on the ship; and they hope that a private word to the Commodore would have the desired effect. A medical man, a friend, and an old shipmate . . .' His voice died away.

'I will not pretend to misunderstand you,' said Stephen, 'but I must tell you that I abhor an informer very much more than I abhor a sodomite: if indeed I can be said to abhor a sodomite *qua* sodomite at all: one has but to think of Achilles and hundreds more. It is true that in our society such connexions are out of place in a man-of-war . . . yet you adduce nothing but probabilities. Is a man's reputation to be blasted on a mere statement of probabilities, and they at second-hand?'

'There is the good of the service,' said Giffard.

'Very true . . .' said Stephen, breaking off to call out, 'Come in.'

'Please sir,' said a ship's boy, 'Mr Killick says ain't you ever going to come and try your frilled shirt? Which he has been standing there with it in his hand this half glass and more.'

'Mary and Joseph,' cried Stephen, clapping his hand to where his warning watch should have been had he not left it in the quarter-gallery. 'Mr Giffard, sir, I beg you will forgive me – may I wait upon you when I have considered?'

The power of running up a cambric shirt to measure, adorning it with a frilled front and then ironing that frill to crisp perfection seemed improbable in so uncouth a creature as Killick; but he was a seaman, and handy with his needle even for a seaman; and neither he nor anyone else thought it out of the way.

It was in this elegant shirt, therefore, that Stephen stood on the *Bellona*'s quarterdeck to await the arrival of the guests, *Thames*, *Aurora*, *Camilla*, *Laurel*, as the captains were called, arrived in close order, to be piped aboard and welcomed; and they were all there when the *Stately*'s barge appeared, steered by Duff's proud coxswain with a midshipman in a gold-laced hat beside him and pulled by ten young bargemen tricked out to the height of nautical elegance and splendour – tight white trousers with ribbons down the seams, embroidered shirts, crimson neckerchiefs, broad-brimmed sennit hats, gleaming pigtails. With Giffard's words in his mind, Stephen looked at them attentively: individually each sailor would have been very well, but since they were all uniformly decorated, he thought it overdone. He was not alone. Jack Aubrey glanced down into the barge after he had received Captain Duff, laughed very heartily and said, 'Upon my word, Mr Duff, you will have to take care of those young ladies' rig, or coarse-minded people will be getting very comical ideas into their heads. They will say "Sod 'em tomorrow" and quote Article XXIX, oh ha, ha, ha, ha!'

The dinner itself went well, and even the Purple Emperor, conscious of his gaffe and devoted to his belly, laid himself out to be agreeable. Attentive trolling from the wardroom lights had provided a handsome young swordfish; the Commodore's livestock three pair of fowls and a sheep, his cellar a considerable quantity of claret, unavoidably rather warm but of a quality to stand it; and the small Jersey cow a syllabub; while there was still some tolerable cheese, with almond cakes to go with the full tide of port.

Stephen enjoyed himself, sitting next to Howard, with whom he talked of Sappho and the delights of the diving-bell, on the one side, and on the other a Marine officer who knew a surprising number of people in the literary world of London and who, to his intense pleasure, told him about a novel by a Mr John Paulton that everyone was reading at present with great applause, a novel dedicated, curiously enough, to a gentleman of the same name as Dr Maturin, a relative, no doubt.

Captain Duff sat immediately opposite him and they exchanged a few amiable words; but the table was too wide and the sound of talk too powerful for more. Yet from time to time, when his neighbours were engaged elsewhere, Stephen considered his face, demeanour, and conversation: Duff was an unusually good-looking, manly fellow of about thirty-five, rather larger than most, with no hint of those traits usually associated with unorthodox affections; he seemed to have been totally unmoved by the Commodore's ribaldry and at times Stephen wondered whether the *Stately*'s officers were not mistaken. He was obviously a friendly man, as were so many sea-officers, willing to please and to be pleased: a good listener. And Stephen knew that he had fought one of his commands, a thirty-two-gun twelve-pounder frigate, with great distinction. Yet there were moments when a certain anxiety seemed to appear, a certain desire for approval.

'If his officers are right,' reflected Stephen, when they had drunk the loyal toast, 'how I hope that Jack's wholly candid and innocent remark will serve as warning enough.'

The whole gathering took coffee on the poop, standing about with little cups in their hands and delighting in the breeze. Before taking his leave of the Commodore, Duff came over and said he hoped he might see something of Dr Maturin ashore, when they reached Sierra Leone. 'I hope so too, I do indeed,' said Stephen, 'and I very much look forward to making acquaintance with the birds, beasts and flowers. We have a young officer aboard who knows the country well, and I have asked him to tell me about them.'

But it was long, long before Mr Whewell could tell the Doctor what he knew about the West African mammals, since day after day he was closeted with the Commodore and his chief officers as the squadron sailed slowly south.

Ordinarily this was the most agreeable part of a voyage in a well-found ship, this rolling down the Trades in warm but not yet oppressive sunshine, never touching sheet nor brace, the people making their hot-weather clothes on deck by day and dancing on the forecastle in the evening; but now everything was changed, utterly changed, changed beyond the memory of the oldest hand aboard. The Commodore, well seconded by most of his captains, started working up the squadron. 'There is not a moment to be lost,' he observed, having heaved out the *Thames*'s signal to make more sail; and indeed there was not. Even his own ship, though far superior in gunnery with her strong contingent of old Surprises, was not nearly as brisk as the *Thames* in lowering, manning and arming all boats, and many a harsh word on this subject did Captain Pullings utter to his lieutenants, master's mates and midshipmen – words that were earnestly passed on, sometimes with an almost excessive warmth. This lowering down of boats at great speed, like the shifting of topgallantmasts in thirteen minutes fifty-five seconds or striking them in two minutes twenty-five seconds, was one of those harbour exercises that commanders on the West Indies station excelled in; and although the *Thames*'s people did not seem to know what to do with their boats once they were in the water apart from pulling them, their speed vexed the rest of the squadron to the very heart.

Day after day they toiled at the great-gun exercise, at small-arms practice, and at this full-blown boat-drill, which often included shipping carronades in their larger craft. And all these activities, which could be, and which were, accurately timed, were of course carried out in addition to all ordinary duties; and although they wore the people into something like a state of torpor in the early days, there was a striking drop in the number of defaulters throughout the squadron, even in the *Thames*, that unhappy ship: almost no drunkenness, no fighting, and no murmuring (a graver crime than either).

Emulation came violently into play from the very beginning, and Stephen once saw his old mild fat and bald friend Joe Plaice fling his hat on the deck, stamping on it with a vile oath, when the blue cutter's midshipman, having worked out the agreed handicap, stated that the *Laurel* had beaten them by six seconds in crossing upper yards. Indeed, Jack Aubrey, who saw the stony looks with which his bargemen were received, sometimes wondered whether the rivalry might not be growing too high altogether; but he had no great time for abstract thought, since he spent the clear of his day with Whewell, John Woodbine (the *Bellona*'s master and an excellent navigator), Mr Adams, and sometimes Tom Pullings, going over the charts, noting all Whewell's observations, collating them with his Admiralty papers, and trying in his inner mind to work out a brief, initially startling campaign against the slavers, a campaign that would impress public opinion. But brief, brief: it had to be brief. He was obsessed with the dread of missing his appointment with the French, the whole real meaning of the expedition, and he knew – who better? – that virtually the whole of the African coast with which he was concerned, particularly the dreaded Bights, was unreliable from the point of view of wind. If he were to cut things at all fine and find the squadron, on its way north for the meeting, caught in the doldrums, sails flaccid, no steerage-way, while the French were racing north-east towards Ireland from some point near the Azores (for they were to make a feint in that direction, as though they were to attack the West Indies), he would hang himself from the maintop. On the other hand, he must do as much as possible of what he was sent to do, and be seen and heard in the act of doing it.

With Gray's death there was a vacancy among the *Bellona*'s lieutenants, and he filled it by giving Whewell an acting-order. As he knew it would, this grieved some of his own young men most bitterly, since an acting-order given by a commodore was almost invariably converted into a full commission by the Admiralty; but he could not do without Whewell's quite exceptional knowledge and contacts, his understanding of affairs, tribal and mercantile, right down the coast, his languages. Furthermore, even before growing used to Whewell's hideous smile he had come to like the man, not only for his clear-minded, intelligent accuracy and his officer-like understanding of the sea, but for himself. These planning sessions often overflowed the set meal-times and Jack and his colleagues would carry on right through dinner or even on occasion skip the sacred meal itself.

This threw Stephen back to his natural place in the ship's economy: the surgeon was a member of the wardroom mess. Yet although the *Bellona*'s wardroom was a long, handsome apartment, with a noble stern-gallery of its own, it was somewhat crowded: as a pennant-ship she carried an extra lieutenant and an extra Marine officer, so that when Stephen appeared, usually rather late, he was the thirteenth guest, which made his messmates and all the servants most uneasy. Then again, he had so rarely eaten there before that they scarcely knew what to make of him: he was known to be the Captain's and the Commodore's particular friend, and he was said to be richer than either – a further cause for reserve, all the more so since he possessed little in the way of small-talk and was often absent in spirit.

In short, he felt something of a restraint on the gathering, which curiously enough contained not a single one of his old shipmates; and since he also found the roaring mirth and interminable anecdotes of two of the Marine lieutenants and the purser's card-tricks somewhat oppressive, he took to coming in towards the end of the meal and either eating a scrap there or taking it away in a napkin to his official surgeon's cabin, far below, on the orlop.

All this time, all this voyage from Corunna, Stephen's entire being had been deeply suffused with happiness, waking and sleeping; a subjacent happiness always ready to become fully conscious. Yet at present it was accompanied rather than tinged with a mild regret for the seafaring life he had known, the life of a village where one knew all the other inhabitants and by force of long acquaintance came to like virtually all of them: a village whose geography, though complex, followed a marine logic of its own and eventually grew as familiar as that of a house.

A two-decker, however, was a town, and a very long commission would be needed to create anything like the same interdependence and fellowship among its six hundred people, counting supernumeraries, if ever it did so at all. He had known the *Worcester*, of course, and the horrible old *Leopard*; but the first was so short and variegated an experience, and the second, little bigger than a heavy frigate, had led to such a wealth of discoveries in natural philosophy among the creatures and the sparse vegetation of the Antarctic, that they scarcely formed the other half of the comparison.

'It is not only the vast size that makes the essential difference,' he reflected, leaving his cabin to take some air before his rounds, 'but the intrusion of another dimension, this additional floor, or deck.'

As the words formed in his mind and as his feet moved him up the ladder so his head rose above the floor, or deck, in question and once again in his sea-going life he was perfectly amazed and rapt in admiration. All the gunports were open wide; brilliant light from the declining sun reflected from the calm, rippling sea flooded the whole vast clean space – a prevailing tone of light brown, subtly varied by the masts – and on either side its exact rows of great thirty-two-pounder guns, while the far end was closed by the canvas screen of his sick-berth, the whole, in its perfect ordered simplicity making an enormous still-life, as satisfying as he had ever seen.

'What kind of an exercise can have brought about this beautiful state of affairs?' he asked. Exercises, exercises of every kind, were always taking place throughout the squadron, as he knew very well from the casualties brought below – sprains, crushed toes, the usual hernia or so, and powder-burns – but what could have caused this splendid luminous vacancy, smelling of salt and tar and slow-match, he could not tell.

The still-life changed as he contemplated it, changed quite surprisingly with the appearance of a small boy who dropped bodily through a hatchway right forward and came running aft. 'There you are, sir,' he cried, perfectly sure of his welcome. 'I have been looking for you everywhere. Commodore's compliments, if you please, and should be happy to see Dr Maturin on the poop at his leisure.'

'Thank you, Mr Wetherby: pray tell the Commodore, with my respects, that as soon as I have looked into the sick-berth I shall do myself the honour of waiting on him upstairs.'

'Why, Stephen, there you are,' cried Jack. 'I have not seen you this age. How do you do?'

'Admirably well, I thank you. My sick-berth gives me great satisfaction. But,' he went on, turning Jack to the light and peering up into his face, 'I cannot congratulate you on your looks.'

'You have never yet congratulated me on my looks at any time: it would make me uneasy if you were to begin now.'

'No. But now the sickly pallor of thought, to which I am not accustomed, is superadded: of thought, study, and watching. Let me see your tongue. Very indifferent. Oh very indifferent; and an ill breath too – fetid. Have you omitted your morning swim, your forenoon climb to the various eminences, your three-mile pacing before quarters?'

'Yes, I have. The first because of the unreasonable number

of sharks – Whewell says they always swarm in slaving waters – and the rest because I have scarcely stirred from the cabin. I have been working out a plan of campaign with great attention and urgency, because, do you see, although I mean to do all that can be reasonably expected in the slavery line, I want to do it quick, leaving all possible time for the rest – you understand me. A pretty set of Jack Puddings we should look, arriving after the fair.'

'I do most earnestly hope that you are satisfied with your progress?'

'Well, Stephen, it sounds boastful, but I must admit I am. With the help of that excellent young man Whewell, Tom and Mr Woodbine and I have worked out a series of movements that, given moderate luck, should be quite successful. The only thing I very much regret is that I see no possibility whatsoever of making a prodigious great thundering din on our first arrival, as their Lordships desire me to do.'

Lowering his voice and steering the Doctor right aft so that they stood by one of the splendid great stern-lanterns, swaying to the even pitch and roll, he went on, 'It may seem wicked, even blasphemous, to say that my orders might have been written by a parcel of landsmen, accustomed to the regularity of travelling by stage-coach, or by navigation on an inland canal: yet on the other hand some of the lords *are* mere landborne politicians, and anyhow the orders pass down through the secretary, that ass Barrow, to a number of clerks who may never have been afloat at all – but all that to one side. I have received orders that make no account of wind or tide before this, and so have all other sea-officers. I do not complain. But what I really cannot understand is that the Ministry should expect me to take the slavers by surprise when our expedition has been advertised to the world in half a dozen daily sheets, including *The Times*. For do not tell *me* that those paragraphs appeared without Whitehall's knowledge. No: the only thing that I can think of doing is to have a full-blown great-gun exercise as soon as we are lying before the town. At least that will make an infernal uproar. But it is vexing, for Whewell tells me that as soon as the preventive squadron was withdrawn the trade started again, even in the Gallinas river, and on Sherbro Island, right next to Freetown, and with a little discretion we might have seized on half a dozen, loading slaves in the estuary. However, I shall send the *Ringle* in tomorrow to have some powder waiting for us. It is only a day's sail for her, with this breeze.'

'May you not be doing the Ministry an injustice, my dear? Conceivably they reflected that whereas the French intelligence people are among the most attentive readers of *The Times* and the *Post*, few slavers in the Bight of Benin subscribe to either; and that the French, convinced that you are busy south of the tropic line – a conviction reinforced by reports of the noise in question – will carry on with their knavish tricks, their plans, in spite of the sailing of this squadron.'

'Oh,' cried Jack. 'Do you really think that could be so?'

'I have known the stratagem succeed: but it has to be used with great delicacy, lest the overreacher find himself overreached.'

'Well, I was certainly overreached, though I have a tolerable knowledge of the world, I believe. There are no doubt some uncommon deep old files in Whitehall, and I had better keep to navigation and the fiddle. Lord,' – laughing heartily – 'there I was, setting up for a political cove.' They paced for a while, and then he said, 'I tell you what it is, Stephen: ever since you told me about that good-natured, honest fellow Hinksey, music has been fairly bubbling up in me. Shall we play this evening?'

Dr Maturin had many of the virtues required in a medical man: he listened to what his patients had to say; he wished even the most repulsive of them well, once they had committed themselves to his care; he was indifferent to their fees; and with a great deal of reading and a great deal of experience, he was fully aware of the narrow limits of his powers – an awareness that on occasion he disguised, but only to keep their spirits up (he was a great believer in the healing powers of cheerfulness, if not of open mirth). Yet he had some faults, and one was a habit of dosing himself, generally from a spirit of inquiry, as in his period of inhaling large quantities of the nitrous oxide and of the vapour of hemp, to say nothing of tobacco, bhang in all its charming varieties in India, betel in Java and the neighbouring islands, qat in the Red Sea, and hallucinating cacti in South America, but sometimes for relief from distress, as when he became addicted to opium in one form or another; and now he was busily poisoning himself with coca-leaves, whose virtue he had learnt in Peru.

These he chewed with a little lime, carrying the leaves in a leather pouch and the lime in a heart-shaped Peruvian silver box: but of late he had seemed to observe a diminution in their powers, possibly caused by long keeping. He did not appear to feel quite the same markedly anaesthetic effect in his mouth and pharynx: it might be no more than the result of long habituation, but he resolved that as soon as the squadron was within reach of Brazil he would send over for a new supply, and this evening, since he wished to play particularly well, he took an unusually large dose. He did play well: they both played well, and they thoroughly enjoyed their music. But whereas the Commodore, heavy with work, port and toasted cheese, went straight to sleep the moment his head touched the pillow of his swinging cot, Stephen found the wakeful coca-leaves as active as ever – they far outdid coffee in banishing even the thought of sleep – and as he wished to write up his notes in the morning he took a powerful sleeping draught, together with a bolus of Java mandragore, and thrust balls of wax deep into his ears against the ship noises, the changing of the watch, the eventual holystoning, scrubbing and swabbing of the decks, the screech and thump of the pumps. Long practice had made him proficient at this exercise; but he was in some ways a simple creature and he had never perceived that on every succeeding Lady Day he was a year older, and that he was now exhibiting a vigorous young man's dose for a middle-aged body.

It was often difficult to wake him in these circumstances. Today it was harder still.

'I beg pardon, sir,' said Wilkins, the senior master's mate, to Harding, now the *Bellona*'s first lieutenant, 'but I can't wake him. I plucked off the clothes – he offered to bite, and then curled up again, though we both hallooed in his ear and shook the cot.'

It was Killick who brought him on deck at last, partly washed, partly clothed, but unshaven; stupid, sullen, blinking in what light there was.

'There you are, Doctor,' cried Jack, very loud. 'Good morning to you. I hope you slept?'

'What's afoot?' asked Stephen, peering heavily about. The squadron was hove to, and in their midst, with her topsails struck, lay a shabby merchantman, wearing Spanish colours, somewhat to the windward of the *Bellona*. As he looked so the breeze wafted a sickening reek across the deck, and he was not surprised to hear Jack say, 'She is a slaver. Mr Whewell knows the vessel, the *Nancy*, formerly belonging to Kingston but lately sold. The master is coming aboard. I should like you to make out his nation if you can, and look at his papers, if they are foreign.' ('Lord, how I hope he is a wrong 'un,' he added in a private undertone.)

Aboard the slaver smoke was already pouring from the galley; large numbers of black, naked women, girls and children stood about the deck; the boat was slowly lowered down, and as the rim of the sun blazed above the horizon the master came across with his papers and an interpreter.

'Do you speak English, sir?' asked Captain Pullings.

'Very little, señor,' said the master in a foreign accent. 'Him interpret.'

'You speak Spanish, however?' said Stephen in that language.

'Oh sí, sí, señor,' with an attempt at cheerful ease.

They exchanged a few sentences. Stephen held out his hand for the passport, and after a glance he tossed it overboard. The man uttered a howl and made as though to dive after it, but checked at the view of the populated sea. 'He is an imposter,' said Stephen. 'An Englishman. He knows no Spanish. His papers are false. You may safely seize the ship.' And to Jack, 'Let us go across.'

Jack nodded and called to Whewell. 'There is nothing like the dawn for these discoveries,' he said as they pulled over the water in his barge. 'Time and again I have found a prize, and to leeward too, just before the first light.'

But his voice changed entirely as they neared the slaver: the stench grew worse, the water still more filthy, and he fell abruptly silent at the sight of two small girls, grey and dead, going over the side. For a moment they were disputed by sharks hardly longer than themselves, until a huge fish, gliding from under the keel, tore them apart.

The negroes did not understand what was happening; they had no notion of rescue, but only of some change of captivity, probably for the worse; they were frightened; at the same time they were desperate for their food and water. Whewell tried to reassure them in a variety of languages and the lingua franca of the Coast: apart from some of the small children, they did not believe him.

The men had not been let out yet, but now the hatches were lifting and the first group came staggering up the ladder, still writhed and bent from their all-night crouch with headroom of two feet six inches at the best. Jack, Stephen, Whewell and Bonden went down into the unbreathable fetor, watched nervously by the slaver's hands, who held their whips in an uncertain, awkward fashion. The slaves farthest aft came out, scarcely looking at them, rubbing knees and elbows and galled heads: they were chained in pairs: their expressions upon the whole were inhuman – apathy with underlying dread – but no evident single emotion.

The files seemed endless, scores and scores of bowed, thin, wretched men, naked and a lightless black; but in time it thinned and almost stopped. Whewell said, 'Now we have reached the sick, no doubt. They are always stowed forward, where there is a little air through the hawse-holes. Perhaps you would like to come and see, Doctor?'

Stephen, who had known some shocking prison infirmaries, lunatic asylums and poor-house wards, had a professional armour; so, from his voyages in a slaver, had Whewell; Jack had none – the gundeck amidships in a hard-fought fleet action, the slaughter-house as it was called, had in no way prepared him for this, and his head swam. He walked forward doggedly after them, bowed under the low beams: he heard Stephen give orders for the removal of the irons, saw him examine several men too weak to move, in the dim light and stifling air, understood him to say that there was dysentery here, that hands were needed, water and swabs.

He reached the deck; the slaver's men looked at him in dismay, and in a strangled, savage, barking voice he ordered six below with buckets and swabs, six to the pumps, and four to look alive there in the galley – all whips overboard. Some of the slaves looked at him, but without much curiosity; some were already washing; most sat there on the deck, still bowed.

'*Bellona*,' he hailed.

'Sir?'

'Send that fellow over, with his men. A file of Marines and an officer; the armourer and his mate. The surgeon's assistants.'

He called for the ship's steward, told him to spread all the cabin bedding out on deck, and as the sick came up, supported or carried, he had them laid upon it. The *Nancy*'s master came aboard. 'Take this swab,' said Jack, bending over his appalled face as he climbed the side. 'Take this swab and clean up below, clean up below, clean up below.'

There was never at any time the least question of disobedience in the slaver: on the contrary, all hands showed an obscurely disgusting zeal. And now, as the Marines took up their station, a double rank right aft, with their muskets at their sides, food was coming from the galley in mess-kits for ten, and the slaves formed their habitual groups, almost filling the deck: five hundred at the least.

'Mr Whewell,' said Jack, 'can you tell them that they are not to be harmed, nor to be sold, but to be set free when we reach Sierra Leone in a couple of days?'

'I shall try, sir, with what smattering I possess.' This he did, loud and clear, in several versions. Half a dozen black men showed some interest, some comprehension: the rest ate wolfishly, their eyes fixed on vacancy or on a world that had no meaning.

'Mr Whewell,' said Jack again, 'are you of opinion that it would be safe to knock off their irons?'

'Yes, sir, so long as the Marines are here. But I believe the hands should be taken off before nightfall: and a strong prize-crew, well-armed, would prevent any trouble in the darkness.'

Jack nodded. 'If there is anything the Doctor needs – boats, hammocks, stretchers or the like' – for Stephen had set up a sick-berth in the ravaged cabin – 'let Captain Pullings know at once. You will be relieved before the end of the watch. Davies,' he said to one of his bargemen, a big, ugly, violent seaman who had followed him from ship to ship, 'you see that those fellows at the pumps and down below are kept busy. You may start them if they are slack in stays.'

He returned to the *Bellona*, took off all his clothes, stood long under a jet of clear water, retired to his cabin and there sat considering, revolving the possibilities open to him, thinking closely, taking notes, and writing two letters to Captain Wood at Sierra Leone, the one official, the other private.

During this time, or part of it, Stephen sat with Whewell on the slaver's capstan, the wind being abaft her quarter and the air clean as the squadron stood south-east. He was reasonably satisfied with his patients; he had put salve and clean linen on many and many an iron-chafed wrist, and there was a somewhat more human feeling on the well-fed deck.

'From your experience, would you say that this vessel was in a very bad condition?' he asked.

'Oh no, not at all,' said Whewell. 'For a ship fourteen days out of Whydah, I should say she was doing rather well. No. It is ugly, of course, and I believe the Commodore was sadly shocked; but there was little dysentery, and that in an early stage and it can be far, far worse. Perhaps the ugliest I ever saw was a brig called the *Gongora* that we chased for three days, off the coast. All that time the slaves were of course kept below – no food, precious little air with her running before the wind – and when at last we took her and opened the hatches there were two hundred dead below: dysentery, starvation, suffocation, misery, and above all fighting before they grew too weak to beat one another to death with their irons. The wretched brig carried almost equal numbers of Fantis and Ashantis, mortal enemies who had been at war, each side selling its prisoners in the same market, and they crammed in together.'

'I beg pardon, sir,' said a tall master's mate, rising up the side, 'but I am come to relieve Mr Whewell. The Commodore wishes to see him when he has washed and changed.'

'Mr Whewell,' said Jack, 'correct me if I am wrong, but I believe it is the rule at Sierra Leone to saw captured and condemned slavers in half, with an estimated auction-price being distributed as prize-money.'

'Yes, sir. Formerly the really fast craft were simply bought by the merchants and used again in the trade.'

'Very well. You have also told the Doctor and me about the Kroomen, described as capital seamen, pilots for various stretches of the Coast, intelligent and reliable.'

'Yes, sir. They have always had that reputation, and I

have found them to deserve it through and through. I have had a great deal to do with them, ever since I was a boy. And what is more, most of them speak Coast English well and understand it even better.'

'I am glad to hear it. Now here are two letters for Captain Wood, the Governor. I ask him to have this ship, this *Nancy*, condemned at once, out of hand, and for her to be moored in the roads once she is empty. And I ask him to have a powder-hoy, a loaded powder-hoy, ready for me when the squadron arrives. If he will do these things, and I have little or no doubt of it, I desire you to use your very best endeavours to recruit at least one good Krooman for each of the squadron's boats from the six-oared cutter up, in order to guide them by night to raid Sherbro Island and perhaps the Gallinas river. Do you think this feasible, Mr Whewell?'

'With this steady leading breeze, perfectly feasible, sir. And I have no fear for the Kroomen. There is a Kroo town in Sierra Leone with some hundreds of them, men I have known these five and twenty years; and they hate slavery – will have nothing to do with it.'

'I am very happy to hear you say so. Mr Adams will give you your order and whatever money you judge necessary for the Kroomen. You will go aboard the *Ringle* as soon as possible and proceed to Sierra Leone without the loss of a minute. Take Mr Reade with you: he handles her beautifully. And you may carry a press of sail, Mr Whewell. Good day to you.'

Chapter Eight

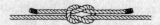

Late in the afternoon dark clouds, remarkably dark clouds, began gathering over the hills behind Freetown; they progressed against the wind for an hour until half the sky was black and the heat still more oppressive. Then much the same happened in the west, out at sea, but now the clouds were darker still, a fine solid black; and as the sea-breeze set in they swallowed the low sun entirely and hurried across to cover the whole sky with a hot, lowering pall.

The sea-breeze also brought in five ships, dimly seen but undoubtedly men-of-war bound for the Cape and India: the powder-hoy that had sailed from the naval yard would certainly have been for them. And since a number of Kroomen had also put off in a schooner it was likely that among them was a merchantman, taking advantage of their protection until she turned off eastwards, trading along the Grain Coast, the Ivory Coast and the Gold Coast for pepper, palm-oil, elephants' teeth and gold-dust. There were some foolish rumours that the preventive squadron was back, rumours based on the bringing-in and instant condemnation of the *Nancy*, now lying in the road; but they were dismissed on the grounds that the *Nancy* had been brought in by the Governor's own sloop, no doubt acting as a privateer – Captain Wood, like his predecessors, could grant a commission: and who was more likely to do so than such a knowing officer? Besides, who had ever heard of the preventive squadron possessing a two-decker? For even in this light – a light that might well presage the end of the world – not one, but *two* of these important ships could be seen.

'Thou art the father of lies,' said a Syrian merchant.

'Nothing whatsoever can be seen in this light, or rather this darkness visible. Though I admit it is very like the death of time.'

'Thou art the offspring of an impotent mole and a dissolute bat,' replied his friend. 'I can distinctly make out two decks on the second from the front: and on the third. They all appear to be bearing down on the *Nancy*.'

'Balls,' said the first merchant. But hardly were these words out before the first of the line turned to starboard until her side was parallel with that of the *Nancy* and at a distance of two hundred yards she let fly with a rolling broadside whose brilliant flashes lit the whole mass of cloud and whose voice, having deafened the town, roared to and fro among the hills. In the space of three astonished exclamations, no more, the whole of this was repeated, but with even greater force, with stronger, longer stabs of fire and the deeper, louder voice of thirty-two-pounder guns: and so it went, right along the line of ships until the last. The silence, with powder-smoke still billowing across the bay, was strangely shocking, and birds flew in every direction. But after the briefest pause there rose a universal sound of shrill amazement from the whole wide-scattered town, followed by conjecture: it was the French; it was the Patriarch Abraham come again; it was the captain of an English man-of-war enforcing the law against slavery. He had caught the wretched Knittel of the *Nancy* sailing under Spanish colours, had chained him and all his men to the mast and was now shooting and burning them to death. This explanation gained general support as the squadron wore and came back again, now thundering and bellowing two ships at a time, so that the spectators, the entire population of Freetown, could scarcely hear their own voices, though raised to a most uncommon pitch. And during the pause between this run and the next, when once again the starboard broadsides uttered their prolonged and deliberate roar, the *Bellona* alone flinging several hundred and twenty-six pounds of iron at each discharge, the news spread from deafened ear to deafened ear that Kande Ngobe, who had a telescope, had clearly seen the mutilated victims in their chains: so had Amadu N'Diaje, the clear-sighted man; so had Suleiman bin Hamad, who stated that some were still alive.

So was the wretched vessel: her side pierced through and through, she lay there yet, very low on the smooth sea, but, since she had never showed a strake below her waterline, still afloat. Yet now, after another prodigious crescendo that lit the sky and the town, filling the streets with shadows, the line moved in for the short-range carronades to come into play, and another voice of war was heard, the high-pitched barking crack of the genuine smasher, firing much faster than the great guns and with heavier shot than most, so fast and so heavy that the slaver could stand no more than a single passage before sliding down and down into sea now strangely thick with sand, as thick as a moderate gruel, the result of conflict between the changing tide and a local current.

'House your guns, house your guns, there,' the cry came down the line, and the grinning crews housed the hot cannon trim and taut. Supper was at last served out, shockingly late: and when all hands had anchored ship in twenty-five-fathom water the watch below turned in, still smiling; for firing live, and at such a target, was one of the most gratifying occupations in a seaman's life.

'No Ministry could have asked for a greater éclat, a greater din,' said Stephen, still rather loud, as they sat in the reconstituted, but still powder-smelling, cabin. 'Nor a more convincing proof of the squadron's presence.'

'It really was a right Guy Fawkes' night,' said Jack. 'I am infinitely obliged to James Wood for arranging things so cleverly and with such discretion – there were a score of details that I had not thought of at all, any one of which would have blown the gaff – that brilliant stroke of sending his own people out to bring the *Nancy* in, for example.'

'A brilliant stroke indeed. Brilliant.'

'Yes. But if the breeze sets in up the coast, as they swear

it will, I believe our Guy Fawkes' night will be put in the shade by tomorrow evening. I believe we may bring off such a stroke against the trade that Wilberforce and . . . what's his name?'

'Romilly?'

'No. The other one.'

'Macaulay.'

'Just so. That Wilberforce and Macaulay will skip and clap their hands and get as drunk as lords.'

Well before the first dog-watch the next day all points of vantage in all the ships and vessels under Jack Aubrey's command were filled with hands gazing fixedly at the cape that closed the bay; for round it, round Cape Sierra Leone itself, their friends, who had slipped away at the height of the gunfire, should soon reappear with the present kindly breeze, bringing with them shore-leave and perhaps the promise of prize-money to make the leave still more delightful. But prize-money to one side, it was the liberty itself that was so wonderfully desirable: there were the delights of palm-trees for those who had never seen them, and the young women of the Coast were said to be friendly. Chastity weighed sadly on all hands; besides, there might be fresh fruit for the picking. But in the present state of things, there was no such thing as liberty for ships moored right out in the bay – the few little blood-boats and the like were fit only for one officer at a time, or at the most two thin ones – no such thing as liberty without the squadron's boats.

The cheering began aboard the *Aurora*, most to seaward of the anchored line, and quickly it spread right along the squadron as all the boats came into view, escorting an improbable number of prizes: at least five schooners, two brigs and a ship.

The Governor's sloop left harbour to guide the prizes in before the eyes of the whole assembled town, even more astonished now than they had been the night before: never had such a catch been seen, nor even anything remotely like it. Those who had interests in the slave-trade, and they were not a few, turned pale or grey or yellow, as was convenient, silent, haggard and mournful, for they recognized each one of the captured vessels – they could not be mistaken. But most of the other inhabitants were excited, full of joy, smiling, talkative, not, except in the case of the Kroomen, from any zeal for the abolitionist cause, but from a candid, heartfelt pleasure at the thought of the money that would flow into and out of the seamen's pockets. The bounty of £60 for a man-slave released, £30 for a woman and £10 for a child would already mean a considerable sum from the *Nancy* alone: from this new and unparalleled haul it would be prodigious, even without the condemned ships themselves. And since Freetown was thoroughly used to the ways of seamen ashore, the townsmen, particularly the keepers of taverns and disorderly-houses, looked forward to their coming with lively pleasure.

This charming anticipation was felt even more strongly aboard, and when in answer to the Commodore's signal the *Ringle* and many of the boats headed for the anchorage and their mother-ships, they were greeted with renewed and even stronger cheers. In a trice they would become liberty-boats, ready and willing to waft Jack ashore, and several members of the watch below hurried off to beautify themselves, whilst others less sure of their deserts, sought out their midshipmen or divisional officers to see what an earnest plea, a becoming deference, might do, and whether fourpence might be advanced.

It was while the talk of coming joys was at its height that a horrid rumour began to spread. First a sour-faced young bosun's mate stumped into the gundeck, plucking his best Barcelona silk handkerchief from his neck. 'No liberty,' he told the world in general. 'No shore-leave after sunset in Sierra Leone. Doctor's fucking orders.'

They told him he was wrong – the rule applied to him alone, because of his ill-conduct: and splay feet: and dismal Jonah face. It was nonsense to say that there should be no liberty. But presently the news was repeated so often and by so many people that it could no longer be disbelieved. No shore-leave anywhere on the Coast after sunset: Doctor's orders, confirmed by Captain and Commodore.

'Damn the Doctor.'

'Rot the Doctor.'

'The Doctor's soul to Hell,' said the lower deck, the midshipmen's berth, and the wardroom.

The Doctor himself, busy sewing up the radiant Whewell's arm – slashed in a brief encounter and roughly bound up with a dead slaver's shirt-tail – listened to his report, his informal verbal report to the Commodore. In consultation with the lieutenant, midshipmen and warrant-officers he had divided the flotilla into four groups of about equal strength, keeping shipmates together as much as possible, two for Sherbro and two for Manga and Loas, quite close on the mainland. 'We were to go to the western market on Sherbro first, the leading boat to paddle in, the chief Krooman to hail quietly, asking was So-and-So in the way, the boat coming alongside as he talked, and the moment it touched we hurried aboard, instantly bundling the anchor-watch below, making the hatches fast and swearing they should be blown to Hell if they lifted a finger, cutting the cable and putting out to sea with as pretty a breeze as you could wish. It was as easy as kiss my hand' – Whewell laughed aloud – 'they had no guard, no notion of any possible danger, and they made no fuss. It was the same with the next three, all prime schooners – we could hardly believe it – and so till we came to the ship. We were a little slow in getting aboard, for she was under way, with all hands on deck, and there was a little trouble – that is where I got this' – nodding to his wound – 'but it amounted to nothing; and having stripped Sherbro, west and east, we joined the others in the offing and proceeded to Manga and Loas, where we did much the same; though I am happy to say, sir, that there they fired on us.'

'Very good,' said Jack with satisfaction, for any vessel firing on a man-of-war, even if she were no larger than a four-oared cutter, was guilty of piracy and therefore forfeit, whatever its colours or nation: condemned without a word. 'But no ill effect, I trust?'

'Only a few flesh-wounds, sir: for as the first brig let fly, a Portuguese, the clouds parted and they was aware how many we were, prizes and all. One tried to cut and run, but that did him no good: the rest, those that were awake, pulled for the shore like smoke and oakum in what boats they had alongside or in tow. So having cleared those two places, sir, we shut their people up below, put prize-crews aboard, and keeping them well under our lee in case of any foolish attempt, we shaped our course for home.'

'Very well done, Mr Whewell, very well done indeed,' said Jack: and after a pause, 'Tell me, what did you do about their papers?'

'Well, sir, I remembered what the Governor said about a legal quibble getting in the way of what was obviously right, and I think they were mostly destroyed in the battle or lost overboard. I did leave a couple of Portuguese captains' manifests and registers alone, to look better: not that it made any odds, since the Portuguese are not protected north of the Line. The pirates I never troubled with, but clapped them in irons directly. And now I come to think of it, sir, there was someone in Government House, one of the gentlemen of the Vice-Admiralty Court, I believe, who observed that a man who had no papers, whose ship had no papers, and who could not certainly identify the person who arrested him was in a hopeless state: he could not make out any kind of a case at all, even with the best of counsel and even if some foolish legal clause was in his favour.'

'That was your view, I believe, Doctor,' said Jack.

'There, Mr Whewell,' said Stephen, cutting his thread and taking no notice of the indiscretion. 'There. I should advise the holding of the limb in a sling for a few days, and the avoidance of anything like excess in meat or drink. A dish of eggs for dinner, or a small grilled fish, followed by a little fruit; and a small bowl of gruel before retiring, thin, but not too thin, will answer very well. And this will answer very well for a sling, too,' he went on, his eye having been caught by Jack's best superfine cambric neckcloth, draped over the back of a chair fresh from Killick's iron. 'There,' he said, inserting the wounded arm with the ease of long practice. 'Now let me ask you to recommend a reliable middle-aged Krooman, given neither to whimsies nor the drink, who will show me the way in Freetown, where I must go shortly after sunset. My dear Commodore, may I beg for a suitable conveyance?'

'My dear Doctor,' said Jack, 'I shall allow you no such thing, nor will Captain Pullings or Mr Harding or anyone else that loves you. Was you to be seen going ashore within half an hour of forbidding the same indulgence to the entire ship's company, you would be the most hated man in the squadron. I do not say they would offer much in the way of physical violence, but their affection would be killed stone dead.'

'If first thing in the morning would do, sir,' said Whewell, 'I have the very man, coming off with papers for me and Mr Adams to sign about the number of slaves released. A Krooman elder by the name of – well, their own names being hard for us to pronounce, we often call them Harry Nimble, or Fatty, or Earl Howe. Mine is known up and down the coast as John Square. The very man for you.'

Square was seaman's hyperbole, but only a pedant could have objected to Rectangular, for Whewell's Krooman was a very broad-shouldered, deep-chested man with short legs and long arms. His small round head was topped by greying wool and his face bore two blue lines on the forehead and another, broader, right across from ear to ear, but on him neither these nor his filed incisors looked any more bizarre than a ruffled shirt on a European. He was as black, or even blue-black, as a man could be, which gave his smile a more than usual brilliance; yet it was clear that he was not to be trifled with in any way.

He came at sunrise, paddling out in one of those flexible, apparently frail canoes that the Kroomen used for landing through the monstrous surf so usual along the coast, ran up the side as nimble as a boy, saluted the quarterdeck and called out, 'Papers for Lieutenant Whewell, sir, if you please,' in a tremendous bass.

He was perfectly willing to take Stephen ashore and show him anything he wished to see in Freetown; and as they made the passage, rising and falling on the long, heavy swell, Stephen asked him whether he knew the inland parts, the wild country, and the animals that lived there. Yes, said he: in his childhood he had lived part of the time at Sino, in the Kroo country, on the coast, but he had an uncle who lived far up the river, and there he spent some years when he was old enough to hunt: his uncle had showed him all manner of creatures – which were lawful, which were holy or at least protected by ju-ju, which were unclean, which were improper for a young unmarried man of his condition; and this knowledge, delightful and necessary in itself, proved of the greatest value later, when he was engaged by a Dutch naturalist to show him the serpents of the region, an engagement that allowed him to buy his first wife, a brilliant dancer and a cook.

'Serpents alone, was it?'

'Oh no, no. Deary me, no. Elephants and shrew-mice, bats, birds, giant scorpions too: but serpents first, and when I showed him a Kroo python, three fathom long, coiled round her eggs, he gave me seven shillings, he was so pleased – seven shillings and a bright red wool hat.'

'I hope he wrote a book. Oh how I hope he wrote a book. Square, will you tell me his name now, the worthy gentleman?'

'Mr Klopstock, sir,' said Square, shaking his head. 'No book.'

'No book at all?'

Square shook his head again. 'Mr Klopstock, he dead.' Poised on the back of a moderate roller he assumed a shrunken appearance, trembled convulsively and made the gesture of one vomiting in the last stages of yellow fever, all perfectly convincing and all within the seconds needed for the wave to curl, run bellowing up the shore and set the canoe down on the sand. Square stepped out, barely wetting his feet, gave Stephen a hand and hauled the canoe above the high-watermark, calling to a little Krooboy to mind it and the paddle in his singularly precise English. The Krooboy could make nothing of his words, however, and he was obliged to repeat them in the local dialect.

'So no book, sir,' said Square gravely as they walked up the strand. 'But he was a very good man, and kind to me. He taught me English, London English.'

'I believe you said he was a Dutchman.'

'Yes, sir; but he spoke English well, and he was happy to come here because he thought we spoke English too. London English. But he showed me prints of cobras, pangolins and shrew-mice, or drew them himself, telling me their names in London English. So I got used to his way of talking: like missionary. Now, sir, where would you like to go?'

'I should like to see the town a little, passing the Governor's house, the fort and the market. Then I should like to see Mr Houmouzios, the money-changer.'

It was a wide, spreading town, with most houses lying well apart in the enclosures of their own, often with palms rising high above their walls. They met few people as they walked along, and John Square, seeing that Stephen was willing to talk, went on, 'And I knew another naturalist, sir, when I was a boy: Mr Afzelius, a Swedish; and he spoke right careful London English too. He was a botany. No book, either, though he was here for years.'

'No book, alas?'

'No book, sir. When the French took the town in ninety-four they burnt his house with the rest, and all his papers and his specimens. It humbugged his heart so cruelly, he never wrote his book.'

They both shook their heads, walking in silence for a

while, until indeed they reached the market: and as they turned the corner they entered another world, crowded, busy, talkative, cheerful, full of colour – stalls with fruit and vegetables of every kind, brilliant in the mounting sun: plantains, bananas, papaws, guavas, oranges, limes, melons, pineapples, pigeon-peas, ockra, cream-fruit, sweet-sops, coco-nuts; and close-woven baskets full of rice, maize, millet, grains of Paradise, as well as yams and cassava and some sugar-cane. Fish in gleaming plenty: tarpon, cavallies, mullets, snappers, yellow-tails, old-maids, ten-pounders (thought rather coarse, said Square, though nourishing), and of course great heaps of oysters. There were grave Arabs walking about, swathed in white, and a few redcoats from the fort, and most stalls had a resident dog or cat; but the world in general was black. There were however varying degrees of darkness, from the Krooman's shining ebony to milk-chocolate brown. 'There is a Zandi from Welle, right down in the Congo,' said Square, nodding discreetly to just such a person, bargaining in passionate Sierra Leone English for a ten-pounder that did not, she claimed, weigh more than eight: 'Niminy-piminy, nutting at all,' she cried. 'And there are some Yoruba. Agbosomi you can always tell by their tattoo: they speak Ewe, same like Attakpami. See the Kondo tribal cuts on those cheeks: quite like the Grebo. There is a Kpwesi from here talking to a Mahi from Dahomey.' He pointed out many more, and said, 'All the nations that were ever sold on the Coast or round even to Mozambique live here: and there, sir, are some Nova Scotia blacks. But you know all about Nova Scotia, sir.'

'I do not,' said Stephen.

'Well, sir, they were slaves in America that fought on the King's side; and when the King's men were beat, they were moved to Nova Scotia: then after about twenty years those that were still alive after all that snow were brought here. Some had learnt Gaelic in those parts.'

'God be with them,' said Stephen. 'Now I should like to see Mr Houmouzios, if you please.'

'Aye aye, sir: right away,' said Square. 'His station is at the far corner there, under the canopy, or awning, as they say.'

Mr Houmouzios was a Greek from some far African diaspora: he sat under his awning at a table covered with saucers holding a great variety of coins, from minute copper objects to Portuguese joes worth four pounds apiece, together with delicate scales and an abacus. To his left sat a small black boy, to his right a bald dog so huge that it might have belonged to another race, a dog that took no notice of anyone at all, except those who might offer to touch the table.

'Monsieur Houmouzios,' said Stephen in French, as it had been agreed long since, 'good day. I have a letter of change for you.'

Houmouzios gazed at him mildly over his spectacles, and replying in a curiously old-fashioned but perfectly fluent Levantine version of the same language bade him welcome to Sierra Leone, looked at the document, said that he never brought such sums into the market and, in the local English, told the boy to fetch Socrates, an aged clerk. As soon as he arrived Houmouzios led Stephen to a singularly beautiful Arab house with fretted shutters and a fountain in the courtyard, and begging him to sit on a raised carpet observed that in these particular transactions a degree of identification was called for: the Doctor would forgive him for respecting this unnecessary form, but it was a superstition with people of his calling.

Stephen smiled, said, 'Oh, of course,' and felt in his pocket for some coins. He found none, and was obliged to borrow six English pennies: these he arranged in two lines and then altered the position of three so that they, always being in contact with two others, formed a circle with the third movement.

'Very good,' said Houmouzios. He drew a purse from under his shirt, told out fifty guineas, and said, 'I have heard from my chief that I may have the honour of receiving messages for you from time to time. Be assured that they too will rest in my bosom.'

'There is another small point,' said Stephen. 'Can you recommend any merchant in Freetown with correspondents in Brazil or Buenos Aires?'

'Now that the trade is illegal there is not much intercourse; but I do carry on a certain amount of banking business with export firms in Bahia – bark, rubber, chocolate, vanilla and the like.'

'Coca-leaves?'

'Certainly.'

'Then please be so good as to order me an arroba of the best upland Peruvian small-leaf. Here are five guineas as earnest-money.'

'By all means. I shall send at the first opportunity, and it should be here within a month or six weeks.'

'You are very good, sir,' said Stephen, and having drunk a cup of coffee he took his leave, pleased with the contact. So often these arrangements, these letter-boxes, had a more than squalid side to them: on occasion an intelligence-agent's life was very dangerous indeed, but what was in a way more wearing was that it almost always brought him into touch with dubious, often semi-criminal characters whose good-fellowship and conniving smiles were profoundly disagreeable. Yet arrangements of this kind, which so often had the air of shady financial deals or adulterous correspondence, were essential: even in a well-regulated embassy or legation or consulate loose talk was so usual that a parallel means of communication was an absolutely necessary evil; and Maturin was certainly not going to endanger the success of the present expedition (which he rated very high) by entrusting the enterprising Governor or his staff with anything in the least confidential.

He found Square sitting on a stone outside, and as they walked back to the strand he said, 'John Square, if you are not engaged for the next few weeks I should like you to sail with me and show me what plants, birds and animals you can whenever we go ashore. I will give you an able seaman's wages and ask Captain Pullings to enter you as a supernumerary.'

'Happy, sir, very happy,' said Square, and they shook hands upon it. After another hundred yards and some thought Dr Maturin said, 'There seemed to be an elegant swamp the other side of the town. If I can deal with my rounds early enough, we might go there this afternoon; and in the following days we may ascend the lofty hill beyond.'

Captain Pullings was quite willing to take Square aboard as a supernumerary for victuals (though not for tobacco, or the purser would grizzle and moan for the rest of the commission), and he said he might stow his canoe in the jolly-boat, as being more suitable for landing the Doctor on so rough a coast.

This was most satisfactory; so was the almost universal cheerfulness as the boats came alongside to carry the liberty-men ashore. There were a few anonymous hoots of 'What cheer, Old Saturnino?' – a nickname given him by some dissolute Maltese hands – but generally it was smiles and nods, yesterday's vehement feelings quite forgotten, while many of his older shipmates asked what they might bring him back.

Yet his rounds were less so. The great cannonade may not have killed all the slavers aboard the *Nancy* (an article of belief throughout Freetown) but it had certainly mangled several of the more impetuous and less nimble first-voyagers belonging to the squadron, in spite of their frequent exercise; and although the *Bellona*'s sick-berth was as clean and airy as that of any line-of-battle ship in the fleet, the singular damp, oppressive heat was not well suited to those who had to lie there. Wind-sails there were, well-spread and efficient wind-sails, but they could not make the air they brought down any fresher than it was on the deck, where people walked about panting and mopping themselves. Several of the wounds and burns threatened to turn ugly, and after dinner – a dinner eaten in the gasping wardroom, for Jack and his captains were all invited by the Governor, and which consisted for the main part of steak and kidney pudding – Stephen returned for another session with his assistants, amiable young men, but slow, lacking in experience. This went on until, just as he was administering a last soothing draught of hellebore, Stephen heard the sound of a returning barge, the wail of bosun's calls as the Commodore and Captain were piped aboard, the thump and clash of Marines presenting arms. 'There, gentlemen,' he said, 'now I believe we may allow the berth to take a little rest. Evans,' he said to the loblolly-boy, an aged farrier who had run away to sea, escaping from a devilish shrew, 'you will call Mr Smith at the least emergency. For my own part,' he added, 'I mean to view the swamp behind the town.'

'Well, my dear, and so you are back, I find,' he said, walking into the great cabin, where Jack was sitting at the stern-window in his shirtsleeves, with his breeches undone at the knees and waist. 'I trust you enjoyed your dinner?'

'James Wood did us proud as Pompous Pilate, bless him,' said Jack. 'Four hours, and never without a glass in my hand. Though Lord, sometimes I feel I am no longer twenty: perhaps it is the heat. Don't you find it damnation hot? Damp, close, oppressive? I suppose not, since you have a coat on.'

'I do not find the heat exorbitant or disagreeable; though I admit the dampness. You portly subjects feel it more than we spare men, men of a more elegant shape. But take comfort: they tell me that the dry season is at hand, when the air, though hotter by far on occasion, is perfectly dry, so dry that the blacks anoint themselves with palm-oil to prevent their skins from cracking: or in default of palm-oil, with tallow. Dry, and sometimes accompanied by an interesting wind, the harmattan; though that may also be the name of the season itself. As for my coat, I wear it because I mean to view the swamp behind the town, and do not choose to risk the falling damps.'

'My dear Stephen, what are you thinking of? Have you forgot your orders that no one was to go ashore after sunset? Though by the way you never told us why. It could not be the falling damps, since there are no falling damps in taverns or bawdy-houses, which is where sailors go by instinct, like the hart to the water-brook.'

'It is because of the miasmata.'

'Are they like miasmas?'

'Much the same, I do assure you, Jack; and they are at their worst after sunset.'

'Look at him now,' said Jack, nodding westwards through the stern-window, where the sun glowed red, his brilliance dimmed by the thick and heavy air. 'He will be down before you have contemplated your swamp for five minutes. No, Stephen. Fair's fair, you know. You cannot deny all hands liberty and then go rioting among the owls and night-birds yourself.'

Jack's total sincerity and conviction overcame Stephen's protests – his cries of special cases – inherent exceptions to be understood – certain qualifications to be taken for granted – and eventually he said, 'Well, I should not have seen much, anyhow; and there is always tomorrow.'

'Stephen,' said Jack, 'I grieve to say it, but as far as your great dismal swamp is concerned, there is no tomorrow. We weigh at the turn of the tide: the Governor says that with this wind the news of our coming and of our capers cannot yet have reached Philip's Island; that there are several slavers due there to complete their cargoes; and that we may catch them in the act of doing so.'

'Oh, indeed,' said Stephen, taken aback.

'We must take every possible advantage before the whole coast is warned. There is not a moment to lose; and as soon as the tide turns we can stem the current and stand out of the bay.'

Stephen could not but agree, and after a moment's cursing of his own tongue for its absolute, domineering, prating folly, its lack of ponderation and decent restraint, which would have led to provisoes, to certain exemptions for the common good, he took a turn on deck, where he was comforted first by an uncommonly numerous school of flying fishes that skimmed well above the surface, quite high in the air, there to be snapped up in the fading light by the frigate-birds, darting and flashing among them with breathtaking rapidity; and second by the fact that the Philip Island river was a fine stream, well known to Square, who said that although at the height of the rainy season it flowed broad and fast, lapping far in among the forest trees, making a fall at its mouth and a great bar, once the very heavy rains were over it began to shrink, leaving a clear bank along which one could walk through the forest, where chimpanzees were often to be seen, and beyond into the more open country, much frequented by elephants. He had also spoken of a small plain above the second set of falls almost entirely covered by baobabs, in which there lived fourteen different kinds of bat, some huge, with monstrous faces.

He was reflecting upon the delightful possibilities – the West African eagle-owl, the blue plantain-eater, the many brilliant weavers and sun-birds, conceivably even the potto, when he heard the cry 'All hands to weigh anchor,' an expected order that was instantly followed by the bosun's call and the powerful voices of his mates roaring 'All hands to weigh anchor' down the hatchways, and he hurried off to be out of the way: well did he know the frightful eagerness and activity set off by this command – the swarms of men racing across the deck regardless of those who might be in their path, the cries, the stretching forth of ropes. Coming into the cabin he found Jack sitting placidly on a locker, treating his fiddle to a fresh set of strings.

'Why, Stephen,' he said, looking up, 'I was so sorry to dash your spirits about the fetid swamp; but I dare say the miasma would have done you as much harm as an ordinary unlearned cove.'

'Not at all, my dear,' said Stephen. 'I contemplated on the delights of the Sinon, the river that comes down by

Philip's Island. I reflected upon the variety of vegetables and animals, of the very real possibility of a potto, and soon recovered my native ebullience.'

'What is a potto?'

'It is a little furry creature that sleeps all day curled up in a ball with its head between its legs and then walks about very, very slowly all night, high in the trees, slowly eating leaves and creeping up on birds as they roost and eating them too. It has immense eyes, which is but reasonable. Some call it the sluggard; some the slow lemur; some the sloth, but quite erroneously, for the two have nothing in common but their modest demeanour, their inoffensive lives. The potto is the most interesting of the primates, from the anatomical point of view. Adanson saw and dissected the potto, and I fairly long to have the same happiness.'

'Adamson of the *Thetis*?'

'No, no. Adanson, with an n. A Frenchman, though to be sure he was of Scotch origin. Surely, Jack, I have told you of Adanson?'

'I believe you have mentioned the gentleman's name,' said Jack, concentrating on the peg of his D string, always awkward and crossgrained in this rough old sea-going instrument, above all in damp weather.

'He was a very great naturalist, as zealous, prolific and industrious as he was unfortunate. I knew him in Paris when I was young, and admired him extremely; so did Cuvier. At that time he was already a member of the Académie des Sciences, but he was very kind to us. When he was little more than a youth he went to Senegal, stayed there five or six years, observing, collecting, dissecting, describing and classifying; and he summarized all this in a brief but eminently respectable natural history of the country, from which I learnt almost everything I know of the African flora and fauna. A valuable book, indeed, and the outcome of intense and long-sustained effort; but I can scarcely venture to name it on the same day as his maximum opus – twenty-seven large volumes devoted to a systematic account of created beings and substances and the relations between them, together with a hundred and fifty volumes more of index, exact scientific description, separate treatises and a vocabulary: *a hundred and fifty volumes*, Jack, with forty thousand drawings and thirty thousand specimens. All this he showed to the Academy. It was much praised, but never published. Yet he continued working on it in poverty and old age, and I like to think he was happy in his immense design, and with the admiration of such men as Jussieu and the *Institut* in general.'

'I am sure he was,' said Jack. 'We are under way,' he cried, as the ship took on a fresh, more lively motion; and Stephen, following his gaze astern, saw the *Thames*, *Aurora* and *Camilla* drop their topsails and fetch the *Bellona*'s wake as the squadron, headed by the *Stately*, moved southeastward into the coming night and a sudden violent squall of rain.

Jack tuned his restrung fiddle: they talked for a while about pitch and how some people maintained that A should sound *thus* – Jack played the note and said, 'I cannot bear it. I hate to think that our grandfathers should be such flats.' After a moment he chuckled, reflecting upon the double meaning of the word, and said, 'That was pretty good, Stephen, don't you think? Such *flats*. You smoked it, of course. But can you think of Corelli playing in that moaning, small-beer-and-water kind of whine?' Then, changing his tone entirely he went on, 'I tell you what, Stephen: being tantamount to a flag-officer is very hard work – infinitely solitary care and toil – and if your expedition don't answer the expectations of a parcel of coves that have never been to sea in their lives you are flogged to death and buried at the crossroads with a stake through your heart; but it has its compensations. There is Tom and everybody else aboard, everybody in all His Majesty's ships and vessels under my command, skipping about, getting wet – look how it is coming down now! – hauling aft – tally and belay – laying aloft – coiling down – bees ain't in it – while we sit here like fine gentlemen, ha, ha, ha! Come, she's on an even keel now; let me call for lights, fetch your 'cello, and we'll have a tune.'

At half-past four in the morning Stephen was woken by an agitated Mr Smith: Abel Black, foretopman, starboard watch, a perfectly ordinary cracked fibula (had stumbled over a misplaced bucket in the dark) was on the point of bursting. There had been retention of urine from a wholly unrelated cause – a common calculus – ever since he was brought below; but he was a shamefaced man, and being far from his messmates, lying there between a couple of unknown larbowlines belonging to the afterguard, he had not liked to mention it early on, while in the night watches he had not liked to disturb the doctors: and now modesty had brought him to a very elegant pass indeed. Stephen knew the condition well, a frequent concomitant of some other seaman's maladies; he was also used to dealing with sailors' wonderfully uneven and complex forms of delicacy; and having dealt with the situation for the time being, he returned to bed. But not to sleep, for just as he was well into his cot and swinging easy, some dreadful voice from the depths said, 'Maturin, Maturin, you had already bored poor Jack Aubrey cruelly with your tedious account of Michel Adanson years ago, prating away in the same earnest even enthusiastic moral improving fashion for half an hour on end and he sitting there smiling and nodding politely saying, "Oh, indeed?" and "Heavens above" oh for shame. You may well blush, but blushing does no good. It is mere remorse of conscience.'

He could not recall the longitude or latitude in which he had done this, nor even in what ocean; but he could hear the sound of his own zealous voice going on and on and on, and Jack's civil replies. 'Do I often do this?' he asked in the darkness. 'Is it habitual, God forbid, or only advancing age? He is a dear, well-bred man, the creature; but will my heart ever forgive him this moral advantage?'

He slept at last, but the recollection was with him, strong

and fresh, when he woke. To dispel it he washed and shaved with particular care – it was, after all, Sunday – and went on deck to take the air. To his astonishment there was no land at all to be seen to larboard nor any of the smaller vessels. The squadron now consisted of the two-deckers and the frigates, and they were all, in a beautifully exact, evenly-spaced line, standing something west of south under topgallantsails with the breeze one or two points free. As he stood there a midshipman reported his reading of the log: 'Eight knots and half a fathom, sir, if you please; and Mr Woodbine reckons the current due easterly a full knot.' The officer, Mr Miller, made some reply, but Stephen missed it, his attention being wholly taken up by an eddy of wind from the forecourse that brought the scent of coffee and toast, of bacon and perhaps of flying fish, freshly fried.

He hurried aft. He had meant to give himself a certain countenance by repeating the pace of the ship and the current, but greed and affection overcame him and he cried, 'Good morning, Jack, God and Mary be with you, and would that be flying fish, freshly fried, at all?'

'A very good morning to you, Stephen. Yes, it is. Pray let me help you to a pair.'

'Jack,' said Stephen, after a while. 'I was astonished to see neither land nor the mass of our smaller companions. Would it be improper to ask how this can have come about? Have they lost their way in the dark, at last? It is but too probable.'

'I am afraid so,' said Jack. 'Yet I am sure that at least one of them had a compass aboard; and in any event, if it is broke they can always follow our light. We have three splendid green lanterns behind, as you have no doubt observed, and I dare say someone lit them.' He raised his voice: 'Killick. Killick, there. Light along another pot of coffee, will you?'

'Which I already got it in my hand, ain't I.' said Killick, outside the door.

'Another cup, Stephen?'

'If you please.'

'We separated when the breeze shifted three points in the middle watch. The brigs and schooners, keeping so much closer to the wind, are sailing right along the coast for Philip's Island when they can and beating when they can't; they are followed by *Laurel* and *Camilla*, a little farther offshore; and we are making a long south-westerly leg, meaning to go about in the afternoon watch, strike the coast beyond the island and snap up any brutes that might be trying to escape or to bear a hand if there is any trouble in the harbour, which I doubt.'

Stephen digested this for a while, and then he said, 'Jack, last night it suddenly came to me that I had told you all about Adanson before, and at great length – his assiduity, his countless books, his misfortune. I beg your pardon. There is nothing more profoundly boring, more deeply saddening, than a repeated tale.'

'I am sure you are right in general. But I do assure you, Stephen, that in this case I never noticed it. To tell the truth, I was so much taken up with my D string, which kept slipping, that I was afraid you might think my inattention uncivil. Yet I tell you what it is, Stephen: I have been talking with Whewell, and I have decided upon my plan of campaign. Should you like to hear it?'

'If you please.'

'Well, it has long seemed to me, and both Whewell and all the officers who were at Sherbro and beyond confirm it, that this is essentially an inshore task, and that there is no place at all for ships of the line or even for frigates unless they are as fast and weatherly as *Surprise*, no place except for the same purpose as those cricket-players who scout out a great way off, like the long-stop or the long field off – I mean far out at sea and to the windward of likely routes of escape, particularly towards the Havana. It is no use lying within sight of the shore: our tall masts can be seen a great way off, all the more since they had watchers stationed on the heights and in very tall trees when the preventive squadron was here, and will have again as soon as they hear of our arrival. On the whole, black men see far better than we do, you know.'

'Sure, I have observed it.'

'So as soon as we have dealt with Philip's Island I am going to station the two-deckers and *Thames* well out to sea, far out of sight of the shore but within signalling distance of one another and of smaller craft interposed: this can cover a most surprising area. At the same time the others will work right along the coast, moving as fast as ever they can to keep ahead of the news that we are here, right along the coast, while we keep pace offshore, from Cape Palmas to the Bight of Benin.'

'*Beware and take care of the Bight of Benin;*

'*There's one comes out for forty goes in,*' Stephen chanted.

'What a fellow you are, Stephen,' cried Jack, in a tone of real displeasure. 'How can you think of singing, or groaning, a foolish unlucky old song like that, aboard a ship that is *going* to the Bight? I wonder at it, after so many years at sea.'

'Why, Jack, I am sorry to have offended you – the Dear knows where I heard it – the words rose of themselves, by mere association. But I shall not sing it again, I promise you.'

'It is not that I am in the least degree superstitious,' said Jack, far from mollified, 'but everyone who knows anything about the sea knows it is a song sung in ships that have come *out* of the Bight, by way of making game of those that are going *in*. Do not sing it again until we are homeward bound, I beg. It might bring bad luck and it is certain to upset the hands.'

'I am very sorry for it, so I am too, and shall never do so again. But tell me about this Bight, Jack: are there sirens along its shores, or terrible reefs? And where is it, at all?'

'I will show you exactly on the charts in the master's day-cabin, when we pass,' said Jack, 'but for the moment,' – reaching for paper and pencil – 'here is a rough idea. I leave the Grain Coast to one side, because the noise we did make at Sherbro and that we shall make at Philip's Island will raise the whole country; but here, going east, is the Ivory Coast, with several promising estuaries and lagoons; then we carry on steadily east and a little north of east right into the Gulf, coming to the Gold Coast, with places like Dixcove and Sekondi and Cape Coast Castle and Winneba, all great markets, and so on to the Slave Coast in this great bay, which is the Bight of Benin itself – the Bight of Biafra is farther on – where the winds grow very troublesome and there is a strong current setting east – the fever very bad, too – wretched waters except for fore-and-aft vessels. But that is where so many slavers go: to Grand Popo and Why-dah. I do not think we can go much beyond Whydah, how-ever, though in the mangrove country beyond there is Brass and Bonny and the Calabars, Old and New. But by then I think we shall have to stand out if ever we can, stand due south for the Line and pick up the south-east trades about St Thomas's Island, which is clear of the Bights and their calms and false breezes. That is my plan: though I forgot to say that *Ringle* and the schooner *Active* will ply inshore and off, continually reporting, either directly or by signal to *Camilla* or *Laurel* to repeat the pennant, since they will lie between us and the inshore craft. And by the way, I am going to break poor Dick's heart by making him change his fine tall man-of-war's topmast for wretched topgallant poles – the same for *Camilla*, so that the watchers on shore will take them for common merchantmen.'

'Then as I understand it,' said Stephen, paying no atten-tion to Captain Richardson's coming distress, 'this vessel, this *Bellona*, is not even to see the coast throughout the entire expedition.'

'Only in the very unlikely case of a row that the brigs and *Camilla* and *Laurel*, mounting sixty guns and more between them, cannot deal with. Though of course one might catch the odd glimpse of mountains from the topgallant crosstrees from time to time.'

233

Stephen turned away, his arm over the back of his chair.

'You are grieving about your potto I am afraid,' said Jack after an awkward silence. 'But you will have a fine run ashore tomorrow, when we have dealt with whatever is lying in the harbour of Philip's Island. And I dare say you could go in occasionally when the *Ringle* comes out to report or carry orders back. Though if it comes to that, you could always exchange with the surgeon of *Camilla*, *Laurel*, or one of the inshore brigs.'

'No. They have tied me to a stake: I cannot fly, but bear-like I must fight the course,' said Stephen with a creditable smile. 'Not a very dreadful course, for all love: it is only that I was so extravagantly indulged in the East Indies and New Holland and Peru. No, not at all. Now one more cup of coffee and I must attend to my calculus, nearly always a difficult subject.'

'So you have suddenly taken to the calculus?' cried Jack. 'How very glad I am – amazed – quite stunned. By just calculus I take it you mean the differential rather than the infinitesimal? If I can be of any help . . .'

'You are very good, my dear,' said Stephen, putting down his cup and rising, 'but I mean the vesical calculus, no more: what is commonly known as a stone in the bladder, the utmost reach of my mathematics. I must be away.'

'Oh,' said Jack, feeling oddly dashed. 'You will not forget it is Sunday?' he called after Stephen's back.

There was little likelihood of Stephen's being able to forget that it was Sunday, for not only did Killick take away and hide his newly-curled and powdered best wig, his newly-brushed second-best coat and breeches, but the loblolly-boy said, 'Asking your pardon, sir, but you ain't forgot it is Sunday?' while both his assistants, separately and tactfully, asked him whether he had remembered it. 'As though I were a brute-beast, unable to tell good from evil, Sunday from common days of the week,' he exclaimed; but his indignation was tempered by a consciousness that he had in fact risen from his cot unaware of this interesting distinction, and that he had shaved close by mere chance. 'Yet I should very soon have made it out,' he said. 'The atmosphere aboard a Sunday man-of-war is entirely different.'

Indeed it was, with five or six hundred men washing, shaving, or being shaved, plaiting their tie-mates' pigtails, drawing clean hammocks, putting on their best clothes for mustering by divisions and then church, all in great haste, all in a bitterly confined space with a heat and humidity great enough to hatch eggs, and all after having brought the ship and everything visible in her to an exemplary state of cleanliness if wooden and of brilliance if metal.

The Anglican aspect of Sunday did not affect Stephen, but the ritual cleanliness did, and he, with his assistants and loblolly-boy, were present, sober, and properly dressed, with their instruments laid out all agleam and their patients rigidly straight in their cots when Captain Pullings and his first lieutenant, Mr Harding, came round to inspect them. So did the convention of the Captain dining with his officers: but this did not take place until after church had been rigged – an awning shaded the quarterdeck, an ensign over an arms-chest to serve as a lectern from which prayers and sermons were delivered if the ship carried a chaplain (which the *Bellona* did not) or by the captain; though a captain might well prefer reading the Articles of War. Stephen therefore had time, after the inspection of the sick-berth, to make his way to the poop, where he had a fine view of the Royal Marines, close on a hundred of them, drawn up exactly in their scarlet and pipe-clayed glory, and of the long, somewhat more wavering lines of seamen, clean and trim, standing in their easy, round-shouldered way, covering the decks fore and aft, a sight that always gave him a certain pleasure.

During the service itself he joined other Catholics for a recital of a Saint Brigid's rosary under the forecastle: they were of all possible colours and origins, and some were momentarily confused by the unusual number of Aves, but wherever they came from their Latin was recognizably the same; there was a sense of being at home; and they recited away in an agreeable unison while from aft came the sound of Anglican hymns and a psalm. They both finished at about the same time, and Stephen walked back to the quarterdeck, overtaking Captain Pullings as he was walking into the coach, where he lived, necessarily resigning the cabin to the Commodore. 'Well, Tom,' he said, 'so you have survived your ordeal?' – As Captain of the *Bellona* he had just read one of South's shorter sermons to the people – 'I have, sir: it comes a little easier, as you said; but sometimes I wish we were just a pack of wicked heathens. Lord, I could do with my dinner, and a drink.'

Dinner, when it came, was quite exceptionally good; and for the best part of an hour before the *Bellona*'s officers and their guests sat down, a hot wind had been blowing off the land – hot, but startlingly dry, so that their uniform no longer clung to them and their appetite revived amazingly.

'This is the first blast of the dry season,' said Whewell, talking to Stephen across the table. 'The two will chop and change for about a week or two, and then I dare say we shall have a right harmattan, the decks covered with brown dust and everything splitting, and then it settles in till Lady Day.'

The conversation ran on dry seasons – far better than wet – the delight of satisfying an enormous thirst – and presently Stephen, turning to his right-hand neighbour, a Marine lieutenant from the *Stately*, said how he admired the soldiers' endurance of either extreme, standing there like images in the sun or the bitter cold, or marching, wheeling and counter-marching with such perfect regularity. 'There is something wonderfully agreeable in the sight of that self-command – or one might almost say relinquishment of self – in that formal, rhythmic precision, the tuck of drum, the stamp and clash of arms. Whether it has anything to do with war or not, I cannot tell; but the spectacle delights me.'

'How I agree with you, sir,' said the Marine. 'And it has always seemed to me that there is something far more to drill than simply training in steadiness and obedience to the word of command. Little do I know of the Pyrrhic dance, yet it pleases me to imagine that it was in the nature of our manoeuvres, only with a clearly-acknowledged, rather than a dimly-perceived, sacred function. The Foot Guards offer a fine example of what I mean, when they troop their colours.'

'The religious element in dancing can scarcely be denied. After all, David danced before the Ark of the Covenant, and in those parts of Spain where the Mozarabic rite is preserved a measured dance still forms part of the Mass.' Here Stephen was called upon to drink a glass of wine with Captain Pullings, while his neighbour joined an animated discussion on the preservation of game at the other end of the table.

The meal wound on: the first lieutenant carved a saddle of mutton and then a leg in a way that did the *Bellona* credit, and the claret decanters pursued their steady round. Yet presently even the subject of putting down pheasants and circumventing poachers was exhausted, and Stephen, finding his Marine disengaged, said, 'One thing that I do remember about the Pyrrhic dance is that it was danced in armour.'

'I am happy to hear you say so, sir,' said the young man with a smile – a strikingly handsome young man – 'for it strengthens my point, since we do the same. To be sure, we admit the degeneration that has taken place since Hector and Lysander and we have reduced our equipment in due proportion; but *mutatis mutandis*, we still drill, or dance, in armour.'

'Do you indeed?' cried Stephen. 'I had never noticed it.'

'Why, this, sir,' said the Royal Marine, tapping his gorget, a little silver crescent hanging on the front of his red coat, 'this is a breast-plate. Somewhat smaller than the breast-plate Achilles wore, but then so are our deserts.' He laughed very cheerfully, seizing a decanter on the wing, filled Stephen's glass and his own. He had not drunk the half before Tom Pullings held up his hand, and in a dead silence the cry from the masthead was repeated, coming down clear and plain through the open hatchways and gunports: 'On deck, there. Land ho! Land broad on the larboard bow.'

'Mr Harding, you will excuse me: I must acquaint the Commodore. Gentlemen, pray carry on with your dinner. In case I do not come back, thank you all for your hospitality.'

He did not come back: and since there was little point in leaving their meat to see very distant land they did carry on. The hot, almost parching wind was blowing stronger and although some officers called for negus or lemon shrub, others quenched their rising thirst with claret, and a fresh dozen had to be brought up.

In time, with the absence of the captain and the presence of a newly-promoted first lieutenant with little natural authority, the talk grew louder and much more free. Stephen and his Marine had to raise their voices for their words to be heard at all – words still connected with such things as the formal dancing of the last age in France and with drill as applied to cavalry and whole fleets – and Stephen was disagreeably aware that his neighbour was drinking, had drunk, too much, and that his attention had wandered to the conversation at the purser's end, where they were talking, often several at once, about sodomy.

'You may say what you like,' said the tall, thin lieutenant, second of the *Thames*, 'but they are never really *men*. They may have pretty ways and read books and so on, but they will not toe the scratch in a fight. I had two in a gun-crew when I was a mid in *Britannia*, and when things grew rather hot they hid between the scuttle-butt and the capstan.'

Other views were heard, other convictions and experiences, some tolerant, even benign, but most more or less violently opposed to sodomites.

'In this atmosphere I scarcely think it would be worth mentioning Patroclus or the Theban Legion,' murmured Stephen, but the Marine was too intent on the general medley of voices to pay attention: he filled another glass and drank it without taking his eyes from the group round the purser.

'You may say what you like,' said the tall, thin lieutenant, 'but even if I had the same tastes I should be very sorry to have to go into action aboard a ship commanded by one of *them*, however stately.'

'If that is a fling against my ship, sir,' cried the Marine, pushing his chair back and standing up, very pale, 'I must ask you to withdraw it at once. The *Stately*'s fighting qualities admit no sort of question.'

'I was not aware that you belonged to *Stately*, sir,' said the lieutenant.

'I see that there are others who do not choose to toe the scratch,' said the Marine; and now there was a general movement to separate the two men, general clamour, general extreme concern. Eventually both were put into their separate boats, the *Stately*'s most unhappily manned by some of her captain's young ladies.

Already the land was high and clear: the hot wind blew as strong and as fair as could be wished and the *Bellona*, *Stately* and *Thames* were nearing the point at which they should cut off any fugitive escaping from Philip's Island. But already signals were passing from the inshore brigs to the pennant by way of the *Laurel* – there were no fugitives to be cut off – the harbour was empty – the slavers were not to appear for three days, they having been delayed at Takondi, and although the barracoons, the great slave-pens, had held many negroes when the inshore force arrived, they had now been marched off.

Jack Aubrey altered course, and by the grace of the tide and the evening breeze his three ships ran straight into the harbour, conned by Square, who knew the inlets and anchorages intimately well. The signal for all captains broke out aboard the *Bellona* before her anchor was down, and the boats converged upon her in the brief tropical dusk.

After he had conferred with them he said to Stephen, 'I intend to stand out to sea again, out of sight, sending the brigs and schooners east along the coast to the Muni lagoon, to stop any coastwise boats or canoes that might carry warning, and to lay those fellows aboard as soon as they are here in the harbour. According to Whewell's predictions and to Square's – a capital seaman, that Square – and to the barometer there is a very fair chance of our catching them, three Dutchmen and a Dane, bound for the Havana. So if you like to go ashore this evening with Square you could have a couple of days naturalizing along your river: there is a little Kroo village where you could pass the night. But you would have to be here on the shore and ready to put off without the loss of a minute at high tide on Wednesday.'

'What time would that be?' asked Stephen, glowing inwardly.

'Why, at seven in the evening, in course,' said Jack, rather impatiently: even now he found Stephen's inability to adapt his mind to the rhythm of moon and tide barely credible in a man of his parts. He paused, considered, and then in quite a different tone he went on, 'Yet Stephen, I cannot but remember what you said about no shore-leave at Freetown after sunset, because of the miasmas and noxious exhalations, and I do beg you will take the utmost care – stay indoors, and walk out only when the day is aired.'

'Thank you for your care of me, my dear,' said Stephen, 'but never let the climate grieve your generous heart. Freetown has a deathly fever-swamp at hand: even horses cannot live long in Freetown. But I shall be walking by a broad brisk river with falls, and miasmata are not to be feared by running water. It is your stagnant pool that engenders fever. Now I must arrange my collecting-bags and paper sheets, choose proper garments – are there leeches? – consult with honest Square and plan our route. In two days, going steady, we might pass his plain with baobabs and monstrous bats and reach the country of the potto and Temminck's pangolin!'

Chapter Nine

It was not until several days after they left Philip's Island that Stephen had a quiet evening in the cabin, to spread his hurried notes and some of his botanical specimens and begin a detailed account of his journey up the Sinon river. He had of course told Jack of the pygmy hippopotamus, the red bush pig, the froward elephant that chased him into a baobab tree, the bay-thighed monkeys, the chimpanzees (mild, curious, though timid), a terrestrial orchid higher than himself, with rose-pink flowers, the Kroo python that Square addressed in a respectful chant and that watched them, turning its head, as they paced meekly by, the seven different hornbills, the two pangolins, the large variety of beetles of course and a scorpion seven and a half inches long, together with sun-birds and weavers.

'And your potto?' asked Jack. 'I hope you saw your potto?'

'I saw him, sure,' said Stephen. 'Clear on a long bare branch tilted to the moon, and he gazing down with his great round eyes. I dare say he advanced a foot or even eighteen inches while I watched him.'

'Did you shoot him?'

'I did not. I am not naturalist enough. Nor would you have done so. But I did shoot a fishing vulture that I prize; and if it prove a nondescript, as I trust it will, I shall name it after the ship.'

Those early days on the island and the opposite shore had been full of activity. There was some malarial fever already among those who had raided Sherbro, and although the captured slavers – they had sailed confidently into the harbour without the least precaution – had no more than half a cargo each, many of the negroes had been aboard since Old Calabar, and some were in a bad way. Now, however, the two Dutchmen and the Dane had been sent off with prize-crews to Freetown, and the two-deckers, together with the slow, heavy-sailing *Thames* and the *Aurora*, had weighed by night, standing out to sea, well out beyond even the highest tree's horizon, to head eastward, to the Bight of Benin, thus setting the Commodore's plan in motion. In the morning those on the *Bellona*'s quarterdeck could make out the *Laurel*'s humble topsails on the larboard beam, and the *Laurel* was in touch with the inshore brigs; all was in train; the ship settled back into ordinary daily life, and Stephen was able to arrange his specimens in some sort of order, skin his birds, and label everything before sheer quantity (it had been a rich expedition) overwhelmed fallible memory. In all this he had John Square's informed and valuable help; but when, after dinner, he sat down to the task of writing an exact account he was alone. Usually, once he had sunk into the proper mood and had marshalled all his facts he wrote quite fast; but now, although the picture of that blessed river, the clear strand between the water and the forest, and a fishing vulture overhead was exactly present in his mind, names, time of day and the sequence of events were less clear by far; and they would not easily yield to what mental effort he could bring to bear. Languor: muscular pain: incipient headache: stupidity.

He had drunk a couple of glasses of wine at dinner and a cup of coffee after, and on the supposition that this one cup had not been enough to counteract the meal he went into the great cabin, where Jack Aubrey was busy at his desk, a pot beside him.

Two more cups did produce a laboured paragraph or two, but this was nothing like the happy spontaneous flow that had been running through his head the day before. A modest ball of coca-leaves (he was husbanding his store) scarcely helped his prose but after a while it did prompt him to go to his looking-glass and put out his tongue. Alas, it was scarlet, as he had half suspected; and his eyes, though bright, had a ferrety look round the edges, while his lips might have been rouged. He felt his pulse: quick and full. He took his bodily temperature with Fahrenheit's thermometer: a little above a hundred, scarcely more than the surrounding air. He reflected for a while and then went below, where he found Mr Smith rolling pills in the dispensary. 'Mr Smith,' he said, 'in Bridgetown I make no doubt you saw many cases of the yellow fever.'

'Oh yes, sir,' said Smith. 'It was our chief killer. The young officers looked to it for promotion. They called it the black vomit, or sometimes yellow jack.'

'Would you say that there was a facies febris markedly typical of the disease?'

'Yes indeed, sir: more so than in almost any other.'

'Then be so good as to come with me when you have finished that board of pills, till I bring you to a good light.'

No light could have been better than the open gunport by which they stood, nor could any young medical man have been more convincing than Mr Smith. After he had looked at Stephen with the closest, most objective attention he quite naturally assumed the physician's liberty, raising his eyelids, desiring him to open his mouth, taking his carotid pulse, and asking the relevant personal questions. At length, look-ing very grave, he said, 'With all the reserves due to my fallibility and relative inexperience, sir, I should say that with one exception you have all the characteristics of a patient in the first stadium of the yellow fever; but I pray I may be mistaken.'

'Thank you for your candour, Mr Smith: what is the exception?'

'The visible anxiety and the strongly-felt oppression about the praecordia, which has never been absent in any of the cases I have seen, and which, in Barbados, is held to be most significant.'

'Perhaps you have never examined a patient fortified by coca, that stoical plant,' said Stephen inwardly, and aloud,

'In spite of that absence, Mr Smith, we will treat the indisposition as a case of nascent yellow fever, and I shall dose myself accordingly. Have we any calumba root left?'

'I doubt it, sir.'

'Then the *radix serpentariae Virginianae* will answer very well. I shall also take a large quantity of bark. And should the disease declare itself, Mr Smith, I formally direct that there should be no bleeding in this case, and no purging whatsoever: there is no plethora. As much warm water just tinged with coffee may be exhibited – as much as possible without gross discomfort. And sponging, mere sponging – no foolish affusion – would be beneficial at the height of the feverish stadium. Do you undertake to follow my direction, William Smith?'

'Yes, sir.' He was about to add something, but thought better of it.

'Otherwise, a dim light with what quiet a man-of-war at sea can provide, and my pouch of coca-leaves beside me is all I wish. In spite of the estimable Dr Lind and several others I do not believe the yellow fever to be infectious. But rather than distress my shipmates I shall live in my cabin on the orlop for the time being. The little booth is in moderately good order, but I should be obliged if you would have it swept to some extent – not swabbed and flogged more or less dry, but *swept*: for the great shining brown West African cockroach, though interesting as an individual, grows tiresome in large numbers; and I fear they are already breeding with us.'

'Very well, sir. I shall come back as soon as the cabin is ready and aired.'

Left to himself Stephen made his slow way to the empty wardroom and sat there beside the rudder-head, gazing astern; for though this deck was denied a stern-gallery it did possess a noble breadth of windows directly overhanging the white turmoil of the *Bellona*'s wake – nothing more hypnotic, and for a while his mind sank into a familiar dreamy vagueness before returning to distinct sequential thought.

The yellow jack was indeed a killer: it was difficult to fix upon any satisfactory figure, though he had heard well-authenticated accounts of a mortality amounting to eighty in a hundred. As for material affairs, he had made what Mr Lawrence described as 'a cast-iron will' before leaving England, with some very solid gentlemen as trustees to look after Diana, Brigid, Clarissa and the others: while as for the less tangible side, his experience as a physician had shown him that all other things being equal patients who gave in, either from terror or pain or a want of spirit, want of appetite for life, did not survive, whereas those with an urgent desire to live without the loss of so much as an hour – those with an enchanting daughter, an ample fortune, a collection of almost certainly unknown phanerogams . . . 'What is it?' he cried.

'Commodore's compliments, sir,' said a red-haired youngster, so young that he was still shedding teeth, 'and would be happy to see the Doctor at his leisure.'

'My duty to the Commodore,' replied Stephen mechanically, 'and shall wait upon him directly.' He sat on for a few minutes and then stood up, dusted himself, straightened his wig and neckcloth and slowly climbed the ladder to the quarterdeck and so aft, his knees feeling strangely weak.

'There you are, Stephen,' cried Jack, while Tom Pullings leapt to his feet and set him a chair, 'how good of you to come so soon. Tom and I wanted you to look over this statement of our proceedings since arriving on the station. Perhaps you could throw in some elegant turns of phrase. Mr Adams writes a capital hand, but he is no better than we are, at your elegant turn of phrase.'

'It is only a rough draft, Doctor,' said Tom.

Stephen read for a while. 'What do you mean by expediently?' he asked. '. . . *proceeded as expediently as possible*.'

'Why, as fast as ever we could sail,' said one; and 'Like *expedition*, you know,' said the other. 'With the greatest expedition.'

'If you do not like *as fast as ever we could sail* . . .' began Stephen.

'No,' said Tom. '*As fast as ever we could sail* is low.'

'Then put *with the utmost celerity*,' said Stephen.

'*Celerity*. There's a word for you,' said Tom, smiling. 'How do you spell it, sir?' A pause. 'How do you . . . are you feeling quite well, sir?'

Startled, they both looked at him with great concern as he sat there gasping. Jack pulled the bell-line and to the answering Grimble he said, 'Pass the word for the surgeon's mate. Tell Killick to ready cot, nightshirt, chamber-pot.'

Both assistant-surgeons reported within the minute, Killick only seconds later, and in the ensuing contention the faint Stephen, weak in body and will, was overwhelmed by kindly insistence. 'Infection be damned,' said the Commodore. 'I had a touch of the yellow jack in Jamaica when I was a boy: I was salted. Besides, it ain't infectious.'

'Doctor, you do look wholly pale,' said Tom Pullings. 'Fresh air is what you need, not the stink of bilge in the orlop.'

He was overwhelmed; and after a certain amount of activity and carefully moderated noise he found himself in his familiar cot, under the shaded poop skylight, with a jug of lukewarm water tinted with coffee in reach, and his coca-leaves. His fever was mounting: his pulse was firm and rapid, his breathing fast: a grateful waft of sea-air passed over his face: he settled himself to the coming trial.

The first Stadium: the opening day of the disease, the kindest, sees much dozing, though in spite of the moderately elevated animal heat the sensation of chill returns. At this time the tongue is moist, rough. The skin moist, with an often profuse sweating.

'Pray, Mr Smith, give me a brief account of the three stadia of this malady, and their separate events. And it would be as well if Mr Macaulay were to listen and to observe the symptoms as you name them,' said Stephen.

'Well, sir, this is the second day of the first stadium, and we may expect a diminution of the animal heat – increasing restlessness and jactitation. We shall find the urine cloudy, troubled, probably bloody – dark, in any event. And although the muscular pains and heavy sweats of yesterday diminish, the patient grows increasingly despondent.'

'It is very well, very valuable, that the patient should be told this. For, gentlemen, you are to consider that if he knows his sadness to be as who should say *mechanical*, a mere part of the disease, common to all sufferers from it, and not the reasoned outcome of the working of his own mind, still less the onset of melancholia or even the result of guilt, he is very much better armed against its attack.'

'Yes, sir,' said Smith. 'Pray show me your tongue. Exactly so. This is the second day, and the middle is brown. Should you like me to hold your shaving-glass, sir?'

'If you please.'

'Tomorrow the roughness and ill colour will abate. But I regret to say that tomorrow, the third day of the first stadium, will also see heavy vomiting and great weakness.'

'The weakness is already strongly marked. Pray set the wine-glass to my lips: I can scarcely raise it, much less keep it steady.'

A party of seamen employed in setting up the foretopmast shrouds, loosened by the onset of the dry season, saw their midshipman reach out for a backstay and slide down on deck, presumably to go to the head. They relaxed, and one of the simpler hands, returning still again to the gossip of the ship, said, 'So the Doctor would not let *us* go ashore for fear of the fever: and it's *him* has got the yellow jack, oh ha, ha, ha! He wouldn't let *us* go, and now he's got it *himself*: God love us.'

'You had better not tell that to Barret Bonden,' said

another, 'or he'll serve you out like he served Dick Roe, as is laughing the other side of his face now. What face he has left.'

> The second stadium: pulse weak and declining, but no fever, indeed, the bodily heat is less than the ordinary degree of warmth. Extreme restlessness and yellow suffusion of the eyes and person. Black vomit. Still greater despondency: prostration: delirium. This stadium lasts an indeterminate number of days before either ceasing entirely or merging with the third.

It was through this prostration and this delirium – a moderate delirium, apparently checked by the coca-leaves and nearer to a waking dream than to the raving of high fever – that Stephen was continuously aware of Jack, a comforting presence, moving quietly about the room, talking now and then in a low voice, giving him a drink, holding him up to be sick, and that in one of his many lucid intervals he heard a hand on the poop say, 'Don't you breathe anywhere near the skylight, mate: surgeon lies just below, and the air that comes off of him is mortal. There is a tree in Java, which if you sleep under it, you wake up dead. This is much the same.'

'Killick says it ain't catching.'

'If it ain't catching why does the poor bugger take in the victuals at a run, holding his breath with a piece of charcoal in his mouth, and then rush out, daubing his face with vinegar and Gregory's cordial, pale and trembling? Not catching, my arse. I seen ward after ward of them die in Kingston, till the very land-crabs was sick and tired of eating them up.'

> The third stadium: pulse, though soft, becomes exceedingly small and unequal: the heat about the praecordia increases much, respiration becomes dif-

ficult with frequent sighs: the patient grows yet more anxious, and extremely restless: sweat flows from the face, neck and breast: deglutination becomes difficult, subsultus tendinum comes on, the patient picks the nap of his bedclothes. Coma may last eight, ten or twelve hours before death.

And then on another day – but how many between? – he heard the voices loud and clear, dreamlike clear: 'Loblolly-boy helped them to sponge him: says he had never seen a body so yellow: like a guinea all over, with purple spots. The doctors say if he don't look up in a couple of days they will put him over the side come Sunday, when church is rigged.'

Sunday came and went with no funeral, and on Tuesday Smith and Macaulay came and said, 'Sir, we are now convinced you have avoided the third stadium. Your pulse, though still faint, is a delight to feel, so regular and true; your excrements a pleasure to inspect. The inner loss of blood has been negligible since Friday, and already your strength is returning: you can almost raise a half-filled glass; your voice reaches the stern-gallery. It will be a long, long, very long while before you can roam the forest again, yet even so we feel that now we may properly congratulate you and give you joy of your recovery.'

'Give you joy, sir, give you joy of your recovery,' said Macaulay, and both gently shook his hand.

Long, long it was before Stephen could roam even the sleeping-cabin, but once he could really walk, and that on a moving deck, with his stick-like calfless legs, strength returned fast, and a remarkable degree of appetite. While long before he could reach the stern-gallery unaided he sickened of the state of invalidity.

'Sickness has innumerable squalors, many of which you know far too well, my dear,' he said when Jack and he were sitting together in the great cabin, 'and among them, in some ways the nastiest, is the sufferer's total selfishness. Admittedly, a body doing all it can to survive will naturally turn in upon itself; but the mind inhabiting that body is so inclined to feast on the indulgence, carrying on and on long after the necessity is gone. To my bitter shame I am almost entirely ignorant of our expedition's success, and even of its whereabouts. From time to time you have told me, in passing, of various captures – emergencies – storms – the all-dreaded harmattan itself – but little did I hear, and little did I retain, of a connected narrative. Be so good as to pass another slice of pineapple.'

'Why, Mr Smith said you were not to be disturbed or excited, above all not to be excited; and anyhow when something really interesting happened, like the *Aurora* and *Laurel* running down the big Havana schooner, you were always fast asleep.'

'Lord, how I slept, indeed: a benign swimming in and out of rosy hibernation – nothing more healing. But will you not tell me how this side of our mission has gone – what stages we have reached – whether your expectations are answered?'

'As far as the stage is concerned, we have almost completed our run along the coast. We have gone as far east into the Gulf as I had planned – perhaps farther than I can afford, in time – right down to the Bight of Benin. We are now lying off the Slave Coast itself, and tomorrow or the next day I hope the inshore brigs will raise Whydah, the great slave-market. Once we have cleaned that up, I shall hand over command of the inshore vessels to Henslow, the senior brig commander, and head for St Thomas to pick up the south-east trades.'

'I remember: then hey for Freetown and the north!'

'Just so. As for our success, I do not think anyone could have expected more or even as much. We have taken eighteen slavers and sent them in with prize-crews: all, or almost all, will be condemned, particularly as most of them, taken unawares, we having run ahead of the news – fired upon us, which constitutes piracy.'

'Well done, upon my honour! That must surely amount to some five thousand black men released. I had no notion that you could accomplish so much.'

'Six thousand one hundred and twenty, counting the women: but there were some Portuguese we had to let go, they having a special status if they load in a Portuguese settlement; and a few doubtfuls; for any commander who seizes a vessel that is not breaking the law is liable to be cast in damages, tremendous damages. Yet even so, it was very well. There were some fine active officers aboard the inshore craft and the boats. Whewell was one of them, of course: he comes off tomorrow for orders about Whydah, and if you feel strong enough I shall ask him to come and read you the log, describing each action in turn. He was in the thick of it, whereas I saw nothing at all, except for the taking of the Havana prize.'

'I should like that of all things. And yet, brother, in spite of this striking success, you look sad and worn and anxious. I do not wish to force the least confidence and if my words are as indiscreet as I fear they may be I shall not resent a civil evasion. But your violin, which has sustained me all these weeks from the stern-gallery, speaks pian-pianissimo and always in D minor. Has the poor ship a hidden leak that cannot be come at? Must she perish?'

Jack gazed at him for a long considering moment and said, 'Sad: yes, I have never liked leading from behind; and the death of many of those young men I have sent in *has* saddened me deeply. Worn and anxious: I have two reasons, two very good reasons for being both worn and anxious. The first is that the winds, having been so favourable for so long, have now turned cruelly baffling, real Bight of Benin weather, and I am very much afraid – so is Whewell – that they may carry on in the same way for months, preventing us from reaching St Thomas until it is too late. The second is that if I do succeed in carrying my squadron up to the rendezvous in time to meet the French, I am not sure how all my ships will behave. It grieves me to say this, Stephen, though a ship being a sounding-board I do not suppose that much of it will be news to you. The fact of the matter is that two, representing forty per cent of our guns and about fifty per cent of our broadside weight of metal, are in very bad order. As a result of all our exercising they can fire tolerably well and they can get their boats over the side tolerably quick; but they are still in very bad order. Neither is in any way what you would call a happy ship; and both are commanded by men who are not fit to command them. The one is a sodomite, or reputed to be a sodomite, and he is utterly at odds with his officers, while discipline among the hands is all to seek; the other is a bloody tyrant, a flogger, and no seaman. If I did not continually check him, he would have a mutiny on his hands, a very ugly mutiny indeed.'

Jack paused, absently cut Stephen another slice of pine-apple, and passed it over. Stephen acknowledged it with a bob of his head but said nothing. It was very unusual for Jack to speak in this way: the flow was not to be interrupted. 'I hate using the ordinary coarse word about Duff, whom I like and who is a fine seaman, and whether he is a sodomite or not I do not give a damn. But as I tried to make him see, you have to check it aboard a man-of-war. A girl on board is a bad thing: half a dozen girls would be Bedlam. But if a man, a man-lover, is an unchecked sodomite, the whole ship's company is his prey. It will not do. I tried to make him see that, but I am not a very eloquent cove and I dare say I put it wrong, being so God-damned tactful, because all that worried him was that his manhood, his courage, his conduct as we say, should be impugned. So long as he was happy to attack, whatever the odds, all was well. It is very difficult. His officers want to arrest him, to bring him to a court-martial, he having angered them so with his favourites. They are said to have witnesses – damning evidence. If he is found guilty he must be hanged: that is the only sentence. It is very bad. Very bad for the service, very bad in every way. I have done what I can in shifting his officers – with the inshore fever and the casualties there have been several promotions – but his ship is still . . .' He shook his head. 'And as for the Purple Emperor, who is not on speaking terms with Duff, by the way, and scarcely with me, he has contrived to gather a set of officers very like himself: not a seaman among them, and even the master needs both watches to put the ship about in anything like a Christian manner. It is the usual West Indies discipline – spit and polish all day long, and flog the last man off the yard, all combined with fine uniforms, brutal ignorance of their profession, and a contempt for bosun captains. Such a band of incompetents as I have never seen gathered together in any one ship belonging to His Majesty.'

Jack had remained silent for so long that Stephen ventured to say, 'Perhaps in the long haul northwards, with constant exercise and colder seas the two sick ships will regain a certain health.'

'I hope so, indeed,' said Jack. 'But it would have to be a most uncommon long haul to bring them to anything like Nelson's standard, a complete change of heart in all hands. And with a man like the Purple Emperor there is no heart to change: no person left: only a set of pompous attitudes. Though to be sure exercise – and we offshore people have been thoroughly idle – and cold seas can do wonders. Stephen, was you to be propped up with cushions, do you think you could hold your 'cello? The sea is smooth. With a couple of turns round your middle, you would not be flung about.'

When Whewell came aboard from the *Cestos*'s cutter he found both Commodore and Captain on the quarterdeck, looking pleased; and when, after the usual obeisances, he asked how the Doctor did, the Commodore nodded his head aft, and Whewell, listening attentively, heard the deep, melodious, though somewhat unsteady voice of the 'cello.

'It takes more than the yellow jack to come to an end of

him,' said the Commodore. 'Come along with me, and when you have made your report, I will take you in. He longs to know how things have been going along, inshore.'

They walked aft, and in the passage Whewell said, 'My report is very brief, sir. Whydah is empty. The news ran ahead of us at last, and there is not a slaver left in the road that we could touch with safety.'

'I am heartily glad of it,' said Jack, and he carried on into the great cabin, where Stephen sat lashed into an elbow-chair, looking like an ancient child. 'Doctor,' cried Jack, 'I have brought you Mr Whewell, who tells me that Whydah is empty. I am heartily glad of it, for we cannot spare officers and men for any more prize-crews – we are far below complement already, with so many of them bowsing up their jibs in Freetown. What is more, it allows us to leave this infernal coast at once, steering for St Thomas and something like breathable air. But since the breeze is dead contrary at present and likely to remain so until after sunset, I shall stand in, say farewell to the brigs and schooners, and then give those scoundrels in the town and the barracoons a salute that will put the fear of God into them. Mr Whewell, I shall send you the log-book rough-sheets so that you can tell the Doctor about each action in turn.'

Orders could be heard on deck, and the patter of feet overhead as the signal-hoists were prepared: already the helm was hard over, and the ship was turning, turning, her motion gradually changing from roll to pitch as she headed for the land. 'Look at that infernal lubber,' cried Whewell, pointing at the *Thames*, two cables' length astern and in the *Bellona*'s wake. Stephen could discern something flapping about among the sails, and a certain deviation either side of the line traced by the pennant-ship; but his seamanship could not name the crime committed, heinous though it must have been.

The rough-sheets came, but before reading them Whewell asked after Square and Stephen's journey up the Sinon river.

'Square was all that could possibly have been wished,' said Stephen. 'I am most grateful to you for the recommendation; and although my little expedition was pitifully short, I saw many wonders and I brought back a wealth of specimens.'

'I wonder whether you saw your potto. I remember you particularly wished to see the potto of those parts.'

'I saw one, sure; and an eminently gratifying sight he was. But I was unable to bring him home.'

'In that case I have one aboard the *Cestos*, if you would like her. But I am afraid she is only the Calabar kind, without a tail: an awantibo. A she-potto. I thought of you at once when I saw her in the market.'

'Nothing, nothing, would give me greater pleasure,' cried Stephen. 'I am infinitely obliged to you, dear Mr Whewell. A Calabar potto within two or three hours' sail, or even less with this beautiful sweet-scented breeze. What joy.'

The activities of the inshore squadron took up the hour or so before dinner, which Whewell ate with the Commodore, the Captain, the first lieutenant and a scrubbed, speechless midshipman: they took their coffee on the poop, supporting Stephen up the ladder; and by now a vast expanse of Africa was to be seen ahead, lagoons glittering along the coast, very tall palms just visible, and greenness, often very dark, stretching away inland until it merged with the indefinite horizon and the sky. The midshipman made his barely-audible blushing acknowledgments and vanished; the superior officers followed him after no more than a glass of brandy; and Whewell said, 'There, on the far bank of the lagoon, about half way along, is Whydah. May I pass you the telescope?'

'If you please. So that is the great slave market: yet I see no port, no harbour.'

'No, sir. Whydah has nothing of that kind. Everything has to be landed or taken off through the frightful surf – see how it breaks! – then run up the beach and so ferried across the lagoon. The Mina, who do it all, have wonderful surf-boats; but even so things get lost.'

'Surely that is a very curious arrangement for a large commercial town?'

'Yes, sir: but there are precious few real ports all along the coast. And then again, Dahomey, that is to say, practically everything we are looking at, is an inland kingdom: their capital is right up-country. They know nothing about the sea and they dislike the coast; but they are a very warlike nation, perpetually raiding their neighbours to capture the slaves they exchange for European goods. So they use Whydah, which is more or less under their rule, as the nearest place, inconvenient though it is; and since they export thousands and thousands of negroes every year, it has grown to be a considerable place, with English, French and Portuguese quarters, and some Arabs and Yorubas.'

'I see a great deal of green among the houses.'

'Oranges and limes and lemons everywhere, sir, a delight after a long passage. I remember squeezing a score together into a bowl and quaffing it straight off, when first I was here. Things were not so cleverly arranged in those days, and there were some goods you had to carry all the way to Abomey, the king's great town, or in the hottest weather to Kana, his smaller place.'

'I do not think I have ever read a description of a great African town – I mean a negro town as opposed to a Moorish.'

'A very curious sight it is, sir. Abomey has a wall six miles round, twenty feet high, with six gates. There is the king's house, a vast great place, surprisingly high, and lined with skulls: skulls on the walls, skulls on posts, skulls everywhere; and jawbones. And then of course there are great numbers of ordinary Ewe houses – they all speak Ewe in those parts – made of mud with thatched roofs; and some what you might call palaces, a market-place of perhaps forty or fifty acres, and a huge spreading barracks.'

'How did the people use you?'

'The Dahomi are a fine, upstanding set of men, civil, though reserved; yet I had the impression that they looked down on me, which they did, of course, being so much taller: but I mean out of pride. Still, I do not remember that any of the men behaved in a way you could object to; and since I had brought a dozen chests of capital iron war-hats for his Amazons, the king ordered me to be given a gold fetiso weighing a good quarter of a pound.'

'Did you say his Amazons, Mr Whewell?'

'Why, yes, sir. The Dahomey Amazons.' And seeing that Stephen was in no way enlightened he went on, 'The most effective part of the king's army is made up of young females, sir, terribly bold and fierce. I never saw more than a thousand at a time, when some particular bands were marching past; but I was assured there were many more. It was for them that I brought the iron war-hats.'

'They are actually warriors, so? Not merely camp-followers?'

'Indeed they are, sir, and by all accounts quite terrible – fearless and terrible. They have the post of honour in battle, and attack first.'

'I am amazed.'

'So was I, sir, when a pack of I suppose female sergeants made me come into their hut and fit them with their war-hats. I was younger then, and not as ill-looking as I am now, and they used me shamefully. I blush for it yet.' He hung his head, regretting having begun the anecdote. Stephen said, 'Your infinitely welcome potto, Mr Whewell, is she as strictly nocturnal as her cousin the Common Potto?'

'Sir, I have no notion at all. She was there in the market, curled up in a ball under some straw in the bottom of a fine brass wire cage, and when I asked what was there the old woman said "Potto". It would have been no satisfaction to anyone not to haggle a little, and I knocked off the equivalent of fourpence for no tail; but in the end she had a price that made her laugh with pleasure and she said I might have some little books and pictures into the bargain. She had been a Popish missionary's housekeeper, you see, and she was selling what he had left. Everything had gone except

257

these books and papers and the potto, which the people of all the nations in Whydah, even the Hausas, suspected of being a Roman fetiso, which might offend the local spirits. I carried her aboard the *Cestos* and just before I turned in I saw her looking at me with eyes like saucers, but she did not seem to like the sight, and she shrank back into the straw almost at once, though I offered her a piece of banana. That is all I know of her, except that she would have been boiled tomorrow if she had not found a customer.'

'You would not have her with you, at all, in that elegant boat, dear Mr Whewell?'

'Oh no. Movement seems to distress her, and we had to beat into a heavy head-sea: but I did bring the drawings and the books.'

The books were an Elzevier Pomponius Mela *De situ orbis*, a breviary worn almost to destruction and a thick notebook filled at one end with equivalents in various African languages and at the other with personal reflexions and what appeared to be drafts of letters. The drawings were painstaking, inexpert representations of the potto in different attitudes, tailless, anxious.

'I am sorry to be disappointing,' said Whewell, 'but the squadron is running in at rather better than eight knots – there, over to starboard, you can see our brigs and schooners – and in a few minutes I must hurry ahead with orders. All ships and vessels are to fire a royal salute of twenty-one guns.'

'Why, for all love? This is not Oak-Apple Day or any other great occasion.'

'In order to impress Whydah and the King of Dahomey: and it can be justified as being the birthday of a member of the royal family – well, almost. Mr Adams ran right through the book and came up with the Duke of Habachtsthal, who was born today: a close cousin, I believe. Anyhow, royal enough for the purpose.'

That ill-omened name was never wholly remote from Stephen's thoughts, but today it had retreated farther than usual, and the sudden, wholly unexpected sound of it cast a singular damp upon his happiness.

Whewell set off for the Whydah road, leaving the drawings and other things by Stephen's side. Presently he took up the notebook, and turning to the back he at once came upon a smaller drawing of both the potto and a creature very like it that he took to be *Lemur tardigradus*, with the following text, apparently meant for a fellow-member of the Congregation of the Holy Ghost:

In her manners she is for the most part gentle, except in the cold season, when her temper seemed wholly changed: and her Creator who made her so sensible to cold, to which she must often have been exposed even in her native forests, gave her her thick fur, which we rarely see in animals in these tropical climates: to me, who not only constantly fed her, but bathed her twice a week in water accommodated to the seasons, and whom she clearly distinguished from others, she was at all times grateful; but when I disturbed her in winter, she was usually indignant, and seemed to reproach me with the uneasiness which she felt, though no possible precaution had been omitted to keep her in a proper degree of warmth. At all times she was pleased with being stroked on the head, and frequently suffered me to touch her extremely sharp teeth; but her temper was always quick, and when she was unreasonably disturbed, she expressed a little resentment, by an obscure murmur, like that of a squirrel.

From half an hour after sunrise to half an hour before sunset, she slept without intermission, rolled up like a hedgehog; and, as soon as she awoke, she began to prepare herself for the labours of her approaching day, licking and dressing herself like a cat, an operation which the flexibility of her neck and limbs enabled her to perform very completely: she was then ready for a slight breakfast, after which she commonly took a short nap; but when the sun was quite set she recovered all her vivacity. A little before daybreak, when my early hours gave me frequent opportunities of observing her, she seemed to solicit my attention, and if I presented my finger to her, she licked or nibbled it with great gentleness, but eagerly took fruit when I offered it, though she seldom ate much at her morning repast; when the day brought back her night, her eyes lost their lustre and strength, and she composed herself for a slumber of ten or eleven hours.

The missionary's writing was difficult to make out, irregular and trembling, the hand of a very sick or aged man, and by the time Stephen had come to the bottom of the page, the *Bellona*, her consort and all the inshore vessels had formed a line of parallel with the shore, lying to on the declining breeze at little more than point-blank range of the immense crowds blackening the strand. He had heard the usual orders, the hoarse cry of Meares the master gunner and his mate, and he knew that a salute was to be fired. Yet nothing had prepared him for the prodigious bellowing uproar that followed the *Bellona*'s first discharge. The people on the strand were equally surprised, or even more so, and several thousand fell flat, covering their heads.

The noise was not quite so great, nor the smoke-banks quite so dense, as they had been at Freetown, but the whole was more concentrated; and when Stephen could hear himself think again he felt that Jack Aubrey was probably right, and that the slave-trade as a whole had received a setback worth a thousand times the cost in powder (shot there was none). For the potto he was not greatly concerned. Creatures that lived within the zone of tropical storms, with the enormous thunder breaking just over their heads, could put up with anything the Royal Navy might be able to offer, particularly those that slept all day with their heads between their knees.

Certainly this was the case with the present potto. When

Whewell and Square brought her aboard and carried her down to Maturin's little cabin on the orlop – he did not trust Jack not to talk loud and chuck her under the chin, which would not do until she was used to life aboard – he sat with her a great while by the light of a single purser's dip. At about sunset she came out, looking nervous to be sure, as any country potto might in new surroundings, but neither shattered nor terrified. She would have nothing to do with his proffered banana, still less with a finger, but she washed to some extent – a very beautiful little creature – and a little before he left he saw one of the far too many local cockroaches walk into her cage. Her immense eyes glowed with an uncommon fire: she paused, motionless until it was within reach, and then seized it with both hands. Yet for eating the animal, which she did with every appearance of appetite, she used but one, and that the left.

'Goodnight, dear potto,' he said, locking the door behind him. His way led him through the after-cockpit, the mid-shipmen's berth, at present filled with a dozen boys and young men, engaged in eating their supper, throwing pieces of biscuit and shouting at one another. They all leapt up at the sight of the Doctor – asked him how he did – said they were very happy to see him on his pins – but he must not overdo it, particularly so soon, and at his age – he must take care – with this blessed topgallant breeze off the land she was pitching into the swell like Leda's swan – and the two senior master's mates, Upex and Tyndall, insisted upon leading him up the ladder to the gundeck, each holding an elbow, so to the upper deck and thence to the quarterdeck, where he was considered safe and capable of walking aft, with the first lieutenant's help, as far as the cabin.

'Heavens, Stephen,' cried Jack, 'I thought you were asleep in the bed-place. I have been walking about on tiptoe and drinking my sherry in an undertone.'

'I was sitting with my potto, in the orlop,' said Stephen, 'she being a nocturnal creature. What amiable young fellows they are in the cockpit.'

'Certainly. They are settling down now, growing far less obnoxious; and there are one or two may become seamen, given fifty years or so. But what a feat, to creep up from the orlop in your state of health. I trust they gave you a hand?'

'Perhaps it was more a question of mutual support,' said Stephen. 'My strength is coming back *hand over fist*. Hand over fist.' He repeated the nautical phrase with a certain complacency.

Yet although he lied shamefully with one half of his mouth, the other spoke Gospel truth: day after day this beautiful wind blew nobly, carrying the squadron out of the accursed Bight under a press of sail, once to the extent of skyscrapers aboard the *Thames* after her signal *make more sail* had been three times repeated, the third repetition emphasized with a windward gun; and day after day Stephen grew brisker, more agile, and (like the potto) greedier.

Many of the sick from the inshore vessels were now aboard the *Bellona* and other ships of the squadron, most with fevers of one kind or another – tertians, double tertians, remittents and quartans for the most part, though there were three cases of the yellow jack – and very soon Dr Maturin was making at least his morning rounds, with Square in attendance to help him up on deck, where he would stand for half a glass or so, revelling with Jack, Tom and all hands present in the squadron's pace as the breeze came whistling in either over the starboard or the larboard bow, no longer a soldier's wind right aft as it had been the first day they sank the shore, but never heading them either, so that they beat steadily towards the Line, making legs a whole watch long.

'This has never been known in the memory of the oldest Guineaman,' said Mr Woodbine, the master, 'and there are some hands who say your potto has brought the ship good luck.'

A Marine officer on the quarterdeck added, 'My servant Joe Andrews tells me that many of the old African hands say there is nothing like a potto for luck: and, after all, there is a potto's field in the Bible, is there not?'

'Is it true,' Jack asked Stephen at supper, 'that Barker and Overly are on the mend?'

'It is, too,' said Stephen, who had sat with them for hours, first persuading their neighbours that the yellow fever was not infectious – they would not speak to the poor men else, nor breathe their breath, but remained turned utterly away – and then assuring the patients themselves that they had a very fair chance if they held on with all their might and never gave way to despair. No one could possibly have had more authority in this instance, and although the third man, very far gone, died almost at once, Barker and Overly were likely to find another way to Heaven.

'Ah,' said Jack, nodding his head, 'that was a famous stroke, bringing your potto aboard.'

'Why, your soul to the Devil, Jack Aubrey, for a vile wicked pagan and an infamously superstitious dog, to be so weak,' cried Stephen, nettled for once.

'Oh, I beg pardon,' said Jack, blushing. 'I did not mean that at all. Not at all. I only meant it comforted the hands. I am sure your physic did them a power of good, too. I make no sort of doubt of it.'

Beating up, beating steadily up into winds mostly west of south, often changeable but never still – none of those wicked clock-calms of the Gulf with its dense fever-bearing mists drifting off the shore – and by the time they raised St Thomas, a cloud-capped peak soaring above the horizon at seventy leagues in the south-south-east a half east, Stephen had put on a stone and his breeches would stay up without a pin.

'There is our salvation,' cried he, having been called from a peaceful sleep to view the peak in question.

'How do you mean, our salvation?' asked Jack suspiciously. He had often been led out of his way or had been attempted to be led out of his way by remote islands said to harbour a cousin of the phoenix, a very curious wren, or the loveless bowers of parthenogenetic lizards (this was in the Aegean), and he had no intention of landing Dr Maturin on St Thomas for another of his timeless rambles: a seaman's eye could already make out the particular cloud-formation of the longed-for south-east trades a great way off on the starboard bow.

'My dear Commodore, how can you be so strange? Is it not I that have been telling you this mortal week and more that I have barely a drachm of cinchona, of Jesuit's bark, left in the dispensary at all? Have not my fever-cases drunk it up day and night? Did not other ships borrow several Winchester quarts? Was not a whole carboy broke by a great oaf I shall not name? And is not St Thomas the island of the world for bark of the finest quality, guaranteed to clear the sick-berth out of hand? And not only bark, but the kindly fruits of the earth, whose lack is now becoming evident?'

'It will mean the loss of a day,' said Jack. 'Though I must admit that I did hear some obscure, muttered complaints about bark, both in quantity and quality.'

'Jesuit's bark is the one sovereign specific against fever,' said Stephen. 'We must have Jesuit's bark.'

In circumstances that he could no longer exactly recall, probably during a feast at the Keppel's Head in Portsmouth, Jack had once said that 'a Jesuit's bark was worse than his bite,' a remark received with infinite mirth, cordial admiration. He smiled at the recollection, and looking at his friend's earnest, guileless face – no parthenogenetic lizards there – he said, 'Very well. But it must be touch and go – just the time to hurry ashore, buy a dozen bottles of bark and away.' 'And don't I wish that may be the case,' he added to himself.

It was not, of course: it never was the case in any but a British port. First there was the matter of the salute: none of His Majesty's ships might salute any foreign fort, governor or local dignitary without having first made certain that the same number of guns would be returned. This meant sending in an officer, accompanied by an interpreter – fortunately Mr Adams had a certain amount of Portuguese. Then there was the question of pratique: after the fifteen covenanted guns had boomed to and fro across Chaves Bay, a man from the captain of the port came out in a handsome galley, and on hearing that the squadron was last from the Slave Coast he looked grave and said that since there had been an outbreak of the plague in Whydah three years ago they would have to perform quarantine before anyone could be allowed on shore. Stephen reasoned with him privately, so convincingly that the regulations were slightly eased: the Doctor and a boat from each ship might spend a few hours ashore, but no one was to go more than a hundred paces from the high-tide mark.

As most people in the squadron expected, the second lieutenant of the *Thames* and the young Marine officer from the *Stately* who had been Stephen's neighbour at dinner took this opportunity, the first, to settle their disagreement. They and their seconds went more than a hundred paces from the shore, but not much, there being a convenient coconut grove at hand. Here the ground was measured out, and at the drop of a handkerchief each young man shot the other in the belly. Each was carried back to his boat, and the question of the *Stately*'s manliness and fighting qualities remained undecided.

'Did you know about this rencontre, Stephen?' asked Jack that evening, when St Thomas was sinking on the southern rim of the sea and the *Bellona* making up for the loss of time with studdingsails aloft and alow, spread to the south-east trades.

'Faith, I was there when the provocation was given.'

'If you had told me, I might have prevented it.'

'Nonsense. There was a direct offence, and the *Stately*'s Marine was bound to resent it. No apology was offered, no withdrawal; and this was the necessary result, as you know very well.'

Jack could not deny it. He shook his head: 'How I hope the young fellow don't die. If he do, poor Duff is like to hang himself. Do you think he will recover? The Stately, I mean.'

'The Dear knows. I have not seen him. It was over before

265

I had done with the apothecary, and all I saw was their blood on the strand. But an abdominal wound very often has a fatal issue, if the viscera are injured.'

In the event both young men died, though not before the second lieutenant, at the urging of the *Thames*'s chaplain, had acknowledged that he was in the wrong and had sent a proper message to Willoughby, the Royal Marine, who returned his thanks and best wishes for a prompt recovery. This reconciliation, however, was confined to those who had fought. The hostility between the two ships increased, and it was made evident on all possible occasions by cries of, 'What ho, the molly-ship' if there was time, or 'The pouffes ahoy,' if there was not, on the part of the *Thames*, and of 'Slack in stays,' or 'Make more sail, there,' from the *Stately*. Not that there were many occasions for rudeness, for although the beautiful trade-wind varied in strength it never declined to anything near enough to one of those calms so usual in the doldrums for ordinary ship-visiting among the hands to be possible, or for it to be easy for the officers of any one ship to invite those of another: nor did the Commodore ever create an artificial calm by lying-to, even on Sundays. He was haunted by the dread of being late; and although on days less blowy than usual he would summon the *Ringle* and run up the line to see how his captains were coming along, he consistently urged his maxim 'Lose not a minute: there is not a minute to be lost', and obeyed it himself even to the point of forbidding the ships he visited to reduce sail to let him come aboard more easily.

He dined once in the *Stately*, and although he had shifted her first lieutenant, the most inveterate against Captain Duff and the man who had wished to arrest him, to the command of a brig, he was sorry to find a marked degree of tension at the captain's table: the officers ill at ease, and Duff, though a good host, anxious and wanting in authority. 'He is a good, kind fellow, and he handles his ship like a prime seaman, but he seems incapable of taking a hint,' said Jack on returning.

Yet this was the one sad day out of the ten – ten, no more;

and but for the heavy-sailing *Thames* it would have been eight – that it took to run up to Freetown, and the rest of the time was delightful sailing, a world to which they had grown so accustomed in the vast stretches of the Pacific and to which they returned as to the natural way of life, with all the shipboard ceremonies and routines in their due order, as exactly marked by bells as those of a monastery. Eight bells in the middle watch, when those whose duty it was to show the sun a spotless deck had to leave their hammocks two hours before he rose; eight bells in the forenoon watch, when the officers fixed the height of the noonday sun and hands were piped to dinner: bells and pipes all day long, with some music too – the drum beating 'Heart of Oak' for the wardroom dinner (though *Aurora*, whose Marine officer had organized a band among his men, did it in a higher style), the drum again for quarters and the retreat, and on most evenings fiddles, bagpipes or a little shrill fife playing for the hands as they danced on the forecastle: bells all night long, too, though somewhat muted. These formal measures and divisions had of course been there during the wearisome creep along the shores of the Gulf, the *Bellona* often lying to, doing nothing; but it was only now that they regained their full significance, and in a surprisingly short time this part of the voyage seemed to have been going on for ever.

For Jack and Stephen too the evening resumed their old familiar pattern of supper and music – occasionally chess or cards if the seas were heavy enough to shake Stephen's control of his 'cello – or rambling talk of common friends, former voyages: rarely about the future, an anxious prospect for both and one they tended to shy away from.

'Jack,' said Stephen, when the ship's pitching had obliged him to lay down his bow: he spoke rather diffidently, knowing how Jack disliked any topic that might reflect discredit on the service, 'would it grieve you to tell me a little more about sodomy in the Navy? One often hears about it; and the perpetual reiteration of the Articles of War with their "unnatural and detestable sin of buggery" makes it seem part of the nautical landscape. Yet apart from your very first command, the brig *Sophie* . . .'

'She was a sloop,' said Jack, quite sharply.

'But she had two masts. I remember them perfectly: one in the front, and the other, if you follow me, behind: whereas a sloop, as you never cease pointing out, has but one, more or less in the middle.'

'If she had no masts at all, or fifty, she would still have been a sloop from the moment my commission had been read aboard her: for I was a commander, a master and commander; and anything a commander commands instantly becomes a sloop.'

'Well, in that *vessel* there was a sailor who could not command his passion – for a goat, as I remember. But apart from that I scarcely remember any instance, and by now I am a very old and experienced salt dog.'

'I do not suppose you do. But when you consider what the lower deck is like – three or four hundred men packed tight – the cloud of witnesses when hammocks are piped down – and the very public nature of the heads – it is difficult to imagine a more unsuitable place for such capers. Yet it does occasionally happen in what few holes and corners a man-of-war possesses, and in cabins. I remember a horrid case off Corsica in '96. *Blanche*, Captain Sawyer, and *Meleager*, Captain Cockburn – George Cockburn – both twelve-pounder thirty-two-gun frigates, had been there in company the year before and something ugly of that kind, involving Sawyer, had taken place. You remember George Cockburn, Stephen?'

'Certainly: a very fine man indeed, the best kind of a sailor.'

'Summoned those men of both ships who knew about it and made them swear to keep the whole damn thing quiet. Yes. But the next year Sawyer began again, calling foremast jacks to his cabin and putting out the light. And of course he favoured these fellows and would not allow his officers to compel them to do their duty – and of course discipline began to go to the dogs. After a good deal of this his first lieutenant called for a court-martial, which was granted, and Sawyer fought back by bringing charges against almost the whole gun-room. Poor George Cockburn was in a horrible position. He had certain evidence of the man's guilt in private letters he had written to him – that Sawyer had written to Cockburn. But they were *private* – as confidential as letters could be. Yet on the other hand, if Sawyer were acquitted, all his officers were ruined, and a man who should not be in command would remain in command. So for the good of the service he showed them, looking like death as he did so and for long after. The judges twisted the evidence round and round, like a kekkle on a cable, and found Sawyer not guilty of the act itself but only of gross indecency, so he was not hanged, but dismissed the service. D'Arcy Preston, a countryman of yours, I believe . . .'

'Of the Gormanston family. I must tell you about their manner of death one day. Pray go on.'

'D'Arcy Preston succeeded him for a short while, and then Nelson, commodore at the time, appointed Henry Hotham, a right taut disciplinarian, for the *Blanche* was still in wretched bad order. Indeed, the people were so far gone in disobedience and loving their ease that they would not receive him. They said he was a damned Tartar and would neither receive him nor hear his commission read: they pointed the forecastle guns aft and turned him out of the ship. Eventually Nelson himself came over, bringing Hotham with him: he told the *Blanche*'s people that they had the best name of any frigate's crew in the Navy – they had taken two heavier frigates in fair fight – and were they now going to rebel? If Captain Hotham used them ill, they were to write him a letter and he would support them. On this they gave three cheers and returned to their duty, while he went back to his ship, leaving Hotham in command. But it did not last: as a crew they were beyond recall, the rot had gone so deep; and as soon as they reached Portsmouth they petitioned to be given another captain or another ship.'

'Were they indulged in either?'

'Of course not. They would have been scattered among any number of short-handed ships. As for our case, or what looks something like our case, I shall advise with James Wood when we reach Freetown, and see what can be done by a thorough shake-up and perhaps some more transfers. But for now let us have another glass of wine – the port stands up wonderfully well in this heat, don't you find? – and go back to our Boccherini.'

They did so; but Jack played indifferently – his heart was no longer in the music, and Stephen wondered how he could have been so heavy, knowing his friend's devotion to the service, as to raise the subject in spite of his own misgivings. He consoled himself with the reflexion that salt water washes all away, that another hundred miles of this perfect sailing would raise Jack's spirits, and that Freetown would see his difficulties resolved.

Freetown on a fine clear afternoon, the immense harbour dotted with ships belonging to the Royal Navy and some Guineamen, who began saluting Commodore Aubrey's pennant with seamanlike promptitude. The *Ringle* had been sent ahead of the squadron, carrying word to the Governor, and as soon as the *Bellona* was comfortably anchored and the whole squadron trim, with yards squared by lifts and braces, Jack, followed by his subordinate commanders, went ashore in style to wait upon his Excellency – number one uniform, presentation sword, gold-laced hat, Nile medal – for as soon as the ship had made his number Government House had thrown out the signal inviting him and his captains to dinner. The *Bellona*'s barge was a fine spectacle, new painted, pulled by as neat a set of bargemen as any in the fleet, most of them Jack's followers from ship to ship, and steered by Bonden, grave, conscious of the occasion, in exactly the same rig as Tom Allen, Nelson's coxswain, whom he resembled, with Mr Wetherby beside him, an infant from the gun-room, who had to be shown how to deal with such ceremonies.

The *Bellona*'s barge (it was in fact her launch, but being

rowed by bargemen and acting as a barge, it assumed the somewhat grander name) pulled fourteen oars, and when these fourteen men were not wholly taken up with the exact regularity of their stroke they looked aft with a certain disapproval: their surgeon and his man had come for the ride, and they let the side down – shabby, unbrushed, and carrying an old green umbrella, badly furled. 'Why that idle sod Killick ever let him out looking like George-a-Green, I cannot tell,' whispered bow oar.

'Never mind,' replied his mate out of the side of his mouth. 'He ain't going to the palace.'

He and Square were in fact going to the market-place to seek out Houmouzios at the earliest possible opportunity and then to hurry over the swamp, there to sit under his umbrella, contemplating the long-legged wading birds – even perhaps the fishing vulture – with his perspective-glass; and he was strangely dashed when, on coming to the money-changer's stall, they found only Socrates, who said that Mr Houmouzios was gone on a journey into the interior, but would be back on Friday.

Stephen was strangely dashed, strangely put about; but having considered for a while he told Square to go and rejoice with his family and walked slowly off in the direction of the fetid swamp, much reduced in this dry season, but still fetid, still a swamp, and with the birds concentrated in a smaller area. And what might he not hope for? Adanson had worked extremely hard, but he had been farther to the north, on the banks of the Senegal; and even Adanson had not turned every egg.

'Doctor, Doctor!' they cried, hallooing far behind.

'They are calling for a doctor, the creatures,' he reflected. 'Don't they wish they may find one? Does the chanting goshawk come so far south, I wonder?'

'Doctor, Doctor!' they called, hoarse with running, and at last he stopped.

'The Commodore says pray come directly,' gasped a midshipman. 'His Excellency invites you to dinner.'

'My compliments and thanks to his Excellency,' said Stephen, 'but regret I am unable to accept.' He moved on towards the fetid swamp.

'Come, sir, that won't do,' said a tall sergeant. 'You will be getting us into cruel trouble. Which we have orders to escort you back, and we shall be brought to the triangle and flogged, else. Come, sir, if you please.'

Stephen looked at the three breathless but determined master's mates, the powerful Marine, and gave in.

'My dear sir,' cried the Governor, 'I beg you will overlook the short notice, the unceremonious invitation, but the last time you were here I did not have the pleasure, the honour, of meeting you; and when my wife heard that Dr Maturin, Dr *Stephen* Maturin, had been in Sierra Leone without dining here she was infinitely distressed, desolated, quite put out . . . allow me to introduce you.' He led Stephen up to a very good-looking young woman, tall, fair, agreeably plump, smiling at him with the utmost benevolence.

'I ask your pardon, ma'am, for appearing before you in this squalid . . .'

'Not in the very least,' she cried, taking both his hands. 'You are covered, *covered* with laurels. I am Edward Heatherleigh's sister, and I have read all your lovely books and papers, including your address to the *Institut*, which Monsieur Cuvier sent over to Edward.'

Edward Heatherleigh, a very shy young man, a naturalist and a member (though rarely seen) of the Royal Society, with a moderate estate in the north of England, where he lived as quietly as possible with this sister, both of them collecting, botanizing, drawing, dissecting, and above all comparing. They had articulated skeletons of all the British mammals, and Edward had told Stephen, one of his few intimates, that she knew bones far better than he did – she was unbeatable on bats.

This passed through or rather appeared in his mind so rapidly that there was no measurable pause before his reply of 'Miss Christine! I am delighted to see you, ma'am; and now I do not mind my squalor in the least.'

Captain James Wood, the Governor, possessed a maiden sister who had looked after much of his official entertaining before his marriage, which was just as well; for although Mrs Governor kept remembering her duty, and doing it, few sailors could engage her real attention when a famous natural philosopher was by.

'You must certainly come tomorrow,' she said as they parted, 'and I will show you my garden and my creatures – I have a chanting goshawk and a brush-tailed porcupine! And perhaps you might like to see my bones.'

'Nothing could possibly give me greater pleasure,' said Stephen, pressing her hand. 'And perhaps we might walk by the swamp.'

'Well, Stephen, you were in luck, upon my word,' said Jack, as they walked down to the boat. 'The only pretty woman of the party, and you completely monopolized her. And in the drawing-room she came and sat at your knee and talked to no one else for hours on end.'

'We had a great deal to talk about. She knows more on the subject of bones and their variations from species to species than any woman I am acquainted with; much more, indeed, than most men, and they professed anatomists. She is sister to Edward Heatherleigh, whom you may have seen at the Royal. A fine young woman.'

'What a pleasure. I love talking to women like that. Caroline Herschel and I used to prattle away about Pomeranian sludge and the last stages of a telescope's mirror half way through the night. But knowing and beautiful too – what bliss. Yet how she ever came to marry James Wood I cannot tell. A fair practical seaman and an excellent fellow, but never an idea in his head; and he is at least twice her age.'

'Other people's marriages are a perpetual source of amazement,' said Stephen.

They walked on, rejecting first the offer of a sedan-chair

and then that of a hammock slung on a pole and carried by two men, a usual conveyance in those parts.

'You too seemed to be enjoying yourselves very heartily at your end of the table,' said Stephen, after a while.

'So we were. There were some people from the vice-admiralty court, and the civil secretary, and they were telling us how well we had done, how very much better than anyone else, how much wealthier we should be when everything was settled up, above all if none of the alleged Americans or Spaniards won an appeal against their decisions, which was most improbable, and how well our hands would do with their undisputed share, which was ready in canvas bags in the treasury – ready to be paid out. And Stephen, now it is the dry season, you will not keep them aboard all night?'

'I will not: though you know very well what the result will be. But, brother, there is a glee radiating from you that was never aroused by prize-money, dearly though you love it. You would never have heard from the Admiralty, at all?'

'Oh no. I should not expect anything yet, if ever: we saved a wonderful amount of time on that last leg. No. I have letters from home' – tapping his bosom – 'and so have you, but from Spain.'

Stephen's letter was from Avila. Clarissa reported a quiet, agreeable life, a healthy, affectionate and biddable child, now garrulous and tolerably correct in English, with some Spanish, but preferring the Irish she spoke with Padeen. She was learning her letters quite well, but was puzzled about which hand to write them with. Stephen's Aunt Petronilla was very kind to Brigid – to them both. Some of the ladies who lived in the convent had carriages and took them for drives, wrapped in furs: it was a severe winter, and two of Stephen's cousins, one coming from Segovia and the other from Madrid, had heard wolves close to the road at noon. She herself was well, mildly happy, reading as she had not read for years, and she liked the nuns' singing: sometimes she went with Padeen (who sent his duty) to the

Benedictine church for the plainchant. Enclosed was a small square piece of paper, not over-clean, with a drawing of a wolf with teeth and some words that Stephen could not make out until he realized that they were Irish written phonetically: *O my father fare well Brigid.*

He sat in the cabin savouring this and drinking thin lime-juice for some considerable time before Jack came in from the stern-gallery, looking equally happy. He said, 'I have had such delightful letters from Sophie, who sends you her dear love, and I mean to answer them this minute – there is a merchantman on the wing for Southampton. Stephen, how do you spell peccavi?'

Christine Heatherleigh had quite charmed Dr Maturin: he lay in his cot that night, swinging to the long Atlantic swell and thinking about his afternoon, and he had a startlingly clear visual image of her speaking earnestly about clavicles in primates, her eyes particularly wide open. 'Can it be that her physical presence has stirred long-dormant emotions in my let us say bosom?' he wondered. The answer 'No. My motives are entirely pure' came at almost the same moment that another part of his mind was considering the gentle pressure of her hand: kindness? her brother's friendship? a certain inclination? 'No,' he replied again, 'my motives being entirely pure she feels perfectly safe with me, middle-aged, ill-formed, wizened from the yellow jack, and can be as free as with her grandfather; or at least an uncle. Yet out of respect for her, and for Government House, I shall desire Killick to unpack, curl and powder my best wig against tomorrow's visit.'

In the morning he rose early, saying, 'I shall not shave until after my rounds and breakfast, when I shall have light enough to shave extremely close.' But when his rounds were over – and they were quite long, with several new cases of an intractable rash that he had never seen elsewhere – the light was still extremely poor. On his way up he met Killick, and speaking loud over the curious circumambient noise, he asked him both to attend to the wig and to lay out his good

275

satin breeches and a clean shirt, adding that he was about to ask the first lieutenant for a boat in the forenoon.

'No forenoon, no, nor no afternoon today, sir. Which there's a smoke on, and you can't hardly breathe on deck: nor no boat could swim. Harmattan, some say, a right Guinea smoke. You won't want no wig.'

No. And had he worn one he would have lost it. The moment he put his head above the level of the quarterdeck his meagre locks were whipped away to the south-west and he understood that the noise he heard was that of a very curious, very furious, north-east wind, hot, extraordinarily parching dry, and so loaded with red-brown dust that at times one could scarcely see twenty yards beyond the side. But those twenty yards of visible sea were whipped to a continuous chopping froth against the swell.

'Smoke, sir,' said Square at his side. 'But only a little one, over tomorrow or the next day.'

'How I hope you are right,' said Stephen. 'I particularly wish to see Mr Houmouzios,' and as he spoke he felt the red dust gritting between his teeth.

A disappointing day, and quite extraordinarily thirsty: yet it did have some wonders of its own. Jack, who as usual was making what observations were possible – observations of temperature at various depths, salinity, humidity of the air and so on for his friend Humboldt – showed Stephen his sea-chest, which had been brought up on to the half-deck so that the joiner might add an additional till or tray, a very stout chest indeed, that had seen and survived almost every kind of weather the world could offer: but the harmattan had split its lid – a broad cleft from one end to the other. 'We are playing the fire-hose on the boats to keep them whole,' he observed in a cheerful roar.

Square was right about the duration, however, and Thursday saw a world which, though ravaged, covered with rufous dust feet deep in sheltered places, and generally flattened, was at least quite calm, and a close-shaven Stephen Maturin, neatly dressed, pulled ashore over a filthy, gently heaving sea. Since he was carrying a gift of sun-birds, or rather their skins arranged with the feathers outwards, as beautiful as any bouquet and far more lasting, he took a sedan-chair to Government House, where he would have sent in his name if Mrs Wood had not thrown up a window with a little shriek and called out to ask him how he did.

She would be down in a minute, she said; and so she was, having paused only to change her shoes and put on a singularly becoming cashmere shawl. 'I am so sorry about this odious harmattan,' she said. 'It has utterly destroyed my garden. But perhaps, when we have had some coffee, you might like to look at some dried specimens, and the bones.'

The bones were indeed worth looking at, beautifully arranged, often articulated with a dexterity few could achieve. 'When we were young,' she said, and Stephen smiled, 'Edward and I used still to put the bat among the primates. But now we do not.'

'I am sure you are right,' said Stephen. 'They are very amiable creatures, yet it appears to me that their next of kin are the insectivores.'

'Just so,' cried she. 'You have but to look at their teeth and their hyoids, whatever Linnaeus may say. The primates are much more interesting. Shall we look at them first? The drawers over there and the tall cupboard are all primates: suppose we were to start with the lowest of the order and work up to the pongo. Here' – opening the bottom drawer, 'is a common potto. *Perodicticus potto*.'

'Ah,' said Stephen, delicately taking up the skeletal hand, 'how I have longed to see these phalanges. Do you happen to know whether in life this aborted index-finger had a nail?'

'He had none, poor dear: he seemed quite conscious of it. I often saw him gazing at his hand, looking puzzled.'

'He lived with you, so?'

'Yes. For nearly eighteen months, and how I wish he were living yet. One grows absurdly attached to a potto.'

Stephen examined the bones in silence for some considerable time, particularly the very curious anterior dorsal vertebrae, and at last he said, 'Dear Mrs Wood, may I ask you to be very kind to me?'

'Dear Dr Maturin,' she replied, blushing, 'you may ask me anything you like.'

'I too am absurdly attached to a potto,' he said, 'a tailless potto from Old Calabar.'

'An awantibo!' she cried, recovering from her surprise.

Stephen bowed. 'She has been grievously on my mind since we left those parts. I cannot in conscience take her north of the tropic line; I have not the resolution to kill and anatomize her; to abandon her to a local tree in unknown surroundings would go against my heart.'

'Oh how well I understand you,' she said, taking his hand in the kindest manner. 'Leave her with me, and I will look after her with the utmost care, for her sake and for yours; and if she dies, as my dear Potto died, you too shall have her bones.'

Friday's market was more than usually crowded, and Stephen's anxiety to find Houmouzios was more than usually keen: the harmattan had cracked not only the Commodore's sea-chest but a large number of other things aboard the *Bellona*, including the caddy in which Stephen kept his small remaining store of coca-leaves: the omnivorous, insatiable Guinea cockroaches had swarmed in, fouling what little they could not eat, and already he was feeling the lack. But there were large numbers of sailors and Marines wandering vaguely about; and a large number, a tribe, of tall stout very black men from some region where it was usual to carry broad-bladed spears and a shining trident stood at gaze, amazed by their first visit to a town: Square heaved them gently aside with his shoulder, opening a path as through a drove of oxen, Stephen followed him, and there at last, beyond a snake-charmer, he saw the familiar canopied stall, the dreadful great bald dog, and, huzzay, Houmouzios.

Socrates was already present, so Houmouzios left him in charge and carried Stephen back to the house at once. At their first greeting he said that he had received the Brazilian leaves, but it was not until the door was closed behind them that he spoke of three messages that had arrived for Dr Maturin.

Stephen thanked him cordially for his trouble, paid for the leaves, put the messages in his pocket and said, 'You have been very kind to me: allow me to suggest the purchase of East India stock as soon as it drops below a hundred and sixteen.'

They parted on excellent terms, and Stephen, with Square carrying the little sack, set off for the strand, the boat, the ship, and the privacy of his cabin and his decoding book; but they had not gone a furlong before the road was blocked by a turbulent mass of seamen, many already drunk, all fighting or about to fight or bawling encouragement at those who were engaged – hands from the *Thames* and the *Stately* having a dust up. Happily a group of moderately sober Bellonas came by, some of them Stephen's old shipmates, and they, forming close about the pair and roaring, 'Make a lane, there,' ran them briskly through unharmed.

Once aboard Stephen hurried below, locked the door and opened the messages in the order of their sending. They were all, of course, from Blaine's office. The code was so familiar that he could almost have done without the key, and the first two were comforting though unremarkable: the French plan was following its course: there had been two unimportant changes of command in minor vessels and one ship substituted for another of equal force. The third, however, stated that a requisition in the Netherlands had provided faster, better, more efficient transports and that the whole operation might be advanced by a week or ten days and that a third line-of-battle ship, the *César*, 74, coming from America might join the French squadron in 42°20'N, 18°30W: there might however be a reduction in the number of French frigates. The message ended with the hope that this might not reach Stephen too late, and it enclosed a fourth sheet written by Blaine himself according to the formula they used for private, personal communication. Stephen recognized the hand, he recognized the shape of the sequences, but he could not make the message out at all, though he was almost certain that one group was the combination Sir Joseph used for Diana's name. He ran clean through the book, a book that he knew backwards in any case; but there was no evident solution.

He put the personal message aside for further study and went in search of Jack, who was in the master's day-cabin with Tom, all three gazing very anxiously at the chronometers, which no longer agreed, harmattan, drought and dust having presumably deranged one or both. In some ways Jack was very quick: one glance at Stephen's face and he was in the great cabin in a moment: he listened in silence, and then said, 'Thank God we heard in time. I shall get under way as soon as possible. Pray see to your medical stores at once.' He summoned Tom: 'Tom, we must be under way in twelve hours, on the first of the ebb. We are short-handed and with so many men ashore, hard to find and bring off, we shall be in real difficulties: send the boats to the last-come merchantmen and press all you can. Stores are fairly good, apart from the gunner's, but watering will take place at once. No liberty, of course. Throw out one signal for all captains and another for the powder-hoys. All Marines to round up stragglers and I shall ask the Governor to use his troops.'

Stephen and his assistants and the potto in her darkened cage went ashore through intense activity: while his young men did all that was needed at the apothecary's, Stephen hurried to Mrs Wood with his charge and took his leave – his forced unwilling leave, as he observed – strangely moved. No young woman could have been kinder.

Back on board he saw the powder-hoys cast off, and in the waist the resigned merchant sailors being assigned to their watch and station. Within eleven and a half hours of

Jack's emphatic order the blue peter broke out at the fore-topmast head: one or two boats and some frantic canoes came racing through the moderate surf; and at the twelfth hour the squadron stood out to sea in a perfect line, steering west-north-west with a full topsail breeze just abaft the beam and the band of the *Aurora* playing loud and clear:

> *Come cheer up my lads, 'tis to glory we steer*
> *To add something new to this wonderful year:*
> *To honour we call you, not press you like slaves,*
> *For who are so free as we sons of the waves?*

Chapter Ten

Commodore Aubrey stood on the main topgallant crosstrees of the *Bellona*, about a hundred and forty feet above the broad grey sea: they were a frail support for a man of his weight and with even this moderate roll and pitch his sixteen or seventeen stone moved continually through a series of irregular swooping curves that might have puzzled an ape, the roll alone swinging him seventy-five feet; but although he was conscious of the starboard watch bending a heavy-weather topsail to the yard below him (the glass was dropping steadily), he was unaware of the movement, the varying centrifugal forces, or the wind howling round his ears, and he stood there as naturally as at home he would have stood on the small landing at the top of the Ashgrove Cottage stairs. He gazed steadily into the north-east, where he could see the *Laurel*'s topsails clear above the horizon, fifteen miles away while the *Laurel*'s lookout commanded a horizon still farther off, where the *Ringle* was lying, at the limit of fair-weather communication: but never a hint of a signal did the *Laurel* show. Slinging his telescope and changing the arm that held him to the topgallant shrouds, he pivoted to scan the south-west ocean. Here the expected cloud-bank obscured much of the lower sky, but he could still make out the white flash of the *Orestes* brig, herself in touch with the *Nimble* cutter, three leagues beyond. At the moment, therefore, he was at the centre of a circle fifty miles across in which no vessel could move unseen; but presently his far-off ships and smallcraft would be moving closer, the sun would set among the south-west clouds, and the night, with almost certain dirty weather, would set in. No moon.

He had been here, with his whole squadron in tolerable shape after an often difficult run from Sierra Leone, some forty degrees of latitude away, eight days before the earliest date that naval intelligence had given for the meeting of the French squadron with their seventy-four, their line-of-battle ship from the west, in 42°20'N, 18°30'W, and during these eight days, with fairly kind winds and clear weather, he had cruised slowly north-east till noon and south-west till sunset each side of centre. Nothing had he seen except for a recent outward-bound Bristol merchantman which had met with never a sail since the chops of the Channel and which was in this out-of-the-way corner of the sea because of a wicked American privateer schooner that was playing Old Harry farther south. But these eight days had had seven nights between them, and an eighth was just at hand.

Another glance into the north-east, and he saw that the *Laurel* was already steering for the squadron, close-hauled on the larboard tack. Another, and much longer, south-west, for that was the vital quarter: if he did not intercept that seventy-four, and if the French commander knew how to handle his ship, the squadron so heavily outnumbered faced disgrace.

He turned, slung his glass again and made his way down, heavy with care. Stephen heard him talking to Tom Pullings in the coach, covered his code-book and the innumerable variations of Blaine's message that he had worked out, shifting numbers, letters, combinations in the hope of finding his old friend's initial mistake and so making sense of his sheet: so far, after many days of the closest application, he had only reached a firmer conviction that the group he half-recognized at first did in fact refer to Diana. He locked his desk-top, wiped the anxiety off his face, and returned to the great cabin. When Jack came in he found him sitting before a tray of birds' skins and labels. Stephen looked up, and after a moment said, 'To a tormented mind there is nothing, I believe, more irritating than comfort. Apart from anything else it often implies superior wisdom in the comforter. But I am very sorry for your trouble, my dear.'

'Thank you, Stephen. Had you told me that there was always a tomorrow, I think I should have thrust your calendar down your throat.'

He sank into a reverie, while Stephen went on sorting and labelling his skins. He had an intimate conviction that the seventy-four had slipped through from the west by night, and that the odds against his squadron would be very great. That was not unexpected in the service. Sir Robert Calder with fifteen of the line had met the combined French and Spanish fleet off Finisterre under Villeneuve with twenty: he was court-martialled and blamed for having taken only two: to be sure, he had left the English coast unguarded and he was censured for misjudgment rather than misconduct; but even so . . . Nelson, with nine seventy-fours, one of which ran aground, came upon Brueys with ten, together with three eighty-gun ships and his own splendid 120-gun *l'Orient*, fourteen battle-ships in all, in the bay of Aboukir, attacked them at once, and burnt, took or destroyed all but two. And on another scale altogether, he himself, commanding a fourteen-gun brig, had boarded and carried a Spanish frigate mounting thirty-two. But then Nelson knew his captains, knew his ships: and he knew the enemy too. 'Never mind manoeuvres,' he had said to Jack one memorable evening, 'always go at them.'

Yes, but at that time the enemy was not a really eminent seaman: he had been shut up in port for years on end, his crew were not used to working a ship quickly in heavy seas (or in any others, quite often) nor to fighting her guns with bloody resolution; and discipline was poor. Now however the case was altered. Nelson would never have advised the captain of the *Java* to go straight at the USS *Constitution*, entirely neglecting manoeuvres.

Nelson had known his captains: the young Jack Aubrey had known the crew of the *Sophie* intimately, after long cruising cooped up together in that little sloop. For all their faults and frequent drunkenness, they could be relied upon to act together without hesitation in the approach to battle and in battle itself, and to deal with frightful odds. On the other hand, the older Jack did *not* know his captains, apart from Howard of the *Aurora* and Richardson of the *Laurel*. Where Duff was concerned, he had no doubt of his personal courage: the trouble there was the possibility of discipline having declined so far as to interfere with the seamanlike working of the ship into action and during the course of it. As for Thomas of the *Thames*, the Emperor, there was no telling: very heavy brutes might prove courageous in battle; but it was quite certain that if he fought, he would not fight his ship intelligently – lack of sense as well as lack of experience guaranteed that. Jack did not worry much about the fighting-spirit of the crew. They had been brought up to a reasonable standard of gunnery, and he had always found that once a ship was thoroughly engaged, the gun-team working fast, all together and with the roundshot flying, the roar of guns and the powder-smoke did away with shyness in the most unpromising. They might sometimes get rid of very tyrannical officers, accidentally-done-a-purpose – but he had never known them stop fighting unless their ship were forced to strike.

No: in this engagement – for engagement there would have to be, whether the other French seventy-four joined or not – the heart of the matter would almost certainly lie in manoeuvres, in ship-handling; and with poor discipline in the *Stately* and poor seamanship in the *Thames* that near-certainty so daunted his heart that when he could not command his mind it kept putting forward plans of attack that reduced the factor almost to the vanishing-point.

'I do not think there is any more futile occupation,' he said aloud, 'than talking about what should be done in a battle at sea until you know the direction and force of the wind, the numbers on both sides, their relative position, the state of the sea, and whether it will take place by day or . . . By God, Stephen, I could swear I smelt toasted cheese. We have not had toasted cheese before our music this last age and more.'

A short pause, and at some distance, through the scent of the sea, the mingled reverberation of taut rigging and the creak of wood, Killick's voice could be heard addressing his mate: 'You heard, Art. You ain't got flannel ears. I said open the door with your arse and let me through.'

Almost immediately after he came crabwise in, holding a splendid silver affair with little fitted dishes of toasted cheese. He put it down on their supper-table with a look of surly triumph and said, 'Which that Bristol cove gave some to Purser's steward. Cheddar. And I got it off of him.'

Stephen scraped the bottom of his second dish as well as he could with a piece of dry biscuit, finished his wine, and said, 'Will I tell you of a point that has been fretting my mind ever since the Bight of Benin, when you told me of your uneasiness about two of the ships? Now I am no great naval strategist . . .'

'Oh, I should never say that.'

Stephen bowed. 'Nor even a tactician . . .'

'After all, everything is relative.'

'Yet one of the vessels in question was a frigate, and I have always understood that when line-of-battle ships are engaged, the frigate's duty is to stand at a distance, to carry messages, to repeat signals, to pick up survivors clinging to the wreckage, and eventually to pursue and harass the frigates of the other side as they attempt to escape; but in no case to join the fray.'

'What you say is perfectly sound where fleet-actions are concerned. Ships of the line do not fire on frigates in a fleet-action – though there was an exception I saw in the Battle of the Nile – so long as the frigates do not fire on them. After all, dogs do not bite bitches: it is much the same. But *we* do not amount to a fleet; and two ships do not form a line of battle. Everything depends on wind and weather, light and darkness, and what sort of a sea is running; but when small squadrons meet there may well be a mêlée in which frigates and even sloops are involved. Be a

286

good fellow and toss me your rosin, will you?' – for by this time they were setting to their music.

'I wonder – I have my own reasons for wondering – that a man of your I might almost say wealth, and of your standing, a member of Parliament, high on the post-captain's list, and well at court, cannot or rather will not afford himself a piece of rosin.'

'You are to consider that I am a family man, Stephen, with a boy to educate and daughters to provide a dowry for, and clothes – half-boots twice and sometimes even three times a year. Tippets. When you come to worry about Brigid's fortune, and Brigid's tippets, you too may economize on rosin. Yes, yes. Don't you find cheese settle the stomach admirably? I believe I shall sleep tonight.'

'I have the same impression,' said Stephen. 'I have omitted my usual very moderate dose of coca-leaves, and I have indulged in two glasses of port extraordinary. Already my eyelids tend to droop. Pray pass the score: I have not really mastered the adagio.'

Toasted cheese is rarely thought of as a soporific, but either the time, the weather or some homely virtue in the cheese, some touch working upon minds extremely worn by anxiety, caused Stephen to sleep right through until the hands were piped to breakfast, while Jack, with one break when his inner watchdog felt the north-west wind increase so that the officer of the watch took a reef in the main and fore topsails, lay gently wheezing until a pale form at his side cried in an adolescent voice breaking with excitement, 'Sir, sir, if you please. *Laurel* signals enemy reported in sight north-north-west about five leagues steering south-westerly.'

'Numbers? Rates?'

'No, sir. It is rather dirty in the north-north-west.'

'Thank you, Mr Hobbs. I shall be on deck directly.'

So he was, joining all the officers and midshipmen, those of the middle watch still in their nightshirts with a coat flung over: and they were all gazing fixedly over the larboard bow, where, in the thin morning light under a grey sky the *Laurel* could be seen hull up already, throwing a fine wave from her cutwater with her press of sail, the signal flying still.

They all broke off to wish the Commodore a good morning. He said to the signal-lieutenant, 'Tell her to ask *Ringle* whether she has any notion of rates and numbers.'

A pause, in which a squall drifted over the north-west horizon.

'Negative, sir,' said a signal-lieutenant at last.

'*Laurel*, repeat to *Ringle*: *approach enemy under American colours. Ascertain numbers, rates. Sink their topsails steering south-east. Report in . . .*' Jack looked intently at the sky '*. . . one hour. Do not acknowledge.* Now to the squadron: *course ENE½E under easy sail.*' One bell in the forenoon watch, and Jack said, 'Captain Pullings, if your people are anything like me, they must be damned hungry by now. Let us all have breakfast.'

It was the welcome shrilling pipe and the thunder of feet on deck that woke Dr Maturin at last: he was therefore at table before anyone else, being no more particular about washing, brushing and shaving than the monks of the Thebaïd. On the quarterdeck Jack led the way aft to the master's day cabin, followed by Tom, the first lieutenant and the master himself, and as they went the sun broke through the eastern clouds.

'Good morning, Commodore,' said Stephen, already deep in eggs and the ship's butcher's capital bacon. 'Good morning, Tom. Here's a pretty state of affairs. I have madly overslept, I have missed my morning rounds, the coffee is almost cold, and there are people running about crying "Oh, oh, the enemy is upon us. What shall we do to be saved?" Can this be true, my dears?'

'Only too true, alas,' said Jack, hanging his head very dolefully. 'And I am sorry to tell you that they are within thirty miles, or even less.'

'Never mind, Doctor,' said Tom. 'The Commodore has a plan that will confound their politics.'

'Would he be prepared to reveal it? To lay it forth in terms suited to the meanest understanding?'

'Let me finish my mutton chop, and gather my wits,' said Jack, 'and I am your man . . . Well,' he said, wiping his mouth at last, 'what I have to offer is all very theoretical, very much the air: naturally, until we know the enemy's force. But I start with three assumptions: first, that he is in search of the missing seventy-four; second, that he will not come to action, encumbered as he is with transports, if he can possibly avoid it; and third, that this north-wester, providential for him at the moment but uncommon in these waters, will back into the much more usual south-west – much more important by far, for my plan – by nightfall or a little later.'

Tom nodded and said, 'That's right.'

'So supposing all these things to be true, I steer somewhat east of east-north-east, keeping him under observation if only this weather stays clear, with *Ringle* lying say ten miles off – an ordinary object, unsuspicious, a small American privateer: there are dozens of the same build and rig – with *Laurel* repeating. Then, once the French commodore is well south of us – Tom, give me the bread-barge, will you?' He broke a biscuit, cleared a space on the table, and said, 'Weevils already? Here, the large piece with the reptile lurking inside, is the rendezvous. This is us, standing gently east. Here are the French, over our horizon and with no frigates scouting out: they are heading for the rendezvous. When they get there, which they should do today with this leading wind, when they get there and find no seventy-four, they turn about and steer for Ireland. By this time, in all likelihood, the wind will have backed into the south of south-west, another leading wind for them. Yes, but here we are' – tapping a piece of biscuit – 'and once they have repassed the parallel of the point we first saw them – once they are to the north of us, why then we have the weather-gage! We have the weather-gage, and in principle we can bring them to action whether they like it or not.'

'That is very satisfactory,' said Stephen, considering the pieces of biscuit. 'And eminently clear. But –' shaking his head – 'it is an odious necessity.'

Stephen's dislike for killing his fellow-men often embarrassed Jack, whose profession it was, and he quickly added, 'Of course, that is only the ideal course of events. A thousand things could throw it out – the wind staying in the north-west or dropping altogether, some busy dog of a privateer who sees us and reports our presence, a reinforcement, the arrival of the other ship of the line, a storm that dismasts us . . . and in any event my predictions may have a strong touch of Old Moore about them . . .'

'If you please, sir,' said yet another midshipman, addressing his captain, 'Mr Soames's compliments, and *Laurel* signals two ships of the line, probably seventy-fours, two frigates in company, a frigate or corvette a league ahead, and four transports, two of them far astern.'

'Thank you, Mr Dormer,' said Tom Pullings. 'I shall come and look at her presently.' He beamed at Stephen, and when the boy had gone he said, 'I don't believe there is anything at all of Old Moore in the Commodore's prediction, sir. I believe we have them . . .'

'Hush, Tom,' said the Commodore. 'There's many a slip, twixt the cup and the sip, you know.'

'How true, sir,' said Tom, touching the wooden bread-barge. 'I nearly said something very improper.' He stood up, returned thanks for his breakfast, and hurried back to the quarterdeck.

In the main, Jack's forecast was sound enough, but so were his reservations. The wind backed south-south-west earlier than he had expected, so that the French squadron had to beat up, tack upon tack, for their rendezvous; then the Commodore Esprit-Tranquil Maistral, a survivor of the enormous expedition destined for Bantry Bay in '96 with no less than seventeen of the line and thirteen frigates, decided to wait for the seventy-four from America until the four-teenth, a particularly lucky day; and even then not to set sail until the most auspicious hour, which was half-past eleven, so that with a thick, dirty night, with a brave topgallant wind on the larboard quarter that bowled them along at a fine rate, he and his ships very nearly ran clear.

During this time, if a space filled with such anxiety could be called a time, the *Bellona* and her fellows had been edging steadily westwards so as to fetch the Frenchman's wake as he proceeded north-north-east for Ireland in three or four days, and they filled the interval with the innumerable tasks always waiting to be done in a ship at sea, and fishing over the side, with moderate success.

The position at which the squadron would lie to, some-what to the south and east of the point the French were expected to reach in three days at the most, had been given to the *Laurel* and the *Ringle*; but in almost twice that space of time, ocean drift, dirty weather and human fallibility deprived the figure of much of its meaning, and it was only when Maistral had been at sea since the fourteenth, that the *Ringle* came tearing close-hauled through a very heavy sea and a black squall at seven bells in the morning watch to bellow and roar that the French had been seen hull-down in the north-east steering north-east, half an hour after sunset yesterday.

For the last day and a half Jack Aubrey had spent almost all the time on deck or at the masthead, saying very little, eating less, pale, withdrawn. Now he breathed again; and now the steady process of cracking on began – preventer backstays, braces, shrouds and stays to enable the ship to bear the press of foul-weather canvas that the people were spreading with such good will.

But it required all this burst of furious seamanlike energy, all this urgent driving of the ship and encouragement of the squadron to prevent him slipping back into bitter self-reproach for having come so near to failure through over-confidence in his own judgment. Much of this activity, once the *Bellona* was in racing trim, was devoted to the *Thames*. He spent a whole day aboard her, showing them quite kindly how to wring an extra knot or even an extra two or three fathoms out of her; but although there was some improvement he had to admit that even when he had done his best she was still slow for a frigate: nothing would cure her but radical measures. It did not appear to him that her hull was particularly ill-formed, but it was quite certain that she could sail no better with her present trim. To take advantage of her lines, she had to be at least a foot and a half by the stern; yet solely to improve her looks, her hold, her ballast, water, stores, everything, had been stowed so that her masts were bolt upright, perpendicular for pretty. The smartest ship on the station, with her yards squared by the lifts and braces and her masts at right angles with the sea, said Thomas: Prince William had often commended her appearance. Jack concealed his opinion of Prince William's judgment of a man-of-war, but said that when they were in the Cove of Cork they would try to bring her by the stern a trifle and make comparative trials; he then said good day, leaving the frigate in a better mood. He had scarcely returned to the *Bellona* before the *Thames*, in her zeal, carried away her foretopgallant mast.

Nevertheless, on the second morning, towards the end of the forenoon watch, the low sky cleared a little and the French sails showed, faint white glimmers on the north-east horizon. Jack contemplated them from the masthead for some considerable time, gathering a general sense of their sailing qualities; and coming down at last he met with Killick's disagreeable, disapproving face. 'Now, sir,' he said, in that familiar whine, 'your good shirt and admiral's uniform has been spread out this last half glass. Which you ain't forgot you are dining with the wardroom today? Even the Doctor remembered it, and changed voluntary.'

The excitement of the chase had done wonders for the wardroom cook: he had lashed in most of his rarest and most costly ingredients – sherry in the turtle soup, port in the sucking-pig's gravy, brandy in one of the Commodore's favourite forecastle dishes, fu-fu, ordinarily made of barley and treacle, but now with honey and cognac.

Jack made an excellent dinner, the first for a great while; the chase, the audible speed of the ship, with water singing loud along her side, the sense of eagerly straining wood, removed much of the restraint imposed by an admiral's uniform in the place of honour, and there was a general sound of cheerful and spontaneous conversation. Several of the officers had seen or more often heard something of Hoche's disastrous attempt on Bantry Bay with an enormous, unmanageable fleet in '96, and while for the most part they avoided shop, they had interesting things to say about that ironbound coast, with its frightful seas in a full south-west gale – the Fastnet rock – the tide-race off the Skelligs – remarks however that might have been better timed if just such a wind were not already blowing, and if a dropping glass did not suggest that it would soon blow harder still.

After coffee Jack suggested that Stephen should put on a tarpaulin jacket and sou'wester – how perfectly named – and come with him to view their quarry from the forecastle, taking his come-up glass with them. It was a wet forecastle, with the spray and even green water of the following seas sweeping right forward to mingle with that flung up by the *Bellona*'s bows as she pitched hawse-deep; but their view was so imperfect that Jack proposed the foretop and called for Bonden.

Stephen protested that he was perfectly recovered, perfectly strong enough for this simple, familiar ascent. Jack hailed somewhat louder, Bonden came at the double, and Stephen submitted, observing privately, 'I thus have the comfort of being raised safely, easily, to this eminence, and at the same time that of retaining my self-respect.'

The eminence of some eighty feet did indeed give them a fine uninterrupted expanse of grey, white-dashed, windwhipped ocean; and there in the north-east were the longlooked-for sails. Not topsails alone, but sometimes courses too, and on occasion a hull rose clear. The *Bellona* had not quite fetched their wake, since the quickest way to do so was to converge upon it in as straight a line as possible rather than make a dog-leg: this meant that from the foretop they still had a slight sideways, glancing view of the French line. Jack passed the telescope. 'Two two-deckers, and a little small thing far ahead,' said Stephen. 'Then four that I take to be troop-ships. And two frigates.'

'Yes,' said Jack. 'How well he handles those troop-ships: all neatly in their station. Their Commodore must be a man of parts. They are fast, even very fast for troop-ships, but I have little doubt we are overhauling them.' He turned a screw on the telescope that separated the two halves of a divided lens and said, 'Now you see two images of the leading two-decker just touching: if they stay like that, we are going at the same speed: if they separate, the chase is going faster: if they overlap, we are gaining. One has to wait quite a while for the effect to be visible.'

Stephen gazed and gazed: after a long pause in which he pointed out a stormy petrel pittering up the side of a foaming roller he looked again and cried, 'They have joined. They overlap!'

'We are certainly gaining quite fast, and I think that if we were to leave the *Thames* to make the best of her way we might be up with them by mid-morning, within sight of land. I think their Commodore will almost certainly heave to and fight there, rather than close among those wicked rocks and on an unknown coast: besides, it might allow him to put his troops ashore under one or both of his frigates.'

'Would our frigates not destroy them?'

'Perhaps. But they might be badly outgunned in weight of metal. One Frenchman is I think a thirty-six-gun ship, almost certainly carrying eighteen-pounders, and the other a thirty-two, with the same. Poor old *Thames* only has twelves, and *Aurora* no more than nines . . .'

Stephen made some other observations, but clearly Jack, gazing at the enemy, was not attending.

'As things stand at present,' he said at last, 'the sooner we engage the better,' and as he turned he called down to Meares, busy just abaft the forecastle, 'I beg you will make sure of those ring-bolts, Master Gunner. They may be sorely tried tomorrow.'

'If they draw, sir,' replied the gunner, looking up with a grin, 'you may draw me, too; and quarter me into the bargain.'

Jack laughed; but on deck he said privately to Stephen, 'As I remember, the Frenchman's orders were for Bantry Bay or the Kenmare river. Do you know either, or the deep inlets all along?'

'Hardly at all, and then only from a landlubber's point of view. I scarcely know west Cork at all. I did stay with the Whites once: not the Whites of Bantry but cousins between Skibereen and Baltimore. And then there was an idle tale of a white-tailed-eagle meeting on Clear Island that took me there. But as a guide I am useless, let alone a pilot, for all love.'

'If things stand as they are, my mind is tolerably clear,' said Jack.

Things did not stand as they were: the wind strengthened, veering westerly, so that they could carry no more than close-reefed topsails; and even those hurried them along at a breakneck pace. As thick a night as could well be imagined, the sky entirely covered by clouds that barely cleared the masthead, frequent rain, often in very heavy squalls. Not the least possibility of an observation, and little reliance could be placed on dead-reckoning.

The *Bellona* had her three great stern-lanterns all ablaze, and from time to time Jack Aubrey left either his fiddle or the game of cards he was playing with Stephen to stand by them on the poop, watching the rain sweep past in their rays or searching the darkness astern for his squadron: at eight bells a suffused glow as the watch changed aboard the *Stately*, and once or twice a small light in what he took to be the *Ringle* right abeam; but almost all the time it was a roaring darkness, another manner of being. After a little while of this the binnacle lamps were so bright when he returned to the quarterdeck that in their mere reflection he recognized the midshipman of the watch, almost extinguished by his waterproof clothes and hat. 'A dirty night, Mr Wetherby,' he said. 'I trust it don't damp your spirits?'

'Oh no, sir,' said the boy, laughing with excitement. 'Ain't it a lark?'

Every few bells he walked – or sometimes clawed his way – on the poop, sensing the changing forces of the air and sea: a great spring tide would flow tomorrow, and already in the countless pressures working on the hull he thought he could discern its first stirring.

'The wind is almost due west now,' he told Stephen, returning from one of these tours, very near the night's end: but Stephen was asleep, bowed in an elbow-chair, his head moving with the roll and pitch of the ship, and she racing through the blackness with him.

For what seemed no more than a moment Jack did the same: but the cry of the lookout on the forecastle: 'Breakers on the starboard bow' pierced through the rising doze, and he was on deck before the messenger could reach him. Miller, the officer of the watch, had already started sheets to reduce the ship's pace, and he and Jack stood listening: through the general din of wind and the crash of tumbling seas there came the grave, regular beat of surf breaking on the shore or on a reef. 'Two blue flares,' said Jack, the agreed signal; and for once, in spite of wind and the omnipresent spray that wetted everything, they soared away at once, their unearthly blue showing clear.

'Indeed the sky is higher, almost clear,' said the lieutenant.

'It will be day in half a glass,' said the master. 'You can make out a glimmer in the east already.'

The glimmer spread: the west wind, though still very strong, bore less rain, more cloud, and presently their night-accustomed eyes made out first a long cape to larboard, cloud still covering all its height above a hundred feet, with islands at the seaward end, and then to starboard the even longer, even more cloudy headland on whose western side the sea was beating with such tremendous, rhythmic solemnity: between them lay a narrow rocky-sided bay reaching away into the land, losing itself in the murk; and as the light increased and the water grew less dark they saw another rounded island some way down, close in on the northern shore. On this side of the island lay two ships. Jack took Miller's glass. They were the French seventy-fours, and as he fixed them, with the utmost intense concentration, he grew more and more convinced that they too were uncertain of their landfall. Indeed, with this visibility, it might have been any one of half a dozen. And that they were trying to make it out, hoping for pre-arranged signals, friendly pilots: they had a green flag flying.

'Do not strike the bell,' he said, stopping the ship's routine: he wanted none of the morning ceremonies at this point.

'No bell it is, sir,' said the quartermaster.

'If you please, sir,' said Miller, pointing to the first island beyond the northern arm of the bay – an island that now proved to be a small group.

'Yes,' said Jack. 'Very good.' For there, in a cove as neat and sheltered and concealed from view as could be wished, invisible from the offing and from the lower bay, there lay the troop-ships and both frigates.

With a fierce pleasure he grasped the situation. The narrow bay ran directly north-east: if the French commodore took his squadron well in, with this wind he could never bring them out. He was trying to make sure whether this was his right destination or not, and already he was most dangerously far along.

All the officers were on deck. 'We have no pilot left from Irish waters?' asked Jack.

'No, sir,' said Miller. 'Even Michael Tierney died in the Bight of Benin. But the master is searching through and through and through his charts – he has called for a sounding.'

'It's all one,' said Jack. 'Beat to quarters.' He ran on to the poop, looking aft. Everyone was present, *Stately* within a cable's length, except for *Thames*, who had sagged right away to the east, almost beyond the other horn closing the bay. The *Ringle*, like a dutiful tender, was rising and falling on the great swell fifty yards on the *Bellona*'s quarter.

'Good morning, William,' he called. 'How are you bearing up?'

'Good morning, sir,' answered Reade. 'Prime, sir, thank you very much.'

Returning, Jack made first *Thames*'s signal to rejoin and then *Stately*'s to come within hail.

The sixty-four came under the *Bellona*'s lee, and in his strong voice Jack said, 'Captain Duff – there lie the French two-deckers. Let us attack them directly; and while we are bearing down let us at least have a bite and a sup. I shall tackle the pennant-ship, if you and *Thames* will look after the other.'

'Very happy, sir,' said Duff, smiling, and his crew gave three cheers.

Before going below Jack gave the *Aurora*, *Camilla* and *Laurel* orders to maintain a discreet watch on the transports and their escort between the islands. He had every hope of snapping them up with neither damage nor casualties if he were successful in the bay.

A spirit-stove and a willing mind can do wonders, even in a heavy sea with a full gale blowing, and Jack Aubrey, leaving Stephen to carry their coffee-pot down into the cockpit, came on deck again warm and well-fed. He was wearing his usual rig: an old uniform coat, threadbare brass-bound hat that had turned many a cut, a heavy cavalry sabre by way of fighting sword, boots and silk stockings (much better in case of a wound). He glanced along the decks, all in the perfect battle-order Captain Pullings knew so well: over to the other side of the bay, where the *Thames* was making good progress: towards the Frenchmen, who for their part had moved from the island towards what seemed to be a cloudy village on the south side, where they lay a-try, perhaps with a kedge out ahead. The *Stately* was keeping a cable's length astern, coming along under the same close-reefed topsails with the same air of competence.

'Shipmates,' said Jack in a conversational voice, but one that carried well over the roar of the wind, 'we are going to attack the pennant-ship from to-windward, while *Stately* goes on to deal with her companion. I am going to engage so close that our roundshot will go through both her sides, to end it quick. And be damned to him who first cries Hold, enough.'

A very hearty cheer indeed, echoed from the *Stately*: and the waft from the match-tubs by each gun drifted in eddies, a scent surpassed only by powder-smoke. Yet the *Thames* had not answered the cheer, though she was no great way off on the southern side. Jack took his glass: she was in trouble: she had contrived to get inshore of a reef and she could neither turn nor advance.

The first ranging shot from the Frenchmen splashed alongside. The next came home, somewhere about the larboard hawse-hole. Tom yawed just enough for the forward starboard guns to reply, and now, in spite of the wind right aft, there was the scent of powder-smoke as well.

How quickly those last few hundred yards fleeted by! At one moment you could still notice a gull or that damn fool of a *Thames*, and the next you were in the full deafening roar of battle yardarm to yardarm, the broadsides losing all unity and merging into a continuous iron bellow. The ships ground together as the Frenchmen tried to board, yelling as they came. They were repelled; and now came a louder, more triumphant cry, then another as the enemy's mizzen went by the board at deck-level, carrying the maintopmast with it. The ship could no longer lie head to wind and she slewed to larboard; but still answering her helm she ran north-east along the shore, keeping up a fire from her undamaged side until, at the very height of flood, eleven minutes after the first shot, she struck, racing high on to the rocky shelf just below the village.

Jack rounded to and called upon her to surrender; and this, after a moment's hesitation, she did. Even if she had been able to bring a gun to bear, which she could not, lying at that dreadful angle on the rock among the surf there was no hope. Yet so far down the bay and in these shallows, the surf was far less dreadful than it looked. The quarter-boats brought the French commodore and his officers across with little difficulty, and carried a prize-crew back, including, at the Frenchman's most earnest request, Stephen Maturin, their own surgeon having been killed – he had wished to see a battle. A nominal prize-crew, and as a last thought a small party of Marines, for even if he had imagined trouble aboard the prize Jack had no time to spare. Below the racing cloud he had just seen *Stately* attempt an extremely brave but perilous manoeuvre, drawing ahead and suddenly tacking across the Frenchman's bows to rake her fore and aft with broadside after broadside. But his ship or his men's skill betrayed him: the *Stately* would not come round. She hung there in irons while the Frenchman pounded her, knocked away her main and mizzen topmasts, and then she fell off to her former starboard tack. The enemy of course bore up and raked her in his turn.

But for the *Bellona*'s approach he must have destroyed or taken her. As it was he let fall his courses and raced close-hauled to the end of the southern headland and out to sea beyond it, just saving both masts and sails, and disappeared, steering eastward and increasing sail without the least care for his friends in their secluded cove.

The reason for this headlong flight appeared a moment later, when two English seventy-fours and a frigate appeared round the northern cape. Jack signalled them to heave to, emphasizing the order with a gun, told Tom to look to the *Stately*, and if she could be left, to make the best of his way towards the troop-ships' cove, and so dropped into *Ringle*.

He went aboard the nearest seventy-four, *Royal Oak*, which received his shabby, battle-stained and indeed bloody person with all the compliments due to his broad pennant, and with very great enthusiasm. 'Gentlemen, I bring you prizes,' he said. 'There is a cove among that group of islands there' – pointing – 'which conceals four French troop carriers and two frigates. I should take them myself, but I have four foot water in the hold and gaining fast, having had a bout with that fellow aground down there – a very determined fighter indeed – and the ship is slow and heavy.'

They treated him with infinite consideration – of course they would do all he desired – they gave him the most cordial joy of his victory – hoped that his people had not suffered and thanked the Lord they had been ordered from Bere Haven on rumours of gunfire – led him to the cabin – would the Commodore care for a dish of tea? of cocoa? Perhaps gin and hot water, or the whiskey of these parts? All this time they were approaching the cove, and now Jack's frigate captains came aboard, passionate for news, grieved for the *Bellona*'s battered state – she could indeed be seen to be wallowing along, her pumps flinging water wide to leeward.

One of the French frigates in the cove chanced it. She cut her cable, squeezed through an improbable gap and ran east before the gale with everything she could set, joining the ship of the line in her way back to France. The rest submitted to the overwhelming force: for by this time the *Bellona* had joined.

'William,' said Jack Aubrey to Reade in the tender, 'pray run down to the Doctor and tell him that Captain Geary is lending us some hands to pump and seeing us back to Bantry to be patched up, and *Warwick* is giving poor *Stately* a tow. Tell him that all is well, and that I hope to ride across and see him in a day or two. It is only a short way across by land – that is how the news of our being here reached Bantry: a boy on an ass to tell them that it was the French at last.'

The French at last: looked for so long, so long promised. Things now seemed to be going astray somewhat; yet here at least was a great French ship and she filled with people, filled with arms.

The tide withdrew, farther and unbelievably far, and the French ship settled, her wounded timbers groaning and even breaking under her weight. Most of the prisoners were confined between decks, but some gave the prize-crew a hand with various tasks, and some helped Stephen transfer the wounded to the Sacred Heart hospital behind and above Duniry. Some of the men of the village had been in one or another of the Irish regiments in the French service before the Revolution, and were still fluent in the language; it was they who learnt the purpose of the expedition and the nature of the ship's cargo for sure. The word spread and by the time Stephen came back from the hospital with Father Boyle there was a noisy, threatening crowd by the stranded ship, her landward side now almost dry. An awkward kind of accommodation-ladder had been shipped, and on a platform at its foot stood a guard of the *Bellona*'s Marines, looking both cross and apprehensive, for not only were the men of the village very near to the point of stoning them, but the foreshore had quantities of seaweed, mud, general filth, and the women, who had already loosed their hair, were perfectly capable of flinging it, wrecking their sacred uniforms.

They made room for Father Boyle and Stephen, the young officer whispering, 'I fear they may try to rush the side.' Half way up the ladder Stephen turned, and speaking in Irish he said, 'Men of Duniry, it is weapons you desire.'

'It is,' they cried. 'And it is weapons we shall have.'

'If you had those weapons, weapons from the man who has kept the Holy Father close prisoner, and who turned Turk in Cairo, worshipping Mahomet, they would be your bane and your certain death, God between us and evil. Do you not know that the whole barony is raised with the news of their coming, the French? The yeomanry of all West Cork and the County Kerry are afoot, and every man found with a musket from this ship must hang. A full gibbet by nightfall, and never a roof with its thatch unburnt.' Turning to the priest he cried, 'Mors in olla, vir Dei: mors in olla. For God's sake urge them to be quiet, Father dear, or there will be widows by the score tomorrow.' And reverting to Irish he said, 'There was the Prophet Eliseus, as our good Father Boyle will tell you, and he and his disciples were offered a meal in the desert: but someone cried out in a great voice, roaring from his chest, "Do not touch it, oh man of God. *There is poison in the pot*." Countrymen, that accursed ship would be the deadly pot for you, so it would, were you to touch it, God forbid.' With this he walked up into the prize, leaving them silent.

Late that night and all next morning the yeomanry, the military and the plain soldiers, with the usual apparatus of triangle, irons and fire, searched Duniry and all the nearby farms and cabins; and nothing did they find but some illicit spirit, which they drank.

At Mass the next day Stephen was greeted with the respect due to the Lord Lieutenant and perhaps more affection: many a man asked would he do the house the honour of taking a tint; and presents of white pudding, cream and carrageen jelly were left for him at the ship. By now all his most critical surgery had been done; and by now the local medical corps had the remaining patients well in hand. He had time to spare, and to walk about, so when one of the many country gentlemen who had come to gaze at the stranded French battleship called from his dogcart, 'Why, Maturin! What a pleasure to see you! It must be years and years . . . Come into this little shebeen and take a glass of sherry; or should you prefer the poteen – perhaps safer? How do you do? I am truly charmed to hear it, upon my honour. So I am. You are on your way to see Diana, I am sure. I was out with her at the end of March, with Ned Taaffe's hounds. We had a famous day, and killed two foxes. House. House, there: two glasses of sherry, if you please, and a little small dry crust to help them down – there would never be an anchovy, at all?'

Stephen looked at the pale wine, raised his glass and said, 'God bless you,' with a bow. He took out his elegant watch and laid it in the light, watching the centre second-hand make its full revolution.

His friend too watched it with close attention. 'You are taking your pulse, I make no doubt?' he said.

'So I am, too,' said Stephen. 'I have had a variety of emotions recently and I wished to assign a number at least to the general effect, to the physical effect, since quality is not subject to measure. My number is one hundred and seventeen to the minute.'

'That is the luckiest number in the world, I believe; a prime number, to be divided or multiplied by no other.'

'You are in the right of it, Stanislas Roche: it is neither too much nor too little. Listen. Will you do me a kindness, now? Will you run me into Bantry in this elegant equipage, till I can hire a horse or a chaise?'

'I will do better than that, since Bantry is in the wrong direction for at least half the way. I will run you into Drimoleague itself: ain't that handsome in me?'

'It is fit to be written in letters of gold,' said Stephen absently.

And absent, painfully so, was his conversation all the way. Fortunately Stanislas had conversation for two: he described his day with Ned Taaffe's hounds – Diana's spirit in negotiating a prodigious number of banks and ditches on a little Arab gelding – every detail of a long chase through the country Stephen had never seen – a chase that ended in some unexpected, surprising manner. 'Ain't you amazed?' asked Stanislas.

'Deeply amazed,' said Stephen, with the utmost truth; but he was slowly coming out of it, setting things in some kind of an order, almost entirely grasping the fact that in a few minutes he might see his heart's desire, whatever the consequences. Diana was staying, had long been staying, with Colonel Villiers, an ancient relative – uncle? Half-uncle? – of her first husband, a gentleman of whom Stephen knew nothing except that he had served in India and that he was devoted to fishing.

'Here we are,' said Stanislas, pulling up. 'We have made splendid time. Be a good fellow and open the gate, will you? There is almost never anyone in the lodge. Oh, but before I forget, as a King's officer you must put on half-mourning. I was in Bantry this morning, as I told you, looking at the *Bellona* and the *Stately* – they had put some sort of a mast into her, the *Stately*, I mean – and to my concern I saw a flag flying at half-mast on it. I sent over to ask whether it meant the gallant Captain Duff had been killed. No, said they; he had only lost a leg. The flag – which indeed was general, as I saw when I looked at the other men-of-war – was because of the death of a royal, or near enough, the Duke of Habachtsthal, who owned Rossnacreena Castle, Lord Lieutenant of the county, and who had cut his throat in London last Thursday – the news was just come over.'

This added an amazement, not indeed of the same stunning importance, but not inconsiderable by any other standard on earth: with that man dead, there would be no difficulty about pardons for Padeen and Clarissa: and Stephen's own fortune would be safe anywhere. He could give Diana a golden crown, if she should like one.

'Stanislas,' said Stephen from the roadside, 'I will not open the gate. I will say farewell here, and thank you as kindly as ever can be. I have not seen Diana this terrible long while, and thousands of miles of sea; and I wish to find her alone.'

'Certainly, certainly. I quite understand. And she too will be amazed.'

'God bless, now, Stanislas.'

He passed through the wicket into a fine broad court, somewhat marred by a twenty-foot stretch of tall grey stone wall fallen into it and the skeleton of a two-ton sloop shored up by the central fountain. Beyond the court the house spread in the brilliant sun before him had two low wings, a three-storey centre with a classical portico and a fine flight of steps, many of them whole.

He had almost reached them – there was a curious liverwort growing between the joints – when the door itself opened and Diana's voice called, 'Are you the bread?'

'I am not,' said Stephen.

She emerged from the darkness, shading her eyes, cried, 'Stephen, my love, is it you?' flew down the steps, missed the last and plunged into his arms, tears running fast.

They sat there, pressed close, and she said, 'You have the wildest way of suddenly appearing when my mind is filled with your name and even your image. But Stephen, my dear, you are so yellow and thin. Do they feed you at all? Have you been ill? You are on leave, I am sure. You must stay here a great while and the Colonel will fill you out with salmon, smoked eels and trout – he will be in before dinner. Lord, I am so happy to see you, my dear. Come now and rest; it is destroyed you are looking. Come up to my bed.'

'Must I come to your bed?'

'Of course you must come to my bed: and you are never to leave it again. Stephen, you must never go to sea any more.'

The Winning Post
at Last

ALAN JUDD

SOMETIMES THINGS come together as they should. They recently have for the novelist and biographer, Patrick O'Brian; within a week of the announcement in the Birthday Honours of his CBE for services to literature, he became the first ever winner of the £10,000 Heywood Hill Literary Prize.

World-wide publishing success already threatens to lionise this energetic and very private octogenarian, but it was clear at the prize-giving that the pleasures of literary recognition do something to render tolerable the passing inconveniences of fame. They do something, too, to make up for decades of unremitting endeavour, for early years of poverty and for numbers of good books written blind – that is, without the comforting assurance of a reading public. It has been a long haul for O'Brian.

Ill-health and parental death resulted in a peripatetic Anglo–Irish childhood, while an education that unusually combined rigour and breadth fed the autodidact in him. Fluency in French, Spanish and Catalan found him useful employment in Intelligence during the Second World War, on which subject he remains firmly discreet, and also led to his marriage to Mary, mother of Count Nikolai Tolstoy. After the war they settled in Wales, then partly for health reasons moved to the coastal village near the Franco-Spanish border where they have lived ever since.

It was easier to be poor in a warm climate.

There was never any question for O'Brian that he should – must – write, and never any wavering or compromise in Mary's essential support. Short stories, reviews, translations and early novels appeared, outstanding amongst which was

Testimonies, an intense and obsessional love story set in rural Wales and now published by HarperCollins. For years, however, it was the translations from French into English – *Papillon*, for instance, and all of de Beauvoir – that kept the wolf from the door. Luck helped; Picasso was a neighbour and became a friend, which subsequently led O'Brian to write a vivid and perceptive biography of him, still acknowledged in Spain (and by the late Lord Clark) as the best.

In 1969 O'Brian published *Master and Commander*, the first of a series of novels – 'tales', he modestly calls them – set in the Royal Navy during the Napoleonic Wars. Although he thought there might be others he no more anticipated that the series would extend to seventeen (so far – the eighteenth is on the way) than that it would ensure his place in the literary pantheon. Indeed, despite early support from such as Mary Renault, T. J. Binyon and John Bayley, the books were not an immediate sensation and actually went out of print in America.

Gradually, however, word-of-mouth, astute publishing, literary merit and – dare one say it? – sheer readability have combined to produce during the last five years a rare tidal wave of literary recognition and commercial success. Sales are now over the million, translations are into nineteen languages, the British Library has published its first bibliography of a living author (with an introduction by William Waldegrave), the University of Indiana is buying the manuscripts and forming an O'Brian study centre, a ship is being built in Chile to the specification of that most often sailed by O'Brian's heroes, his American publishers (Norton) issue a regular newsletter and in the Cayman Isles there is a dining club called the Patrick O'Brian Widows, formed by ladies whose husbands are addicted. Better known admirers include people as diverse as Iris Murdoch and Max Hastings, Antonia Byatt and Charlton Heston.

Master and Commander begins in Port Mahon where the impoverished Lieutenant Jack Aubrey and the impoverished physician, Stephen Maturin, meet and fall out at a concert. Next morning, in the euphora of a longed-for but unexpected promotion to command, Jack offers Stephen a place as ship's surgeon, so beginning a friendship that will surely prove one of the most enduring and endearing in our literature. They are quite different: Jack is English, beefy, cheerful and generous, a fool ashore but a genius afloat; Stephen is Irish–Catalan, moody, subtle, brilliant, a passionate naturalist (O'Brian is also the biographer of Sir Joseph Banks) and a determined spy against Napoleon. They are united by sympathy, respect, acknowledgement of difference, a sense of fairness and justice and affection. All this is suggested more in the spaces between words than expressed directly, except when they make music together. In the portrayal of this friendship we learn something of all friendship, just as in the series as a whole we learn of loyalty and betrayal, love and mutability, interest and humour.

These novels are neither Forester nor Marryat, though O'Brian pays the respect due to both. There is adventure and there are battles. The historic furniture and vernacular you can trust absolutely because O'Brian is so steeped in his period but there is also something of his heroine, Jane Austen. He writes with her irony, humour and moral toughness, almost as she might have written of the adventures of her naval brothers. Above all, they are accessible novels, so well written that you settle into each as into a warm bath, knowing you are in good, considerate hands. In evoking so vividly what it was like to be alive then, O'Brian shows by reflection elements of what it is to be alive now, and of how we should live. He achieves that simultaneous dislocation and bridging that is the essence of all imaginative art and is what distinguishes it from everything else.

The Heywood Hill Literary Prize was the suggestion of the Duke of Devonshire, a director of the bookshop. The judges were John Saumarez Smith, Mark Amory and Roy Jenkins. It is awarded not for somebody's latest work, but for a 'lifetime's contribution to the enjoyment of books' and could easily have gone to a publisher such as Rupert Hart-Davis or the late Jock Murray. For an author to win it his or her books must have held up well over a period of years among the customers of Heywood Hill; in the words of John Saumarez Smith, '*we wanted to strike a blow for reading*'.

There is a feeling that one or two well-known prize-giving bodies have lost sight of what they think of as the reading aspect of books.

O'Brian was handed his award by another admirer, Tom Stoppard, amidst the bucolic elegance of a large mixed crowd on the lawn at Chatsworth. The sun shone, the bands played cheerfully, the literati were littered about and the gliterati glittered – though not as brightly as the chains adorning the assembled mayors of Derbyshire. The RAF laid on a timely unintended fly-past, the Chatsworth dogs proved that if you're handsome enough you can scrounge any number of free lunches and at the end a lady danced extempore upon a table.

It was, O'Brian told us, his first literary award; in fact, his first prize of any sort since he was given a pen-knife by the headmaster of his prep school in Paignton for keeping on running when everyone else was way ahead and out of sight. Well, they're out of sight now, but no longer ahead, and Patrick O'Brian is running still.

This essay first appeared in
Patrick O'Brian: Critical Appreciations and a Bibliography,
A. E. Cunningham (ed), British Library, 1993.